When the three were ~~together~~
Liem, the militiaman, announced, "We discovered a microprint reader among the dead man's effects."

"You remember today's earthquake?" Peggol asked Radnal.

"Yes, and there was another one yesterday, a smaller one," Radnal answered. "They happen all the time down here. You just go on about your business."

"Sensible," Peggol. "Sensible under most circumstances, anyway. But not now."

"Why not?" Radnal demanded.

"Because, if what was on Dokhor of Kellef's microprint reader is true, someone is trying to engineer a special earthquake."

Radnal's frown drew his heavy eyebrows together above his nose. "I still don't know what you're talking about."

Liem said, "Somebody has smuggled the parts for a starbomb into Trench Park."

The tour guide gaped. "That's insane. What do they want to do, blow up the last big herd of humpless camels in the world?"

"He has more in mind than that," Liem answered. "You see, the bomb is on one of the fault lines nearest the Barrier Mountains."

The mountain range that held back the Western Ocean. The night was warm and dry, but cold sweat prickled on Radnal's back and under his arms. If the mountains fell, the deaths, the devastation, would be incalculable. His voice shook as he asked, "What do we do about it?"

"Good question," Peggol said, astringent as usual. "We don't know who planted it, where it is, or if it's ready. Other than that, we're fine."

DOWN
IN THE
BOTTOMLANDS
(AND OTHER PLACES)

Harry Turtledove
&
L. Sprague de Camp

A Baen Books Original

Baen Publishing Enterprises
P.O. Box 1403
Riverdale, NY 10471

ISBN: 0-671-57835-9

Cover art by Larry Elmore

First printing, October 1999

Distributed by Simon & Schuster
1230 Avenue of the Americas
New York, NY 10020

Typeset by Brilliant Press
Printed in the United States of America

DEDICATION

From Harry Turtledove:
To L. Sprague de Camp,
with thanks for the inspiration

CONTENTS

Down in the Bottomlands

Harry Turtledove

A double handful of tourists climbed down from the omnibus, chattering with excitement. From under the long brim of his cap, Radnal vez Krobir looked them over, comparing them with previous groups he'd led through Trench Park. About average, he decided: an old man spending money before he died; younger folks searching for adventure in an overcivilized world; a few who didn't fit into an obvious category and might be artists, writers, researchers, or anything else under the sun.

He also looked over the women in the tour group with a different sort of curiosity. He was in the process of buying a bride from her father, but he hadn't done it; legally and morally, he remained a free agent. Some of the women were worth looking over, too: a couple of tall, slim, dark Highheads from the eastern lands who stuck by each other, and another of Radnal's own Strongbrow race, shorter, stockier, fairer, with deep-set light eyes under heavy brow ridges.

One of the Highhead girls gave him a dazzling smile. He smiled back as he walked toward the group, his wool robes flapping around him. "Hello, friends," he called. "Do you all understand Tarteshan? Ah, good."

Cameras clicked as he spoke. He was used to that; people from every tour group wasted pictures on him, though he wasn't what they'd come to see. He went into his usual welcoming speech:

"On behalf of the Hereditary Tyranny of Tartesh and the staff of Trench Park, I'm pleased to welcome you here today. If you haven't read my button, or if you just speak Tarteshan but don't know our syllabary, my name is Radnal vez Krobir. I'm a field biologist with the park, doing a two-year stretch of guide duty."

"Stretch?" said the woman who'd smiled at him. "You make it sound like a sentence in the mines."

"I don't mean it like that—quite." He grinned his most disarming grin. Most of the tourists grinned back. A few stayed sober-faced, likely the ones who suspected the gibe was real and the grin put on. There was some truth in that. He knew it, but the tourists weren't supposed to.

He went on, "In a bit, I'll take you over to the donkeys for the trip down into the Trench itself. As you know, we try to keep our mechanical civilization out of the park so we can show you what all the Bottomlands were like not so long ago. You needn't worry. The donkeys are very sure-footed. We haven't lost one—or even a tourist—in years."

This time, some of the chuckles that came back were nervous. Probably only a couple of this lot had ever done anything so archaic as getting on the back of an animal. Too bad for the ones just thinking about that now. The rules were clearly stated. The pretty

Highhead girls looked particularly upset. The placid donkeys worried them more than the wild beasts of the Trench.

"Let's put off the evil moment as long as we can," Radnal said. "Come under the colonnade for half a daytenth or so and we'll talk about what makes Trench Park unique."

The tour group followed him into the shade. Several people sighed in relief. Radnal had to work to keep his face straight. The Tarteshan sun was warm, but if they had trouble here, they'd cook down in the Trench. That was their lookout. If they got heatstroke, he'd set them right again. He'd done it before.

He pointed to the first illuminated map. "Twenty million years ago, as you'll see, the Bottomlands didn't exist. A long stretch of sea separated what's now the southwest section of the Great Continent from the rest. Notice that what were then two lands' masses first joined in the east, and a land bridge rose *here*." He pointed again, this time more precisely. "This sea, now a long arm of the Western Ocean, remained."

He walked over to the next map, drawing the tourists with him. "Things stayed like that until about six and a half million years ago. Then, as that southwest section of the Great Continent kept drifting northward, a new range gradually pushed up *here*, at the western outlet of that inland sea. When it was cut off from the Western Ocean, it began to dry up: it lost more water by evaporation than flowed into it from its rivers. Now if you'll come along . . ."

The third map had several overlays, in different shades of blue. "The sea took about a thousand years to turn into the Bottomlands. It refilled from the Western Ocean several times, too, as tectonic forces lowered the Barrier Mountains. But for about the last five and a half million years, the Bottomlands have had about the form we know today."

The last map showed the picture familiar to any

child studying geography: the Trench of the Bottomlands furrowing across the Great Continent like a
surgical scar, requiring colors needed nowhere else
on the globe to show relief.

Radnal led the tourists out to the donkey corral.
The shaggy animals were already bridled and saddled.
Radnal explained how to mount, demonstrated, and
waited for the tourists to mess it up. Sure enough,
both Highhead girls put the wrong foot in the stirrup.

"No, like this," he said, demonstrating again. "Use
your left foot, then swing over."

The girl who had smiled at him succeeded on the
second try. The other balked. "Help me," she said.
Breathing out through his beaky nose in lieu of sighing, Radnal put his hands on her waist and all but
lifted her into the saddle as she mounted. She giggled.
"You're so strong. He's so strong, Evillia." The other
Highhead girl—presumably Evillia—giggled too.

Radnal breathed out again, harder. Tarteshans and
other folk of Strongbrow race who lived north of the
Bottomlands and down in them *were* stronger than
most Highheads, but generally weren't as agile. So
what, either way?

He went back to work: "Now that we've learned
to mount our donkeys, we're going to learn to dis-
mount." The tourists groaned, but Radnal was inexo-
rable. "You still have to carry your supplies from the
omnibus and stow them in the saddlebags. I'm your
guide, not your servant." The Tarteshan words carried overtones of *I'm your equal, not your slave*.

Most of the tourists dismounted, but Evillia stayed
up on her donkey. Radnal strode over to her; even
his patience was fraying. "This way." He guided her
through the necessary motions.

"Thank you, freeman vez Krobir," she said in
surprisingly fluent Tarteshan. She turned to her friend.
"You're right, Lofosa; he *is* strong."

Radnal felt his ears grow hot under their coat of

down. A brown-skinned Highhead from south of the Bottomlands rocked his hips back and forth and said, "I'm jealous of you." Several tourists laughed.

"Let's get on with it," Radnal said. "The sooner we get the donkeys loaded, the sooner we can begin and the more we'll see." That line never failed; you didn't become a tourist unless you wanted to see as much as you could. As if on cue, the driver brought the omnibus around to the corral. The baggage doors opened with a hiss of compressed air. The driver started chucking luggage out of the bins.

"You shouldn't have any problems," Radnal said. Everyone's gear had been weighed and measured beforehand, to make sure the donkeys wouldn't have to bear anything too bulky or heavy. Most people easily shifted their belongings to the saddlebags. The two Highhead girls, though, had a night demon of a time making everything fit. He thought about helping them, but decided not to. If they had to pay a penalty for making the supply donkeys carry some of their stuff, it was their own fault.

They did get everything in, though their saddlebags bulged like a snake that had just swallowed a half-grown humpless camel. A couple of other people stood around helplessly, with full bags and gear left over. Smiling a smile he hoped was not too predatory, Radnal took them to the scales and collected a tenth of a unit of silver for every unit of excess weight.

"This is an outrage," the dark brown Highhead man said. "Do you know who I am? I am Moblay Sopsirk's son, aide to the Prince of Lissonland." He drew himself up to his full height, almost a Tarteshan cubit more than Radnal's.

"Then you can afford the four and three tenths," Radnal answered. "*I* don't keep the silver. It all goes to upkeep for the park."

Grumbling still, Moblay paid. Then he stomped off

and swung aboard his animal with more grace than
Radnal had noticed him possessing. Down in Lissonland, the guide remembered, important people sometimes rode stripehorses for show. He didn't understand
that. He had no interest in getting onto a donkey
when he wasn't going down into Trench Park. As long
as there were better ways of doing things, why not
use them?

Also guilty of overweight baggage were a middle-
aged Tarteshan couple. They were overweight themselves, too, but Radnal couldn't do anything about
that. Eltsac vez Martois protested, "The scale at home
said we were all right."

"If you read it right," Nocso zev Martois said to
her husband. "You probably didn't."

"Whose side are you on?" he snarled. She
screeched at him. Radnal waited till they ran down,
then collected the silver due the park.

When the tourists had remounted their donkeys,
the guide walked over to the gate on the far side of
the corral, swung it open, and replaced the key in
a pouch he wore belted round his waist under his
robe. As he went back to his own animal, he said,
"When you ride through there, you enter the park
itself, and the waivers you signed come into play.
Under Tarteshan law, park guides have the authority of military officers within the park. I don't intend
to exercise it any more than I have to; we should get
along just fine with simple common sense. But I am
required to remind you the authority is there." He
also kept a repeating handcannon in one of his
donkey's saddlebags, but didn't mention that.

"Please stay behind me and try to stay on the trail,"
he said. "It won't be too steep today; we'll camp tonight
at what was the edge of the continental shelf. Tomorrow we'll descend to the bottom of the ancient sea,
as far below mean sea level as a medium-sized mountain is above it. That will be more rugged terrain."

The Strongbrow woman said, "It will be hot, too, much hotter than it is now. I visited the park three or four years ago, and it felt like a furnace. Be warned, everyone."

"You're right, freelady, ah—" Radnal said.

"I'm Toglo zev Pamdal." She added hastily, "Only a distant collateral relation, I assure you."

"As you say, freelady." Radnal had trouble keeping his voice steady. The Hereditary Tyrant of Tartesh was Bortav vez Pamdal. Even his distant collateral relations needed to be treated with sandskink gloves. Radnal was glad Toglo had had the courtesy to warn him who she was—or rather, who her distant collateral relation was. At least she didn't seem the sort who would snoop around and take bad reports on people back to the friends she undoubtedly had in high places.

Although the country through which the donkeys ambled was below sea level, it wasn't very far below. It didn't seem much different from the land over which the tourists' omnibus had traveled to reach the edge of Trench Park: dry and scrubby, with thornbushes and palm trees like long-handled feather dusters.

Radnal let the terrain speak for itself, though he did remark, "Dig a couple of hundred cubits under the soil hereabouts and you'll find a layer of salt, same as you would anywhere in the Bottomlands. It's not too thick here on the shelf, because this area dried up quickly, but it's here. That's one of the first clues geologists had that the Bottomlands used to be a sea, and one of the ways they map the boundaries of the ancient water."

Moblay Sopsirk's son wiped his sweaty face with a forearm. Where Radnal, like any Tarteshan, covered up against the heat, Moblay wore only a hat, shoes, and a pocketed belt to carry silver, perhaps a small knife or toothpick, and whatever else he thought he couldn't do without. He was dark enough that he didn't need to worry about skin cancer, but he didn't look very comfortable, either.

He said, "Were some of that water back in the Bottomlands, Radnal, Tartesh would have a better climate."

"You're right," Radnal said; he was resigned to foreigners using his familial name with uncouth familiarity. "We'd be several hundredths cooler in summer and warmer in winter. But if the Barrier Mountains fell again, we'd lose the great area that the Bottomlands encompass and the mineral wealth we derive from them: salt, other chemicals left by evaporation, and the petroleum reserves that wouldn't be accessible through deep water. Tarteshans have grown used to heat over the centuries. We don't mind it."

"I wouldn't go that far," Toglo said. "I don't think it's an accident that Tartesan air coolers are sold all over the world."

Radnal found himself nodding. "You have a point, freelady. What we get from the Bottomlands, though, outweighs fuss over the weather."

As he'd hoped, they got to the campsite with the sun still in the sky and watched it sink behind the mountains to the west. The tourists gratefully descended from their donkeys and stumped about, complaining of how sore their thighs were. Radnal set them to carrying lumber from the metal racks that lined one side of the site.

He lit the cookfires with squirts from a squeeze bottle of starter fuel and a flint-and-steel lighter. "The lazy man's way," he admitted cheerfully. As with his skill on a donkey, that he could start a fire at all impressed the tourists. He went back to the donkeys, dug out ration packs which he tossed into the flames. When their tops popped and began to vent steam, he fished them out with a long-handled fork.

"Here we are," he said. "Peel off the foil and you have Tarteshan food—not a banquet fit for the gods, perhaps, but plenty to keep you from starving and meeting them before your time."

Evillia read the inscription on the side of her pack. "These are military rations," she said suspiciously. Several people groaned.

Like any other Tarteshan freeman, Radnal had done his required two years in the Hereditary Tyrant's Volunteer Guard. He came to the ration packs' defense: "Like I said, they'll keep you from starving."

The packs—mutton and barley stew, with carrots, onions, and a heavy dose of ground pepper and garlic—weren't too bad. The two Martoisi inhaled theirs and asked for more.

"I'm sorry," Radnal said. "The donkeys carry only so many. If I give you another pack each, someone will go hungry before we reach the lodge."

"We're hungry now," Nocso zev Martois said.

"That's right," Eltsac echoed. They stared at each other, perhaps surprised at agreeing.

"I'm sorry," Radnal said again. He'd never had anyone ask for seconds before. Thinking that, he glanced over to see how Toglo zev Pamdal was faring with such basic fare. As his eyes flicked her way, she crumpled her empty pack and got up to throw it in a refuse bin.

She had a lithe walk, though he could tell little of the shape of her body because of her robes. As young—or even not so young—men will, he wandered into fantasy. Suppose he was dickering with *her* father over bride price instead of with Markaf vez Putun, who acted as if his daughter Wello shat silver and pissed petrol . . .

He had enough sense to recognize when he was being foolish, which is more than the gods grant most. Toglo's father undoubtedly could make a thousand better matches for her than a none-too-special biologist.

Confrontation with brute fact didn't stop him from musing, but did keep him from taking himself too seriously.

He smiled as he pulled sleepsacks out of one of the pack donkeys' panniers. The tourists took turns with a foot pump to inflate them. With the weather so warm, a good many tourists chose to lie on top of the sleepsacks rather than crawl into them. Some kept on the clothes they'd been wearing, some had special sleep clothes, and some didn't bother with clothes. Tartesh had a moderately strong nudity taboo: not enough to give Radnal the horrors at naked flesh, but plenty to make him eye Evillia and Lofosa as they carelessly shed shirts and trousers. They were young, attractive, and even well-muscled for Highheads. They seemed more naked to him because their bodies were less hairy than those of Strongbrows. He was relieved his robe hid his full response to them.

Speaking to the group, he said, "Get as much sleep as you can tonight. Don't stay up gabbing. We'll be in the saddle most of the day tomorrow, on worse terrain than we saw today. You'll do better if you're rested."

"Yes, clanfather," Moblay Sopsirk's son said, as a youngster might to the leader of his kith grouping— but any youngster who sounded as sassy as Moblay would get the back of his clanfather's hand across his mouth to remind him not to sound that way again.

But, since Radnal had spoken good sense, most of the tourists did try to go to sleep. They did not know the wilds but, with the possible exception of the Martoisi, they were not fools: few fools accumulated for an excursion to Trench Park. As he usually did the first night with a new group, Radnal disregarded his own advice. He was good at going without sleep and, being familiar with what lay ahead, would waste no energy on the trip down to the Trench itself.

An owl hooted from a hole in a palm trunk. The

air smelled faintly spicy. Sage and lavender, oleander, laurel, thyme—many local plants had leaves that
secreted aromatic oils. Their coatings reduced water
loss—always of vital importance here—and made the
leaves unpalatable to insects and animals.

The fading campfires drew moths. Every so often,
their glow would briefly light up other, larger shapes:
bats and nightjars swooping down to take advantage
of the feast set out before them. The tourists took
no notice of insects or predators. Their snores rang
louder than the owl's cries. After a few trips as tour
guide, Radnal was convinced practically everyone
snored. He supposed he did, too, though he'd never
heard himself do it.

He yawned, lay back on his own sleepsack with
hands clasped behind his head, looked up at the stars,
displayed as if on black velvet. There were so many
more of them here than in the lights of the big city:
yet another reason to work in Trench Park. He
watched them slowly whirl overhead; he'd never found
a better way to empty his mind and drift toward
sleep.

His eyelids were getting heavy when someone rose
from his—no, her—sleepsack: Evillia, on her way to
the privy shed behind some bushes. His eyes opened
wider; in the dim firelight, she looked like a moving statue of polished bronze. As soon as her back
was to him, he ran his tongue over his lips.

But instead of getting back into her sack when she
returned, Evillia squatted by Lofosa's. Both Highhead
girls laughed softly. A moment later, they both
climbed to their feet and headed Radnal's way. Lust
turned to alarm—what were they doing?

They knelt down, one on either side of him. Lofosa
whispered, "We think you're a fine chunk of man."
Evillia set a hand on the tie of his robe, began to
undo it.

"*Both* of you?" he blurted. Lust was back, impossible

to disguise since he lay on his back. Incredulity came
with it. Tarteshan women—even Tarteshan tarts—
weren't so brazen (he thought how Evillia had
reminded him of smoothly moving bronze); nor were
Tarteshan men. Not that Tarteshan men didn't enjoy
lewd imaginings, but they usually kept quiet about
them.

The Highhead girls shook with more quiet laughter,
as if his reserve were the funniest thing imaginable.
"Why not?" Evillia said. "Three can do lots of interesting things two can't."

"But—" Radnal waved to the rest of the tour
group. "What if they wake up?"

The girls laughed harder; their flesh shifted more
alluringly. Lofosa answered, "They'll learn something."

Radnal learned quite a few things. One was that,
being on the far side of thirty, his nights of keeping
more than one woman happy were behind him,
though he enjoyed trying. Another was that, what with
sensual distractions, trying to make two women happy
at once was harder than patting his head with one
hand and rubbing his stomach with the other. Still
another was that neither Lofosa nor Evillia carried
an inhibition anywhere about her person.

He felt himself flagging, knew he'd be limp in more
ways than one come morning. "Shall we have mercy
on him?" Evillia asked—in Tarteshan, so he could
understand her teasing.

"I suppose so," Lofosa said. "This time." She
twisted like a snake, brushed her lips against Radnal's.
"Sleep well, freeman." She and Evillia went back to
their sleepsacks, leaving him to wonder if he'd
dreamed they were with him but too worn to believe
it.

This time, his drift toward sleep was more like a
dive. But before he yielded, he saw Toglo zev Pamdal
come back from the privy. For a moment, that meant
nothing. But if she was coming back now, she must

have gone before, when he was too occupied to notice . . . which meant she must have seen him so occupied.

He hissed like an ocellated lizard, though green wasn't the color he was turning. Toglo got back into her sleepsack without looking either at him or the two Highhead girls. Whatever fantasies he'd had about her shriveled. The best he could hope for come morning was the cool politeness someone of prominence gives an underling of imperfect manners. The worst . . .

What if she starts screaming to the group? he wondered. He supposed he could grit his teeth and carry on. *But what if she complains about me to the Hereditary Tyrant?* He didn't like the answers he came up with; *I'll lose my job* was the first that sprang to mind, and they went downhill from there.

He wondered why Moblay Sopsirk's son couldn't have got up to empty his bladder. Moblay would have been envious and admiring, not disgusted as Toglo surely was.

Radnal hissed again. Since he couldn't do anything about what he'd already done, he tried telling himself he would have to muddle along and deal with whatever sprang from it. He repeated that to himself several times. It didn't keep him from staying awake most of the night, no matter how tired he was.

The sun woke the tour guide. He heard some of the group already up and stirring. Though still sandy-eyed and clumsy with sleep, he made himself scramble out of his sack. He'd intended to get moving first, as he usually did, but the previous night's exertion and worry overcame the best of intentions.

To cover what he saw as a failing, he tried to move twice as fast as usual, which meant he kept making small, annoying mistakes: tripping over a stone and almost falling, calling the privy the campfire and the campfire the privy, going to a donkey that carried only fodder when he wanted breakfast packs.

He finally found the smoked sausages and hard bread. Evillia and Lofosa grinned when they took out the sausages, which flustered him worse. Eltsac vez Martois stole a roll from his wife, who cursed him with a dockwalloper's fluency and more than a dock-walloper's volume.

Then Radnal had to give breakfast to Toglo zev Pamdal. "Thank you, freeman," she said, more at ease than he'd dared hope. Then her gray eyes met his. "I trust you slept well?"

It was a conventional Tarteshan morning greeting, or would have been, if she hadn't sounded—no, Radnal decided, she couldn't have sounded amused. "Er—yes," he managed, and fled.

He knew only relief at handing the next breakfast to a Strongbrow who put away a sketch pad and charcoal to take it. "Thank you," the fellow said. Though he seemed polite enough, his guttural accent and the striped tunic and trousers he wore proclaimed him a native of Morgaf, the island kingdom off the northern coast of Tartesh—and the Tyranny's frequent foe. Their current twenty-year bout of peace was as long as they'd enjoyed in centuries.

Normally, Radnal would have been cautious around a Morgaffo. But now he found him easier to confront than Toglo. Glancing at the sketch pad, he said, "That's a fine drawing, freeman, ah—"

The Morgaffo held out both hands in front of him in his people's greeting. "I am Dokhnor of Kellef, freeman vez Krobir," he said. "Thank you for your interest."

He made it sound like *stop spying on me*. Radnal hadn't meant it that way. With a few deft strokes of his charcoal stick, Dokhnor had picked out the features of the campsite: the fire pits, the oleanders in front of the privy, the tethered donkeys. As a biologist who did field work, Radnal was a fair hand with a piece of charcoal. He wasn't in Dokhnor's class, though. A military engineer couldn't have done better.

That thought triggered his suspicions. He looked at the Morgaffo more closely. The fellow carried himself as a soldier would, which proved nothing. Lots of Morgaffos were soldiers. Although far smaller than Tartesh, the island kingdom had always held its own in their struggles. Radnal laughed at himself. If Dokhnor was an agent, why was he in Trench Park instead of, say, at a naval base along the Western Ocean?

The Morgaffo glowered. "If you have finished examining my work, freeman, perhaps you will give someone else a breakfast."

"Certainly," Radnal answered in a voice as icy as he could make it. Dokhnor certainly had the proverbial Morgaffo arrogance. Maybe that proved he wasn't a spy—a real spy would have been smoother. Or maybe a real spy would think no one would expect him to act like a spy, and act like one as a disguise. Radnal realized he could extend the chain to as many links as his imagination could forge. He gave up.

When all the breakfast packs were eaten, all the sleepsacks deflated and stowed, the group headed over to remount their donkeys for the trip into Trench Park itself. As he had the night before, Radnal warned, "The trail will be much steeper today. As long as we take it slow and careful, we'll be fine."

No sooner were the words out of his mouth than the ground quivered beneath his feet. Everyone stood stock-still; a couple of people exclaimed in dismay. The birds, on the other hand, all fell silent. Radnal had lived in earthquake country his whole life. He waited for the shaking to stop, and after a few heart-beats it did.

"Nothing to get alarmed at," he said when the quake was over. "This part of Tartesh is seismically active, probably because of the inland sea that dried up so long ago. The crust of the earth is still adjusting to the weight of so much water being gone. There are a lot of fault lines in the area, some quite close to the surface."

Dokhnor of Kellef stuck up a hand. "What if an earthquake should—how do you say it?—make the Barrier Mountains fall?"

"Then the Bottomlands would flood." Radnal laughed. "Freeman, if it hasn't happened in the last five and a half million years, I won't lose sleep worrying that it'll happen tomorrow, or any time I'm down in Trench Park."

The Morgaffo nodded curtly. "That is a worthy answer. Carry on, freeman."

Radnal had an impulse to salute him—he spoke with the same automatic assumption of authority that Tarteshan officers employed. The tour guide mounted his own donkey, waited until his charges were in ragged line behind him. He waved. "Let's go."

The trail down into Trench Park was hacked and blasted from rock that had been on the bottom of the sea. It was only six or eight cubits wide, and frequently switched back and forth. A motor with power to all wheels might have negotiated it, but Radnal wouldn't have wanted to be at the tiller of one that tried.

His donkey pulled up a gladiolus and munched it. That made him think of something about which he'd forgotten to warn his group. He said, "When we get lower into the park, you'll want to keep your animals from browsing. The soil down there has large amounts of things like selenium and tellurium along with the more usual minerals—they were concentrated there as the sea evaporated. That doesn't bother a lot of the Bottomlands plants, but it *will* bother—and maybe kill—your donkeys if they eat the wrong ones."

"How will we know which ones are which?" Eltsac zev Martois called.

He fought the urge to throw Eltsac off the trail and let him tumble down into Trench Park. The idiot tourist would probably land on his head, which by all evidence was too hard to be damaged by a fall of a mere few thousand cubits. And Radnal's job was riding herd on idiot tourists. He answered, "Don't let your donkey forage at all. The pack donkeys carry fodder, and there'll be more at the lodge."

The tour group rode on in silence for a while. Then Toglo zev Pamdal said, "This trail reminds me of the one down into the big canyon through the western desert in the Empire of Stekia, over on the Double Continent."

Radnal was both glad Toglo would speak to him and jealous of the wealth that let her travel—just a collateral relation of the Hereditary Tyrant's, eh? "I've only seen pictures," he said wistfully. "I suppose there is some similarity of looks, but the canyon was formed differently from the Bottomlands: by erosion, not evaporation."

"Of course," she said. "I've also only seen pictures myself."

"Oh." Maybe she was a distant relative, then. He went on, "Much more like the big canyon are the gorges our rivers cut before they tumble into what was deep seabottom to form the Bitter Lakes in the deepest parts of the Bottomlands. There's a small one in Trench Park, though it often dries up—the Dalorz River doesn't send down enough water to maintain it very well."

A little later, when the trail twisted west around a big limestone boulder, several tourists exclaimed over the misty plume of water plunging toward the floor of the park. Lofosa asked, "Is that the Dalorz?"

"That's it," Radnal said. "Its flow is too erratic to make it worth Tartesh's while to build a power station where it falls off the ancient continental shelf, though we've done that with several other bigger rivers. They supply more than three fourths of our electricity: another benefit of the Bottomlands."

A few small spun-sugar clouds drifted across the sky from west to east. Otherwise, nothing blocked the sun from beating down on the tourists with greater force every cubit they descended. The donkeys kicked up dust at every footfall.

"Does it ever rain here?" Evillia asked.

"Not very often," Radnal admitted. "The Bottomlands desert is one of the driest places on earth. The Barrier Mountains pick off most of the moisture that blows from the Western Ocean, and the other mountain ranges that stretch into the Bottomlands from the north catch most of what's left. But every two or three years Trench Park does get a downpour. It's the most dangerous time to be there—a torrent can tear through a wash and drown you before you know it's coming."

"But it's also the most beautiful time," Toglo zev Pamdal said. "Pictures of Trench Park after a rain first made me want to come here, and I was lucky enough to see it myself on my last visit."

"May I be so fortunate," Dokhnor of Kellef said. "I brought colorsticks as well as charcoal, on the off chance I might be able to draw post-rain foliage."

"The odds are against you, though the freelady was lucky before," Radnal said. Dokhnor spread his hands to show his agreement. Like everything he did, the gesture was tight, restrained, perfectly controlled. Radnal had trouble imagining him going into transports of artistic rapture over desert flowers, no matter how rare or brilliant.

He said, "The flowers are beautiful, but they're only the tip of the iceberg, if you'll let me use a wildly inappropriate comparison. All life in Trench Park depends on water, the same as everywhere else. It's adapted to get along with very little, but not none. As soon as any moisture comes, plants

and animals try to pack a generation's worth of
growth and breeding into the little while it takes
to dry up."

About a quarter of a daytenth later, a sign set by
the side of the trail announced that the tourists were
farther below sea level than they could go anywhere
outside the Bottomlands. Radnal read it aloud and
pointed out, rather smugly, that the salt lake which
was the next most submerged spot on dry land lay
close to the Bottomlands, and might almost be considered an extension of them.

Moblay Sopsirk's son said, "I didn't imagine anyone would be so proud of this wasteland as to want
to include more of the Great Continent in it." His
brown skin kept him from roasting under the desert
sun, but sweat sheened his bare arms and torso.

A little more than halfway down the trail, a wide
flat rest area was carved out of the rock. Radnal let
the tourists halt for a while, stretch their legs and ease
their weary hindquarters, and use the odorous privy.
He passed out ration packs, ignored his charges'
grumbles. He noticed Dokhnor of Kellef ate his meal
without complaint.

He tossed his own pack into the bin by the privy,
then, a couple of cubits from the edge of the trail,
peered down onto the floor of the Bottomlands. After
one of the rare rains, the park was spectacular from
here. Now it just baked: white salt pans, gray-brown
or yellow-brown dirt, a scattering of faded green
vegetation. Not even the area around the lodge was
watered artificially; the Tyrant's charter ordained that
Trench Park be kept pristine.

As they came off the trail and started along the
ancient sea bottom toward the lodge, Evillia said, "I
thought it would be as if we were in the bottom of
a bowl, with mountains all around us. It doesn't really
feel that way. I can see the ones we just came down,
and the Barrier Mountains to the west, but there's

nothing to the east and hardly anything to the south—just a blur on the horizon."

"I expected it would look like a bowl, too, the first time I came here," Radnal said. "We are in the bottom of a bowl. But it doesn't look that way because the Bottomlands are broad compared to their depth—it's a big, shallow bowl. What makes it interesting is that its top is at the same level as the bottom of most other geological bowls, and its bottom deeper than any of them."

"What are those cracks?" Toglo zev Pamdal asked, pointing down to breaks in the soil that ran across the tour group's path. Some were no wider than a barleycorn; others, like open, lidless mouths, had gaps of a couple of digits between their sides.

"In arid terrain like this you'll see all kinds of cracks in the ground from mud drying unevenly after a rain," Radnal said. "But the ones you've noticed do mark a fault line. The earthquake we felt earlier probably was triggered along this fault: it marks where two plates in the earth's crust are colliding."

Nocso zev Martois let out a frightened squeak. "Do you mean that if we have another earthquake, those cracks will open and swallow us down?" She twitched her donkey's reins, as if to speed it up and get as far away from the fault line as she could.

Radnal didn't laugh; the Tyranny paid him for not laughing at tourists. He answered gravely, "If you worry about something that unlikely, you might as well worry about getting hit by a skystone, too. The one has about as much chance of happening as the other."

"Are you *sure*?" Lofosa sounded anxious, too.

"I'm sure." He tried to figure out where she and Evillia were from: probably the Krepalgan Unity, by their accent. Krepalga was the northwesternmost Highhead nation; its western border lay at the eastern edge of the Bottomlands. More to the point, it was earthquake country too. If this was all Lofosa knew about quakes, it didn't say much for her brains.

And if Lofosa didn't have a lot of brains, what did that say about her and Evillia picking Radnal to amuse themselves with? No one cares to think of a sexual partner's judgment as faulty, for that reflects upon him.

Radnal did what any sensible man might have done: he changed the subject. "We'll be at the lodge soon, so you'll want to think about getting your things out of your bags and into your sleep cubicles."

"What I want to think about is getting clean," Moblay Sopsirk's son contradicted.

"You'll each be issued a small bucket of water every day for personal purposes," he said, and over-rode a chorus of groans: "Don't complain—our brochures are specific about this. Almost all the fresh water in Trench Park comes down the trail we rode, on the backs of these donkeys. Think how much you'll relish a hot soak when we come out of the park."

"Think how much we'll *need* a hot soak when we come out of the park," said the elderly Strongbrow man Radnal had tagged as someone spending the silver he'd made in his earlier years (to his embarrassment, he'd forgotten the fellow's name). "It's not so bad for these Highheads here, since their bodies are mostly bare, but all my hair will be a greasy mess by the time this excursion is done." He glared at Radnal as if it were his fault.

Toglo zev Pamdal said, "Don't fret, freeman vez Maprab." Benter vez Maprab, that's who he was, Radnal thought, shooting Toglo a grateful glance. She was still talking to the old Strongbrow: "I have a jar of waterless hair cleaner you can just comb out. It's more than I'd need; I'll share some with you."

"Well, that's kind of you," Benter vez Maprab said, mollified. "Maybe I should have brought some myself."

You certainly should, you old fool, instead of complaining, Radnal thought. He also noted that Toglo had figured out what she'd need before she started her trip. He approved; he would have done the same had he been tourist rather than guide. Of course, if he'd arranged to forget his own waterless hair cleaner, he could have borrowed some from her. He exhaled through his nose. Maybe he'd been too practical for his own good.

Something small and dun-colored darted under his donkey's hooves, then bounced away toward a patch of oleander. "What was that?" several people asked as it vanished among the fallen leaves under the plants.

"It's one of the species of jerboa that live down here," Radnal answered. "Without more than two heartbeats' look, I couldn't tell you which. There are many varieties, all through the Bottomlands. They lived in arid country while the inland sea still existed, and evolved to get the moisture they need from their food. That preadapted them to succeed here, where free water is so scarce."

"Are they dangerous?" Nocso zev Martois asked.

"Only if you're a shrub," Radnal said. "No, actually, that's not quite true. Some eat insects, and one species, the bladetooth, hunts and kills its smaller relatives. It filled the small predator niche before carnivores proper established themselves in the Bottomlands. It's scarce today, especially outside Trench Park, but it is still around, often in the hottest, driest places where no other meat eaters can thrive."

A little later, the tour guide pointed to a small, nondescript plant with thin, greenish-brown leaves. "Anyone tell me what that is?"

He asked that question whenever he took a group along the trail, and had only got a right answer once, just after a rain. But now Benter vez Maprab said confidently: "It's a Bottomlands orchid, freeman vez

Krobir, and a common type at that. If you'd shown us a red-veined one, that would have been worth fussing over."

"You're right, freeman, it *is* an orchid. It doesn't look much like the ones you see in more hospitable climates, though, does it?" Radnal said, smiling at the elderly Strongbrow—if he was an orchid fancier, that probably explained why he'd come to Trench Park.

Benter only grunted and scowled in reply—evidently he'd had his heart set on seeing a rare red-veined orchid his first day at the park. Radnal resolved to search his bags at the end of the tour: carrying specimens out of the park was against the law.

A jerboa hopped up, started nibbling on an orchid leaf. Quick as a flash, something darted out from behind the plant, seized the rodent, and ran away. The tourists bombarded Radnal with questions: "Did you see that?" "What was it?" "Where'd it go?"

"That was a koprit bird," he answered. "Fast, wasn't it? It's of the butcherbird family, but mostly adapted to life on the ground. It can fly, but it usually runs. Because birds excrete urea in more or less solid form, not in urine like mammals, they've done well in the Bottomlands." He pointed to the lodge, which was only a few hundred cubits ahead now. "See? There's another koprit bird on the roof, looking around to see what it can catch."

A couple of park attendants came out of the lodge. They waved to Radnal, sized up the tourists, then helped them stable their donkeys. "Take only what you'll need tonight into the lodge," said one, Fer vez Canthal. "Leave the rest in your saddlebags for the trip out tomorrow. The less packing and unpacking, the better."

Some tourists, veteran travelers, nodded at the good advice. Evillia and Lofosa exclaimed as if they'd never heard it before. Frowning at their naiveté,

Radnal wanted to look away from them, but they were too pretty.

Moblay Sopsirk's son thought so, too. As the group started from the stable to the lodge, he came up behind Evillia and slipped an arm around her waist. At the same moment, he must have tripped, for his startled cry made Radnal whirl toward them.

Moblay sprawled on the dirt floor of the stable. Evillia staggered, flailed her arms wildly, and fell down on top of him, hard. He shouted again, a shout which lost all its breath as she somehow hit him in the pit of the stomach with an elbow while getting back to her feet.

She looked down at him, the picture of concern. "I'm so sorry," she said. "You startled me."

Moblay needed a while before he could sit, let alone stand. At last, he wheezed, "See if I ever touch you again," in a tone that implied it would be her loss.

She stuck her nose in the air. Radnal said, "We should remember we come from different countries and have different customs. Being slow and careful will keep us from embarrassing one another."

"Why, freeman, were you embarrassed last night?" Lofosa asked. Instead of answering, Radnal started to cough. Lofosa and Evillia laughed. Despite what Fer vez Canthal had said, both of them were just toting their saddlebags into the lodge. Maybe they hadn't a lot of brains. But their bodies, those smooth, oh so naked bodies, were something else again.

The lodge was not luxurious, but boasted mesh screens to keep out the Bottomlands bugs, electric lights, and fans which stirred the desert air even if they did not cool it. It also had a refrigerator. "No ration packs tonight," Radnal said. The tourists cheered.

The cooking pit was outdoors: the lodge was warm

enough without a fire inside. Fer vez Canthal and the
other attendant, Zosel vez Glesir, filled it with chunks
of charcoal, splashed light oil over them, and fired
them. Then they put a disjointed lamb carcass on a
grill and hung it over the pit. Every so often, one
of them basted it with a sauce full of pepper and
garlic. The sauce and melting fat dripped onto the
coals. They sputtered and hissed and sent up little
clouds of fragrant smoke. Spit streamed in Radnal's
mouth.

The refrigerator also held mead, date wine, grape
wine, and ale. Some of the tourists drank boisterously.
Dokhnor of Kellef surprised Radnal by taking only
chilled water. "I am sworn to the Goddess," he
explained.

"Not my affair," Radnal answered, but his sleeping suspicions woke. The Goddess was the deity the
Morgaffo military aristocracy most commonly followed.
Maybe a traveling artist was among her worshipers,
but Radnal did not find it likely.

He did not get much time to dwell on the problem Dokhnor presented. Zosel vez Glesir called him
over to do the honors on the lamb. He used a big
pair of eating sticks to pick up each piece of meat
and transfer it to a paper plate.

The Martoisi ate like starving cave cats. Radnal
felt guilty; maybe ordinary rations weren't enough
for them. Then he looked at how abundant flesh
stretched the fabric of their robes. Guilt evaporated.
They weren't wasting away.

Evillia and Lofosa had poured down several mugs
of date wine. That soon caused them difficulties.
Krepalgans usually ate with knife and skewer; they
had trouble manipulating their disposable pairs of
wooden eating sticks. After cutting her meat into bite-
sized chunks, Lofosa chased them around her plate
but couldn't pick them up. Evillia managed that, but
dropped them on the way to her mouth.

They both seemed cheerful drunks, and laughed at their mishaps. Even stiff-necked Dokhnor unbent far enough to try to show them how to use sticks. His lesson did not do much good, though both Highhead girls moved close enough to him to make Radnal jealous. Evillia said, "You're so deft. Morgaffos must use them every day."

Dokhnor tossed his head in his people's negative. "Our usual tool has prongs, bowl, and a sharp edge, all in one. The Tarteshans say we are a quiet folk because we risk cutting our tongues whenever we open our mouths. But I have traveled in Tartesh, and learned what to do with sticks."

"Let me try again," Evillia said. This time, she dropped the piece of lamb on Dokhnor's thigh. She picked it up with her fingers. After her hand lingered on the Morgaffo's leg long enough to give Radnal another pang, she popped the gobbet into her mouth.

Moblay Sopsirk's son began singing in his own language. Radnal did not understand most of the words, but the tune was wild and free and easy to follow. Soon the whole tour group was clapping time. More songs followed. Fer vez Canthal had a ringing baritone. Everyone in the group spoke Tarteshan, but not everyone knew Tartesh's songs well enough to join in. As they had for Moblay, those who could not sing clapped.

When darkness fell, gnats emerged in stinging clouds. Radnal and the group retreated to the lodge, whose screens held the biters away. "Now I know why you wear so many clothes," Moblay said. "They're armor against insects." The dark brown Highhead looked as if he didn't know where to scratch first.

"Of course," Radnal said, surprised Moblay had taken so long to see the obvious. "If you'll hold still for a couple of heartbeats, we have a spray to take away the itch."

Moblay sighed as Radnal sprayed painkiller onto him. "Anyone want another song?" he called.

This time, he got little response. Being under a roof inhibited some people. It reminded others of their long day; Toglo zev Pamdal was not the only tourist to wander off to a sleeping cubicle. Dokhnor of Kellef and old Benter vez Maprab had discovered a war board and were deep in a game. Moblay went over to watch. So did Radnal, who fancied himself a war player.

Dokhnor, who had the blue pieces, advanced a footsoldier over the blank central band that separated his side of the board from his opponent's. "Across the river," Moblay said.

"Is that what Lissonese name the gap?" Radnal said. "With us, it's the Trench."

"And in Morgaf, it's the Sleeve, after the channel that separates our islands from Tartesh," Dokhnor said. "No matter what we call it, though, the game's the same all over the world."

"It's a game that calls for thought and quiet," Benter said pointedly. After some thought, he moved a counselor (that was the name of the piece on the red side of board; its blue equivalent was an elephant) two squares diagonally.

The old Tarteshan's pauses for concentration grew more frequent as the game went on. Dokhnor's attack had the red governor scurrying along the vertical and horizontal lines of his fortress, and his guards along the diagonals, to evade or block the blue pieces. Finally Dokhnor brought one of his cannons in line with the other and said, "That's the end."

Benter glumly nodded. The cannon (the red piece of identical value was called a catapult) was hard to play well: it moved vertically and horizontally, but had to jump over one other piece every time. Thus the rear cannon, not the front, threatened the red governor. But if Benter interposed a guard or one of his chariots, that turned the forward cannon into the threat.

"Nicely played," Benter said. He got up from the war table, headed for a cubicle.

"Care for a game, either of you?" Dokhnor asked the spectators.

Moblay Sopsirk's son shook his head. Radnal said, "I did, till I saw you play. I don't mind facing someone better than I am if I have some chance. Even when I lose, I learn something. But you'd just trounce me, and a little of that goes a long way."

"As you will." Dokhnor folded the war board, poured the disks into their bag. He replaced bag and board on their shelf. "I'm for bed, then." He marched off to the cubicle he'd chosen.

Radnal and Moblay glanced at each other, then toward the war set. By unspoken consent, they seemed to decide that if neither of them wanted a go at Dokhnor of Kellef, playing each other would be rude. "Another night," Radnal said.

"Fair enough." Moblay yawned, displaying teeth that gleamed all the whiter against his brown skin. He said, "I'm about done over—no, it's 'done in' in Tarteshan, isn't it?—anyhow. See you in the morning, Radnal."

Again the tour guide controlled his annoyance at Moblay's failure to use the polite particle vez. At first when foreigners forgot that trick of Tarteshan grammar, he'd imagined himself deliberately insulted. Now he knew better, though he still noticed the omission.

A small light came on in Dokhnor's cubicle: a battery-powered reading lamp. The Morgaffo wasn't reading, though. He sat with his behind on the sleeping mat and his back against the wall. His sketch pad lay on his bent knees. Radnal heard the faint skritch-skritch of charcoal on paper.

"What's he doing?" Fer vez Canthal whispered. A generation's peace was not enough time to teach most Tarteshans to trust their island neighbors.

"He's drawing," Radnal answered, as quietly. Neither of them wanted to get Dokhnor's attention. The reply could have come out sounding innocent. It didn't. Radnal went on, "His travel documents say he's an artist." Again, tone spoke volumes.

Zosel vez Glesir said, "If he really were a spy, Radnal vez, he'd carry a camera, not a sketch pad. Everyone carries a camera into Trench Park—he wouldn't even get noticed."

"True," Radnal said. "But he doesn't act like an artist. He acts like a member of the Morgaffo officer caste. You heard him—he's sworn to their Goddess."

Fer vez Canthal said something lewd about the Morgaffo Goddess. But he lowered his voice even further before he did. An officer from Morgaf who heard his deity offended might make formal challenge. Then again, in Tartesh, where dueling was illegal, he might simply commit murder. The only thing certain was that he wouldn't ignore the insult.

"We can't do anything to him—or even about him—unless we find out he *is* spying," Zosel vez Glesir said.

"Yes," Radnal said. "The last thing Tartesh wants is to hand Morgaf an incident." He thought about what would happen to someone who fouled up so gloriously. Nothing good, that was sure. Then something else occurred to him. "Speaking of the Tyrant, do you know who's in this group? Freelady Toglo zev Pamdal, that's who."

Zosel and Fer whistled softly. "Good thing you warned us," Zosel said. "We'll stay round her like cotton round cut glass."

"I don't think she cares for that sort of thing," Radnal said. "Treat her well, yes, but don't fall all over yourselves."

Zosel nodded. Fer still had Dokhnor of Kellef on his mind. "If he *is* a spy, what's he doing in Trench Park instead of somewhere important?"

"I thought of that myself," Radnal said. "Cover, maybe. And who knows where he's going after he leaves?"

"I know where *I'm* going," Zosel said, yawning: "To bed. If you want to stay up all night fretting about spies, go ahead."

"No, thanks," Fer answered. "A spy would have to be crazy or on holiday to come to Trench Park. If he's crazy, we don't have to worry about him, and if he's on holiday, we don't have to worry about him then, either. So I'm going to bed, too."

"If you think I'll stay talking to myself, you're *both* crazy," Radnal said. All three Tarteshans got up. Dokhnor of Kellef's reading lamp went out, plunging his cubicle into blackness. Radnal dimmed the lights in the common room.

He flopped down onto his sleeping mat with a long sigh. He would sooner have been out in the field, curled up in a sleepsack under gnat netting. This was the price he paid for doing what he wanted most of the time. He knew his own snores would soon join the tourists'.

Then two female shapes appeared in the entrance to his cubicle. *By the gods, not again*, he thought as his eyes opened wide, which showed how tired he was. He said, "Don't you believe in sleep?"

Evillia laughed softly, or maybe Lofosa. "Not when there are better things to do," Lofosa said. "We have some new ideas, too. But we can always see who else is awake."

Radnal almost told her to go ahead, and take Evillia with her. But he heard himself say "No" instead. The night before had been educational beyond his dreams, the stuff people imagined when they talked about the fringe benefits of a tour guide's job. Until last night, he'd reckoned those stories imaginary: in his two years as a guide, he'd never cavorted with a tourist before. Now . . . he grinned as he felt himself rising to the occasion.

The Highhead girls came in. As they'd promised, the threesome tried some new things. He wondered how long their inventiveness could last, and if he could last as long. He was sure he'd enjoy trying.

His stamina and the girls' ingenuity flagged together. He remembered them getting up from the mat. He thought he remembered them going out into the common room. He was sure he didn't remember anything after that. He slept like a log from a petrified forest.

When the scream jarred him awake, his first muzzy thought was that only a few heartbeats had passed. But a glance at his pocket clock as he closed his robe told him sunrise was near. He dashed out into the common room.

Several tourists were already out there, some dressed, some not. More emerged every moment, as did the other two Trench Park staffers. Everyone kept saying, "What's going on?"

Though no one directly answered the question, no one needed to. As naked as when she'd frolicked with Radnal, Evillia stood by the table where Benter vez Maprab and Dokhnor of Kellef had played war. Dokhnor was there, too, but not standing. He lay sprawled on the floor, head twisted at an unnatural angle.

Evillia had jammed a fist in her mouth to stifle another scream. She took it out, quavered, "Is—is he dead?"

Radnal strode over to Dokhnor, grabbed his wrist, felt for a pulse. He found none, nor was the Morgaffo breathing. "He's dead, all right," Radnal said grimly.

Evillia moaned. Her knees buckled. She toppled onto Radnal's bent back.

When Evillia fainted, Lofosa screamed and ran forward to try to help. Nocso zev Martois screamed, too, even louder. Moblay Sopsirk's son hurried toward

Radnal and Evillia. So did Fer vez Canthal and Zosel vez Glesir. So did Toglo zev Pamdal. So did another tourist, a Highhead who'd spoken very little on the way down to the lodge.

Everyone got in everyone else's way. Then the quiet Highhead stopped being quiet and shouted, "I am a physician, the six million gods curse you! Let me through!"

"Let the physician through," Radnal echoed, sliding Evillia off him and to the ground as gently as he could. "Check her first, freeman Golobol," he added, pleased he'd hung onto the doctor's name. "I'm afraid you're too late to help Dokhnor now."

Golobol was almost as dark as Moblay, but spoke Tarteshan with a different accent. As he turned to Evillia, she moaned and stirred. "She will be all right, oh yes, I am sure," he said. "But this poor fellow—" As Radnal had, he felt for Dokhnor's pulse. As Radnal had, he failed to find it. "You are correct, sir. This man is dead. He has been dead for some time."

"How do you know?" Radnal asked.

"You felt of him, not?" the physician said. "Surely you noticed his flesh has begun to cool. It has, oh yes."

Thinking back, Radnal *had* noticed, but he'd paid no special attention. He'd always prided himself on how well he'd learned first-aid training. But he wasn't a physician, and didn't automatically take everything into account as a physician would. His fit of chagrin was interrupted when Evillia let out a shriek a hunting cave cat would have been proud of.

Lofosa bent by her, spoke to her in her own language. The shriek cut off. Radnal started thinking about what to do next. Golobol said, "Sir, look here, if you would."

Golobol was pointing to a spot on the back of Dokhnor's neck, right above where it bent gruesomely. Radnal had to say, "I don't see anything."

"You Strongbrows are a hairy folk, that is why," Golobol said. "Here, though—see this, ah, discoloration, is that the word in your language? It is? Good. Yes. This discoloration is the sort of mark to be expected from a blow by the side of the hand, a killing blow."

Despite Bottomlands heat, ice formed in the pit of Radnal's stomach. "You're telling me this was murder."

The word cut through the babble filling the common room like a scalpel. There was chaos one heartbeat, silence the next. Into that abrupt, intense silence, Golobol said, "Yes."

"Oh, by the gods, what a mess," Fer vez Canthal said.

Figuring out what to do next became a lot more urgent for Radnal. Why had the gods (though he didn't believe in six million of them) let someone from *his* tour group get murdered? And why, by all the gods he did believe in, did it have to be the Morgaffo? Morgaf would be suspicious—if not hostile—if any of its people met foul play in Tartesh. And if Dokhnor of Kellef really was a spy, Morgaf would be more than suspicious. Morgaf would be furious.

Radnal walked over to the radiophone. "Whom will you call?" Fer asked.

"First, the park militia. They'd have to be notified in any case. And then—" Radnal took a deep breath. "Then I think I'd best call the Hereditary Tyrant's Eyes and Ears in Tarteshem. Murder of a Morgaffo sworn to the Goddess is a deeper matter than the militia can handle alone. Besides, I'd sooner have an Eye and Ear notify the Morgaffo plenipo than try doing it myself."

"Yes, I can see that," Fer said. "Wouldn't want Morgaffo gunboats running across the Sleeve to raid our coasts because you said something wrong. Or—" The lodge attendant shook his head. "No, not even the island king would be crazy enough to start tossing starbombs over something this small." Fer's voice turned anxious. "Would he?"

"I don't think so." But Radnal sounded anxious, too. Politics hadn't been the same since starbombs came along fifty years before. Neither Tartesh nor Morgaf had used them, even in war against each other, but both countries kept building them. So did eight or ten other nations, scattered across the globe. If another big war started, it could easily become The Big War, the one everybody was afraid of.

Radnal punched buttons on the radiophone. After a couple of static bursts, a voice answered: "Trench Park militia, Subleader vez Steries speaking."

"Gods bless you, Liem vez," Radnal said; this was a man he knew and liked. "Vez Krobir here, over at the tourist lodge. I'm sorry to have to tell you we've had a death. I'm even sorrier to have to tell you it looks like murder." Radnal explained what had happened to Dokhnor of Kellef.

Liem vez Steries said, "Why couldn't it have been anyone else but the Morgaffo? Now you'll have to drag in the Eyes and Ears, and the gods only know how much hoorah will erupt."

"My next call was to Tarteshem," Radnal agreed.

"It probably should have been your first one, but never mind," Liem vez Steries said. "I'll be over there with a circumstances man as fast as I can get a helo in the air. Farewell."

"Farewell." Radnal's next call had to go through a human relayer. After a couple of hundred heartbeats, he found himself talking with an Eye and Ear named Peggol vez Menk. Unlike the park militiaman, Peggol kept interrupting with questions, so the conversation took twice as long as the other one had.

When Radnal was through, the Eye and Ear said, "You did right to involve us, freeman vez Krobir. We'll handle the diplomatic aspects, and we'll fly a team down there to help with the investigation. Don't let anyone leave the—lodge, did you call it? Farewell."

The radiophone had a speaking diaphragm in the console, not the more common—and more private— ear-and-mouth handset. Everyone heard what Peggol vez Menk said. Nobody liked it. Evillia said, "Did he mean we're going to have to stay cooped up here— with a murderer?" She started trembling. Lofosa put an arm around her.

Benter vez Maprab had a different objection: "See here, freeman, I put down good silver for a tour of Trench Park, and I intend to have that tour. If not, I shall take legal measures."

Radnal stifled a groan. Tarteshan law, which relied heavily on the principle of trust, came down hard on those who violated contracts in any way. If the old Strongbrow went to court, he'd likely collect enormous damages from Trench Park—and from Radnal, as the individual who failed to deliver the service contracted for.

Worse, the Martoisi joined the outcry. A reasonably upright and upstanding man, Radnal had never had to hire a pleader in his life. He wondered if he had enough silver to pay for a good one. Then he wondered if he'd ever have any silver again, once the tourists, the courts, and the pleader were through with him.

Toglo zev Pamdal cut through the hubbub: "Let's wait a few heartbeats. A man is dead. That's more important than everything else. If the start of our tour is delayed, perhaps Trench Park will regain equity by delaying its end to give us the full touring time we've paid for."

"That's an excellent suggestion, freelady zev Pamdal," Radnal said gratefully. Fer and Zosel nodded.

A distant thutter in the sky grew to a roar. The militia helo kicked up a small dust storm as it set down between the stables and the lodge. Flying

pebbles clicked off walls and windows. The motor shut
down. As the blades slowed, dust subsided.

Radnal felt as if a good god had frightened a night
demon from his shoulders. "I don't think we'll need
to extend your time here by more than a day," he
said happily.

"How will you manage that, if we're confined here
in this gods-forsaken wilderness?" Eltsac vez Martois
growled.

"That's just it," Radnal said. "We *are* in a wilderness. Suppose we go out and see what there is to see
in Trench Park—where will the culprit flee on
donkeyback? If he tries to get away, we'll know who
he is because he'll be the only one missing, and we'll
track him down with the helo." The tour guide
beamed. The tourists beamed back—including, Radnal
reminded himself, the killer among them.

Liem vez Steries and two other park militiamen
walked into the lodge. They wore soldierly versions
of Radnal's costume: their robes, instead of being
white, were splotched in shades of tan and light green,
as were their long-brimmed caps. Their rank badges
were dull; even the metal buckles of their sandals
were painted to avoid reflections.

Liem set a recorder on the table Dokhnor and
Benter vez Maprab had used for war the night before.
The circumstances man started taking pictures with
as much abandon as if he'd been a tourist. He asked,
"Has the body been moved?"

"Only as much as we needed to make sure the man
was dead," Radnal answered.

"We?" the circumstances man asked. Radnal introduced Golobol. Liem got everyone's statement on the
wire: first Evillia, who gulped and blinked back tears
as she spoke, then Radnal, then the physician, and
then the other tourists and lodge attendants. Most of
them echoed one another: they'd heard a scream, run
out, and seen Evillia standing over Dokhnor's corpse.

Golobol added, "The woman cannot be responsible for his death. He had been deceased some while, between one and two daytenths, possibly. She, unfortunate one, merely discovered the body."

"I understand, freeman," Liem vez Steries assured him. "But because she did, her account of what happened is important."

The militiaman had just finished recording the last statement when another helo landed outside the lodge. The instant its dust storm subsided, four men came in. The Hereditary Tyrant's Eyes and Ears looked more like prosperous merchants than soldiers: their caps had patent-leather brims, they closed their robes with silver chains, and they sported rings on each index finger.

"I am Peggol vez Menk," one of them announced. He was short and, by Tarteshan standards, slim; he wore his cap at a dapper angle. His eyes were extraordinarily shrewd, as if he were waiting for someone around him to make a mistake. He spotted Liem vez Steries at once, and asked, "What's been done thus far, Subleader?"

"What you'd expect," the militiaman answered: "Statements from all present, and our circumstances man, Senior Trooper vez Sofana there, has taken some pictures. We didn't disturb the body."

"Fair enough," the Eye and Ear said. One of his men was flashing more photos. Another set a recorder beside the one already on the table. "We'll get a copy of your wire, and we'll make one for ourselves— maybe we'll find questions you missed. You haven't searched belongings yet?"

"No, freeman." Liem vez Steries' voice went wooden. Radnal wouldn't have wanted someone to steal and duplicate his work, either. Eyes and Ears, though, did as they pleased. Why not? They watched Tartesh, but who watched them?

"We'll take care of it." Peggol vez Menk sat down at the table. The photographer stuck in a fresh clip of film, then followed the two remaining Eyes and Ears into the sleeping cubicle nearest the entrance.

It was Golobol's. "Be careful, oh please I beg you," the physician exclaimed. "Some of my equipment is delicate."

Peggol said, "I'll hear the tale of the woman who discovered the body." He pulled out a notepad, glanced at it. "Evillia." A little calmer now, Evillia retold her story using, so far as Radnal could tell, the same words she had before. If Peggol found any new questions, he didn't ask them.

After about a tenth of a daytenth, it was Radnal's turn. Peggol did remember his name without needing to remind himself. Again, his questions were like the ones Liem vez Steries had used. When he asked the last one, Radnal had a question of his own: "Freeman, while the investigation continues, may I take my group out into the Bottomlands?" He explained how Benter vez Maprab had threatened to sue, and why he thought even a guilty tourist unlikely to escape.

The Eye and Ear pulled at his lower lip. He let the hair beneath it grow out in a tuft, which made him seem to have a protruding chin like a Highhead's. When he released the lip, it went back with a liquid plop. Under his tilted cap, he looked wise and cynical. Radnal's hopes plunged. He waited for Peggol to laugh at him for raising the matter.

Peggol said, "Freeman, I know you technically enjoy military rank, but suppose you discover who the killer is, or he strikes again. Do you reckon yourself up to catching him and bringing him back for trial and decapitation?"

"I—" Radnal stopped before he went any further. The ironic question reminded him this wasn't a game. Dokhnor of Kellef might have been a spy, he was dead now, and whoever had killed him might kill again—*might kill* me, *if I find out who he is*, he thought. He said, "I don't know. I'd like to think so, but I've never had to do that sort of thing."

Something like approval came into Peggol vez Menk's eyes. "You're honest with yourself. Not everyone can say that. Hmm—it wouldn't be just your silver involved in a suit, would it? No, of course not; it would be Trench Park's, too, which means the Hereditary Tyrant's."

"Just what I was thinking," Radnal said, with luck patriotically. His own silver came first with him. He was honest enough with himself to be sure of that— but he didn't have to tell it to Peggol.

"I'm sure you were," the Eye and Ear said, his tone dry. "The Tyrant's silver really does come first with me. How's this, then? Suppose you take the tourists out, as you've contracted to do. But suppose I come with you to investigate while my comrades keep working here? Does that seem reasonable?"

"Yes, freeman; thank you," Radnal exclaimed.

"Good," Peggol said. "My concubine has been nagging me to bring her here. Now I'll see if I want to do that." He grinned knowingly. "You see, I also keep my own interests in mind."

The other Eyes and Ears had methodically gone from one sleeping cubicle to the next, examining the tourists' belongings. One of them brought a codex out of Lofosa's cubicle, dropped it on the table in front of Peggol vez Menk. The cover was a color photo of two good-looking Highheads fornicating. Peggol flipped through it. Variations on the same theme filled every page.

"Amusing," he said, "even if it should have been seized when its owner entered our domains."

"I like that!" Lofosa sounded indignant. "You sanctimonious Strongbrows, pretending you don't do the same things—and enjoy them, too. I ought to know."

Radnal hoped Peggol would not ask how she knew.

He was certain she would tell him, in detail; she and
Evillia might have been many things, but not shy. But
Peggol said, "We did not come here to search for filth.
She might have worn out Dokhnor with that volume,
but she didn't kill him with it. Let her keep it, if she
enjoys telling the world what should be kept private."

"Oh, rubbish!" Lofosa scooped up the codex and
carried it back to her cubicle, rolling her hips at every
step as if to contradict Peggol without another word.

The Eyes and Ears brought out nothing more from
her sleep cubicle or Evillia's for their chief to inspect.
That surprised Radnal; the two women had carried
in everything but the donkey they'd ridden. He
shrugged—they'd probably filled their saddlebags with
feminine fripperies and junk that could have stayed
behind in their Tarteshan hostel if not in Krepalga.

Then he stopped thinking about them—the Eye
and Ear who'd gone into Dokhnor's cubicle whistled.
Peggol vez Menk dashed in there. He came out with
his fist tightly closed around something. He opened
it. Radnal saw two six-pointed gold stars: Morgaffo
rank badges.

"So he *was* a spy," Fer vez Canthal exclaimed.

"He may have been," Peggol said. But when he
got on the radiophone to Tarteshem, he found Dokhnor of Kellef had declared his battalion leader's rank
when he entered the Tyranny. The Eye and Ear
scowled. "A soldier, yes, but not a spy after all, it
would appear."

Benter vez Maprab broke in: "I wish you'd finish
your pawing and let us get on with our tour. I haven't
that many days left, so I hate to squander one."

"Peace, freeman," Peggol said. "A man is dead."

"Which means he'll not complain if I see the much-
talked-about wonders of Trench Park." Benter glared
as if he were the Hereditary Tyrant dressing down
some churlish underling.

Radnal, seeing how Benter reacted when thwarted,

wondered if he'd broken Dokhnor's neck for no better reason than losing a game of war. Benter might be old, but he wasn't feeble. And he was sure to be a veteran of the last war with Morgaf, or the one before that against Morgaf and the Krepalgan Unity both. He would know how to kill.

Radnal shook his head. If things kept on like this, he'd start suspecting Fer and Zosel next, or his own shadow. He wished he hadn't lost the tour guides' draw. He would sooner have been studying the metabolism of the fat sand rat than trying to figure out which of his charges had just committed murder.

Peggol vez Menk said, "We shall have to search the outbuildings before we begin. Freeman vez Krobir already told you we'd go out tomorrow. My professional opinion is that no court would sustain a suit over one day's delay when compensational time is guaranteed."

"Bah!" Benter stomped off. Radnal caught Toglo zev Pamdal's eye. She raised one eyebrow slightly, shook her head. He shifted his shoulders in a tiny shrug. They both smiled. In every group, someone turned out to be a pain in the backside. Radnal let his smile expand, glad Toglo wasn't holding his sport with Lofosa and Evillia against him.

"Speaking of outbuildings, freeman vez Krobir," Peggol said, "there's just the stables, am I right?"

"That and the privy, yes," Radnal said.

"Oh, yes, the privy." The Eye and Ear wrinkled his nose. It was even more prominent than Radnal's. Most Strongbrows had big noses, as if to counterbalance their long skulls. Lissonese, whose noses were usually flattish, sometimes called Tarteshans Snouts on account of that. The name would start a brawl in any port on the Western Ocean.

Fer vez Canthal accompanied one of Peggol's men to the stables; the Eye and Ear obviously needed support against the ferocious, blood-crazed donkeys inside—that was what his body language said, anyhow. When Peggol ordered him out, he'd flinched as if told to invade Morgaf and bring back the king's ears.

"You Eyes and Ears don't often deal with matters outside the big cities, do you?" Radnal asked.

"You noticed that?" Peggol vez Menk raised a wry eyebrow. "You're right; we're urbanites to the core. Threats to the realm usually come among crowds of masking people. Most that don't are a matter for the army, not us."

Moblay Sopsirk's son went over to the shelf where the war board was stored. "If we can't go out today, Radnal, care for the game we didn't have last night?"

"Maybe another time, freeman vez Sopsirk," the tour guide said, turning Moblay's name into its nearest Tarteshan equivalent. Maybe the brown man would take the hint and speak a bit more formally to him. But Moblay didn't seem good at catching hints, as witness his advances toward Evillia and this even more poorly timed suggestion of a game.

The Eye and Ear returned from the stable without the solution to Dokhnor's death. By his low-voiced comments to his friends, he was glad he'd escaped the den of vicious beasts with his life. The Trench Park staffers tried to hide their sniggers. Even a few of the tourists, only two days better acquainted with donkeys than the Eye and Ear, chuckled at his alarm.

Something on the roof said *hig-hig-hig!* in a loud, strident voice. The Eye and Ear who'd braved the stables started nervously. Peggol vez Menk raised his eyebrow again. "What's that, freeman vez Krobir?"

"A koprit bird," Radnal said. "They hardly impale people on thornbushes."

"No, eh? That's good to hear." Peggol's dry cough served him for a laugh.

The midday meal was ration packs. Radnal sent Liem vez Steries a worried look: the extra mouths at

the lodge would make supplies run out faster than
he'd planned for. Understanding the look, Liem said,
"We'll fly in more from the militia outpost if we have
to."

"Good."

Between them, Peggol vez Menk and Liem vez
Steries spent most of the afternoon on the radiophone.
Radnal worried about power, but not as much. Even
if the generator ran out of fuel, solar cells would take
up most of the slack. Trench Park had plenty of
sunshine.

After supper, the militiamen and Eyes and Ears
scattered sleepsacks on the common room floor.
Peggol set up a watch schedule that gave each of his
and Liem's men about half a daytenth each. Radnal
volunteered to stand a watch himself.

"No," Peggol answered. "While I do not doubt your
innocence, freeman vez Krobir, you and your colleagues formally remain under suspicion here. The
Morgaffo plenipo could protest were you given a post
which might let you somehow take advantage of us."

Though that made some sense, it miffed Radnal.
He retired to his sleeping cubicle in medium dud-
geon, lay down, and discovered he could not sleep.
The last two nights, he'd been on the edge of dropping off when Evillia and Lofosa called. Now he was
awake, and they stayed away.

He wondered why. They'd already shown they
didn't care who watched them when they made love.
Maybe they thought he was too shy to do anything
with militiamen and Eyes and Ears outside the
entrance. A few days before, they would have been
right. Now he wondered. They took fornication so
much for granted that they made any other view of
it seem foolish.

Whatever their reasons, they stayed away. Radnal
tossed and turned on his sleepsack. He thought about
going out to chat with the fellow on watch, but

decided not to: Peggol vez Menk would suspect he was up to something nefarious if he tried. That annoyed him all over again, and drove sleep further away than ever. So did the Martoisi's furious row over how one of them—Eltsac said Nocso, Nocso said Eltsac—had managed to lose their only currycomb.

The tour guide eventually dozed off, for he woke with a start when the men in the common room turned up the lights just before sunrise. For a heart-beat or two, he wondered why they were there. Then he remembered.

Yawning, he grabbed his cap, tied the belt on his robe, and headed out of the cubicle. Zosel vez Glesir and a couple of tourists were already in the common room, talking with the militiamen and the Eyes and Ears. Conversation flagged when Lofosa emerged from her sleeping cubicle without dressing first.

"A tough job, this tour guide business must be," Peggol vez Menk said, sounding like everyone else who thought a guide did nothing but roll on the sleepsack with his tourists.

Radnal grunted. This tour, he hadn't done much with Lofosa or Evillia but roll on the sleepsack. *It's not usually like that*, he wanted to say. He didn't think Peggol would believe him, so he kept his mouth shut. If an Eye and Ear didn't believe something, he'd start digging. If he started to dig, he'd keep digging till he found what he was looking for, regardless of whether it was really there.

The tour guide and Zosel dug out breakfast packs. By the time they came back, everyone was up, and Evillia had succeeded in distracting some of the males from Lofosa. "Here you are, freelady," Radnal said to Toglo zev Pamdal when he got to her.

No one paid her any particular attention; she was just a Tarteshan woman in a concealing Tarteshan robe, not a foreign doxy wearing nothing much.

Radnal wondered if that irked her. Women, in his experience, did not like being ignored.

If she was irked, she didn't show it. "I trust you slept well, freeman vez Krobir?" she said. She did not even glance toward Evillia and Lofosa. If she meant anything more by her greeting than its words, she also gave no sign of that—which suited Radnal perfectly.

"Yes. I trust you did likewise," he answered.

"Well enough," she said, "though not as well as I did before the Morgaffo was killed. A pity he'll not be able to make his sketches—he had talent. May his Goddess grant him wind and land and water in the world to come: that's what the islanders pray for, not so?"

"I believe so, yes," Radnal said, though he knew little of Morgaffo religious forms.

"I'm glad you've arranged for the tour to continue despite the misfortune that befell him, Radnal vez," she said. "It can do him no harm, and the Bottomlands are fascinating."

"So they are, fr—" Radnal began. Then he stopped, stared, and blinked. Toglo hadn't used formal address, but the middle grade of Tarteshan politesse, which implied she felt she knew him somewhat and didn't disapprove of him. Considering what she'd witnessed at the first night's campsite, that was a minor miracle. He grinned and took a like privilege: "So do I, Toglo zev."

About a tenth of a daytenth later, as he and Fer carried empty ration packs to the disposal bin, the other Trench Park staffer elbowed him in the ribs and said, "You have *all* the women after you, eh, Radnal vez?"

Radnal elbowed back, harder. "Go jump in the Bitter Lake, Fer vez. This group's nothing but trouble. Besides, Nocso zev Martois thinks I'm part of the furniture."

"You wouldn't want her," Fer replied, chuckling. "I was just jealous."

"That's what Moblay said," Radnal answered. Having anyone jealous of him for being sexually attractive was a new notion, one he didn't care for. By Tarteshan standards, drawing such notice was faintly disreputable, as if he'd got rich by skirting the law. It didn't bother Evillia and Lofosa—they reveled in it. *Well*, he asked himself, *do you really want to be like Evillia and Lofosa, no matter how ripe their bodies are?* He snorted through his nose. "Let's go back inside, so I can get my crew moving."

After two days of practice, the tourists thought they were seasoned riders. They bounded onto their donkeys, and had little trouble guiding them out of their stalls. Peggol vez Menk looked almost as apprehensive as his henchman who'd gone to search the stable. He drew in his white robe all around him, as if fearing to have it soiled. "You expect me to ride one of these creatures?" he said.

"You were the one who wanted to come along," Radnal answered. "You don't have to ride; you could always hike along beside us."

Peggol glared. "Thank you, no, freeman vez Krobir." He pointedly did *not* say *Radnal vez*. "Will you be good enough to show me how to ascend one of these perambulating peaks?"

"Certainly, freeman vez Menk." Radnal mounted a donkey, dismounted, got on again. The donkey gave him a jaundiced stare, as if asking him to make up his mind. He dismounted once more, and took the snort that followed as the asinine equivalent of a resigned shrug. To Peggol, he said, "Now you try, freeman."

Unlike Evillia or Lofosa, the Eye and Ear managed to imitate Radnal's movements without requiring the tour guide to take him by the waist (just as well, Radnal thought—Peggol wasn't smooth and supple like the Highhead girls). He said, "When back in Tartesham, freeman vez Krobir, I shall stick exclusively to motors."

"When I'm in Tarteshem, freeman vez Menk, I do the same," Radnal answered.

The party set out a daytenth after sunrise: not as early as Radnal would have liked but, given the previous day's distractions, the best he could expect. He led them south, toward the lowlands at the core of Trench Park. Under his straw hat, Moblay Sopsirk's son was already sweating hard.

Something skittered into hiding under the fleshy leaves of a desert spurge. "What did we just nearly see there, freeman?" Golobol asked.

Radnal smiled at the physician's phrasing. "That was a fat sand rat. It's a member of the gerbil family, one specially adapted to feed off succulent plants that concentrate salt in their foliage. Fat sand rats are common throughout the Bottomlands. They're pests in areas where there's enough water for irrigated agriculture."

Moblay said, "You sound like you know a lot about them, Radnal."

"Not as much as I'd like to, freeman vez Sopsirk," Radnal answered, still trying to persuade the Lissonese to stop being so uncouthly familiar. "I study them when I'm not being a tour guide."

"I hate all kinds of rats," Nocso zev Martois said flatly.

"Oh, I don't know," Eltsac said. "Some rats are kind of cute." The two Martoisi began to argue. Everyone else ignored them.

Moblay said, "Hmp. Fancy spending all your time studying rats."

"And how do you make *your* livelihood, freeman?" Radnal snapped.

"Me?" Flat-nosed, dark, and smooth, Moblay's face was different from Radnal's in every way. But the tour guide recognized the blank mask that appeared on it for a heartbeat: the expression of a man with something to hide. Moblay said, "As I told you, I am aide

to my prince, may his years be many." He had said
that, Radnal remembered. It might even be true, but
he was suddenly convinced it wasn't the whole truth.

Benter vez Maprab couldn't have cared less about
the fat sand rat. The spiny spurge under which it hid,
however, interested him. He said, "Freeman vez
Krobir, perhaps you will explain the relationship
between the plants here and the cactuses in the
deserts of the Double Continent."

"There is no relationship to speak of." Radnal gave
the old Strongbrow an unfriendly look. *Try to make
me look bad in front of everyone, will you?* he
thought. He went on, "The resemblances come from
adapting to similar environments. That's called con-
vergent evolution. As soon as you cut them open,
you'll see they're unrelated: spurges have a thick white
milky sap, while that of cactuses is clear and watery.
Whales and fish look very much alike, too, but that's
because they both live in the sea, not because they're
kin."

Benter hunched low over his donkey's back. Radnal
felt like preening, as if he'd overcome a squadron of
Morgaffo marine commandos rather than one queru-
lous old Tarteshan.

Some of the spines of the desert spurge held a
jerboa, a couple of grasshoppers, a shoveler skink, and
other small, dead creatures. "Who hung them out to
dry?" Peggol vez Menk asked.

"A koprit bird," Radnal answered. "Most butcher-
birds make a larder of things they've caught but haven't
got round to eating yet."

"Oh." Peggol sounded disappointed. Maybe he'd
hoped someone in Trench Park enjoyed tormenting
animals, so he could hunt down the miscreant.

Toglo zev Pamdal pointed to the impaled lizard,
which looked to have spent a while in the sun. "Do
they eat things as dried up as that, Radnal vez?"

"No, probably not," Radnal said. "At least, I

wouldn't want to." After he got his small laugh, he continued, "A koprit bird's larder isn't just things it intends to eat. It's also a display to other koprit birds. That's especially true in breeding season—it's as if the male says to prospective mates, 'Look what a hunter I am.' Koprits don't display only live things they've caught, either. I've seen hoards with bright bits of yarn, wires, pieces of sparkling plastic, and once even a set of old false teeth, all hung on spines."

"False teeth?" Evillia looked sidelong at Benter vez Maprab. "Some of us have more to worry about than others." Stifled snorts of laughter went up from several tourists. Even Eltsac chuckled. Benter glared at the Highhead girl. She ignored him.

High in the sky, almost too small to see, were a couple of moving black specks. As Radnal pointed them out to the group, a third joined them. "Another feathered optimist," he said. "This is wonderful country for vultures. Thermals from the Bottomlands floor make soaring effortless. They're waiting for a donkey—or one of us—to keel over and die. Then they'll feast."

"What do they eat when they can't find tourists?" Toglo zev Pamdal asked.

"Humpless camels, or boar, or anything else dead they spy," Radnal said. "The only reason there aren't more of them is that the terrain is too barren to support many large-bodied herbivores."

"I've seen country that isn't," Moblay Sopsirk's son said. "In Duvai, east of Lissonland, the herds range the grasslands almost as they did in the days before mankind. The past hundred years, though, hunting has thinned them out. So the Duvains say, at any rate; I wasn't there then."

"I've heard the same," Radnal agreed. "It isn't like that here."

He waved to show what he meant. The Bottomlands were too hot and dry to enjoy a covering of grass. Scattered over the plain were assorted varieties of succulent spurges, some spiny, some glossy with wax to hold down water loss. Sharing the landscape with them were desiccated-looking bushes—thorny burnets, oleander, tiny Bottomlands olive plants (they were too small to be trees).

Smaller plants huddled in shadows round the base of the bigger ones. Radnal knew seeds were scattered everywhere, waiting for the infrequent rains. But most of the ground was as barren as if the sea had disappeared yesterday, not five and a half million years before.

"I want all of you to drink plenty of water," Radnal said. "In weather like this, you sweat more than you think. We've packed plenty aboard the donkeys, and we'll replenish their carrying bladders tonight back at the lodge. Don't be shy—heatstroke can kill you if you aren't careful."

"Warm water isn't very satisfying to drink," Lofosa grumbled.

"I am sorry, freelady, but Trench Park hasn't the resources to haul a refrigerator around for anyone's convenience," Radnal said.

Despite Lofosa's complaint, she and Evillia both drank regularly. Radnal scratched his head, wondering how the Krepalgan girls could seem so fuzz-brained but still muddle along without getting into real trouble.

Evillia had even brought along some flavoring packets, so while everyone else poured down blood-temperature water, she had blood-temperature fruit punch instead. The crystals also turned the water the color of blood. Radnal decided he could do without them.

They got to the Bitter Lake a little before noon. It was more a salt marsh than a lake; the Dalorz River did not drop enough water off the ancient continental shelf to keep a lake bed full against the tremendous evaporation in the eternally hot, eternally dry Bottomlands. Salt pans gleamed white around pools and patches of mud.

"Don't let the donkeys eat *anything* here," Radnal warned. "The water brings everything from the underground salt layer to the surface. Even Bottomlands plants have trouble adapting."

That was emphatically true. Despite the water absent everywhere else in Trench Park, the landscape round the Bitter Lake was barren even by Bottomlands standards. Most of the few plants that did struggle to grow were tiny and stunted.

Benter vez Maprab, whose sole interest seemed to be horticulture, pointed to one of the exceptions. "What's that, the ghost of a plant abandoned by the gods?"

"It looks like it," Radnal said: the shrub had skinny, almost skeletal branches and leaves. Rather than being green, it was white with sparkles that shifted as the breeze shook it. "It's a saltbush, and it's found only around the Bitter Lake. It deposits the salts it picks up from ground water as crystals on all its above-ground parts. That does two things: it gets rid of the salt, and having the reflective coating lowers the plant's effective temperature."

"It also probably keeps the saltbush from getting eaten very often," Toglo zev Pamdal said.

"Yes, but with a couple of exceptions," Radnal said. "One is the humpless camel, which has its own ways of getting rid of excess salt. The other is my little friend the fat sand rat, although it prefers desert spurges, which are juicier."

The Strongbrow woman looked around. "One of the things I expected to see when I came down here, both the first time and now, was lots of lizards and snakes and tortoises. I haven't, and it puzzles me. I'd have thought the Bottomlands would be a perfect place for cold-blooded creatures to live."

"If you look at dawn or dusk, Toglo zev, you'll see

plenty. But not in the heat of the day. Cold-blooded isn't a good term for reptiles: they have a *variable* body temperature, not a constant one like birds or mammals. They warm themselves by basking, and cool down by staying out of the midday sun. If they didn't, they'd cook."

"I know just how they feel." Evillia ran a hand through her thick dark hair. "You can stick eating tongs in me now, because I'm done all the way through."

"It's not so bad as that," Radnal said. "I'm sure it's under fifty hundredths, and it can get above fifty even here. And Trench Park doesn't have any of the deepest parts of the Bottomlands. Down another couple of thousand cubits, the extreme temperatures go above sixty."

The non-Tarteshans groaned. So did Toglo zev Pamdal and Peggol vez Menk. Tarteshem had a relatively mild climate; temperatures there went past forty hundredths only from late spring to early fall.

With morbid curiosity, Moblay Sopsirk's son said, "What is the highest temperature ever recorded in the Bottomlands?"

"Just over sixty-six," Radnal said. The tourists groaned again, louder.

Radnal led the line of donkeys around the Bitter Lake. He was careful not to get too close to the little water actually in the lake at this time of year. Sometimes a salt crust formed over mud; a donkey's hoof could poke right through, trapping the animal and slicing its leg against the hard, sharp edge of the crust.

After a while, the tour guide asked, "Do you have all the pictures you want?" When no one denied it, he said, "Then we'll head back toward the lodge."

"Hold on." Eltsac vez Martois pointed across the Bitter Lake. "What are those things over there?"

"I don't see anything, Eltsac," his wife said. "You

must be looking at a what-do-you-call it, a mirage."
Then, grudgingly, a heartbeat later: "Oh."

"It's a herd of humpless camels," Radnal said
quietly. "Try not to spook them."

The herd was a little one, a couple of long-necked
males with a double handful of smaller females and
a few young ones that seemed all leg and awkward-
ness. Unlike the donkeys, they ambled over the crust
around the Bitter Lake. Their hooves were wide and
soft, spreading under their weight to keep them from
falling through.

A male stood guard as the rest of the herd drank
at a scummy pool of water. Golobol looked distressed.
"That horrid liquid, surely it will poison them," he
said. "I would not drink it to save my life." His round
brown face screwed up in disgust.

"If you drank it, it would end your days all the
sooner. But humpless camels have evolved along with
the Bottomlands; their kidneys are wonderfully effi-
cient at extracting large amounts of salt."

"Why don't they have humps?" Lofosa asked.
"Krepalgan camels have humps." By her tone, what
she was used to was right.

"I know Krepalgan camels have humps," Radnal
said. "But the camels in the southern half of the
Double Continent don't, and neither do these. With
the Bottomlands beasts, I think the answer is that any
lump of fat—which is what a hump is—is a liability
in getting rid of heat."

"In the days before motors, we used to ride our
Krepalgan camels," Evillia said. "Has anyone ever
tamed your humpless ones?"

"That's a good question," Radnal said, beaming to
hide his surprise at her coming up with a good question. He went on, "It has been tried many times, in
fact. So far, it's never worked. They're too stubborn
to do what a human being wants. If we had domes-
ticated them, you'd be riding them now instead of

these donkeys; they're better suited to the terrain here."

Toglo zev Pamdal scratched her mount's ears. "They're also uglier than donkeys."

"Freelady—uh, Toglo zev—I can't argue with you," Radnal said. "They're uglier than anything I can think of, with dispositions to match."

As if insulted by words they couldn't have heard, the humpless camels raised their heads and trotted away from the Bitter Lake. Their backs went up and down, up and down, in time to their rocking gait. Evillia said, "In Krepalga, we sometimes call camels desert barques. Now I see why: riding on one looks like it would make me seasick."

The tourists laughed. So did Radnal. Making a joke in a language that wasn't Evillia's took some brains. Then why, Radnal wondered, did she act so empty-headed? But he shrugged; he'd seen a lot of people *with* brains do impressively stupid things.

"Why don't the camels eat all the forage in Trench Park?" Benter vez Maprab asked. He sounded as if his concern was for the plants, not the humpless camels.

"When the herds get too large for the park's resource, we cull them," Radnal answered. "This ecosystem is fragile. If we let it get out of balance, it would be a long time repairing itself."

"Are any herds of wild humpless camels left outside Trench Park, Radnal vez?" Toglo asked.

"A few small ones, in areas of the Bottomlands too barren for people," the tour guide said. "Not many, though. We occasionally introduce new males into this herd to increase genetic diversity, but they come from zoological parks, not the wild." The herd receded rapidly, shielded from clear view by the dust it kicked up. "I'm glad we had a chance to see them, if at a distance. That's why the gods made long lenses for cameras. But now we should head back to the lodge."

❖   ❖   ❖

The return journey north struck Radnal as curiously unreal. Though Peggol vez Menk rode among the tourists, they seemed to be pretending as hard as they could that Dokhnor of Kellef had not died, that this was just an ordinary holiday. The alternative was always looking over a shoulder, remembering the person next to you might be a murderer.

The person next to someone *was* a murderer. Whoever it was, he seemed no different from anyone else. That worried Radnal more than anything.

It even tainted his pleasure from talking with Toglo zev Pamdal. He had trouble imagining her as a killer, but he had trouble imagining anyone in the tour group a killer—save Dokhnor of Kellef, who was dead, and the Martoisi, who might want to kill each other.

He got to the point where he could say "Toglo zev" without prefacing it with "uh." He really wanted to ask her (but lacked the nerve) how she put up with him after watching him at play with the two Highhead girls. Tarteshans seldom thought well of those who made free with their bodies.

He also wondered what he'd do if Evillia and Lofosa came into his cubicle tonight. He'd throw them out, he decided. Edifying a tour group was one thing, edifying the Park Militia and the Eyes and Ears another. But what they did was *so* edifying . . . Maybe he wouldn't throw them out. He banged a fist onto his knee, irritated at his own fleshly weakness.

The lodge was only a couple of thousand cubits away when his donkey snorted and stiffened its legs against the ground. "Earthquake!" The word went up in Tarteshan and other languages. Radnal felt the ground jerk beneath him. He watched, and marveled at, the Martoisi clinging to each other atop their mounts.

After what seemed a daytenth but had to be an interval measured in heartbeats, the shaking ceased. Just in time, too; Peggol vez Menk's donkey, panicked

by the tremor, was about to buck the Eye and Ear
into a thornbush. Radnal caught the beast's reins,
calmed it.

"Thank you, freeman vez Krobir," Peggol said.
"That was bad."

"You didn't make it any better by letting go of the
reins," Radnal told him. "If you were in a motor,
wouldn't you hang on to the tiller?"

"I hope so," Peggol said. "But if I were in a motor,
it wouldn't try to run away by itself."

Moblay Sopsirk's son looked west, toward the
Barrier Mountains. "That was worse than the one
yesterday. I feared I'd see the Western Ocean pouring in with a wave as high as the Lion God's mane."

"As I've said before, that's not something you're
likely to have to worry about," Radnal said. "A quake
would have to be *very* strong and at exactly the wrong
place to disturb the mountains."

"So it would." Moblay did not sound comforted.

Radnal dismissed his concern with the mild scorn
you feel for someone who overreacts to a danger
you're used to. Over in the Double Continent, they
had vast and deadly windstorms. Radnal was sure one
of those would frighten him out of his wits. But the
Stekians probably took them in stride, as he lost no
sleep over earthquakes.

The sun sank toward the spikes of the Barrier
Mountains. As if bloodied by their pricking, its rays
grew redder as Bottomlands shadows lengthened.
More red sparkled from the glass and metal and
plastic of the helos between the lodge and the stables.
Noticing them made Radnal return to the here-and-
now. He wondered how the militiamen and Eyes and
Ears had done in their search for clues.

They came out as the tour group approached. In
their tan, speckled robes, the militiamen were almost
invisible against the desert. The Eyes and Ears, with
their white and gold and patent leather, might have

been spotted from ten thousand cubits away, or from the mountains of the moon.

Liem vez Steries waved to Radnal. "Any luck? Do you have the killer tied up in pink string?"

"Do you see any pink string?" Radnal turned back to face the group, raised his voice: "Let's get the donkeys settled. They can't do it for themselves. When they're fed and watered, we can worry about ourselves." *And about everything that's been going on*, he added to himself.

The tourists' dismounting groans were quieter than they'd been the day before; they were growing hardened to riding. Poor Peggol vez Menk assumed a bowlegged gait most often seen in rickets victims. "I was thinking of taking yesterday off," he said lugubriously. "I wish I had—someone else would have taken your call."

"You might have drawn a worse assignment," Radnal said, helping him unsaddle the donkey. The way Peggol rolled his eyes denied that was possible.

Fer vez Canthal and Zosel vez Glesir came over to help see to the tour group's donkeys. Under the brims of their caps, their eyes sparked with excitement. "Well, Radnal vez, we have a good deal to tell *you*," Fer began.

Peggol had a sore fundament, but his wits still worked. He made a sharp chopping gesture. "Freeman, save your news for a more private time." A smoother motion, this time with upturned palm, pointed out the chattering crowd still inside the stables. "Someone may hear something he should not."

Fer looked abashed. "Your pardon, freeman; no doubt you are right."

"No doubt." Peggol's tone argued that he couldn't be anything but. From under the shiny brim of his cap, his gaze flicked here and there, measuring everyone in turn with the calipers of his suspicion. It came

to Radnal, and showed no softening. Resentment
flared in the tour guide, then dimmed. He knew he
hadn't killed anyone, but the Eye and Ear didn't.

"I'll get the firepit started," Fer said.

"Good idea," Eltsac vez Martois said as he walked
by. "I'm hungry enough to eat one of those humpless
camels, raw and without salt."

"We can do better than that," Radnal said. He
noted the I-told-you-so look Peggol sent Fer vez
Canthal: if a tourist could overhear one bit of casual
conversation, why not another?

Liem vez Steries greeted Peggol with a formal
military salute he didn't use five times a year—his body
went tetanus-rigid, while he brought his right hand
up so the tip of his middle finger brushed the brim
of his cap. "Freeman, my compliments. We've all
heard of the abilities of the Hereditary Tyrant's Eyes
and Ears, but until now I've never seen them in action.
Your team is superb, and what they found—" Unlike
Fer vez Canthal, Liem had enough sense to close his
mouth right there.

Radnal felt like dragging him into the desert to pry
loose what he knew. But years of slow research had
left him a patient man. He ate supper, sang songs,
chatted about the earthquake and what he'd seen on
the journey to and from the Bitter Lake. One by one,
the tourists sought their sleepsacks.

Moblay Sopsirk's son, however, sought him out for
a game of war. For politeness' sake, Radnal agreed
to play, though he had so much on his mind that he
was sure the brown man from Lissonland would
trounce him. Either Moblay had things on his mind,
too, or he wasn't the player he thought he was. The
game was a comedy of errors which had the spectators biting their lips to keep from blurting out
better moves. Radnal eventually won, in inartistic
style.

Benter vez Maprab had been an onlooker. When

the game ended, he delivered a two-sentence verdict which was also obituary: "A wasted murder. Had the Morgaffo seen that, he'd've died of embarrassment." He stuck his nose in the air and stalked off to his sleeping cubicle.

"We'll have to try again another time, when we're thinking straighter," Radnal told Moblay, who nodded ruefully.

Radnal put away the war board and pieces. By then, Moblay was the only tourist left in the common room. Radnal sat down next to Liem vez Steries, not across the gaming table from the Lissonese. Moblay refused to take the hint.

Finally Radnal grabbed the rhinoceros by the horn: "Forgive me, freeman, but we have a lot to discuss among ourselves."

"Don't mind me," Moblay said cheerfully. "I'm not in your way, I hope. And I'd be interested to hear how you Tarteshans investigate. Maybe I can bring something useful back to my prince."

Radnal exhaled through his nose. Biting off words one by one, he said, "Freeman vez Sopsirk, you are a subject of this investigation. To be blunt, we have matters to discuss which you shouldn't hear."

"We also have other, weightier, things to discuss," Peggol vez Menk put in. "Remember, freeman, this is not your principality."

"It never occurred to me that you might fear I was guilty," Moblay said. "*I* know I'm not, so I assumed you did, too. Maybe I'll try and screw the Krepalgan girls, since it doesn't sound like Radnal will be using them tonight."

Peggol raised an eyebrow. "Them?" He packed a world of question into one word.

Under their coat of down, Radnal's ears went hot. Fortunately, he managed to answer a question with a question: "What could be weightier than learning who killed Dokhnor of Kellef?"

Peggol glanced from one sleeping cubicle to the next, as if wondering who was feigning slumber. "Why don't you walk with me in the cool night air? Sub-leader vez Steries can come with us; he was here all day, and can tell you what he saw himself—things I heard when I took my own evening walk, and which I might garble in reporting them to you."

"Let's walk, then," Radnal said, though he wondered where Peggol vez Menk would find cool night air in Trench Park. Deserts above sea level cooled rapidly when the sun set, but that wasn't true in the Bottomlands.

Getting out in the quiet dark made it seem cooler. Radnal, Peggol, and Liem walked without saying much for a couple of hundred cubits. Only when they were out of earshot of the lodge did the park militiaman announce, "Freeman vez Menk's colleagues discovered a microprint reader among the Morgaffo's effects."

"Did they, by the gods?" Radnal said. "Where, Liem vez? What was it disguised as?"

"A stick of artist's charcoal." The militiaman shook his head. "I thought I knew every trick in the codex, but that's a new one. Now we can rub the plenipo's nose in it if he fusses about losing a Morgaffo citizen in Tartesh. But even that's a small thing, next to what the reader held."

Radnal stared. "Heading off a war with Morgaf is small?"

"It is, freeman vez Krobir," Peggol vez Menk said. "You remember today's earthquake—"

"Yes, and there was another one yesterday, a smaller one," Radnal interrupted. "They happen all the time down here. No one except a tourist like Moblay Sopsirk's son worries about them. You reinforce your buildings so they won't fall down except in the worst shocks, then go on about your business."

"Sensible," Peggol said. "Sensible under most circumstances, anyway. Not here, not now."

"Why not?" Radnal demanded.

"Because, if what was on Dokhnor of Kellef's microprint reader is true—always a question when we're dealing with Morgaffos—someone is trying to engineer a special earthquake."

Radnal's frown drew his heavy eyebrows together above his nose. "I still don't know what you're talking about."

Liem vez Steries inclined his head to Peggol vez Menk. "By your leave, freeman—?" When Peggol nodded, Liem went on, "Radnal vez, over the years somebody—has smuggled the parts for a starbomb into Trench Park."

The tour guide gaped at his friend. "That's insane. If somebody smuggled a starbomb into Tartesh, he'd put it by the Hereditary Tyrant's palace, not here. What does he want, to blow up the last big herd of humpless camels in the world?"

"He has more in mind than that," Liem answered. "You see, the bomb is underground, on one of the fault lines nearest the Barrier Mountains." The militiaman's head swiveled to look west toward the sawbacked young mountain range . . .

. . . the mountain range that held back the Western Ocean. The night was warm and dry, but cold sweat prickled on Radnal's back and under his arms. "They want to try to knock the mountains down. I'm no geologist—can they?"

"The gods may know," Liem answered. "I'm no geologist either, so I don't. This I'll tell you: the Morgaffos seem to think it would work."

Peggol vez Menk cleared his throat. "The Hereditary Tyrant discourages research in this area, lest any positive answers fall into the wrong hands. Thus our studies have been limited. I gather, however, that such a result might be obtained."

"The freeman's colleagues radiophoned a geologist known to be reliable," Liem amplified. "They put to him some of what was on the microprint reader, as a theoretical exercise. When they were through, he sounded ready to wet his robes."

"I don't blame him." Radnal looked toward the Barrier Mountains, too. What had Moblay said? *A wave as high as the Lion God's mane*. If the mountains fell at once, the wave might reach Krepalga before it halted. The deaths, the devastation, would be incalculable. His voice shook as he asked, "What do we do about it?"

"Good question," Peggol said, astringent as usual. "We don't know whether it's really there, who planted it if it is, where it is, or if it's ready. Other than that, we're fine."

Liem's voice turned savage: "I wish all the tourists were Tarteshans. Then we could question them as thoroughly as we needed, until we got truth from them."

Thoroughly, Radnal knew, was a euphemism for *harshly*. Tarteshan justice was more pragmatic than merciful, so much so that applying it to foreigners would strain diplomatic relations and might provoke war. The tour guide said, "We couldn't even be properly thorough with our own people, not when one of them is Toglo zev Pamdal."

"I'd forgotten." Liem made a face. "But you can't suspect *her*. Why would the Hereditary Tyrant's relative want to destroy the country he's Hereditary Tyrant of? It makes no sense."

"I don't suspect her," Radnal said. "I meant we'll have to use our heads here; we can't rely on brute force."

"I suspect everyone," Peggol vez Menk said, matter-of-factly as if he'd said, *It's hot tonight*. "For that matter, I also suspect the information we found among Dokhnor's effects. It might have been planted there to provoke us to question several foreign tourists thoroughly and embroil us with their governments. Morgaffo duplicity knows no bounds."

"As may be, freeman, but dare we take the chance that this is duplicity, not real danger?" Liem said.

"If you mean, *dare we ignore the danger?*—of course not," Peggol said. "But it might be duplicity."

"Would the Morgaffos kill one of their own agents to mislead us?" Radnal asked. "If Dokhnor were alive, we'd have no idea this plot was afoot."

"They might, precisely because they'd expect us to doubt they were so coldhearted," Peggol answered. Radnal thought the Eye and Ear would suspect someone of stealing the sun if a morning dawned cloudy. That was what Eyes and Ears were for, but it made Peggol an uncomfortable companion.

"Since we can't question the tourists thoroughly, what shall we do tomorrow?" Radnal said.

"Go on as we have been," Peggol replied unhappily. "If any of them makes the slightest slip, that will justify our using appropriate persuasive measures." Not even a man who sometimes used torture in his work was easy saying the word out loud.

"I can see one problem coming soon, freeman vez Menk—" Radnal said.

"Call me Peggol vez," the Eye and Ear interrupted. "We're in this mess together; we might as well treat each other as friends. I'm sorry—go ahead."

"Sooner or later, Peggol vez, the tour group will want to go west, toward the Barrier Mountains—and toward the fault line where this starbomb may be. If it requires some finishing touches, that will give whoever is supposed to handle them his best chance. If it is someone in the tour group, of course."

"When were you thinking of doing this?" If he'd sounded unhappy before, he was lugubrious now.

Radnal didn't cheer him up: "The western swing was on the itinerary for tomorrow. I could change it, but—"

"But that would warn the culprit—if there is a culprit—we know what's going on. Yes." Peggol fingered the tuft of hair under his lip. "I think you'd better make the change anyhow, Radnal vez." Having heard Radnal use his name with the polite particle, he could do likewise. "Better to alert the enemy than offer him a free opportunity."

Liem vez Steries began, "Freeman vez Menk—"

The Eye and Ear broke in again: "What I told Radnal also holds for you."

"Fair enough, Peggol vez," Liem said. "How could Morgaf have got wind of this plot against Tartesh without our having heard of it, too? I mean no disrespect, I assure you, but this matter concerns me." He waved toward the Barrier Mountains, which suddenly seemed a much less solid bulwark than they had before.

"The question is legitimate, and I take no offense. I see two possible answers," Peggol said. (Radnal had a feeling the Eye and Ear saw at least two answers to every question.) "One is that Morgaf may be doing this deceitfully to incite us against our other neighbors, as I said before. The other is that the plot is real, and whoever dreamed it up approached the Morgaffos so they could fall on us after the catastrophe."

Each possibility was logical; Radnal wished he could choose between them. Since he couldn't, he said, "There's nothing we can do about it now, so we might as well sleep. In the morning, I'll tell the tourists we're going east, not west. That's an interesting excursion, too. It—"

Peggol raised a hand. "Since I'll see it tomorrow, why not keep me in suspense?" He twisted this way and that. "You can't die of an impacted fundament, can you?"

"I've never heard of it happening, anyhow." Radnal hid a smile.

"Maybe I'll be a medical first, and get written up in all the physicians' codices." Peggol rubbed the afflicted parts. "And I'll have to go riding again tomorrow, eh? How unfortunate."

"If we don't get some sleep soon, we'll both be dozing in the saddle," Radnal said, yawning. "It must be a couple of daytenths past sunset by now. I thought Moblay would never head for his cubicle."

"Maybe he was just fond of you, Radnal." Liem vez Steries put a croon in the guide's name that burlesqued the way the Lissonese kept leaving off the polite particle.

Radnal snapped, "Night demons carry you off, Liem vez, the ideas you come up with." He waited for the militiaman to taunt him about Evillia and Lofosa, but Liem left that alone. He wondered what ideas the two girls from the Krepalgan Unity had come up with, and whether they'd use them with him tonight. He hoped not—as he'd told Peggol, he did need sleep. Then he wondered if putting sleep ahead of fornication meant he was getting old.

If it did, too bad, he decided. Along with Peggol and Liem, he walked back to the lodge. The other militiamen and Eyes and Ears reported in whispers—all quiet.

Radnal turned a curious ear toward Evillia's sleep cubicle, then Lofosa's, and then Moblay Sopsirk's son's. He didn't hear moans or thumpings from any of them. He wondered whether Moblay hadn't propositioned the Krepalgan girls, or whether they'd turned him down. Or maybe they'd frolicked and gone back to sleep. No, that last wasn't likely; the Eyes and Ears would have been smirking about the eye- and earful they'd got.

Yawning again, Radnal went into his own sleep cubicle, took off his sandals, undid his belt, and lay down. The air-filled sleepsack sighed beneath him like a lover. He angrily shook his head. Two nights with

Lofosa and Evillia had filled his mind with lewd notions.

He hoped they would leave him alone again. He knew their dalliance with him was already an entry in Peggol vez Menk's dossier; having the Eye and Ear watch him at play—or listen to him quarreling with them when he sent them away—would not improve the entry.

Those two nights, he'd just been falling asleep when Evillia and Lofosa joined him. Tonight, nervous about whether they'd come, and about everything he'd heard from Peggol and Liem, he lay awake a long time. The girls stayed in their own cubicles.

He dozed off without knowing he'd done so. His eyes flew open when a koprit bird on the roof announced the dawn with a raucous *hig-hig-hig!* He needed a couple of heartbeats to wake fully, realize he'd been asleep, and remember what he'd have to do this morning.

He put on his sandals, fastened his belt, and walked into the common room. Most of the militiamen and Eyes and Ears were already awake. Peggol wasn't; Radnal wondered how much knowing he snored would be worth as blackmail. Liem vez Steries said quietly, "No one murdered last night."

"I'm glad to hear it," Radnal said, sarcastic and truthful at the same time.

Lofosa came out of her cubicle. She still wore what Radnal assumed to be Krepalgan sleeping attire, namely skin. Not a hair on her head was mussed, and she'd done something to her eyes to make them look bigger and brighter than they really were. All the men stared at her, some more openly, some less.

She smiled at Radnal and said in a voice like silver bells, "I hope you didn't miss us last night, freeman vez Krobir. It would have been as much fun as the other two, but we were too tired." Before he could answer (he would have needed a while to find an answer), she went outside to the privy.

The tour guide looked down at his sandals, not daring to meet anyone's eyes. He listened to the small coughs that meant the others didn't know what to say to him, either. Finally Liem remarked, "Sounds as though she knows you well enough to call you Radnal vez."

"I suppose so," Radnal muttered. In physical terms, she'd been intimate enough with him to leave off the *vez*. Her Tarteshan was good enough that she ought to know it, too. She'd managed to embarrass him even more by combining the formal address with such a familiar message. She couldn't have made him look more foolish if she'd tried for six moons.

Evillia emerged from her cubicle, dressed, or undressed, like Lofosa. She didn't banter with Radnal, but headed straight for the privy. She and Lofosa met each other behind the helos. They talked for a few heartbeats before each continued on her way.

Toglo zev Pamdal walked into the common room as Lofosa returned from outside. Lofosa stared at the Strongbrow woman, as if daring Toglo to remark on her nakedness. A lot of Tarteshans, especially female Tarteshans, would have remarked on it in detail.

Toglo said only, "I trust you slept well, freelady?" From her casual tone, she might have been talking to a neighbor she didn't know well but with whom she was on good terms.

"Yes, thank you." Lofosa dropped her eyes when she concluded she couldn't use her abundantly displayed charms to bait Toglo.

"I'm glad to hear it," Toglo said, still sweetly. "I wouldn't want you to catch cold on holiday."

Lofosa took half a step, then jerked as if poked by a pin. Toglo had already turned to greet the others in the common room. For a heartbeat, maybe two,

Lofosa's teeth showed in a snarl like a cave cat's. Then she went back into her cubicle to finish getting ready for the day.

"I hope I didn't offend her—too much," Toglo said to Radnal.

"I think you handled yourself like a diplomat," he answered.

"Hmm," she said. "Given the state of the world, I wonder whether that's a compliment." Radnal didn't answer. Given what he'd heard the night before, the state of the world might be worse than Toglo imagined.

His own diplomatic skills got a workout after breakfast, when he explained to the group that they'd be going east rather than west. Golobol said, "I find the change from the itinerary most distressing, yes." His round brown face bore a doleful expression.

Benter vez Maprab found any change distressing. "This is an outrage," he blustered. "The herbaceous cover approaching the Barrier Mountains is far richer than that to the east."

"I'm sorry," Radnal said, an interesting mixture of truth and lie: he didn't mind annoying Benter, but would sooner not have had such a compelling reason.

"I don't mind going east rather than west today," Toglo zev Pamdal said. "As far as I'm concerned, there are plenty of interesting things to see either way. But I would like to know *why* the schedule has been changed."

"So would I," Moblay Sopsirk's son said. "Toglo is right—what are you trying to hide, anyhow?"

All the tourists started talking—the Martoisi started shouting—at once. Radnal's own reaction to the Lissonese man was a wish that a trench in Trench Park went down a lot deeper, say, to the red-hot center of the earth. He would have shoved Moblay into it. Not only was he a boor, to use a woman's name without the polite particle (using it uninvited even with the particle would have been an undue liberty), he was a snoop and a rabble-rouser.

Peggol vez Menk slammed his open hand down on the table beside which Dokhnor of Kellef had died. The boom cut through the chatter. Into sudden silence, Peggol said, "Freeman vez Krobir changed your itinerary at my suggestion. Aspects of the murder case suggest that course would in the best interests of Tartesh."

"This tells us nothing, not a thing." Now Golobol sounded really angry, not just upset at breaking routine. "You say these fine-sounding words, but where is the meaning behind them?"

"If I told you everything you wished to know, freeman, I would also be telling those who should not hear," Peggol said.

"Pfui!" Golobol stuck out his tongue.

Eltsac vez Martois said, "I think you Eyes and Ears think you're little tin demigods."

But Peggol's pronouncement quieted most of the tourists. Ever since starbombs came along, nations had grown more anxious about keeping secrets from one another. That struck Radnal as worrying about the cave cat after he'd carried off the goat, but who could tell? There might be worse things than starbombs.

He said, "As soon as I can, I promise I will tell all of you everything I can about what's going on." Peggol vez Menk gave him a hard look; Peggol wouldn't have told anyone his own name if he could help it.

"What *is* going on?" Toglo echoed.

Since Radnal was none too certain himself, he met that comment with dignified silence. He did say, "The longer we quarrel here, the less we'll have the chance to see, no matter which direction we end up choosing."

"That makes sense, freeman vez Krobir," Evillia said. Neither she nor Lofosa had argued about going east as opposed to west.

Radnal looked around the group, saw more resignation than outrage. He said, "Come now, freemen, freeladies, let's head for the stables. There are many fascinating things to see east of the lodge—and to hear, also. There's the Night Demons' Retreat, for instance."

"Oh, good!" Toglo clapped her hands. "As I've said, it rained the last time I was here. The guide was too worried about flash floods to take us out there. I've wanted to see that ever since I read Hicag zev Ginfer's frightener codex."

"You mean *Stones of Doom*?" Radnal's opinion of Toglo's taste fell. Trying to stay polite, he said, "It wasn't as accurate as it might have been."

"I thought it was trash," Toglo said. "But I went to school with Hicag zev and we've been friends ever since, so I had to read it. And she certainly makes the Night Demons' Retreat sound exotic, whether there's a breeze of truth in what she writes or not."

"Maybe a breeze—a mild breeze," Radnal said.

"I read it, too. I thought it was very exciting," Nocso zev Martois said.

"The tour guide thinks it's garbage," her husband told her.

"I didn't say *that*," Radnal said. Neither Martois listened to him; they enjoyed yelling at each other more.

"Enough of your own breeze. If we must do this, let's do it, at least," Benter vez Maprab said.

"As you say, freeman." Radnal wished the Night Demons' Retreat really held night demons. With any luck, they'd drag Benter into the stones and no one in the tour group would ever see—or have to listen to—him again. But such convenient things happened only in codices.

❖   ❖   ❖

The tourists were getting better with the donkeys. Even Peggol seemed less obviously out of place on donkeyback than he had yesterday. As the group rode away from the lodge, Radnal looked back and saw park militiamen and Eyes and Ears advancing on the stables to go over them again.

He made himself forget the murder investigation and remember he was a tour guide. "Because we're off earlier this morning, we're more likely to see small reptiles and mammals that shelter against the worst heat," he said. "Many of them—"

A sudden little *flip* of sandy dirt a few cubits ahead made him stop. "By the gods, there's one now." He dismounted. "I think that's a shoveler skink."

"A what?" By now, Radnal was used to the chorus that followed whenever he pointed out one of the more unusual denizens of the Bottomlands.

"A shoveler skink," he repeated. He crouched down. Yes, sure enough, there was the lure. He knew he had an even-money chance. If he grabbed the tail end, the lizard would shed the appendage and flee. But if he got it by the neck—

He did. The skink twisted like a piece of demented rubber, trying to wriggle free. It also voided. Lofosa made a disgusted noise. Radnal took such things in stride.

After thirty or forty heartbeats, the skink gave up and lay still. Radnal had been waiting for that. He carried the palm-sized lizard into the midst of the tourists. "Skinks are common all over the world, but the shoveler is the most curious variety. It's a terrestrial equivalent of the anglerfish. Look—"

He tapped the orange fleshy lump that grew on the end of a spine about two digits long. "The skink buries itself under sand, with just this lure and the tip of its nose sticking out. See how its ribs extend to either side, so it looks more like a gliding animal than one that lives underground? It has specialized musculature, to make those long rib ends bend what we'd think of as the wrong way. When an insect comes along, the lizard tosses dirt on it, then twists around and snaps it up. It's a beautiful creature."

"It's the ugliest thing I ever saw," Moblay Sopsirk's son declared.

The lizard didn't care one way or the other. It peered at him through little beady black eyes. If the variety survived another few million years—if the Bottomlands survived another couple of moons, Radnal thought nervously—future specimens might lose their sight altogether, as had already happened with other subterranean skinks.

Radnal walked out of the path, put the lizard back on the ground. It scurried away, surprisingly fast on its short legs. After six or eight cubits, it seemed to melt into the ground. Within moments, only the bright orange lure betrayed its presence.

Evillia asked, "Do any bigger creatures go around looking for lures to catch the skinks?"

"As a matter of fact, yes," Radnal said. "Koprit birds can see color; you'll often see shoveler skinks impaled in their hoards. Big-eared nightfoxes eat them, too, but they track by scent, not sight."

"I hope no koprit birds come after me," Evillia said, laughing. She and Lofosa wore matching red-orange tunics—almost the same shade as the shoveler skink's lure—with two rows of big gold buttons, and red plastic necklaces with gold clasps.

Radnal smiled. "I think you're safe enough. And now that the lizard is safe, for the time being, shall we go—? No, wait, where's freeman vez Maprab?"

The old Strongbrow emerged from behind a big, wide-spreading thornbush a few heartbeats later, still refastening the belt to his robe. "Sorry for the delay, but I thought I'd answer nature's call while we paused here."

"I just didn't want to lose you, freeman." Radnal

stared at Benter as he got back onto his donkey. This was the first apology he'd heard from him. He wondered if the tourist was well.

The group rode slowly eastward. Before long, people began to complain. "Every piece of Trench Park looks like every other piece," Lofosa said.

"Yes, when will we see something different?" Moblay Sopsirk's son agreed. Radnal suspected he would have agreed if Lofosa said the sky were pink; he slavered after her. He went on, "It's all hot and flat and dry; even the thornbushes are boring."

"Freeman, if you wanted to climb mountains and roll in snow, you should have gone someplace else," Radnal said. "That's not what the Bottomlands have to offer. But there are mountains and snow all over the world; there's nothing like Trench Park anywhere. And if you tell me this terrain is like what we saw yesterday around the Bitter Lake, freeman, freelady"—he glanced over at Lofosa—"I think you're both mistaken."

"They certainly are," Benter vez Maprab chimed in. "This area has very different flora from the other one. Note the broader-leafed spurges, the oleanders—"

"They're just plants," Lofosa said. Benter clapped a hand to his head in shock and dismay. Radnal waited for him to have another bad-tempered fit, but he just muttered to himself and subsided.

About a quarter of a daytenth later, Radnal pointed toward a gray smudge on the eastern horizon. "There's the Night Demons' Retreat. I promise it's like nothing you've yet seen in Trench Park."

"I hope it shall be interesting, oh yes," Golobol said.

"I loved the scene where the demons came out at sunset, claws dripping blood," Nocso zev Martois said. Her voice rose in shivery excitement.

Radnal sighed. "*Stones of Doom* is only a frightener, freelady. No demons live inside the Retreat, or come out at sunset or any other time. I've passed the night in a sleepsack not fifty cubits from the stonepile, and

I'm still here, with my blood inside me where it belongs."

Nocso made a face. No doubt she preferred melodrama to reality. Since she was married to Eltsac, reality couldn't seem too attractive to her.

The Night Demons' Retreat was a pile of gray granite, about a hundred cubits high, looming over the flat floor of the Bottomlands. Holes of all sizes pitted the granite. Under the merciless sun, the black openings reminded Radnal of skulls' eyes looking at him.

"Some holes look big enough for a person to crawl into," Peggol vez Menk remarked. "Has anybody ever explored them?"

"Yes, many people," Radnal answered. "We discourage it, though, because although no one's ever found a night demon, they're a prime denning place for vipers and scorpions. They also often hold bats' nests. Seeing the bats fly out at dusk to hunt bugs doubtless helped start the legend about the place."

"Bats live all over," Nocso said. "There's only one Night Demons' Retreat, because—"

The breeze, which had been quiet, suddenly picked up. Dust skirled over the ground. Radnal grabbed for his cap. And from the many mineral throats of the Night Demons' Retreat came a hollow moaning and wailing that made the hair on his body want to stand on end.

Nocso looked ecstatic. "There!" she exclaimed. "The cry of the deathless demons, seeking to be free to work horror on the world!"

Radnal remembered the starbomb that might be buried by the Barrier Mountains, and thought of horrors worse than any demons could produce. He said, "Freelady, as I'm sure you know, it's just wind playing some badly tuned flutes. The softer rock around the Retreat weathered away, and the Retreat itself has taken a lot of sandblasting. Whatever bits that weren't as hard as the rest are gone, which explains how and why the openings formed. And now, when the wind blows across them, they make the weird sounds we just heard."

"Hmp!" Nocso said. "If there are gods, how can there not be demons?"

"Freelady, speak to a priest about that, not to me." Radnal swore by the gods of Tartesh but, like most educated folk of his generation, had little other use for them.

Peggol vez Menk said, "Freelady, the question of whether night demons exist does not necessarily have anything to do with the question of whether they haunt the Night Demons' Retreat—except that if there be no demons, they are unlikely to be at the Retreat."

Nocso's plump face filled with rage. But she thought twice about telling off an Eye and Ear. She turned her head and shouted at Eltsac instead. He shouted back.

The breeze swirled around, blowing bits of grit into the tour guide's face. More unmusical notes emanated from the Night Demons' Retreat. Cameras clicked. "I wish I'd brought along a recorder," Toglo zev Pamdal said. "What's interesting here isn't how this place looks, but how it sounds."

"You can buy a wire of the Night Demons' Retreat during a windstorm at the gift shop near the entrance to Trench Park."

"Thank you, Radnal vez; I may do that on my way out. It would be even better, though, if I could have recorded what I heard with my own ears." Toglo's glance slipped to Eltsac and Nocso, who were still barking at each other. "Well, some of what I heard."

Evillia said, "This Night Demons' Retreat was on the sea floor?"

"That's right. As the dried muck and salt that surrounded it eroded, it was left alone here. Think of it as a miniature version of the mountain plains that stick up from the Bottomlands. In ancient days, they were islands. The Retreat, of course, was below the surface back then."

And may be again, he thought. He imagined fish peering into the holes in the ancient granite, crabs scuttling in to scavenge the remains of snakes and sand rats. The picture came to vivid life in his mind. That bothered him; it meant he took this menace seriously.

He was so deep in his own concerns that he needed a couple of heartbeats to realize the group had fallen silent. When he did notice, he looked up in a hurry, wondering what was wrong. From a third of the way up the Night Demons' Retreat, a cave cat looked back.

The cave cat must have been asleep inside a crevice until the tourists' racket woke it. It yawned, showing yellow fangs and pink tongue. Then, with steady amber gaze, it peered at the tourists once more, as if wondering what sauce would go well with them.

"Let's move away from the Retreat," Radnal said quietly. "We don't want it to think we're threatening it." That would have been a good trick, he thought. If the cave cat did decide to attack, his handcannon would hurt it (assuming he was lucky enough to hit), but it wouldn't kill. He opened the flap to his saddlebag just the same.

For once, all the tourists did exactly as they were told. Seeing the great predator raised fears that went back to the days of man-apes just learning to walk erect.

Moblay Sopsirk's son asked, "Will more of them be around? In Lissonland, lions hunt in prides."

"No, cave cats are solitary except during mating season," Radnal answered. "They and lions have a common ancestor, but their habits differ. The Bottomlands don't have big herds that make pride hunting a successful survival strategy."

Just when Radnal wondered if the cave cat was going back to sleep, it exploded into motion. Long gray-brown mane flying, it bounded down the steep slope of the Night Demons' Retreat. Radnal yanked out his handcannon. He saw Peggol vez Menk also had one.

But when the cave cat hit the floor of the Bottomlands, it streaked away from the tour group. Its grayish fur made it almost invisible against the desert. Cameras clicked incessantly. Then the beast was gone.

"How beautiful," Toglo zev Pamdal breathed. After a moment, she turned more practical: "Where does he find water?"

"He doesn't need much, Toglo zev," he answered. "Like other Bottomlands creatures, he makes the most of what he gets from the bodies of his prey. Also"— he pointed north—"there are a few tiny springs in the hills. Back when it was legal to hunt cave cats, a favorite way was to find a spring and lay in wait until the animal came to drink."

"It seems criminal," Toglo said.

"To us, certainly," Radnal half-agreed. "But to a man who's just had his flocks raided or a child carried off, it was natural enough. We go wrong when we judge the past by our standards."

"The biggest difference between past and present is that we moderns are able to sin on a much larger scale," Peggol said. Maybe he was thinking of the buried starbomb. But recent history held enough other atrocities to make Radnal have trouble disagreeing.

Eltsac vez Martois said, "Well, freeman vez Krobir, I have to admit that was worth the price of admission."

Radnal beamed; of all the people from whom he expected praise, Eltsac was the last. Then Nocso chimed in: "But it would have been even more exciting if the cave cat had come toward us and he'd had to shoot at it."

"I'll say," Eltsac agreed. "I'd love to have that on film."

Why, Radnal wondered, did the Martoisi see eye to eye only when they were both wrong? He said, "With respect, I'm delighted the animal went the other way. I'd hate to fire at so rare a creature, and I'd hate even more to miss and have anyone come to harm."

"Miss?" Nocso said the word as if it hadn't occurred to her. It probably hadn't; people in adventure stories shot straight whenever they needed to.

Eltsac said, "Shooting well isn't easy. When I was drafted into the Voluntary Guards, I needed three tries before I qualified with a rifle."

"Oh, but that's you, not a tour guide," Nocso said scornfully. "He has to shoot well."

Through Eltsac's outraged bellow, Radnal said, "I will have you know, I have never fired a handcannon in all my time at Trench Park." He didn't add that, given a choice between shooting at a cave cat and at Nocso, he'd sooner have fired on her.

The wind picked up again. The Night Demons' Retreat made more frightful noises. Radnal imagined how he would have felt if he were an illiterate hunter, say, hearing those ghostly wails for the first time. He was sure he'd've fouled his robes from fear.

But even so, something else also remained true: judging by the standards of the past was even more foolish when the present offered better information. If Nocso believed in night demons for no better reason than that she'd read an exciting frightener about them, that only argued she didn't have the sense the gods gave a shoveler skink. Radnal smiled. As far as he could tell, she *didn't* have the sense the gods gave a shoveler skink.

"We'll go in the direction opposite the one the cave cat took," Radnal said at last. "We'll also stay in a tight group. If you ask me, anyone who goes wandering off deserves to be eaten."

The tourists rode almost in one another's laps. As far as Radnal could tell, the eastern side of the Night Demons' Retreat wasn't much different from the western. But he'd been here tens of times already. Tourists could hardly be blamed for wanting to see as much as they could.

"No demons over here, either, Nocso," Eltsac vez Martois said. His wife stuck her nose in the air. Radnal wondered why they stayed married—for that matter, he wondered why they'd got married—when they sniped at each other so. Pressure from their kith groupings, probably. It didn't seem a good enough reason.

So why was he haggling over bride price with Wello zev Putun's father? The Putuni were a solid family in the lower aristocracy, a good connection for an up-and-coming man. He couldn't think of anything wrong with Wello, but she didn't much stir him, either. Would she have read *Stones of Doom* without recognizing it for the garbage it was? Maybe. That worried him. If he wanted a woman with whom he could talk, would he need a concubine? Peggol had one. Radnal wondered if the arrangement made him happy. Likely not—Peggol took a perverse pleasure in not enjoying anything.

Thinking of Wello brought Radnal's mind back to the two nights of excess he'd enjoyed with Evillia and Lofosa. He was sure he wouldn't want to marry a woman whose body was her only attraction, but he also doubted the wisdom of marrying one whose body didn't attract him. What he needed—

He snorted. *What I need is for a goddess to take flesh and fall in love with me . . . if she doesn't destroy my self-confidence by letting on she's a goddess.* Finding such a mate—especially for a bride price less than the annual budget of Tartesh—seemed unlikely. Maybe Wello would do after all.

"Are we going back by the same route we came?"
Toglo zev Pamdal asked.

"I hadn't planned to," Radnal said. "I'd aimed to
swing further south on the way back, to give you the
chance to see country you haven't been through
before." He couldn't resist adding, "No matter how
much the same some people find it."

Moblay Sopsirk's son looked innocent. "If you mean
me, Radnal, I'm happy to discover new things. I just
haven't come across that many here."

"Hmp," Toglo said. "I'm having a fine time here.
I was glad to see the Night Demons' Retreat at last,
and also to hear it. I can understand why our ancestors believed horrid creatures dwelt inside."

"I was thinking the same thing only a couple of
hundred heartbeats ago," Radnal said.

"What a nice coincidence." A smile brightened her
face. To Radnal's disappointment, she didn't stay
cheerful long. She said, "This tour is so marvelous,
I can't help thinking it would be finer still if Dokhnor
of Kellef were still alive, or even if we knew who
killed him."

"Yes," Radnal said. He'd spent much of the day
glancing from one tourist to the next, trying to figure out who had broken the Morgaffo's neck. He'd
even tried suspecting the Martoisi. He'd dismissed
them before, as too inept to murder anybody quietly.
But what if their squawk and bluster only disguised
devious purposes?

His laugh came out dusty as Peggol vez Menk's.
He couldn't believe it. Besides, Nocso and Eltsac were
Tarteshans. They wouldn't want to see their country
ruined. Or could they be paid enough to want to
destroy it?

Nocso looked back toward the Night Demons'
Retreat just as a koprit bird flew into one of the holes
in the granite. "A demon! I saw a night demon!" she
squalled.

Radnal laughed again. If Nocso was a spy and a saboteur, he was a humpless camel. "Come on," he called. "Time to head back."

As he'd promised, he took his charges to the lodge by a new route. Moblay Sopsirk's son remained unimpressed. "It may not be the same, but it isn't much different."

"Oh, rubbish!" Benter vez Maprab said. "The flora here are quite distinct from those we observed this morning."

"Not to me," Moblay said stubbornly.

"Freeman vez Maprab, by your interest in plants of all sorts, were you by chance a scholar of botany?" Radnal asked.

"By the gods, no!" Benter whinnied laughter. "I ran a train of plant and flower shops until I retired."

"Oh. I see." Radnal did, too. With that practical experience, Benter might have learned as much about plants as any scholar of botany.

About a quarter of a daytenth later, the old man reined in his donkey and went behind another thornbush. "Sorry to hold everyone up," he said when he returned. "My kidneys aren't what they used to be."

Eltsac vez Martois guffawed. "Don't worry, Benter vez. A fellow like you knows you have to water the plants. Haw, haw!"

"You're a bigger jackass than your donkey," Benter snapped.

"Freemen, please!" Radnal got the two men calmed down and made sure they rode far from each other. He didn't care if they went at each other three heartbeats after they left Trench Park, but they were his responsibility till then.

"You earn your silver here, I'll say that for you," Peggol observed. "I see fools in my line of work, but I'm not obliged to stay polite to them." He lowered his voice. "When freeman vez Maprab went behind

the bush now, he didn't just relieve himself. He also
bent down and pulled something out of the ground.
I happened to be off to one side."

"Did he? How interesting." Radnal doubted Benter
was involved in the killing of Dokhnor of Kellef. But
absconding with plants from Trench Park was also a
crime, one the tour guide was better equipped to deal
with than murder. "We won't do anything about it
now. After we get back to the lodge, why don't you
have your men search Benter vez's belongings again?"

Amusement glinted in Peggol's eyes. "You're looking
forward to this."

"Who, me? The only thing that could be better
would be if it were Eltsac vez instead. But he hasn't
a brain in his head or anywhere else about his
person."

"Are you sure?" Peggol had been thinking along
the same lines as Radnal. He'd probably started well
before Radnal had, too. That was part of his job.

But Radnal came back strong: "If he had brains,
would he have married Nocso zev?" That won a laugh
which didn't sound dusty. He added, "Besides, all he
knows about thornbushes is not to ride into them,
and he's not certain of that."

"Malice agrees with you, Radnal vez."

By the time the lodge neared, Golobol was complaining along with Moblay. "Take away the Night
Demons' Retreat, oh yes, and take away the cave cat
we saw there, and what have you? Take away those
two things and it is a nothing of a day."

"Freeman, if you insist on ignoring everything
interesting that happens, you can turn any day dull,"
Toglo observed.

"Well said!" Being a tour guide kept Radnal from
speaking his mind to the people he led. This time,
Toglo had done it for him.

She smiled. "Why come see what the Bottomlands
are like if he isn't happy with what he finds?"

"Toglo zev, some are like that in every group. It makes no sense to me, but there you are. If I had the money to see the Nine Iron Towers of Mashyak, I wouldn't whine because they aren't gold."

"That is a practical attitude," Toglo said. "We'd be better off if more people felt as you do."

"We'd be better off if—" Radnal shut up. *If we didn't fear a starbomb was buried somewhere around here* was how he'd been about to end the sentence. That wasn't smart. Not only would it frighten Toglo (or worry her; she didn't seem to frighten easily), but Peggol vez Menk would come down on him like he didn't know what for breaching security.

All at once, he knew how Peggol would come down on him: like the Western Ocean, pouring into the Bottomlands over the broken mountains. He tried to laugh at himself; he didn't usually come up with such literary comparisons. Laughter failed. The simile was literary, but it might be literal as well.

"We'd be better off if what, Radnal vez?" Toglo asked. "What did you start to say?"

He couldn't tell her what he'd started to say. He wasn't glib enough to invent something smooth. To his dismay, what came out of his mouth was, "We'd be better off if more people were like you, Toglo zev, and didn't have fits at what they saw other people doing."

"Oh, that. Radnal vez, I didn't think anyone who was doing that was hurting anyone else. You all seemed to be enjoying yourselves. It's not something I'd care to do where other people might see, but I don't see I have any business getting upset about it."

"Oh." Radnal wasn't sure how to take Toglo's answer. He had, however, already pushed his luck past the point where it had any business going, so he kept quiet.

Something small skittered between spurges. Something larger bounded along in hot pursuit. The pursuit ended in a cloud of dust. Forestalling the inevitable chorus of *What's that?*, Radnal said, "Looks like a bladetooth just made a kill." The carnivorous rodent crouched over its prey; the tour guide pulled out a monocular for a closer look. "It's caught a fat sand rat."

"One of the animals you study?" Moblay said. "Are you going to blast it with your handcannon to take revenge?"

"*I* think you should," Nocso zev Martois declared. "What a vicious brute, to harm a defenseless furry beast."

Radnal wondered if he should ask how she'd enjoyed her mutton last night, but doubted she would understand. He said, "Either carnivores eat meat or they starve. A bladetooth isn't as cuddly as a fat sand rat, but it has its place in the web of life, too."

The bladetooth was smaller than a fox, tan above and cream below. At first glance, it looked like any other jerboa, with hind legs adapted for jumping, big ears, and a long, tufted tail. But its muzzle was also long, and smeared with blood. The fat sand rat squirmed feebly. The bladetooth bit into its belly and started feeding nonetheless.

Nocso moaned. Radnal tried to figure out how her mind worked. She was eager to believe in night demons that worked all manner of evils, yet a little real predation turned her stomach. He gave up; some inconsistencies were too big for him to understand how anyone managed to hold both halves of them at once.

He said, "As I remarked a couple of days ago, the bladetooth does well in the Bottomlands because jerboas had already adapted to conditions close to these while this part of the world was still under water. Its herbivorous relatives extract the water they must have from leaves and seeds, while it uses the tissues of the animals it captures. Even during our rare rains, no bladetooth has ever been seen to drink."

"Disgusting." Nocso's plump body shook as she shuddered. Radnal wondered how long her carcass would give a bladetooth the fluids it needed. *A long time*, he thought.

Moblay Sopsirk's son whooped. "There's the lodge! Cold water, cold ale, cold wine—"

As they had the evening before, the Eyes and Ears and the militiamen came out to await the tour group's return. The closer the donkeys came, the better Radnal could see the faces of the men who had stayed behind. They all looked thoroughly grim.

This time, he did not intend to spend a couple of daytenths wondering what was going on. He called, "Fer vez, Zosel vez, take charge of the tourists. I want to catch up on what's happened here."

"All right, Radnal vez," Fer answered. But his voice was no more cheerful than his expression.

Radnal dismounted and walked over to Liem vez Steries. He was not surprised when Peggol vez Menk fell into step with him. Their robes rustled as they came up to the militia subleader. Radnal asked, "What's the word, Liem vez?"

Liem's features might have been carved from stone. "The word is interrogation," he said quietly. "Tomorrow."

"By the gods." Radnal stared. "They're taking this seriously in Tarteshem."

"You'd best believe it." Liem wiped his sweaty face with his sleeve. "See those red cones past the cookpit? That's the landing site we laid out for the helo that's due in the morning."

"But—interrogation." Radnal shook his head. The Eyes and Ears' methods were anything but gentle. "If we interrogate foreigners, we're liable to touch off a war."

"Tarteshem knows this, Radnal vez," Liem said. "My objections are on the wire up there. I have been overruled."

"The Hereditary Tyrant and his advisors must think

the risks and damages of war are less than what
Tartesh would suffer if the starbomb performs as those
who buried it hope," Peggol said.

"But what if it's not there, or if it is but none of
the tourists knows about it?" Radnal said. "Then we'll
have antagonized the Krepalgan Unity, Lissonland, and
other countries as well, and for what? Nothing. Get
on the radiophone, Peggol vez; see if they'll change
their minds."

Peggol shook his head. "No, for two reasons. One
is that this policy will have come down from a level
far higher than I can influence. I am only a field
agent; I have no say in grand strategy. The other is
that your radiophone is too public. I do not want to
alert anyone that he is about to be interrogated."

Radnal had to concede that made sense as far as
security went. But he did not like it any better. Then
something else occurred to him. He turned to Liem
vez Steries. "Am I going to be, uh, interrogated, too?
What about Zosel vez and Fer vez? And what about
Toglo zev Pamdal? Are the interrogators going to work
on one of the Hereditary Tyrant's relatives?"

"I don't know any of those answers," the militiaman said. "The people I spoke with in Tartesh
wouldn't tell me." His eyes flicked to Peggol. "I
suppose they didn't care to be too public, either."

"No doubt," Peggol said. "Now we have to act as
normally as we can, not letting on that we'll have
visitors in the morning."

"I'd have an easier time acting normal if I knew
I wouldn't be wearing thumbscrews tomorrow,"
Radnal said.

"After such ordeals, the Hereditary Tyrant gener-
ously compensates innocents," Peggol said.

"The Hereditary Tyrant is generous." That was all
Radnal could say while talking to an Eye and Ear.
But silver, while it worked wonders, didn't fully make
up for terror and pain and, sometimes, permanent

injury. The tour guide preferred remaining as he was to riches and a limp.

Liem remarked, "Keeping things from the tourists won't be hard. Look what they're doing."

Radnal turned, looked, and snorted. His charges had turned the area marked off with red cones into a little game field. All of them except prim Golobol ran around throwing somebody's sponge rubber ball back and forth and trying to tackle one another. If their sport had rules, Radnal couldn't figure them out.

Moblay Sopsirk's son, stubborn if unwise, kept his yen for Evillia and Lofosa. Careless of the abrasions to his nearly naked hide, he dragged Lofosa into the dirt. When she stood up, her tunic was missing some of its big gold buttons. She remained indifferent to the flesh she exposed. Moblay had got grit in his eyes and stayed on the ground a while.

Evillia lost buttons, too; Toglo zev Pamdal's belt broke, as did Nocso zev Martois'. Toglo capered with one hand holding her robes closed. Nocso didn't bother. Watching her jounce up and down the improvised pitch, Radnal wished she were modest and Toglo otherwise.

Fer vez Canthal asked, "Shall I get supper started?"

"Get the coals going, but wait for the rest," Radnal said. "They're having such a good time, they might as well enjoy themselves. They won't have any fun tomorrow."

"Neither will we," Fer answered. Radnal grimaced and nodded.

Benter vez Maprab tackled Eltsac vez Martois and stretched the bigger, younger man in the dust. Benter sprang to his feet, swatted Evillia on the backside. She spun round in surprise.

"The old fellow has life in him yet," Peggol said, watching Eltsac rise, one hand pressed to a bloody nose.

"So he does." Radnal watched Benter. He might

be old, but he was spry. Maybe he could have broken Dokhnor of Kellef's neck. Was losing a game of war reason enough? Or was he playing the same deeper game as Dokhnor?

Only when the sun slid behind the Barrier Mountains and dusk enfolded the lodge did the tourists give up their sport. The cones shone with a soft pink phosphorescent glow of their own. Toglo tossed the ball to Evillia, saying, "I'm glad you got this out, freelady. I haven't enjoyed myself so much—and so foolishly—in a long time."

"I thought it would be a good way for us to unwind after riding and sitting around," Evillia answered.

She had a point. If Radnal ever led tourists down here again—if the lodge wasn't buried under thousands of cubits of sea—he'd have to remember to bring along a ball himself. He frowned in self-reproach. He should have thought of that on his own instead of stealing the idea from someone in his group.

"If I was thirsty before, I'm drier than the desert now," Moblay boomed. "Where's that ale?"

"I'll open the refrigerator," Zosel vez Glesir said. "Who else wants something?" He cringed from the hot, sweaty tourists who dashed his way. "Come, my friends! If you squash me, who will get the drinks?"

"We'll manage somehow," Eltsac vez Martois said, the first sensible remark he'd made.

Fer vez Canthal had the coals in the firepit glowing red. Zosel fetched a cut-up pig carcass and a slab of beef ribs. Radnal started to warn him about going through the stored food so prodigally, but caught himself. If people fell into the interrogators' hands tomorrow, no need to worry about the rest of the tour.

Radnal ate heartily, and joined in songs after supper. He managed to forget for hundreds of heartbeats what awaited when morning came. But every so often, realization came flooding back. Once his voice faltered so suddenly that Toglo glanced over to see what had happened. He smiled sheepishly and tried to do better.

Then he looked at her. He couldn't imagine her being connected with the plot to flood the Bottomlands. He had trouble imagining Eyes and Ears interrogating her as they would anyone else. But he hadn't thought they would risk international incidents to question foreign tourists, either. Maybe that meant he didn't grasp how big the emergency was. If so, Toglo might be at as much risk as anyone.

Horken vez Sofana, the circumstances man from the Trench Park militia, came up to the tour guide. "I was told you wanted Benter vez Maprab's saddlebags searched, freeman vez Krobir. I found—these." He held out his hand.

"How interesting. Wait here, Senior Trooper vez Sofana." Radnal walked over to where Benter was sitting, tapped him on the shoulder. "Would you please join me, freeman?"

"What is it?" Benter growled, but he came back with Radnal.

The tour guide said, "I'd like to hear how these red-veined orchids"—he pointed to the plants in Horken vez Sofana's upturned palm—"appeared in your saddlebags. Removal of any plants or animals, especially rare varieties like these, is punishable by fine, imprisonment, stripes, or all three."

Benter vez Maprab's mouth opened and closed silently. He tried again: "I—I would have raised them carefully, freeman vez Krobir." He was so used to complaining himself, he did not know how to react when someone complained of him—and caught him in the wrong.

Triumph turned hollow for Radnal. What were a couple of red-veined orchids when the whole Bottomlands might drown? The tour guide said, "We'll confiscate these, freeman vez Maprab. Your gear will be searched again when you leave Trench Park. If we find no more contraband, we'll let this pass. Otherwise—I'm sure I need not paint you a picture."

"Thank you—very kind." Benter fled.

Horken vez Sofana sent Radnal a disapproving look. "You let him off too lightly."

"Maybe, but the interrogators will take charge of him tomorrow."

"Hmm. Compared to everything else, stealing plants isn't such a big thing."

"Just what I was thinking. Maybe we ought to give them back to the old lemonface so they'll be somewhere safe if—well, you know the ifs."

"Yes." The circumstances man looked thoughtful. "If we gave them back now, he'd wonder why. We don't want that, either. Too bad, though."

"Yes." Discovering he worried about saving tiny pieces of Trench Park made Radnal realize he'd begun to believe in the starbomb.

The tourists began going off to their sleeping cubicles. Radnal envied their ignorance of what lay ahead. He hoped Evillia and Lofosa would visit him in the quiet darkness, and didn't care what the Eyes and Ears and militiamen thought. The body had its own sweet forgetfulness.

But the body had its own problems, too. Both women from Krepalga started trotting back and forth to the privy every quarter of a daytenth, sometimes even more than that. "It must have been something I ate," Evillia said, leaning wearily against the doorpost after her third trip. "Do you have a constipant?"

"The aid kit should have some." Radnal rummaged through it, found the orange pills he wanted. He brought them to her with a paper cup of water. "Here."

"Thank you." She popped the pills into her mouth, drained the cup, threw back her head to swallow. "I hope they help."

"So do I." Radnal had trouble keeping his voice casual. When she'd straightened to take the constipant, her left breast popped out of her tunic. "Freelady, I think you have fewer buttons than you did when the game ended."

Evillia covered herself again, an effort almost undermined when she shrugged. "I shouldn't be surprised. Most of those that didn't get pulled off took some yanks." She shrugged again. "It's only skin. Does it bother you?"

"You ought to know better than that," he said, almost angrily. "If you were feeling well—"

"If I were feeling well, I would enjoy feeling good," she agreed. "But as it is, Radnal vez—" At last she called him by his name and the polite particle. A grimace crossed her face. "As it is, I hope you will forgive me, but—" She hurried back out into the night.

When Lofosa made her next dash to the privy, Radnal had the pills waiting for her. She gulped them almost on the dead run. She'd lost some new buttons herself. Radnal felt guilty about thinking of such things when she was in distress.

After a game of war with Moblay that was almost as sloppy as their first, Radnal went into his cubicle. He didn't have anything to discuss with Liem or Peggol tonight; he knew what was coming. Somehow, he fell asleep anyway.

"Radnal vez." A quiet voice jerked him from slumber. It was neither Lofosa nor Evillia bending over him promising sensual delights. Peggol vez Menk stood in the entryway.

Radnal came fully awake. "What's gone wrong?" he demanded.

"Those two Highhead girls who don't believe in wearing clothes," Peggol answered.

"What about them?" Radnal asked, confused.

"They went off to the privy a while ago, and

neither of them came back. My man on watch woke me before he went out to see if they were all right. They weren't there, either."

"Where could they have gone?" Radnal had had idiot tourists wander on their own, but never in the middle of the night. Then other possible meanings for their disappearance crossed his mind. He jumped up. "And why?"

"This also occurred to me," Peggol said grimly. "If they don't come back soon, it will have answered itself."

"They can't go far," Radnal said. "I doubt they'll have thought to get on donkeys. They could hardly tell one end of the beasts from the—" The tour guide stopped. If Evillia and Lofosa were other than they seemed, who could tell what they knew?

Peggol nodded. "We are thinking along the same lines." He plucked at the tuft of hair under his mouth. "If this means what we fear, much will depend on you to track them down. You know the Bottomlands, and I do not."

"Our best tools are the helos," Radnal said. "When it's light, we'll sweep the desert floor a hundred times faster than we could on donkeyback."

He kept talking for another few words, but Peggol didn't hear him. He didn't hear himself, either, not over the sudden roar from outside. They dashed for the outer door. They pushed through the Eyes and Ears and militiamen who got there first. Tourists pushed them from behind.

Everyone stared at the blazing helos.

Radnal stood in disbelief and dismay for a couple of heartbeats. Peggol vez Menk's shout brought him to himself: "We have to call Tarteshem *right now!*" Radnal spun round, shoved and elbowed by the tourists in his way, and dashed for the radiophone. The amber ready light didn't come on when he hit the switch. He ducked under the table to see if any connections were loose. "Hurry up!" Peggol yelled.

"The demon-cursed thing won't come on," Radnal yelled back. He picked up the radiophone itself. It rattled. It wasn't supposed to. "It's broken."

"It's *been* broken," Peggol declared.

"How could it have been broken, with Eyes and Ears and militiamen in the common room all the time?" the tour guide said, not so much disagreeing with Peggol as voicing his bewilderment to the world.

But Peggol had an answer: "If one of those Krepalgan tarts paraded through here without any clothes— and they both ran back and forth all night—we might not have paid attention to what the other one was doing. Bang it . . . mmm, more likely reach under it with the right little tool . . . and you wouldn't need more than five heartbeats."

Radnal would have needed more than five heartbeats, but he wasn't a saboteur. If Evillia and Lofosa were— He couldn't doubt it, but it left him sick inside. They'd used him, used their bodies to lull him into thinking they were the stupid doxies they pretended to be. And it had worked . . . He wanted to wash himself over and over; he felt he'd never be clean again.

Liem vez Steries said, "We'd better make sure the donkeys are all right." He trotted out the door, ran around the crackling hulks of the flying machines. The stable door was closed against cave cats. The militiaman pulled it open. Through the crackle of the flames, Radnal heard a sharp report, saw a flash of light. Liem crashed to the ground. He lay there unmoving.

Radnal and Golobol the physician sprinted out to him. The firelight told them all they needed to know. Liem would not get up again, not with those dreadful wounds.

The tour guide went into the stables. He knew something was wrong, but needed a moment to realize what. Then the quiet hit him. The donkeys were not shifting in their stalls, nipping at the straw, or making any of their other small noises.

He looked into the stall by the broken door. The donkey there lay on its side. Its flanks neither rose nor fell. Radnal ran to the next, and the next. All the donkeys were dead—except for three, which were missing. One for Evillia, the tour guide thought, one for Lofosa, and one for their supplies.

No, they weren't fools. "I am," he said, and ran back to the lodge.

He gave the grim news to Peggol vez Menk. "We're in trouble, sure enough," Peggol said, shaking his head. "We'd be worse off, though, if the interrogation team weren't coming in under a daytenth. We can go after them in that helo. It has its own cannon, too; if they don't yield, goodbye. By the gods, I hope they don't."

"So do I." Radnal cocked his head to one side. A grin split his face. "Isn't that the helo now? Why is it early?"

"I don't know," Peggol answered. "Wait a heartbeat, maybe I do. If Tarteshem called and got no answer, they might have decided something was wrong and sent the helo straightaway."

The racket of engine and rotors swelled. The pilot must have spotted the fires and put on full speed. Radnal hurried outside to greet the incoming Eyes and Ears. The helo's black silhouette spread huge across the sky; as Peggol had implied, this was a military machine, not just a utility flier. It made for the glowing cones that marked the landing area.

Radnal watched it settle toward the ground. He remembered Evillia and Lofosa running around in the landing zone, laughing, giggling, and . . . losing buttons. He waved his arms, dashed toward the cones. "No!" he screamed. "Wait!"

Too late. Dust rose in choking clouds as the helo

touched the ground. The tour guide saw the flash under one skid, heard the report. The skid crumpled. The helo heeled over. A rotor blade dug into the ground, snapped, thrummed past Radnal's head. Had it touched him, his head would have gone with it.

The side panel of the helo came down on the Bottomlands floor. Another sharp report—and suddenly flames were everywhere. The Eyes and Ears trapped inside the helo screamed. Radnal tried to help them, but the heat would not let him approach. The screams soon stopped. He smelled the thick odor of charring flesh. The fire burned on.

Peggol vez Menk hurried out to Radnal. "I tried to stop them," the tour guide said brokenly.

"You came closer than I, a reproach I shall carry to my grave," Peggol answered. "I did not see that danger, much as I should have. Some of those men were my friends." He slammed a fist against his thigh. "What now, Radnal vez?"

Die when the waters come, was the first thought that crossed the tour guide's mind. Mechanically, he went through the obvious: "Wait till dawn. Try to find their trail. Pack as much water on our backs as we can and go after them afoot."

"Afoot?" Peggol said.

Radnal realized he hadn't explained about the donkeys. He did, then went on, "Leave one man here for when another helo comes. Give the tourists as much water as they can carry and send them up the trail. Maybe they'll escape the flood."

"What you say sounds sensible. We'll try it," Peggol said. "Anything else?"

"Pray," Radnal told him. He grimaced, nodded, turned away.

Moblay Sopsirk's son got through the Eyes and Ears and trotted up to Radnal and Peggol. "Freeman vez Krobir—" he began.

Radnal rolled his eyes. He was about to wish a

night demon on Moblay's head, but stopped. Instead, he said, "Wait a heartbeat. You named me properly." What should have been polite surprise came out as accusation.

"So I did." Something about Moblay had changed. In the light of the blazing helos, he looked . . . not like Peggol vez Menk, since he remained a short-nosed, brown-skinned Highhead, but of the same type as the Eye and Ear—tough and smart, not just las-civious and overfamiliar. He said, "Freeman vez Krobir, I apologize for irritating you, but I wanted to remain as ineffectual-seeming as I could. Names are one way of doing that. I am an aide to my Prince: I am one of his Silent Servants."

Peggol grunted. He evidently knew what that meant. Radnal didn't, but he could guess: something like an Eye and Ear. He cried, "Is there anyone in this cursed tour group *not* wearing a mask?"

"More to the point, why drop the mask now?" Peggol asked.

"Because my Prince, may the Lion God give him many years, does not want the Bottomlands flooded," Moblay said. "We wouldn't suffer as badly as Tartesh, of course; we own only a strip of the southernmost part. But the Prince fears the fighting that would follow."

"Who approached Lissonland with word of this?" Peggol said.

"We learned from Morgaf," Moblay answered. "The island king wanted us to join the attack on Tartesh after the flood. But the Morgaffos denied the plot was theirs, and would not tell us who had set the starbomb here. We suspected the Krepalgan Unity, but had no proof. That was one reason I kept sniff-ing around the Krepalgan women." He grinned. "Another should be obvious."

"Why Krepalga?" Peggol wondered aloud. "The Unity didn't join Morgaf against us in the last war.

What could they want enough to make them risk a war with starbombs?"

Radnal remembered the lecture he'd given on how the Bottomlands came to be, remembered also his fretting about how far an unchecked flood might reach. "I know part of the answer to that, I think," he said. Peggol and Moblay both turned to him. He went on, "If the Bottomlands flood, the new central sea would stop about at Krepalga's western border. The Unity would have a whole new coastline, and be in a better position than either Tartesh or Lissonland to exploit the new sea."

"The flood wouldn't get to Krepalga for a long time," Moblay protested.

"True," Radnal said, "but can you imagine stopping it before it did?" He visualized the map again. "I don't think you could, not against that weight of water."

"I think you're right." Peggol nodded decisively. "That may not be all Krepalga has in mind, but it'll be part. The Unity must have been planning this for years; they'll have looked at all the consequences they could."

"Let me help you now," Moblay said. "I heard freeman vez Krobir say the donkeys are dead, but what one walking man may do, I shall."

Radnal would have taken any ally who presented himself. But Peggol said, "No. I am grateful for your candor and suspect you are truthful now, but dare not take the chance. One walking man could do much harm as well as good. Being of the profession, I trust you understand."

Moblay bowed. "I feared you would say that. I do understand. May the Lion God go with you."

The three men walked back to the lodge. The tourists rained questions on Radnal. "No one has told us anything, not a single thing," Golobol complained. "What is going on? Why are helos exploding to left and then to right? Tell me!"

Radnal told him—and everyone else. The stunned silence his words produced lasted perhaps five heartbeats. Then everybody started yelling. Nocso zev Martois' voice drowned all others: "Does this mean we don't get to finish the tour?"

More sensibly, Toglo zev Pamdal said, "Is there any way we can help you in your pursuit, Radnal vez?"

"Thank you, no. You'd need weapons; we haven't any to give you. Your best hope is to make for high ground. You ought to leave as soon as you load all the water you can carry. Lie up in the middle of the day when the sun is worst. With luck, you'll be up at the old continental shelf in, oh, a day and a half. If the flood's held off that long, you ought to be safe for a while there. And a helo may spot you as you travel."

"What if the flood comes when we're still down here?" Eltsac vez Martois demanded. "What then, freeman Know-It-All?"

"Then you have the consolation of knowing I drowned a few heartbeats before you. I hope you enjoy it," Radnal said. Eltsac stared at him. He went on, "That's all the stupidity I have time for now. Let's get you people moving. Peggol vez, we'll send a couple of Eyes and Ears back, too. Your men won't be much help traveling cross-country. Come to that, you—"

"No," Peggol said firmly. "My place is at the focus. I shan't lag, and I shoot straight. I'm not the worst tracker, either."

Radnal knew better than to argue. "All right."

The water bladders would have gone on the donkeys. Radnal filled them from the cistern while the militiamen and Eyes and Ears cut straps to fit them to human shoulders. The eastern sky was bright pink by the time they finished. Radnal tried to give no tourists loads of more than a third of their body weight: that was as much as anyone could carry without breaking down.

Nocso vez Martois said, "With all this water, how can we carry food?"

"You can't," Radnal snapped. He stared at her. "You can live off yourself a while, but you can't live without water." Telling off his tourists was a new, heady pleasure. Since it might be his last, he enjoyed it while he could.

"I'll report your insolence," Nocso shrilled.

"That is the least of my worries." Radnal turned to the Eyes and Ears who were heading up the trail with the tourists. "Try to keep them together, try not to do too much at midday, make sure they all drink— and make sure you do, too. Gods be with you."

An Eye and Ear shook his head. "No, freeman vez Krobir, with *you*. If they watch you, we'll be all right. But if they neglect you, we all fail."

Radnal nodded. To the tourists, he said, "Good luck. If the gods are kind, I'll see you again at the top of Trench Park." He didn't mention what would happen if the gods bumbled along as usual.

Toglo said, "Radnal vez, if we see each other again, I will use whatever influence I have for you."

"Thanks," was all Radnal could say. Under other circumstances, getting patronage from the Hereditary Tyrant's relative would have moved him to do great things. Even now, it was kindly meant, but of small weight when he first had to survive to gain it.

A sliver of red-gold crawled over the eastern horizon. The tourists and the Eyes and Ears trudged north. A koprit bird on the rooftop announced the day with a cry of *hig, hig, hig!*

Peggol ordered one of the remaining Eyes and Ears to stay at the lodge and send westward any helos that came. Then he said formally, "Freeman vez Krobir, I place myself and freeman vez Potos, my colleague here, under your authority. Command us."

"If that's how you want it," Radnal answered,

shrugging. "You know what we'll do: march west until we catch the Krepalgans or drown, whichever comes first. Nothing fancy. Let's go."

Radnal, the two Eyes and Ears, the lodge attendants, and the surviving militiamen started from the stables. The morning light showed the tracks of three donkeys heading west. The tour guide took out his monocular, scanned the western horizon. No luck—dips and rises hid Evillia and Lofosa.

Fer vez Canthal said, "There's a high spot maybe three thousand cubits west of here. You ought to look from there."

"Maybe," Radnal said. "If we have a good trail, though, I'm likelier to rely on that. I begrudge wasting even a heartbeat's time, and spotting someone isn't easy even if he wants to be found. Remember that poor fellow who wandered off from his group four years ago? They used helos, dogs, everything, but they didn't find his corpse until a year later, and then by accident."

"Thank you for pumping up my hopes," Peggol said.

"Nothing wrong with hope," Radnal answered, "but you knew the odds were bad when you decided to stay."

The seven walkers formed a loose skirmish line, about five cubits apart from one another. Radnal, the best tracker, took the center; at his right was Horken vez Sofana, at his left Peggol. He figured they had the best chance of picking up the trail if he lost it.

That likelihood grew with every step. Evillia and Lofosa hadn't gone straight west. He quickly found that out. Instead, they'd jink northwest for a few hundred cubits, then southwest a few hundred more, in a deliberate effort to throw off pursuit. They also chose the hardest ground they could find, which made the donkeys' tracks tougher to follow.

Radnal's heart sank every time he had to cast about

before they found the hoofprints again. His group lost ground with every step; the Krepalgans rode faster than they could walk.

"I have a question," Horken vez Sofana: "Suppose the starbomb goes off and the mountains fall. How are these two women supposed to get away?"

Radnal shrugged; he had no idea. "Did you hear that, Peggol vez?" he asked.

"Yes," Peggol said. "Two possibilities spring to mind—"

"I might have guessed," Radnal said.

"Hush. As I was saying before you crassly interrupted, one is that the starbomb was supposed to have a delayed detonation, letting the perpetrators escape. The other is that these agents knew the mission was suicidal. Morgaf has used such personnel; so have we, once or twice. Krepalga might find such servants, however regrettable that prospect seems to us."

Horken gave a slow, deliberate nod. "What you say sounds convincing. They might have first planned a delay to let them escape, then shifted to sacrificing themselves when they found we were partway on to them."

"True," Peggol said. "And they may yet be planning to escape. If they somehow secreted away helium cylinders, for instance, they might inflate several prophylactics and float out of the Bottomlands."

Radnal wondered for a heartbeat if he was serious. Then the tour guide snorted. "I wish I could stay so cheerful at death's door."

"Death will find me whether I am cheerful or not," Peggol answered. "I will go forward as boldly and as long as I can."

Conversation flagged. The higher the sun rose, the hotter the desert became, the more anything but putting one foot in front of the other seemed more trouble than it was worth. Radnal wiped sweat from his eyes as he slogged along.

The water bladder on his back started out as heavy as any pack he'd ever toted. He wondered how long he could go on with such a big burden. But the bladder got lighter every time he refilled his canteen. He made himself keep drinking—not getting water in as fast as he sweated would be suicidal. Unlike the fanatic Morgaffos Peggol had mentioned, he wanted to live if he could.

He'd given everyone about two days' worth of water. If he didn't catch up to Lofosa and Evillia by the end of the second day . . . He shook his head. One way or another, it wouldn't matter after that.

As noon neared, he ordered the walkers into the shade of a limestone outcrop. "We'll rest a while," he said. "When we start again, it ought to be cooler."

"Not enough to help," Peggol said. But he sat down in the shade with a grateful sigh. He took off his stylish cap, sadly felt of it. "It'll make a dishrag after this—nothing better."

Radnal squatted beside him, too hot to talk. His heart pounded. It seemed so loud, he wondered if it would give out on him. Then he realized most of that beating rhythm came from outside. Fatigue fell away. He jumped up, doffed his own cap and waved it in the air. "A helo!"

The rest of the group also got up and waved and yelled. "It's seen us!" Zosel vez Glesir said. Nimbly as a dragonfly, the helo shifted direction in midair and dashed straight toward them. It set down about fifty cubits from the ledge. Its rotors kept spinning; it was ready to take off again at any moment.

The pilot leaned out the window, bawled something in Radnal's direction. Through the racket, he had no idea what the fellow said. The pilot beckoned him over.

The din and dust were worse under the whirling rotor blades. Radnal had to lean on tiptoe against the helo's hot metal skin before he made out the pilot's words: "How far ahead are the cursed Krepalgans?"

"They had better than a daytenth's start, and they're on donkeyback. Say, up to thirty thousand cubits west of here." Radnal repeated himself several times before the pilot nodded and ducked back into his machine.

"Wait!" Radnal screamed. The pilot stuck his head out again. Radnal asked, "Did you come across my group heading toward the trail up the old continental shelf?"

"Yes. Somebody ought to be picking them up right about now."

"Good," Radnal bellowed. The pilot tossed him a portable radiophone. He seized it; now he was no longer cut off from the rest of the search.

They sped. The helo shot into the air, sped away westward. The tour guide knew relief: even if he drowned, the people he'd led would be safe.

"Now that this helo's here, do we need to go on?" asked Impac vez Potos, the Eye and Ear with Peggol.

"You'd best believe it, freeman." Radnal recounted the story of the lost tourist who'd stayed lost. "No matter how many helos search, they'll be covering a big area and trying to find people who don't want to be found. We stay in the hunt till it's over. By the way the Krepalgans fooled us all, they won't make things easy."

"Shall we keep resting, or head out now?" Peggol asked.

Radnal chewed on that for a few heartbeats. If the helo was here, that meant the people at Tarteshem knew from its radiophone how bad things were. And *that* meant helos would swarm here as fast as they could take off, which meant his group would probably be able to get supplies. But he didn't want to lose people to heatstroke, either, a risk that came with exertion in the desert.

"We'll give it another tenth of a daytenth," he said at last.

He was first up when the rest ended. The other

six rose with enough groans and creaking joints for an army of invalids. "We'll loosen up as we get going," Fer vez Canthal said hopefully.

A little later, panic ran through Radnal when he lost the trail. He waved for Peggol and Horken vez Sofana. They scoured the ground on hands and knees, but found nothing. Rock-hard dirt stretched in all directions for a couple of hundred cubits. "If they pulled up a bush and swept away their tracks, we'll have a night demons' time picking them up again," Horken said.

"We won't try," Radnal declared. The rest of the searchers looked at him in surprise. He went on, "We're wasting time here, right?" No one disagreed. "So here is the last place we want to stay. We'll do a search spiral. Zosel vez, you stand here to mark this spot. Sooner or later, we'll find the trail again."

"You hope," Peggol said quietly.

"Yes, I do. If you have a better plan, I'll be grateful to hear it." The Eye and Ear shook his head and, a moment later, dropped his eyes.

While Zosel stood in place, the other searchers tramped in a widening spiral. After a hundred heart-beats, Impac vez Potos shouted: "I've found it!"

Radnal and Horken hurried to see what he'd come across. "Where?" Radnal asked. Impac pointed to a patch of ground softer than most in the area. Sure enough, it held marks. The more experienced men squatted to take a better look. They glanced up together; their eyes met. Radnal said, "Freeman vez Potos, those are the tracks of a bladetooth. If you look carefully, you can see where it dragged its tail in the dirt. Donkeys never do that."

"Oh," Impac said in a small, sad voice.

Radnal sighed. He hadn't bothered mentioning that the tracks were too small for donkeys' and didn't look like them, either. "Let's try once more," he said. The spiral resumed.

When Impac yelled again, Radnal wished he hadn't tried to salve his feelings. If he stopped them every hundred heartbeats, they'd never find anything. This time, Horken stayed where he was. Radnal stalked over to Impac. "Show me," he growled.

Impac pointed once more. Radnal filled his lungs to curse him for wasting their time. The curse remained unspoken. There at his feet lay the unmistakable tracks of three donkeys. "By the gods," he said.

"They are right this time?" Impac asked anxiously.

"Yes. Thank you, freeman." Radnal shouted to the other searchers. The seven headed southwest, following the recovered trail. Fer vez Canthal went up to Impac and slapped him on the back. Impac beamed as if he'd performed bravely in front of the Hereditary Tyrant. Considering the service he'd just done Tartesh, he'd earned the right.

He was also lucky, Radnal thought. But he'd needed courage to call out a second time after being ignominiously wrong the first, and sharp eyes to spot both sets of tracks, even if he couldn't tell what they were once he'd found them. So more than luck was involved. Radnal slapped Impac's back, too.

Sweat poured off Radnal. As it evaporated from his robes, it cooled him a little, but not enough. Like a machine taking on fuel, he drank again and again from the bladder on his back.

Now the sun was in his face. He tugged his cap over his eyes, kept his head down, and tramped on. When the Krepalgans tried doubling back, he spotted the ruse instead of following the wrong trail and wasting hundreds of precious heartbeats.

By then, the western sky was full of helos. They roared about in all directions, sometimes low enough to kick up dust. Radnal wanted to strangle the pilots who flew that way; they might blow away the trail, too. He yelled into the radiophone. The low-flying helos moved higher.

A big transport helo set down a few hundred cubits in front of the walkers. A door in its side slid open. A squadron of soldiers jumped down and hurried west.

"Are they close or desperate?" Radnal wondered.

"Desperate, certainly," Peggol said. "As for close, we can hope. We haven't drowned yet. On the other hand"—he always thought of the other hand—"we haven't caught your two sluts, either."

"They weren't mine," Radnal said feebly. But he remembered their flesh sliding against his, the way their breath had caught, the sweat-salty taste of their skin.

Peggol read his face. "Aye, they used you, Radnal vez, and they fooled you. If it makes you feel better, they fooled me, too; I thought they kept their brains in their twats. They outsmarted me with the fornication books in their gear and the skin they showed. They used our prudishness against us—how could anyone who acts that way be dangerous? It's a ploy that won't work again."

"Once may have been plenty." Radnal wasn't ready to stop feeling guilty.

"If it was, you'll pay full atonement," Peggol said.

Radnal shook his head. Dying when the Bottomlands flooded wasn't atonement enough, not when that flood would ruin his nation and might start an exchange of starbombs that would wreck the world.

The ground shivered under his feet. Despite the furnace heat of the desert floor, his sweat went cold. "Please, gods, make it stop," he said, his first prayer in years.

It stopped. He breathed again. It was just a little quake; he would have laughed at tourists for fretting over it. At any other time, he would have ignored it. Now it nearly scared him to death.

A koprit bird cocked its head, peered down at him from a thornbush that held its larder.

Hig-hig-hig! it said, and fluttered to the ground. Radnal wondered if it could fly fast enough or far enough to escape a flood.

The radiophone let out a burst of static. Radnal thumbed it to let himself transmit: "Vez Krobir here."

"This is Combat Group Leader Turand vez Nital. I wish to report that we have encountered the Krepalgan spies. Both are deceased."

"That's wonderful!" Radnal relayed the news. His companions raised a weary cheer. Then he remembered again his nights with Evillia and Lofosa. And *then* he realized Combat Group Leader vez Nital hadn't sounded as overjoyed and relieved as he should have. Slowly, he said, "What's wrong?"

"When encountered, the Krepalgans were moving eastward."

"Eastw— Oh!"

"You see the predicament?" Turand said. "They appear to have completed their work and to have been attempting to escape. Now they are beyond questioning. Please keep your transmission active so a helo can home on you and bring you here. You look to be Tartesh's best hope of locating the bomb before its ignition. I repeat, please maintain transmission."

Radnal obeyed. He looked at the Barrier Mountains. They seemed taller now than they had when he set out. How long would they keep standing tall? The sun was sliding down toward them, too. How was he supposed to search after dark? He feared tomorrow morning would be too late.

He passed on to his comrades what the officer had said. Horken vez Sofana made swimming motions. Radnal stooped for a pebble, threw it at him.

A helo soon landed beside the seven walkers. Someone inside opened the sliding door. "Come on!" he bawled. "Move it, move it!"

Moving it as fast as they could, Radnal and the

rest scrambled into the helo. It went airborne before
the fellow at the door had it fully closed. A couple
of hundred heartbeats later, the helo touched down
hard enough to rattle the tour guide's teeth. The
crewman at the door undogged it and slid it open.
"Out!" he yelled.

Out Radnal jumped. The others followed. A few
cubits away stood a man in a uniform robe similar
but not identical to the one the militia wore. "Who's
freeman vez Krobir?" he said. "I'm Turand vez Nital."

"I'm vez Krobir. I—" Radnal broke off. Two bodies
lay behind the Tarteshan soldier. Radnal gulped. He'd
seen corpses on their funeral pyres, but never before
sprawled out like animals waiting to be butchered.
He said the first thing that popped into his head:
"They don't look like you shot them."

"We didn't," the officer said. "When they saw they
couldn't escape, they took poison."

"They *were* professionals," Peggol murmured.

"As may be," Turand growled. "This one"—he
pointed at Evillia—"wasn't gone when we got to her.
She said, 'You're too late,' and then died, may night
demons gnaw her ghost forever."

"We'd better find that cursed bomb fast, then,"
Radnal said. "Can you take us to where the Krepalgans were cornered?"

"This very heartbeat," Turand said. "Come with me.
It's only three or four hundred cubits from here." He
moved at a trot that left the worn walkers gasping
in his wake. At last he stopped and waited impatiently
for them to catch up. "This is where we found them."

"And they were coming east, you said?" Radnal
asked.

"That's right, though I don't know for how long,"
the officer answered. "Somewhere out there is the
accursed starbomb. We're scouring the desert, but this
is *your* park. Maybe, your eye will fall on something
they'd miss. If not—"

"You needn't go on," Radnal said. "I almost fouled my robe when we had that little tremor a while ago. I thought I'd wash ashore on the Krepalgan border, ten million cubits from here."

"If you're standing on a starbomb when it goes off, you needn't fear the flood afterwards," Turand said.

"Gak." Radnal hadn't thought of that. It would be quick, anyhow.

"Enough chatter," Horken vez Sofana said. "If we're to search, let us search."

"Search, and may the gods lend your sight wings," Turand said.

The seven walkers trudged west again. Radnal did his best to follow the donkey's trail, but the soldiers' footprints often obscured them. "How are we supposed to track in this confusion?" he cried. "They might as well have turned a herd of humpless camels loose here."

"It's not quite so bad as that," Horken said. Stooping low, he pointed to the ground. "Look, here's a track. Here's another, a few paces on. We can do it. We have to do it."

Radnal knew the senior trooper was right; he felt ashamed of his own outburst. He found the next hoofprint himself, and the one after that. Those two lay on opposite sides of a fault-line crack; when he saw that, he knew the starbomb couldn't rest too far away. But he felt time pressing hard on his shoulders.

"Maybe the soldiers will have found the starbomb by now," Fer vez Canthal said.

"We can't count on it. Look how long it took them to find the Krepalgans. We have to figure it's up to us." Radnal realized the weight on him wasn't just time. It was also responsibility. If he died now, he'd die knowing he'd failed.

And yet, while the searchers stirred through Trench Park, the animals of the Bottomlands kept living their

usual lives; they could not know they might perish
in the next heartbeat. A koprit bird skittered across
the sand a few paces in front of Radnal. A clawed
foot stabbed down.

"It's caught a shoveler skink," he said, as if the hot,
worn men with him were members of his group.

The lizard thrashed, trying to get away. Sand flew
every which way. But the koprit bird held on with
its claws, tore at the skink with its beak, and smashed
it against the ground until its writhing ceased. Then
it flew to a nearby thornbush with its victim.

It impaled the skink on a long, stout thorn. The
lizard was the latest addition to its larder, which also
included two grasshoppers, a baby snake, and a jerboa. And, as koprit birds often did, this one used the
thornbush's spikes to display bright objects it had
found. A yellow flower, now very dry, must have hung
there since the last rains. And not far from the lizard, the koprit bird had draped a couple of red-orange
strings over a thorn.

Radnal's eyes came to them, passed by, snapped
back. They weren't strings. He pointed. "Aren't those
the necklaces Evillia and Lofosa wore yesterday?" he
asked hoarsely.

"They are." Peggol and Horken said it together.
They both had to notice and remember small details.
They sounded positive.

When Peggol tried to take the necklaces off their
thorn, the koprit bird furiously screeched *hig-hig!*
Claws outstretched, it flew at his face. He staggered
backwards, flailing his arms.

Radnal waved his cap as he walked up to the
thornbush. That intimidated the bird enough to keep
it from diving on him, though it kept shrieking. He
grabbed the necklaces and got away from the larder
as fast as he could.

The necklaces were heavier than he'd expected, too
heavy for the cheap plastic he'd thought them to be.

He turned one so he could look at it end-on. "It's got a copper core," he said, startled.

"Let me see that." Again Peggol and Horken spoke together. They snatched a necklace apiece. Then Peggol broke the silence alone: "Detonator wire."

"Absolutely," Horken agreed. "Never seen it with red insulator, though. Usually it would be brown or green for camouflage. This time, it was camouflaged as jewelry."

Radnal stared from Horken to Peggol. "You mean, these wires would be hooked to the cell that would send the charge to the starbomb when the timer went off?"

"That's just what we mean," Peggol said. Horken vez Sofana solemnly nodded.

"But they can't now, because they're here, not there." Fumbling for words, Radnal went on, "And they're here because the koprit bird thought they were pretty, or maybe it thought they were food—they're about the color of a shoveler skink's lure—and pulled them loose and flew away with them." Realization hit then: "That koprit bird just saved Tartesh!"

"The ugly thing almost put my eye out," Peggol grumbled. The rest of the group ignored him. One or two of them cheered. More, like Radnal, stood quietly, too tired and dry and stunned to show their joy.

The tour guide needed several heartbeats to remember he carried a radiophone. He clicked it on, waited for Turand vez Nital. "What do you have?" the officer barked. Radnal could hear his tension. He'd felt it too, till moments before.

"The detonation wires are off the starbomb," he said, giving the good news first. "I don't know where that is, but it won't go off without them."

After static-punctuated silence, Turand said slowly, "Are you daft? How can you have the wires without the starbomb?"

"There was this koprit bird—"

"What?" Turand's roar made the radiophone vibrate in Radnal's hand. As best he could, he explained. More silence followed. At last, the soldier said, "You're certain this is detonator wire?"

"An Eye and Ear and the Trench Park circumstances man both say it is. If they don't recognize the stuff, who would?"

"You're right." Another pause from Turand, then: "A koprit bird, you say? Do you know that I never heard of koprit birds until just now?" His voice held wonder. But suddenly he sounded worried again, saying, "Can you be sure the wire wasn't left there to fool us one last time?"

"No." Fear knotted Radnal's gut again. Had he and his comrades come so far, done so much, only to fall for a final deception?

Horken let out a roar louder than Turand's had been. "I've found it!" he screamed from beside a spurge about twenty cubits away. Radnal hurried over. Horken said, "It couldn't have been far, because koprit birds have territories. So I kept searching, and—" He pointed down.

At the base of the spurge lay a small timer hooked to an electrical cell. The timer was upside down; the koprit bird must have had quite a fight tearing loose the wires it prized. Radnal stooped, turned the timer over. He almost dropped it—the needle that counted off the daytenths and heartbeats lay against the zero knob.

"Will you look at that?" he said softly. Impac vez Potos peered over his shoulder. The junior Eye and Ear clicked his tongue between his teeth.

"A koprit bird," Horken said. He got down on hands and knees, poked around under every plant and stone within a couple of cubits of the spurge. Before a hundred heartbeats went by, he let out a sharp, wordless exclamation.

Radnal got down beside him. Horken had tipped over a chunk of sandstone about as big as his head. Under it was a crack in the earth that ran out to either side. From the crack protruded two drab brown wires.

"A koprit bird," Horken repeated. The helos and men would have been too late. But the koprit bird, hungry or out to draw females into its territory, had spotted something colorful, so—

Radnal took out the radiophone. "We've found the timer. It is separated from the wires which, we presume, lead to the starbomb. The koprit bird took away the wires the Krepalgans used to attach the timer."

"A koprit bird." Now Turand vez Nital said it. He sounded as dazed as any of the rest of them, but quickly pulled himself together again: "That's excellent news, as I needn't tell you. I'll send a crew to your location directly, to begin excavating the starbomb. Out."

Peggol vez Menk had been examining the timer, too. His gaze kept returning to the green needle bisecting the zero symbol. He said; "How deep do you suppose the bomb is buried?"

"It would have to be pretty deep, to trigger the fault," Radnal answered. "I couldn't say how deep; I'm no savant of geology. But if Turand vez Nital thinks his crew will dig it up before nightfall, he'll have to think again."

"How could Krepalga have planted it here?" Impac vez Potos said. "Wouldn't you Trench Park people have noticed?"

"Trench Park is a big place," Radnal said.

"I know that. I ought to; I've walked enough of it," Impac said wearily. "Still—"

"People don't frequent this area, either," Radnal persisted. "I've never led a group anywhere near here. No doubt the Krepalgans took risks doing whatever they did, but not enormous risks."

Peggol said, "We shall have to ensure such deadly danger cannot return again. Whether we should expand the militia, base regular soldiers here, or set up a station for Eyes and Ears, that I don't know— we must determine which step offers the best security. But we will do something."

"You also have to consider which choice hurts Trench Park least," Radnal said.

"That will be a factor," Peggol said, "but probably a small one. Think, Radnal vez: if the Barrier Mountains fall and the Western Ocean pours down on the Bottomlands, how much will that hurt Trench Park?"

Radnal opened his mouth to argue more. Keeping the park in its natural state had always been vital to him. Man had despoiled so much of the Bottomlands; this was the best—almost the only—reminder of what they'd been like. But he'd just spent days wondering whether he'd drown in the next heartbeat, and all of today certain he would. And if he'd drowned, his country would have drowned with him. Set against that, a base for soldiers or Eyes and Ears suddenly seemed a small thing. He said not another word.

Radnal hadn't been in Tarteshem for a long time, though Tartesh's capital wasn't far from Trench Park. He'd never been paraded through the city in an open-topped motor while people lined the sidewalks and cheered. He should have enjoyed it. Peggol vez Menk, who sat beside him in the motor, certainly did. Peggol smiled and waved as if he'd just been chosen high priest.

After so long in the wide open spaces of the Bottomlands, though, and after so long in his own company or that of small tour groups, riding through the midst of so much tight-packed humanity more nearly overwhelmed than overjoyed Radnal. He looked nervously at the buildings towering over the avenue. It felt more as if he were passing through a canyon than anything man-made.

"Radnal, Radnal!" the crowds chanted, as if everybody knew him well enough to use his name in its most naked, intimate form. They had another cry, too: "Koprit bird! Koprit bird! The gods praise the koprit bird!"

That took away some of his nervousness. Seeing his grin, Peggol said, "Anyone would think they'd seen the artist's new work."

"You're right," Radnal answered. "Maybe it's too bad *the* koprit bird isn't here for the ceremony after all."

Peggol raised that eyebrow of his. "You talked them out of capturing it."

"I know. I did the right thing," Radnal said. Putting the koprit bird that stole the detonator wires in a cage didn't seem fitting. Trench Park existed to let its creatures live wild and free, with as little interference from mankind as possible. The koprit bird had made it possible for that to go on. Caging it afterwards struck Radnal as ungrateful.

The motor drove onto the grounds of the Hereditary Tyrant's palace. It pulled up in front of the gleaming building that housed Bortav vez Pamdal. A temporary stage and a podium stood on the lawn near the road. The folding chairs that faced it were full of dignitaries from Tartesh and other nations.

No Krepalgans sat in those chairs. The Hereditary Tyrant had sent the plenipo from the Krepalgan Unity home, ordered all Krepalgan citizens out of Tartesh, and sealed the border. So far, he'd done nothing more than that. Radnal both resented and approved of his caution. In an age of starbombs, even the attempted murder of a nation had to be dealt with cautiously, lest a successful double murder follow.

A man in a fancy robe came up to the motor,

bowed low. "I am the protocol officer. If you will come with me, freemen—?"

Radnal and Peggol came. The protocol officer led them onto the platform, got them settled, and hurried away to see to the rest of the seven walkers, whose motors had parked behind the one from which the tour guide and the Eye and Ear had dismounted.

Peering at the important people who were examining him, Radnal got nervous again. He didn't belong in this kind of company. But there in the middle of the second row sat Toglo zev Pamdal, who smiled broadly and waved at him. Seeing someone he knew and liked made it easier for him to wait for the next part of the ceremony.

The Tarteshan national hymn blared out. Radnal couldn't just sit. He got up and put his hand over his heart until the hymn was done. The protocol officer stepped up to the podium and announced, "Freemen, freeladies, the Hereditary Tyrant."

Bortav vez Pamdal's features adorned silver, smiled down from public buildings, and were frequently on the screen. Radnal had never expected to see the Hereditary Tyrant in person, though. In the flesh, Bortav looked older than he did on his images, and not quite so firm and wise: like a man, in other words, not a demigod.

But his ringing baritone proved all his own. He spoke without notes for a quarter of a daytenth, praising Tartesh, condemning those who had tried to lay her low, and promising that danger would never come again. In short, it was a political speech. Since Radnal cared more about the kidneys of the fat sand rat than politics, he soon stopped paying attention.

He almost missed the Hereditary Tyrant calling out his name. He started and sprang up. Bortav vez Pamdal beckoned him to the podium. As if in a dream, he went.

Bortav put an arm around his shoulder. The Hereditary Tyrant was faintly perfumed. "Freemen, free-ladies, I present Radnal vez Krobir, whose sharp eye spotted the evil wires which proved the gods had not deserted Tartesh. For his valiant efforts in preserving not only Trench Park, not only the Bottomlands, but all Tartesh, I award him five thousand units of silver and to declare that he and all his heirs are henceforward recognized as members of our nation's aristocracy. Freeman vez Krobir!"

The dignitaries applauded. Bortav vez Pamdal nodded, first to the microphone, then to Radnal. Making a speech frightened him worse than almost anything he'd gone through in the Bottomlands. He tried to pretend it was a scientific paper: "Thank you, Your Excellency. You honor me beyond my worth. I will always cherish your kindness."

He stepped back. The dignitaries applauded again, perhaps because he'd been so brief. Away from the mike, the Hereditary Tyrant said, "Stay up here by me while I reward your colleagues. The other presentation for you is at the end."

Bortav called up the rest of the seven walkers, one by one. He raised Peggol to the aristocracy along with Radnal. The other five drew his praise and large sums of silver. That seemed unfair to Radnal. Without Horken, for instance, they wouldn't have found the electrical cell and timer. And Impac had picked up the trail when even Radnal lost it.

He couldn't very well protest. Even as the hero of the moment, he lacked the clout to make Bortav listen to him. Moreover, he guessed no one had informed the Hereditary Tyrant he'd been fornicating with Evillia and Lofosa a few days before they went out to detonate the buried starbomb. Bortav vez Pamdal was a staunch conservative about morals. He wouldn't have elevated Radnal if he'd known everything he did in Trench Park.

To salve his conscience, Radnal reminded himself that all seven walkers would have easier lives because of today's ceremony. It was true. He remained not quite convinced it was enough.

Zosel vez Glesir, last to be called to the podium, finished his thank-you and went back to his place. Bortav vez Pamdal reclaimed the microphone. As the applause for Zosel died away, the Tyrant said, "Our nation should never forget this near brush with disaster, nor the efforts of all those within Trench Park who turned it aside. To commemorate it, I here display for the first time the insigne Trench Park will bear henceforward."

The protocol officer carried a cloth-covered square of fiberboard, not quite two cubits on a side, over to Radnal. He murmured, "The veil unfastens from the top. Hold the emblem up so the crowd can see it as you lower the veil."

Radnal obeyed. The dignitaries clapped. Most of them smiled; a few even laughed. Radnal smiled, too. What better way to symbolize Trench Park than a koprit bird perching on a thornbush?

Bortav vez Pamdal waved him to the microphone once more. He said, "I thank you again, Your Excellency, now on behalf of all Trench Park staff. We shall bear this insigne proudly."

He stepped away from the microphone, then turned his head and hissed to the protocol officer, "What do I do with this thing?"

"Lean it against the side of the podium," the unflappable official answered. "We'll take care of it." As Radnal returned to his seat, the protocol officer announced, "Now we'll adjourn to the Grand Reception Hall for drinks and a luncheon."

Along with everyone else, Radnal found his way to the Grand Reception Hall. He took a glass of sparkling wine from a waiter with a silver tray, then stood around accepting congratulations from important officials. It was like being a tour guide: he knew most of what he should say, and improvised new answers along old themes.

In a flash of insight, he realized the politicians and bureaucrats were doing the same thing with him. The whole affair was formal as a figure dance. When he saw that, his nervousness vanished for good.

Or so he thought, until Toglo came smiling up to him. He dipped his head. "Hello, freelady, it's good to see you again."

"If I was Toglo zev through danger in Trench Park, I remain Toglo zev here safe in Tarteshem." She sounded as if his formality disappointed her.

"Good," he said. Despite her pledge of patronage before she hiked away from the lodge, plenty of people friendly to Trench Park staff in the Bottomlands snubbed them if they met in the city. He hadn't thought she was that type, but better safe.

As if by magic, Bortav vez Pamdal appeared at Radnal's elbow. The Hereditary Tyrant's cheeks were a little red; he might have had more than one glass of sparkling wine. He spoke as if reminding himself: "You already know my niece, don't you, freeman vez Krobir?"

"Your—niece?" Radnal stared from Bortav to Toglo. She'd called herself a distant collateral relation. *Niece* didn't fit that definition.

"Hope you enjoy your stay here." Bortav slapped Radnal on the shoulder, breathed wine into his face, and ambled off to hobnob with other guests.

"You never said you were his niece," Radnal said. Now that he was suddenly an aristocrat, he might have imagined talking to the clanfather of the Hereditary Tyrant's distant collateral relative. But to talk to Bortav vez Pamdal's brother or sister-husband . . . impossible. Maybe that made him sound peevish.

"I'm sorry," Toglo answered. Radnal studied her, expecting the apology to be merely for form's sake.

But she seemed to mean it. She said, "Bearing my clan name is hard enough anyway. It would be harder yet if I told everyone how close a relative of the Hereditary Tyrant's I am. People wouldn't treat me like a human being. Believe me, I know." By the bitterness in her voice, she did.

"Oh," Radnal said slowly. "I never thought of that, Toglo zev." Her smile when he used her name with the polite particle made him feel better.

"You should have," she told him. "When folk hear I'm from the Pamdal clan, they either act as if I'm made of glass and will shatter if they breathe on me too hard, or else they try to see how much they can get out of me. I don't care for either one. That's why I minimize the kinship."

"Oh," Radnal's snort of laughter was aimed mostly at himself. "I always imagined being attached to a rich and famous clan made life simpler and easier, not the other way round. I never thought anything bad might be mixed with that. I'm sorry, for not realizing it."

"You needn't be," she said. "I think you'd have treated me the same even if you'd known from the first heartbeat who my uncle happened to be. I don't find that often, so I treasure it."

Radnal said, "I'd be lying if I told you I didn't think about which family you belonged to."

"Well, of course, Radnal vez. You'd be stupid if you didn't think about it. I don't expect that; until the koprit bird, I thought the gods were done with miracles. But whatever you were thinking, you didn't let it get in the way."

"I tried to treat you as much like everyone else as I could," he said.

"I thought you did wonderfully," she answered. "That's why we became friends so fast down in Trench Park. It's also why I'd like us to stay friends now."

"I'd like that very much," Radnal said, "provided

you don't think I'm saying so to try and take advantage of you."

"I don't think you'd do that." Though Toglo kept smiling, her eyes measured him. She'd said she'd had people try to take advantage of her before. Radnal doubted those people had come off well.

"Being who you are makes it harder for me to tell you I also liked you very much, down in the Bottomlands," he said.

"Yes, I can see that it might," Toglo said. "You don't want me to think you seek advantage." She studied Radnal again. This time, he studied her, too. Maybe the first person who'd tried to turn friendship to gain had succeeded; she was, he thought, a genuinely nice person. But he would have bet his five thousand units of silver that she'd sent the second such person packing. Being nice didn't make her a fool.

He didn't like her less for that. Maybe Eltsac vez Martois was attracted to fools, but Eltsac was a fool himself. Radnal had called himself many names, but fool seldom. The last time he'd thought that about himself was when he found out what Lofosa and Evillia really were. Of course, when he made a mistake, he didn't do it halfway.

But he'd managed to redeem himself—with help from that koprit bird.

Toglo said, "If we do become true friends, Radnal vez, or perhaps even more than that"—a possibility he wouldn't have dared mention himself, but one far from displeasing—"promise me one thing."

"What?" he asked, suddenly wary. "I don't like friendship with conditions. It reminds me too much of our last treaty with Morgaf. We haven't fought the islanders in a while, but we don't trust them, or they us. We saw that in the Bottomlands, too."

She nodded. "True. Still, I hope my condition isn't too onerous."

"Go on." He sipped his sparkling wine.

"Well, then, Radnal vez Krobir, the *next* time I see you in a sleepsack with a couple of naked Highhead girls—or even Strongbrows—you will have to consider our friendship over."

Some of the wine went up his nose. That only made him choke worse. Dabbing at himself with a linen square gave him a few heartbeats to regain composure. "Toglo zev, you have a bargain," he said solemnly.

They clasped hands.

The Wheels of If

L. Sprague de Camp

King Oswiu of Northumbria squirmed in his chair. In the first place these synods bored him. In the second, his mathematics comprised the ability to add and subtract numbers under twenty on his fingers. Hence all this argument among the learned clerics, assembled in Whitby in the year of Our Lord 664, about the date of Easter and the phases of the moon and cycles of 84 and 532 years, went over the King's head completely.

What did the exact date of Easter matter, anyhow? If they wanted to, why couldn't the Latins celebrate their Easter when they wanted, and the Ionans celebrate theirs? The Ionans had been doing all right, as far as Oswiu could see. And then this Wilfrid of York had to bring in his swarms of Latin priests, objecting to this and that as schismatic, heretical, etc. They were abetted by Oswiu's queen, Eanfled, which put poor Oswiu in an awkward position. He not only wanted peace in the family, but also hoped to attain

to Heaven some day. Moreover, he liked the Abbot
Colman, leader of the Ionans. And he certainly didn't
want any far-off Bishop of Rome sticking his nose into
his affairs. On the other hand . . .

King Oswiu came to with a jerk. Father Wilfrid
was speaking to him directly: ". . . the arguments of
my learned friend—" he indicated the Abbot Colman
of Lindisfarne "—are very ingenious, I admit. But that
is not the fundamental question. The real decision is,
shall we accept the authority of His Holiness of Rome,
like good Christians, or—"

"Wait a minute, wait a minute," interrupted Oswiu.
"Why must we accept Gregory's authority to be good
Christians? I'm a good Christian, and I don't let any
foreign—"

"The question, my lord, is whether one can be a
good Christian and a rebel against—"

"I am too a good Christian!" bristled Oswiu.

Wilfrid of York smiled. "Perhaps you remember the
statement of our Savior to Peter, the first Bishop of
Rome? Thou art Peter; and upon this rock I will build
my Church; and the gates of Hell shall not prevail
against it. And I will give unto thee the keys of the
Kingdom of Heaven; and whatsoever thou shalt bind
on earth shall be bound in Heaven; and whatsoever
thou shalt loose on earth shall be loosed in Heaven.'
You see?"

Oswiu thought. That put a different light on the
matter. If this fellow Peter actually had the keys of
Heaven . . .

He turned to the Abbot Colman and asked: "Is that
a correct quotation?"

"It is, my lord. But—"

"Just a minute, just a minute. You'll get me all confused again if you start arguing. Now, can you quote
a text showing that equivalent powers were granted
to Saint Columba?"

The grave Irishman's face registered sudden dismay. He frowned in concentration so intense that one could almost hear the wheels.

"Well?" said Oswiu. "Speak up!"

Colman sighed. "No, my lord, I cannot. But I can show that it is the Latins, not we, who are departing from—"

"That's enough, Colman!" Oswiu's single-track mind, once made up, had no intention of being disturbed again. "I have decided that from this day forth the Kingdom of Northumbria shall follow the Latin practice concerning Easter. And that we shall declare our allegiance to the Roman Bishop Gregory, lest, when I come to the gates of Heaven, there would be none to open them for me—he being my adversary who has the keys. The synod is adjourned."

King Oswiu went out, avoiding the reproachful look that the Abbot sent after him. It was a dirty trick on Colman, who was a very decent chap. But after all, it wouldn't do to antagonize the heavenly doorman. And maybe now Eanfled would stop nagging him . . .

Allister Park rubbed his eyes and sat up in bed, as he usually did. He noticed nothing wrong until he looked at the sleeve of his pajamas.

He could not recall ever having had a pair of pajamas of that singularly repulsive green. He couldn't recall having changed to clean pajamas the night before. In short, he couldn't account for these pajamas at all.

Oh, well, probably Eunice or Mary had given them to him, and he'd put them on without thinking. He yawned, brushing his mouth with the back of his hand.

He jerked his hand away. Then he cautiously felt his upper lip.

He got out of bed and made for the nearest mirror. There was no doubt about it. He had a mustache.

He had not had a mustache when he went to bed the night before.

'Abd-ar-Rahman, Governor of Cordoba for the Khalifah Hisham ibn 'Abd-al-Malik, Lord of Damascus, Protector of the Faithful, etc., etc., paced his tent like a caged leopard with claustrophobia. He hated inactivity, and to him the last six days of tentative skirmishing had been just that.

He glowered over his pepper-and-salt beard at his chiefs, sitting cross-legged in an ellipse on the rugs. "Well?" he barked.

Yezid spoke up. "But a little longer, Commander-in-Chief, and the Franks will melt away. The infidels have little cavalry, save Gothic and Aquitanian refugees. Without cavalry, they cannot keep themselves fed. Our horse can range the country, supplying us and cutting off help from our enemies. There is no God but God."

Ya'qub snorted. "How long do you think our men will abide this fearful Frankish climate? The winter is almost upon us. I say strike now, while their spirits are still up. This rabble of Frankish farmers on foot will show some rare running. Have the armies of the Faithful come this far by sitting in front of their enemies and making grimaces at them?"

Yezid delivered an impressive snort of his own. "Just the advice one would expect from a dog of a Ma'adite. This Karel, who commands the infidels, is no fool—"

"Who's a dog?" yelped Ya'qub, jumping up. "Pig of a Yemenite—"

'Abd-ar-Rahman yelled at them until they subsided. One major idea of this foray into Francia was to bury the animosity between members of the two parties. Yezid's starting a quarrel on political grounds put the Governor in an embarrassing position, as he was a Yemenite himself. He was still undecided. An intelligent man, he could see the sense to Yezid's Fabian *advice. Emotionally, however, he burned to get to grips with the army of Charles, Mayor of Austrasia. And Yezid should be punished for his insulting remark.*

"I have decided," said 'Abd-ar-Rahman, "that, while there is much to be said on both sides, Ya'qub's advice is the sounder. Nothing hurts an army's spirit like waiting. Besides, God has planned the outcome of the battle anyway. So why should we fear? If He decides that we shall win, we shall win.

"Therefore tomorrow, Saturday, we shall strike the Franks with all our force. God is God, and Mohammed is His prophet . . ."

But the next night 'Abd-ar-Rahman lay dead by the banks of the River Vienne, near Tours, with his handsome face waxy in the starlight and blood in his pepper-and-salt beard. The Austrasian line had held. Yezid, who had been right, was dead likewise, and so was Ya'qub, who had been wrong. And the surviving Arabs were fleeing back to Narbonne and Barcelona.

Allister Park opened the door of his apartment and grabbed up his *Times*. Sure enough, the date was Monday April 11th, just as it ought to have been. The year was right, too. That ruled out the possibility of amnesia.

He went back to the mirror. He was still a slightly stout man in his middle thirties, with pale-blue eyes and thinning sandy hair. But he wasn't the same man. The nose was different. So were the eyebrows. The scar under the chin was gone. . . .

He gave up his self-inspection and got out his clothes. At that juncture he got another shock. The clothes weren't his. Or rather, they were clothes for a man of his size, and of the quality that a self-indulgent bachelor with an income of $12,000 a year would buy. Park didn't object to the clothes. It was just that they weren't *his* clothes.

Park gave up speculation about his sanity for the nonce; he had to get dressed. Breakfast? He was sick of the more cardboard-like cereals. To hell with it; he'd make himself some French toast. If it put another inch on his middle, he'd sweat it off Sunday at the New York Athletic Club.

The mail was thrust under his door. He finished knotting his necktie and picked it up. The letters were all addressed to a Mr. Arthur Vogel.

Then Allister Park, really awake, did look around. The apartment was built on the same plan as his own, but it wasn't the same. The furniture was different. Lots of little things were different, such as a nick in the wall that shouldn't be there.

Park sat down and smoked a cigarette while he thought. There was no evidence of kidnapping, which, considering his business, was not too unlikely a possibility. He'd gone to bed Sunday night sober, alone, and reasonably early. Why should he wake up in another man's apartment? He forgot for the moment that he had also awakened with another man's face. Before he had time to remember it, the sight of the clock jostled him into action. No time for French toast—it would have to be semi-edible cardboard after all.

But the real shock awaited him when he looked for his briefcase. There was none. Neither was there any sign of the sheaf of notes he had so carefully drawn up on the conduct of the forthcoming Antonini case. That was more than important. On his convicting the Antonini gang depended his nomination for District Attorney for the County of New York next fall. The present DA was due to get the bipartisan nomination to the Court of General Sessions at the same time.

He was planning, with thoroughly dishonorable motives, to invite Martha up for dinner. But he didn't want to have dinner with her until he'd cleared this matter up. The only trouble with calling her up was

that the address book didn't have her name in it—
or indeed the name of anybody Park had ever heard
of. Neither was she listed in the phone book.

He dialed CAnal 6-5700. Somebody said: "Department of Hospitals."

"Huh? Isn't this CAnal 6-5700?"

"Yes, this is the Department of Hospitals."

"Well what's the District Attorney's office then?"
Hell, I ought to know my own office phone.

"The District Attorney's office is WOrth 2-2200."

Park groggily called WOrth 2-2200. "Mr. Park's
office, please."

"What office did you ask for, please?"

"The office of Assistant District Attorney Park!"
Park's voice took on the metallic rasp. "Racket Bureau
to you, sister."

"I'm sorry, we have no such person."

"Listen, young lady, have you got a Deputy Assistant DA named Frenczko? John Frenczko? You spell
it with a z."

Silence. "No, I'm sorry, we have no such person."
Allister Park hung up.

The old building at 137 Center was still there. The
Racket Bureau was still there. But they had never
heard of Allister Park. They already had an Assistant
DA of their own, a man named Hutchison, with
whom they seemed quite well satisfied. There was no
sign of Park's two deputies, Frenczko and Burt.

As a last hope, Park went over to the Criminal
Courts Building. If he wasn't utterly mad, the case
of *People v. Cassidy*, extortion, ought to come up as
soon after ten as it would take Judge Segal to read
his calendar. Frenczko and Burt would be in there,
after Cassidy's hide.

But there was no Judge Segal, no Frenczko, no
Burt, no Cassidy. . . .

❖   ❖   ❖

"Very interesting, Mr. Park," soothed the psychiatrist. "Very interesting indeed. The most hopeful feature is that you quite realize your difficulty, and come to me now—"

"What I want to know," interrupted Park, "is: was I sane up to yesterday, and crazy since then, or was I crazy up to then and sane now?"

"It seems hard to believe that one could suffer from a coherent set of illusions for thirty-six years," replied the psychiatrist. "Yet your present account of your perceptions seems rational enough. Perhaps your memory of what you saw and experienced today is at fault."

"But I want to get straightened out! My whole political future depends on it! At least—" he stopped. *Was* there such an Antonini gang? *Was* there a nomination awaiting an Allister Park if they were convicted?

"I know," said the psychiatrist gently. "But this case isn't like any I ever heard of. You go ahead and wire Denver for Allister Park's birth certificate. We'll see if there is such a person. Then come back tomorrow. . . ."

Park awoke, looked around, and groaned. The room had changed again. But he choked off his groan. He was occupying a twin bed. In its mate lay a fair-to-middling handsome woman of about his own age.

His groan had roused her. She asked: "How are you feeling, Wally?"

"I'm feeling fine," he mumbled. The significance of his position was soaking in. He had some trouble suppressing another groan. About marriage, he was an adherent of the why-buy-a-cow philosophy, as he had had occasion to make clear to many women by way of fair warning.

"I hope you are," said the woman anxiously. "You acted so queer yesterday. Do you remember your appointment with Dr. Kerr?"

"I certainly do," said Park. Kerr was not the name of the psychiatrist with whom he had made the appointment.

The woman prepared to dress. Park gulped a little. For years he'd managed to get along without being mixed up with other men's wives, ever since . . .

And he wished he knew her name. A well-mannered man, under those circumstances, wouldn't refer to the woman as "Hey, you."

"What are we having for breakfast, sweetie-pie?" he asked with a sickly grin. She told him, adding: "You never called me that before, dear." When she started toward him with an expectant smile, he jumped out of bed and dressed with frantic haste.

He ate silently. When the woman inquired why, he pointed to his mouth and mumbled: "Canker sore. It hurts to talk."

He fled as soon as he decently could, without learning his "wife's" name. His wallet told him his name was Wallace Heineman, but little else about himself. If he wanted to badly enough, he could no doubt find out whom he worked for, who his friends were, which if any bank he had money in, etc. But if these daily changes were going to continue, it hardly seemed worthwhile. The first thing was to get back to that psychiatrist.

Although the numbers of the streets were different, the general layout was the same. Half an hour's walking brought him to the block where the psychiatrist's office had been. The building had been on the southeast corner of Fifty-seventh and Eighth. Park could have sworn the building that now occupied that site was different.

However, he went up anyway. He had made a careful note of the office number. His notebook had been missing that morning, like all the rest of his (or rather Arthur Vogel's) things. Still, he remembered the number.

The number turned out to be that of a suite of offices occupied by Williamson, Ostendorff, Cohen, Burke, and Williamson, Attorneys. No, they had never heard of Park's brain-man. Yes, Williamson, Ostendorff, Cohen, Burke, and Williamson had occupied those offices for years.

Park came out into the street and stood a long time, thinking. A phenomenon that he had hitherto noticed only vaguely now puzzled him: the extraordinary number of Union Jacks in sight.

He asked the traffic cop about it. The cop looked at him. "King's buithday," he said.

"What king?"

"Why, *our* king of course. David the Fuist." The cop touched his finger to the peak of his cap.

Park settled himself on a park bench with a newspaper. The paper was full of things like references to the recent Anglo-Russian war, the launching of the *Queen Victoria*, His Majesty's visit to a soap factory ("Where he displayed a keen interest in the technical problems involved in . . ."), the victory of Massachusetts over Quebec in the Inter-Colonial football matches (Massachusetts a colony? And football in April?), the trial of one Diedrichs for murdering a man with a cross-cut saw. . . .

All this was very interesting, especially the Diedrichs case. But Allister Park was more concerned with the whereabouts and probable fate of the Antonini gang. He also thought with gentle melancholy of Mary and Eunice and Dorothy and Martha and Joan and . . . But that was less important than the beautiful case he had dug up against such a slimy set of public enemies. Even Park, despite the cynical view of humanity that public prosecutors get, had felt a righteous glow when he tallied up the evidence and knew he had them.

And the nomination was not to be sneezed at either. It just happened that he was available when it was a Protestant's turn at that nomination. If he missed out, he'd have to wait while a Catholic and a Jew took theirs. Since you had to be one or the other to get nominated at all, Park had become perforce a church member and regular if slightly hypocritical goer.

His plan was, after a few terms as DA, to follow the incumbent DA onto the bench. You would never have guessed it, but inside Allister Park lingered enough of the idealism that as a young lawyer he had brought from Colorado to give the bench an attractiveness not entirely comprised of salary and social position.

He looked in his pockets. There was enough there for one good bender.

Of the rest of the day, he never could remember much afterwards. He did remember giving a pound note to an old woman selling shoelaces, leading a group of drunks in a song about one Columbo who knew the world was round-o (unexpurgated), and trying to take a fireman's hose away from him on the ground that the city was having a water shortage.

He awoke in another strange room, without a trace of a hangover. A quick look around assured him that he was alone.

It was time, he thought, that he worked out a system for the investigation of his identity on each successive morning. He learned that his name was Wadsworth Noe. The pants of all the suits in his closet were baggy knee pants, plus fours.

Something was going *ping*, *ping*, *ping*, like one of those tactful alarm clocks. Park located the source of the noise in a goose-necked gadget on the table, which he finally identified as a telephone. As the transmitter and receiver were built into a single unit on the end of the gooseneck, there was nothing to lift off the hook. He pressed a button in the base. A voice spoke: "Waddy?"

"Oh—yeah. Who's this?"

"This is your little bunnykins."

Park swore under his breath. The voice sounded female and young; and had a slight indefinable accent. He stalled: "How are you this morning?"

"Oh, I'm fine. How's my little butterball?"

Park winced. Wadsworth Noe had a figure even more portly than Allister Park's. Park, with effort, infused syrup into his voice: "Oh, I'm fine too, sweetie-pie. Only I'm lonesome as all hell."

"Oh, isn't that too bad! Oo poor little thing! Shall I come up and cook dinner for my precious?"

"I'd love it." A plan was forming in Park's mind. Hitherto all these changes had taken place while he was asleep. If he could get somebody to sit around and watch him while he stayed up . . .

The date was made. Park found he'd have to market.

On the street, aside from the fact that all the men wore plus fours and wide-brimmed hats, the first thing that struck him was the sight of two dark men in uniform. They walked in step down the middle of the sidewalk. Their walk implied that they expected people to get out of their way. People got. As the soldiers passed him, Park caught a sentence in a foreign language, sounding like Spanish.

At the market everyone spoke with that accent Park had heard over the phone. They fell silent when another pair of soldiers entered. These loudly demanded certain articles of food. A clerk scurried around and got the order. The soldiers took the things and departed without paying.

Park thought of going to a library to learn about the world he was in. But if he were going to shift again, it would hardly be worthwhile. He bought a *New York Record*, noticing that the stand also carried a lot of papers in French and Spanish.

Back in his apartment he read of His Majesty

Napoleon V, apparently emperor of New York City
and God knew what else!

His little bunnykins turned out to be a smallish
dark girl, not bad-looking, who kissed him soundly.
She said: "Where have you been the last few days,
Waddy? I haven't heard from you for simply *ages*! I
was beginning to think you'd forgotten me. Oo hasn't
forgotten, has oo?"

"Me forget? Why, sweetie-pie, I couldn't any more
forget you than I could forget my own name." (And
what the hell's that? he asked himself. Wordsworth—
no, Wadsworth Noe. Thank God.) "Give us another
kiss."

. . . She looked at him. "What makes you talk so
funny, Waddy?"

"Canker sore," said Allister Park.

"O-o-o, you poor angel. Let me see it."

"It's all right. How about that famous dinner?"

At least Wadsworth Noe kept a good cellar. After
dinner Park applied himself cautiously to this. It gave
an excuse for just sitting. Park asked the girl about
herself. She chattered on happily for some hours.

Then her conversation began to run dry. There
were long silences.

She looked at him quizzically. "Are you worrying
about something, Waddy? Somehow you seem like a
different man."

"No," he lied. "I'm not worrying."

She looked at the clock. "I suppose I ought to go,"
she said hesitantly.

Park sat up. "Oh, please don't!"

She relaxed and smiled. "I didn't *think* you'd let
me. Just wait." She disappeared into the bedroom and
presently emerged in a filmy nightgown.

Allister Park was not surprised. But he was concerned. Attractive as the girl was, the thought of

solving his predicament was more so. Besides, he was already sleepy from the liquors he had drunk.

"How about making some coffee, sweetie-pie?" he asked.

She acquiesced. The making and drinking of the coffee took another hour. It was close to midnight. To keep the ball rolling, Park told some stories. Then the conversation died down again. The girl yawned. She seemed puzzled and a bit resentful.

She asked: "Are you going to sit up all night?"

That was just what Park intended to do. But while he cast about for a plausible reason to give, he stalled: "Ever tell you about that man Wugson I met last week? Funniest chap you ever saw. He has a big bunch of hairs growing out the end of his nose. . . ."

He went on in detail about the oddities of the imaginary Mr. Wugson. The girl had an expression of what-did-I-do-to-deserve-this. She yawned again.

Click! Allister Park rubbed his eyes and sat up. He was on a hard knobby thing that might, by gross misuse of the language, be called a mattress. His eyes focussed on a row of iron bars.

He was in jail.

Allister Park's day in jail proved neither interesting nor informative. He was marched out for meals and for an hour of exercise. Nobody spoke to him except a guard who asked: "Hey there, chief, who ja think you are today, huh? Julius Caesar?"

Park grinned. "Nope. I'm God, this time."

This was getting to be a bore. If one could do this flitting about from existence to existence voluntarily, it might be fun. As it was, one didn't stay put long enough to adjust oneself to any of these worlds of— illusion?

The next day he was a shabby fellow sleeping on a park bench. The city was still New York—no it wasn't; it was a different city built on the site of New York.

He had money for nothing more than a bottle of milk and a loaf of bread. These he bought and consumed slowly, while reading somebody's discarded newspaper. Reading was difficult because of the queer spelling. And the people had an accent that required the closest attention to understand.

He spent a couple of hours in an art museum. The guards looked at him as if he were something missed by the cleaners. When it closed he went back to his park bench and waited. Night came.

A car—at least, a four-wheeled power vehicle—drew up and a couple of cops got out. Park guessed they were cops because of their rhinestone epaulets. One asked: "Are you John Gilby?" He pronounced it: "Air yew Thawn Gilbü?"

But Allister Park caught his drift. "Damned if I know, brother. Am I?"

The cops looked at each other. "He's him, all right," said one. To Park: "Come along."

Park learned, little by little, that he was not wanted for anything more serious than disappearance. He kept his own counsel until they arrived at the stationhouse.

Inside was a fat woman. She jumped up and pointed at him, crying raucously: "That's him! That's the dirty deserter, running off and leaving his poor wife to starve! The back of me hand to you, you dirty—"

"Please, Mrs. Gilby!" said the desk sergeant.

The woman was not to be silenced. "Heaven curse the day I met you! Sergeant darlin', what can I do to put the dirty loafer in jail where he belongs?"

"Well," said the sergeant uncomfortably, "you can charge him with desertion, of course. But don't you think you'd better go home and talk it over? We don't want to—"

"Hey!" cried Park. They looked at him. "I'll take jail, if you don't mind—"

Click! Once again he was in bed. It was a real bed

this time. He looked around. The place had the
unmistakable air of a sanitarium or hospital.

Oh, well. Park rolled over and went to sleep.

The next day he was still in the same place. He
began to have hopes. Then he remembered that, as
the transitions happened at midnight, he had no
reason for assuming that the next one would not
happen the following midnight.

He spent a very boring day. A physician came in,
asked him how he was, and was gone almost before
Park could say "Fine." People brought him his meals.
If he'd been sure he was going to linger, he'd have
made vigorous efforts to orient himself and to get
out. But as it was, there didn't seem any point.

The next morning he was still in bed. But when
he tried to rub his eyes and sit up, he found that
his wrists and ankles were firmly tied to the four
posts. This wasn't the same bed, nor the same room;
it looked like a room in somebody's private house.

And at the foot of the bed sat the somebody: a
small gray-haired man with piercing black eyes that
gleamed over a sharp nose.

For a few seconds Allister Park and the man looked
at each other. Then the man's expression underwent
a sudden and alarming change, as if internal pain had
gripped him. He stared at his own clothes as if he
had never seen them before. He screamed, jumped
up, and dashed out of the room. Park heard his feet
clattering down stairs, and the slam of a front door;
then nothing.

Allister Park tried pulling at his bonds, but the
harder he pulled, the tighter they gripped. So he tried
not pulling, which brought no results either.

He listened. There was a faint hiss and purr of
traffic outside. He must be still in a city, though, it
seemed, a fairly quiet one.

A stair creaked. Park held his breath. Somebody

was coming up, and without unnecessary noise. More than one man, Park thought, listening to the creaks.

Somebody stumbled. From far below a voice called up a question that Park couldn't catch. There were several quick steps and the smack of a fist.

The door of Park's room was ajar. Through the crack appeared a vertical strip of face, including an eye. The eye looked at Park and Park looked at the eye.

The door jerked open and three men pounced into the room. They wore floppy trousers and loose blouses that might have come out of a Russian ballet. They had large, flat, pentagonal faces, red-brown skins and straight black hair. They peered behind the door and under the bed.

"What the hell?" asked Allister Park.

The largest of the three men looked at him. "You're not hurt, Hallow?"

"No. But I'm damn sick of being tied up."

The large man's face showed a flicker of surprise. The large man cut Park's lashings. Park sat up, rubbing his wrists, and learned that he was wearing a suit of coarse woolen underwear.

"Where's the rascally Noggle?" asked the large brown man. Although he rolled his r's like a Scot, he did not look like a Scot. Park thought he might be an Asiatic or an American Indian.

"You mean the little gray-haired bird?"

"Sure. You know, the scoundrel." He pronounced the *k* in "know."

"Suppose I do. When I woke up he was in that chair. He looked at me and beat it out of here as if all the bats of Hell were after him."

"Maybe he's gone daft. But the weighty thing is to get you out." One of the men got a suit out of the closet, resembling the three men's clothes, but somber gray.

Allister Park dressed. The tenseness of the men made him hurry, though he didn't take all this very seriously yet.

Working his feet into the elastic-sided shoes with the big metal buckles, Park asked: "How long have I been here?"

"You dropped from the ken of a man a week ago today," replied the large man with a keen look.

A week ago today he had been Allister Park, assistant district attorney. The next day he hadn't been. It was probably not a mere coincidence.

He started to take a look at his new self in the mirror. Before he could do more than glimpse a week's growth of beard, two of the men were gently pulling his arms toward the door. There was something deferential about their urgency. Park went along. He asked: "What do I do now?"

"That takes a bit of thinking on," said the large man. "It might not be safe for you to go home. Shh!" He stole dramatically down the stairs ahead of them. "Of course," he continued, "you could put in a warrant against Joseph Noggle."

"What good would that do?"

"Not much, I fear. If Noggle was put up to this by MacSvensson, you can be sure the lazy knicks wouldn't find him."

Park had more questions, but he didn't want to give himself away any sooner than he had to.

The house was old, decorated in a curious geometrical style, full of hexagons and spirals. On the ground floor sat another brown man in a rocking chair. In one hand he held a thing like an automobile grease gun, with a pistol grip. Across the room sat another man, with a black eye, looking apprehensively at the gun-thing.

The one in the chair got up, took off his bonnet, and made a bow toward Park. He said: "Haw, Hallow. Were you hurt?"

"He'll live over it, glory be to Patrick," said the big one, whom the others addressed as "Sachem." This person now glowered at the man with the black eye. "Nay alarums, understand? Or—" he drew the tip of his forefinger in a quick circle on the crown of his head. It dawned on Park that he was outlining the part of the scalp that an Indian might remove as a trophy.

They quickly went out, glancing up and down the street. It was early morning; few people were visible. Park's four companions surrounded him in a way that suggested that, much as they respected him, he had better not make a break.

The sidewalk had a wood-block paving. At the curb stood a well-streamlined automobile. The engine seemed to be in the rear. From the size of the closed-in section, Park guessed it to be huge.

They got in. The instrument board had more knobs and dials than a transport plane. The Sachem started the car noiselessly. Another car blew a resonant whistle, and passed them wagging a huge tail of water vapor. Park grasped the fact that the cars were steam-powered. Hence the smooth, silent operation; hence also the bulky engine and the complex controls.

The buildings were large but low; Park saw none over eight or ten stories. The traffic signals had sema-phore arms with "STAI" and "COM" on them.

"Where are you taking me?" asked Park.

"Outside the burg bounds, first," said the Sachem. "Then we'll think on the next."

Park wondered what was up; they were still res-pectful as all Hell, but there was something ominous about their haste to get outside the "burg bounds," which Park took to be the city limits. He said, experi-mentally, "I'm half starved."

A couple of the brown men echoed these senti-ments, so the Sachem presently stopped the car at a restaurant. Park looked around it; except for that odd geometric style of decoration, it was much like other restaurants the world over.

"What's the program?" he asked the Sachem. Park had known some heavy drinkers in his time, but never one who washed his breakfast pancakes down with whiskey, as the large brown man was now doing.

"That'll be seen," said the Sachem. "What did Noggle try to do to you?"

"Never did find out."

"There's been an under talk about the swapping of minds. I wonder if—where are you going?"

"Be right back," said Park, heading for the men's room. In another minute the Sachem would have cornered him on the question of identity. They watched him go. Once in the men's room, he climbed onto a sink, opened a window, and squirmed out into the adjacent alley. He put several blocks between himself and his convoyers before he slowed down.

His pockets failed to tell him whose body he had. His only mark of identification was a large gold ring with a Celtic cross. He had a few coins in one pocket, wherewith he bought a newspaper.

Careful searching disclosed the following item:

BISJAP STIL MISING

At a læt aur jestrdai nee toocan had ben faund of yi mising Bisjap Ib Scoglund of yi Niu Belfast Bisjapric of yi Celtic Cristjan Tjörtj, hwuuz vanisjing a wiik agoo haz sterd yi börg. Cnicts sai yai aar leeving nee steen öntornd in yæir straif tu fained yi hwarabouts of yi mising preetjr, hwuuz lösti swink on bihaaf of yi Screlingz haz bimikst him in a fiirs yingli scöfal . . .

It looked to Park as though some German or Norwegian had tried to spell English—or what passed for English in this city—phonetically according to the rules of his own language, with a little Middle English or Anglo-Saxon thrown in. He made a tentative translation:

BISHOP STILL MISSING

At a late hour yesterday no token (sign?) had been found of the missing Bishop Ib Scoglund of the New Belfast Bishopric of the Celtic Christian Church, whose vanishing a week ago has stirred the burg (city?). Cnicts (police?) say they are leaving no stone unturned in their strife (effort?) to find the whereabouts of the missing preacher . . .

It sounded like him, all right. What a hell of a name, Ib Scoglund! The next step was to find where he lived. If they had telephones, they ought to have telephone directories . . .

Half an hour later Park approached the bishop's house. If he were going to change again at midnight, the thing to do would be to find some quiet place, relax, and await the change. However, he felt that the events of the week made a pattern, of which he thought he could see the beginnings of an outline. If his guesses were right, he had arrived at his destination.

The air was moderately warm and a bit sticky, as New York City air might well be in April. A woman passed him, leading a floppy-eared dog. She was stout and fiftyish. Although Park did not think that a skirt that cleared her knees by six inches became her, that was what was being worn.

As he turned the corner onto what ought to be his block, he sighted a knot of people in front of a house. Two men in funny steeple-crowned hats sat in an open car. They were dressed alike, and Park guessed they were policemen.

Park pulled his bonnet—a thing like a Breton

peasant's hat—over one side of his face. He walked past on the opposite side of the street, looking unconcerned. The people were watching No. 64, his number.

There was an alley on one side of the house. Park walked to the next corner, crossed, and started back toward No. 64. He had almost reached the entrance to the alley when one of the men spotted him. With a cry of "There's the bishop himself!" the men on the sidewalk—there were four—ran toward him. The men in the funny hats got out of their vehicle and followed.

Park squared his shoulders. He had faced down wardheelers who invaded his apartment to tell him to lay off certain people, or else. However, far from being hostile, these shouted: "Wher-r-re ya been, Hallow?" "Were you kidnapped?" "Ja lose your recall?" "How about a wording?" All produced pads and pencils.

Park felt at home. He asked: "Who's it for?"

One of the men said: "I'm from the *Sooth*."

"The what?"

"The *New Belfast Sooth*. We've been upholding you on the Skrelling question."

Park looked serious. "I've been investigating conditions."

The men looked puzzled. Park added: "You know, looking into things."

"Oh," said the man from the *Sooth*. "Peering the kilters, eh?"

The men in the funny hats arrived. One of the pair asked: "Any wrongdoings, Bishop? Want to mark in a slur?"

Park, fumbling through the mazes of this dialect, figured that he meant "file a complaint." He said: "No, I'm all right. Thanks anyway."

"But," cried the hat, "are you *sure* you don't want to mark in a slur? We'll take you to the lair if you do."

"No, thank you," said Park. The hats sidled up to him, one on either side. In the friendliest manner they took his arms and gently urged him toward the car, saying: "Sure you want to mark in a slur. We was sent special to get you so you could. If somebody kidnapped you, you must, or it's helping wrongdoing, you know. It's just a little way to the lair—"

Park had been doing some quick thinking. They had an ulterior reason for wanting to get him to the "lair" (presumably a police station); but manhandling a bishop, especially in the presence of reporters, just wasn't done. He wrenched loose and jumped into the doorway of No. 64. He snapped: "I haven't got any slurs, and I'm not going to your lair, get me?"

"Aw, but Hallow, we wasn't going to hurt you. Only if you have a slur, you have to mark it in. That's the law, see?" The man, his voice a pleading whine, came closer and reached for Park's sleeve. Park cocked a fist, saying: "If you want me for anything, you can get a warrant. Otherwise the *Sooth*'ll have a story about how you tried to kidnap the bishop, and how he knocked the living bejesus out of you!" The reporters made encouraging noises.

The hats gave up and got back in their car. With some remark about ". . . he'll sure give us hell," they departed.

Park pulled the little handle on the door. Something went *bong, bong* inside. The reporters crowded around, asking questions. Park, trying to look the way a bishop should, held up a hand. "I'm very tired, gentlemen, but I'll have a statement for you in a few days."

They were still pestering him when the door opened. Inside, a small monkeylike fellow opened his mouth. "Hallow Colman keep us from harm!" he cried.

"I'm sure he will," said Park gravely, stepping in. "How about some food?"

"Surely, surely," said Monkey-face. "But—but what on earth has your hallowship been doing? I've been fair sick with worry."

"Peering the kilters, old boy, peering the kilters." Park followed Monkey-face upstairs, as if he had intended going that way of his own accord. Monkey-face doddered into a bedroom and busied himself with getting out clean clothes.

Park looked at a mirror. He was—as he had been throughout his metamorphoses—a stocky man with thinning light hair, in the middle thirties. While he was not Allister Park, neither was he very different from him.

The reddish stubble on his face would have to come off. In the bathroom Park found no razor. He stumbled on a contraption that might be an electric razor. He pushed the switch experimentally, and dropped the thing with a yell. It had bitten a piece out of his thumb. Holding the injured member, Park cut loose with the condemnatory vocabulary that ten years of work among New York City's criminal class had given him.

Monkey-face stood in the doorway, eyes big. Park stopped his swearing long enough to rasp: "Damn your lousy little soul, don't stand there! Get me a bandage!"

The little man obeyed. He applied the bandage as though he expected Park to begin the practice of cannibalism on him at any moment.

"What's the matter?" said Park. "I won't bite you!"

Monkey-face looked up. "Begging pardon, your hallowship, but I thock you wouldn't allow the swearing of aiths in your presence. And now such frickful aiths I never did hear."

"Oh," said Park. He remembered the penetrating look the Sachem had given his mild damns and hells. Naturally a bishop would not use such language—at least not where he could be overheard.

"You'd better finish my shave," he said.

Monkey-face still looked uneasy. "Begging your forgiveness again, Hallow, but what makes you talk such a queer speech?"

"Canker sore," growled Park.

Shaved, he felt better. He bent a kindly look on Monkey-face. "Listen," he said, "your bishop has been consorting with low uncouth persons for the past week. So don't mind it if I fall into their way of speaking. Only don't tell anybody, see? Sorry I jumped on you just now. D'you accept my apology?"

"Yes—yes, of course, Hallow."

"All right, then. How about that famous breakfast?"

After breakfast he took his newspaper and the pile of mail into the bishop's well-equipped library. He looked up "Screling" in the "Wördbuk" or dictionary. A "Screling" was defined as one of the aboriginal inhabitants of Vinland.

"Vinland" stirred a faint chord; something he'd learned in school. The atlas contained a map of North America. A large area in the north and east thereof, bounded on the west and south by an irregular line running roughly from Charleston to Winnipeg, was labeled the Bretwaldate of Vinland. The remaining two-thirds of the continent comprised half a dozen political areas, with such names as Dacoosja, Tjeroogia, Aztecia. Park, referring back to the dictionary, derived these from Dakota, Cherokee, Aztec, etcetera.

In a couple of hours telephone calls began coming in. Monkey-face, according to his instructions, told one and all that the bishop was resting up and couldn't be disturbed. Park meanwhile located a pack of pipes in the library, and a can of tobacco. He got out several pads of paper and sharpened a dozen pencils.

Monkey-face announced lunch. Park told him to bring it in. He announced dinner. Park told him to bring it in. He announced bedtime. Park told him to go soak his head. He went, clucking. He had never seen a man work with such a fury of concentration for so long at a stretch, let alone his master. But then, he had never seen Allister Park reviewing the evidence for a big criminal case.

History, according to the encyclopedia, was much the same as Park remembered it down to the Dark Ages. Tracing down the point at which the divergence took place, he located the fact that King Oswiu of Northumbria had decided in favor of the Celtic Christian Church at the Synod of Whitby, 664 A.D. Park had never heard of the Synod or of King Oswiu. But the encyclopedia ascribed to this decision the rapid spread of the Celtic form of Christianity over Great Britain and Scandinavia. Hence it seemed to Park that probably, in the history of the world he had come from, the king had decided the other way.

The Roman Christian Church had held most of its ground in northern Europe for a century more. But the fate of its influence there had been sealed by the defeat of the Franks by the Arabs at Tours. The Arabs had occupied all southern Gaul before they were finally stopped, and according to the atlas they were still there. The Pope and the Lombard duchies of Italy had at once placed themselves under the protection of the Byzantine emperor Leo the Iconoclast. (A Greek-speaking "Roman" Empire still occupied Anatolia and the Balkans, under a Serbian dynasty.)

A Danish king of England named Gorm had brought both the British Isles and Scandinavia under his rule, as Knut had done in Park's world. But Gorm's kingdom proved more durable than Knut's; the connection between England and Scandinavia had survived, despite intervals of disunion and civil war, down to the present. North America was discovered by one Ketil Ingolfsson in 989 A.D. Enough Norse, English, and Irish colonists had migrated thither during the Eleventh Century to found a permanent colony, from which the Bretwaldate of Vinland had grown. Their language, while descended from Anglo-Saxon, naturally contained fewer words of Latin and French origin than Park's English.

The Indians—"Screlingz" or Skrellings—had not proved a pushover, as the colonists had neither the gunpowder nor the numbers that the whites of Park's history had had. By the time the whites had reached the present boundaries of Vinland, expelling or enslaving the Skrellings as they went, the remaining natives had acquired enough knowledge of ferrous metallurgy and organized warfare to hold their own. Those that remained in Vinland were no longer slaves, but were still a suppressed class suffering legal and economic disabilities. He, Bishop Ib Scoglund, was a crusader for the removal of these disabilities. ("Hallow" was simply a respectful epithet, meaning about the same as "Reverend.")

An Italian named Caravello had invented the steam engine about 1790, and the Industrial Revolution had followed as a matter of course. . . .

It was the following morning, when Park, having caught the three hours of sleep that sufficed for him when necessary, was back at the books, that Monkey-face (right name: Eric Dunedin) came timidly in. He coughed deferentially. "The pigeon came with a writing from Thane Callahan."

Park frowned up from his mountain of printed matter. "Who? Never mind; let's see it." He took the note. It read (spelling conventionalized):

> Dear Hallow: Why in the name of the Blood Witnesses of Belfast did you run away from us yesterday? The papers say you have

gone back home; isn't that risky? Must have a
meeting with you forthwith; shall be at Bridget's
Beach this noon, waiting. Respectfully, R. C.

Park asked Dunedin: "Tell me, is Callahan a tall
heavy guy who looks like an In—a Skrelling?"

Dunedin looked at him oddly. By this time Park
was getting pretty well used to being looked at oddly.
Dunedin said: "But he *is* a Skrelling, Hallow; the
Sachem of all the Skrellings of Vinland."

"Hm. So he'll meet me at this beach—why the
devil can't he come here?"

"Ooooh, but Hallow, bethink what happened to him
the last time the New Belfast knicks caught him!"

Whatever that was, Park reckoned he owed the
Sachem something for the rescue from the clutches
of the mysterious Mr. Noggle. The note didn't sound
like one from a would-be abductor to his escaped
prey. But just in case, Park went out to the modest episcopal automobile (Dunedin called it a "wain")
and put a wrench in his pocket. He told Dunedin:
"You'll have to drive this thing; my thumb's still
sore."

It took a few minutes to get steam up. As they
rolled out of the driveway, a car parked across the
street started up too. Park got a glimpse of the men
therein. While they were in civilian clothes, as he
was, they had a grim plainclothesman look about
them.

After three blocks the other car was still behind
them. Park ordered Dunedin to go around the block.
The other car followed.

Park asked: "Can you shake those guys?"

"I—I don't know, your hallowship. I'm not very
good at fast driving."

"Slide over then. How in hell do you run this
thing?"

"You mean you don't know—"

"Never mind!" roared Park. "Where's the accelerator or throttle or whatever you call it?"

"Oh, the strangle. There." Dunedin pointed a frankly terrified finger. "And the brake—"

The wain jumped ahead with a rush. Park spun it around a couple of corners, getting the feel of the wheel. The mirror showed the other car still following. Park opened the "strangle" and whisked around the next corner. No sooner had he straightened out than he threw the car into another dizzy turn. The tires screeched and Dunedin yelped as they shot into an alleyway. The pursuers whizzed by without seeing them.

An egg-bald man in shirtsleeves popped out of a door in the alley. "Hi," he said, "this ain't no hitching place." He looked at Park's left front fender, clucking. "Looks like you took off some paint."

Park smiled. "I was just looking for a room, and I saw your sign. How much are you asking?"

"Forty-five a month."

Park made a show of writing this down. He asked: "What's the address, please?"

"One twenty-five Isleif."

"Thanks. I'll be back, maybe." Park backed out, with a scrape of fender against stone, and asked Dunedin directions. Dunedin, gray of face, gave them. Park looked at him and chuckled. "Nothing to be scared of, old boy. I knew I had a good two inches clearance on both sides."

The Sachem awaited Park in the shade of the bathhouse. He swept off his bonnet with a theatrical flourish. "Haw, Hallow! A fair day for our tryst." Park reflected that on a dull day you could smell Rufus Callahan's breath almost as far as you could see Rufus Callahan. He continued: "The west end's best for talk. I have a local knick watching in case Greenfield sends a prowler. Did they follow you out?"

Park told him, meanwhile wondering how to handle
the interview so as to make it yield the most information. They passed the end of the bathhouse, and
Allister Park checked his stride. The beach was covered with naked men and women. Not *quite* naked;
each had a gaily colored belt of elastic webbing
around his or her middle. Just that. Park resumed his
walk at Callahan's amused look.

Callahan said: "If the head knick, Lewis, weren't
a friend of mine, I shouldn't be here. If I ever did
get pulled up—well, the judges are all MacSvensson's
men, just as Greenfield is." Park remembered that
Offa Greenfield was mayor of New Belfast. Callahan
continued: "While MacSvensson's away, the pushing
eases a little."

"When's he due back?" asked Park.

"In a week maybe." Callahan waved an arm toward
distant New Belfast. "What a fair burg, and what a
wretched wick to rule it! How do you like it?"

"Why, I live there, don't I?"

Callahan chuckled. "Wonderful, my dear Hallow,
wonderful. In another week nobody'll know you aren't
his hallowship at all."

"Meaning what?"

"Oh, you needn't look at me with that wooden face.
You're nay mair Bishop Scoglund than I am."

"Yeah?" said Park noncommittally. He lit one of
the bishop's pipes.

"How about a jinn?" asked Callahan.

Park looked at him, until the Sachem got out a
cigarette.

Park lit it for him, silently conceding one to the
opposition. How was he to know that a jinn was a
match? He asked: "Suppose I was hit on the head?"

The big Skrelling grinned broadly. "That mick
spoil your recall, in spots, but it wouldn't give you
that frickful word-tone you were using when we
befreed you. I see you've gotten rid of most of it,

by the way. How did you do that in thirty-some hours?"

Park gave up. The man might be just a slightly drunken Indian with a conspiratorial manner, but he had the goods on Allister. He explained: "I found a bunch of records of some of my sermons, and played them over and over on the machine."

"My, my, you are a cool one! Joe Noggle mick have done worse when he picked your mind to swap with the bishop's. Who are you, in sooth? Or perhaps I should say who *were* you?"

Park puffed placidly. "I'll exchange information, but I won't give it away."

When Callahan agreed to tell Park all he wanted to know, Park told his story. Callahan looked thoughtful. He said: "I'm nay brain-wizard, but they do say there's a theory that every time the history of the world hinges on some decision, there are two worlds, one that which would happen if the card fell one way, the other that which would follow from the other."

"Which is the *real* one?"

"That I can't tell you. But they do say Noggle can swap minds with his thocks, and I don't doubt it's swapping between one of these possible worlds and another they mean."

He went on to tell Park of the bishop's efforts to emancipate the Skrellings, in the teeth of the opposition of the ruling Diamond Party. This party's strength was mainly among the rural squirearchy of the west and south, but it also controlled New Belfast through the local boss, Ivor MacSvensson. If Scoglund's amendment to the Bretwaldate's constitution went through at the next session of the national Thing, as seemed likely if the Ruby Party ousted the Diamonds at the forthcoming election, the squirearchy might revolt. The independent Skrelling nations of the west and south had been threatening intervention on behalf of their abused minority. (That sounded

familiar to Park, except that, if he took what he had
read and heard at its face value, the minority really
had something to kick about this time.) The Diamonds wouldn't mind a war, because in that case the
elections, which they expected to lose, would be
called off . . .

"You're not listening, Thane Park, or should I say
Hallow Scoglund?"

"Nice little number," said Park, nodding toward a
pretty blonde girl on the beach.

Callahan clucked. "Such a wording from a strict
wed-less!"

"*What?*"

"You're a pillar of the church, aren't you?"

"Oh, my Lord!" Park hadn't thought of that angle.
The Celtic Christian Church, despite its libertarian
tradition, was strict on the one subject of sex.

"Anyhow," said Callahan, "what shall we do with
you? For you're bound to arouse mistrust."

Park felt the wrench in his pocket. "*I* want to get
back. Got a whole career going to smash in my own
world."

"Unless the fellow who's running your body knows
what to do with it."

"Not much chance." Park could visualize Frenczko
or Burt frantically calling his apartment to learn why
he didn't appear; the unintelligible answers they would
get from the bewildered inhabitant of his body; the
cops screaming up in the struggle-buggy to cart the
said body off to Belleview; the headline: "PROSECU-
TOR BREAKS DOWN." So they yanked me here as
a bit of dirty politics, eh? I'll get back, but mean-
time I'll show 'em some *real* politics!

Callahan continued: "The only man who could
unswap you is Joseph Noggle, and he's in his own
daffybin."

"Huh?"

"They found him wandering about, clean daft. It's

a good deed you didn't put in a slur against him; they'd have stripped you in court in nay time."

"Maybe that's what they wanted to do."

"That's an idea! That's why they were so anxious for you to go to the lair. I don't doubt they'll be watching for to pull you up on some little charge; it won't matter whether you're guilty or not. Once they get hold of you, you're headed for Noggle's inn. What a way to get rid of the awkward bishop without pipe or knife!"

When Callahan had departed with another flourish, Park looked for the girl. She had gone too. The day was blistering, and the water inviting. Since you didn't need a bathing suit to swim in Vinland, why not try it?

Park returned to the bathhouse and rented a locker. He stowed his clothes, and looked at himself in the nearest mirror. The bishop didn't take half enough exercise, he thought, looking at the waistline. He'd soon fix *that*. No excuse for a man's getting out of shape that way.

He strolled out, feeling a bit exposed with his white skin among all these bronzed people, but not showing it in his well-disciplined face. A few stared. Maybe it was his whiteness; maybe they thought they recognized the bishop. He plunged in and headed out. He swam like a porpoise, but shortness of breath soon reminded him that the bishop's body wasn't up to Allister Park's standards. He cut loose with a few casual curses, since there was nobody to overhear, and swam back.

As he dripped out onto the sand, a policeman approached, thundering: "You! You're under stoppage!"

"What for?"

"Shameful outputting!"

"But look at those!" protested Park, waving at the other bathers.

"That's just it! Come along, now!"

Park went, forgetting his anger in concern as to the best method of avoiding trouble. If the judges were MacSvensson men, and MacSvensson was out to expose him . . . He dressed under the cop's eagle eye, thanking his stars he'd had the foresight to wear non-clerical clothes.

The cop ordered: "Give your name and address to the bookholder."

"Allister Park, 125 Isleif Street, New Belfast."

The clerk filled out a blank; the cop added a few lines to it. Park and the cop went and sat down for a while, waiting. Park watched the legal procedure of this little court keenly.

The clerk called: "Thane Park!" and handed the form up to the judge. The cop went over and whispered to the judge. The judge said: "All women will kindly leave the courtroom!" There were only three; they went out.

"Allister Park," said the judge, "you are marked with shameful outputting. How do you plead?"

"I don't understand this, your honor—I mean your ærness," said Park. "I wasn't doing anything the other people on the beach weren't."

The judge frowned. "Knick Woodson says you afterthockly exposed—uh—" The judge looked embarrassed. "You afterthockly output your—uh—" he lowered his voice. "Your navel," he hissed. The judge blushed.

"Is that considered indecent?"

"Don't try to be funny. It's not in good taste. I ask you again, how do you plead?"

Park hesitated a second. "Do you recognize the plea of *non vult*?"

"What's that? Latin? We don't use Latin here."

"Well then—a plea that I didn't mean any harm, and am throwing myself on the mercy of the court."

"Oh, you mean a plea of good will. That's not usually used in a freerighter's court, but I don't see why you can't. What's your excuse?"

"You see, your honor, I've been living out in Dakotia for many years, and I've rather gotten out of civilized habits. But I'll catch on quickly enough. If you want a character reference, my friend Ivor MacSvensson will give me one."

The judge's eyebrows went up, like a buzzard hoisting its wings for the takeoff. "You ken Thane MacSvensson?"

"Oh, sure."

"Hrrrmph. Well. He's out of town. But—uh—if that's so, I'm sure you're a good burger. I hereby sentence you to ten days in jail, sentence withheld until I can check your mooding, and thereafter on your good acting. You are free."

Like a good thane's thane, Eric Dunedin kept his curiosity to himself. This became a really heroic task when he was sent out to buy a bottle of soluble hair dye, a false mustache, and a pair of phoney spectacles with flat glass panes in them.

There was no doubt about it; the boss was a changed man since his reappearance. He had raised Dunedin's salary, and except for occasional outbursts of choler treated him very considerately. The weird accent had largely disappeared; but this hard, inscrutable man wasn't the bishop Dunedin had known.

Park presented himself in his disguise to the renting agent at 125 Isleif. He said: "Remember me? I was here this morning asking about a room." The man said sure he remembered him; he never forgot a face. Park rented a small two-room apartment, calling himself Allister Park. Later in the evening he took some books, a folder of etchings, and a couple of suitcases full of clothes over. When he returned to the bishop's house he found another car with a couple of large watchful men waiting at the curb. Rather than risk contact with a hostile authority, he went back to his new apartment and read. Around midnight he dropped in at a small hash house for a cup of coffee. In fifteen minutes he was calling the waitress "sweetie-pie." The etchings worked like a charm.

Dunedin looked out the window and announced: "Two wains and five knicks, Hallow. The twoth wain drew up just now. The men in it look as if they'd eat their own mothers without salt."

Park thought. He had to get out somehow. He had looked into the subject of search warrants, illegal entry, and so forth, as practiced in the Bretwaldate of Vinland, and was reasonably sure the detectives wouldn't invade his house. The laws of Vinland gave what Park thought was an impractically exaggerated sanctity to a man's home, but he was glad of that as things were. However, if he stepped out, the pack would be all over him with charges of drunken driving, conspiracy to violate the tobacco tax, and anything else they could think of.

He telephoned the "knicks' branch," or police department, and spoke falsetto: "Are you the knicks? Glory be to Patrick and Bridget! I'm Wife Caroline Chisholm, at 79 Mercia, and we have a crazy man running up and down the halls naked with an ax. Sure he's killed my poor husband already; spattered his brains all over the hall he did, and I'm locked in my room and looking for him to break in any time." Park stamped on the floor, and continued: "Eeek! That's the monster now, trying to break the door down. Oh, hurry, I pray. He's shouting that he's going to chop me in little bits and feed me to his cat! . . . Yes, 79 Mercia. Eeeee! Save me!"

He hung up and went back to the window. In five minutes, as he expected, the gongs of the police wains sounded, and three of the vehicles skidded around the corner and stopped in front of No. 79, down the block. Funny hats tumbled out like oranges from a burst paper bag, and raced up the front steps with guns and ropes enough to handle Gargantua. The five who had been watching the house got out of their cars too and ran down the block.

Allister Park lit his pipe, and strode briskly out the front door, down the street away from the disturbance, and around the corner.

Park was announced, as Bishop Scoglund, to Dr. Edwy Borup. The head of the Psychophysical Institute was a smallish, bald, snaggle-toothed man, who smiled with an uneasy cordiality.

Park smiled back. "Wonderful work you've been doing, Dr. Borup." After handing out a few more vague compliments, he got down to business. "I understand that poor Dr. Noggle is now one of your patients?"

"Umm—uh—yes, Reverend Hallow. He is. Uh—his lusty working seems to have brock on a brainly breakdown."

Park sighed. "The good Lord will see him through, let us hope. I wonder if I could see him? I had some small kenning of him before his trouble. He once told me he'd like my spiritual guidance, when he got around to it."

"Well—umm—I'm not sure it would be wise—in his kilter—"

"Oh, come now, Dr. Borup; surely thocks of hicker things would be good for him . . ."

The sharp-nosed, gray-haired man who had been Joseph Noggle sat morosely in his room, hardly bothering to look up when Park entered.

"Well, my friend," said Park, "what have they been doing to you?"

"Nothing," said the man. His voice had a nervous

edge. "That's the trouble. Every day I'm a different man in a different sanitarium. Each day they tell me that two days previously I got violent and tried to poke somebody in the nose. *I* haven't poked *nobody* in the nose. Why in God's name don't they *do* something? Sure, I know I'm crazy. I'll cooperate, if they'll *do* something."

"There, there," said Park. "The good Lord watches over all of us. By the way, what were you before your trouble started?"

"I taught singing."

Park thought several "frickful aiths." If a singing teacher, or somebody equally incompetent for his kind of work, were in his body now . . .

He lit a pipe and talked soothingly and inconsequentially to the man, who though not in a pleasant mood, was too grateful for a bit of company to discourage him. Finally he got what he was waiting for. A husky male nurse came in to take the patient's temperature and tell Park that his time was up.

Park hung around, on one excuse or another, until the nurse had finished. Then he followed the nurse out and grasped his arm.

"What is it, Hallow?" asked the nurse.

"Are you poor Noggle's regular attendant?"

"Yes."

"Got any kinfolk, or people you like specially, in the priesthood?"

"Yes, there's my Aunt Thyra. She's a nun at the New Lindisfarne Abbey."

"Like to see her advanced?"

"Why—I guess so; yes. She's always been pretty good to me."

"All right. Here's what you do. Can you get out, or send somebody out, to telephone Noggle's condition to me every morning before noon?"

The nurse guessed he could. "All right," snapped Park. "And it won't do anybody any good if anybody knows you're doing it, understand?" He realized that his public-prosecutor manner was creeping back on him. He smiled benignly. "The Lord will bless you, my son."

Park telephoned Dunedin; asked him to learn the name of somebody who dwelt on the top floor of the apartment house next door, and to collect one ladder, thirty feet of rope, and one brick. He made him call back the name of the top-floor tenant. "But Hallow, what in the name of Patrick do you want a brick for . . ."

Park, chuckling, told him he'd learn. When he got off the folkwain at Mercia Street, he didn't walk boldly up to his own house. He entered the apartment house next door and said he was calling on Mrs. Figgis, his clericals constituting adequate credentials. When the elevator-man let him out on the top floor, he simply climbed to the roof and whistled for Monkey-face. He directed Dunedin in the tieing of the end of the rope to the brick, the heaving thereof to the roof of the apartment house, and the planting of the ladder to bridge the ten-foot gap. After that it was a simple matter for Park to lower himself to his own roof, without being intercepted by the watchdogs in front of his house.

As soon as he got in, the phone rang. A sweetness-and-light voice at the other end said: "This is Cooley, Hallow. Every time I've called your man has said you were out or else that you couldn't be bothered!"

"That's right," said Park. "I was."

"Yes? Anyway, we're all giving praises to the Lord that you were spared."

"That's fine," said Park.

"It surely is a wonderful case of how His love watches over us—"

"What's on your mind, Cooley?" said Park, sternly repressing a snarl of impatience.

"Oh—uh—what I meant was, will you give your usual sermon next Sunday?"

Park thought quickly. If he could give a sermon and get away with it, it ought to discourage the people who were trying to prove the bishop loony. "Sure I will. Where are you calling from?"

"Why—uh—the vestry." Some damned assistant, thought Park. "But, Hallow, won't you come up tonight? I'm getting some of the parishioners together in the chapel for a homish thanksgiving stint—with hymns of—"

"I'm afraid not," said Park. "Give 'em my love anyway. There goes my doorbell. Bye."

He marched into the library, muttering. Dunedin asked: "What is it, Hallow?"

"Gotta prepare a goddam sermon," said Park, taking some small pleasure at his thane's thane's expression of horror.

Fortunately the bishop was an orderly man. There were manuscripts of all his sermons for the past five years, and phonograph records (in the form of magnetized wire) of several. There was also plenty of information about the order of procedure in a Celtic Christian service. Park set about concocting a sermon out of fragments and paragraphs of those the bishop had delivered during the past year, playing the spools of wire over and over to learn the bishop's inflections. He wished he had some way of getting the bishop's gestures, too.

He was still at it next day when he dimly heard his doorbell. He thought nothing of it, trusting to Dunedin to turn the visitor away, until Monkey-face came in and announced that a pair of knicks awaited without.

Park jumped up. "Did you let 'em in?"

"No, Hallow, I thought—"

"Good boy! I'll take care of 'em."

❖   ❖   ❖

The larger of the two cops smiled disarmingly. "Can we come in, Hallow, to use your wiretalker?"

"Nope," said Park. "Sorry."

The knick frowned. "In that case we gotta come in anyway. Mistrust of unlawful owning of pipe." He put his foot in the door crack.

A pipe, Park knew, was a gun. He turned and stamped on the toe of the shoe, hard; then slammed the door shut as the foot was jerked back. There were some seconds of "frickful aiths" wafting through the door, then the pounding of a fist against it.

"Get a warrant!" Park yelled through the door. The noise subsided. Park called Dunedin and told him to lock the other entrances. Presently the knicks departed. Park's inference, based upon what he had been able to learn of Vinland law, that they would not force an entrance without a warrant, had proved correct. However, they would be back, and there is nothing especially difficult about "finding" an illegal weapon in a man's house, whether he had one before or not.

So Park packed a suitcase, climbed to the roof of the adjoining apartment, and went down the elevator. The elevator man looked at him in a marked manner. Once in the street, he made sure nobody was looking, and slapped on his mustache and glasses. He pulled his bonnet well down to hide his undyed hair, and walked over to Allister Park's place. There he telephoned Dunedin, and directed him to call the city editors of all the pro-bishop newspapers and tip them off that an attempt to frame the bishop impended. He told Dunedin to let the reporters in when they came; the more the better. Preferably there should be at least one in every room. Now, he thought, let those flatfeet try to sneak a gun into one of my bureau drawers so they can "find" it and raise a stink.

He spent the night at the apartment, and the next day, having gotten his sermon in shape, he paid a visit to his church. He found a functionary of some sort in an office, and told him that he, Allister Park, was considering getting married in St. Columbanus', and would the functionary (a Th. Morgan) please show him around? Th. Morgan was pleased to; Dr. Cooley usually did that job, but he was out this afternoon. Park looked sharply through his phoney spectacles, memorizing the geography of the place. He wished now he'd passed up the sermon for one more week, and had instead attended next Sunday's service as Allister Park, so that he could see how the thing was done. But it was too late now. Morgan broke in on his thoughts: "There's Dr. Cooley now, Thane Park; wouldn't you like to meet him?"

"Ulp," said Park. "Sorry; got to see a man. Thanks a lot." Before the startled cleric could protest, Park was making for the door as fast as he could go without breaking into a run. The plump, rosy young man in pince-nez, whom Park saw out of the corner of his eye, must be Cooley. Park had no intention of submitting his rather thin disguise to his assistant's inspection.

He telephoned the bishop's home. The other people in the lunchroom were startled by the roar of laughter that came through the glass of his telephone booth as Dunedin described the two unhappy cops trying to plant a gun in his house under the noses of a dozen hostile wise-cracking reporters. Monkey-face added: "I—I took the freedom, your hallowship, of finding out that two of the newsers live right near here. If the knicks try that again, and these newsers are at home, we could wirecall them over."

"You're learning fast, old boy," said Park. "Guess I can come home now."

It was Saturday when Dunedin answered a call from the Psychophysical Institute. He cocked an eye upward, whence came a series of irregular whams as if trunks were being tossed downstairs. "Yes," he said. "I'll get him." As he wheezed upstairs, the whams gave way to a quick, muffled drumming. If anything were needed to convince him that something drastic had happened to his master's mind, the installation and regular use of a horizontal bar and a punching bag in a disused room was it.

Park, in a pair of sweat-soaked shorts, turned his pale eyes. Good old Monkey-face. Park, who treated subordinates with great consideration, never told Dunedin what he thought he looked like.

"It's the man at the Psychophysical Institute," announced Dunedin.

The male nurse announced that, for a change, Joseph Noggle was claiming to be Joseph Noggle.

Park grabbed his bonnet and drove the steamer over. Borup asked: "But, my dear, dear Hallow, why must you—uh—see this one patient? There are plenty mair who could use your ghostly guidance."

Fool amateur, thought Park. If he doesn't want me to know why he wants to keep Noggle locked up, why doesn't he say he's violent or something? This way he's giving away his whole game. But aloud he gave a few smooth, pious excuses, and got in to see his man.

The original, authentic Noggle had a quick, nervous manner. It didn't take him more than a minute to catch on to who Park-Scoglund was.

"Look here," he said. "Look here. I've got to get out. I've got to get at my books and onmarkings. If I don't get out now, while I'm in my own body, I shan't be able to stop this damned merry-go-round for another six days!"

"You mean, my son, that you occupy your own body every six days? What happens the rest of the time?"

"The rest of the time I'm going around the wheel, indwelling ane after another of the bodies of the other men on my wheel. And the minds of these other men are following me around likewise. So every ane of the six bodies has each of our six minds in it in turn every six days."

"I see." Park smiled benignly. "And what's this wheel you talk about?"

"I call it my wheel of if. Each of the other five men on it are the men I should most likely have been *if* certain things had been otherwise. For instance, the man in whose body my mind dwelt yesterday was the man I should most likely have been if King Egbert had fallen off his horse in 1781."

Park didn't stop to inquire about King Egbert or the sad results of his poor equestrianism. He asked softly: "How did your wheel get started in the first place?"

"It was when I tried to stop yours! Law of keeping of psychic momentum, you know. I got careless, and the momentum of your wheel was overchanged to mine. So I've been going around ever since. Now look here, whatever your name is, I've got to get out of here, or I'll never get stopped. I ordered them to let me out this morning, but all they'd say was that they'd see about it tomorrow. Tomorrow my body'll be occupied by some other wheel-mate, and they'll say I'm crazy again. Borup won't let me go anyway if he can help it; he likes my job. But you've got to use your inflowing as bishop—"

"Oh," said Park silkily, "I've got to use my influence, eh? Just one more question. Are we all on wheels? And how many of these possible worlds are there?"

"Yes, we're all on wheels. The usual number of rooms on a wheel is fourteen—that's the number on yours—though it sometimes varies. The number of worlds is infinite, or almost, so that the chances that anybody on my wheel would be living in the same world as anybody on yours is pretty small. But that's not weightful. The weightful thing is to get me out so—"

"Ah yes, that's the weightful thing, isn't it? But suppose you tell me why you started my wheel in the first place?"

"It was just a forseeking in the mental control of wheels."

"You're lying," said Park softly.

"Oh, I'm lying, am I? Well then, reckon out your own reason."

"I'm sorry that you take this attitude, my son. How can I help you if you won't put your trust in me and in God?"

"Oh, come on, don't play-act. You're not the bishop, and you know it."

"Ah, but I *was* a churchman in my former being." Park fairly oozed holiness. "That's not odd, is it? Since I was the man the bishop would most likely have been if King Oswiu had chosen for the Romans, and the Arabs had lost the battle of Tours."

"You'd hold yourself bound by professional confidence?"

Park looked shocked. "What a thock! Of course I would."

"All right. I'm something of a sportsman, you know. About a month ago I got badly pinched by the ponies, and I—ah—borrowed a little heading on my pay from the Institute's funds. Of course I'd have paid it back; it was really quite an honest deed. But I had to make a few little—ah—rightings in the books, because otherwise one who didn't understand the conditions might have drawn the wrong thocks from them.

"Ivor MacSvensson somehow found out, and threatened to put me in jail if I didn't use my mental powers to start your wheel of if going until it had made a half-turn, and then stop it. With another man's mind in the bishop's body, it ought to be easy to prove the bishop daft; in any event his inflowing would be

destroyed. But as you know, it didn't work out quite
that way. You seemingly aren't in anybody's custody.
So you'll have to do something to get me out."

Park leaned forward and fixed Noggle with the
bishop's fish-pale eyes. He said harshly: "You know,
Noggle, I admire you. For a guy who robs his hospital, and then to get out of it goes and starts fourteen men's minds spinning around, ruining their lives
and maybe driving some of them crazy or to self-
killing, you have more gall than a barn rat. You sit
there and tell me, one of your victims, that I'll have
to do something to get you out. Why, damn your lousy
little soul, if you ever *do* get out I'll give you a case
of lumps that'll make you think somebody dropped
a mountain on you!"

Noggle paled a bit. "Then—then you weren't a
churchman in your own world?"

"Hell, no! My business was putting lice like you
in jail. And I still ock to be able to do that here, with
what you so kindly told me just now."

Noggle swallowed as this sank in. "But—you promised—"

Park laughed unpleasantly. "Sure I did. I never let
a little thing like a promise to a crook keep me awake
nights."

"But you want to get back, don't you? And I'm the
only one who can send you back, and you'll have to
get me out of here before I can do anything—"

"There is that," said Park thoughtfully. "But I don't
know. Maybe I'll like it here when I get used to it.
I can always have the fun of coming around here
every sixth day and giving you the horse-laugh."

"You're—a devil!"

Park laughed again. "Thanks. You thought you'd
get some poor bewildered dimwit in Scoglund's body,
didn't you? Well, you'll learn just how wrong you
were." He stood up. "I'll let you stay here a while
more as Dr. Borup's prize looney. Maybe when you've

been taken down a peg we can talk business. Meanwhile, you might form a club with those other five guys on your wheel. You could leave notes around for each other to find. So long, Dr. Svengali!"

Ten minutes later Park was in Borup's office, with a bland episcopal smile on his face. He asked Borup, apropos of nothing in particular, a lot of questions about the rules involving commitment and release of inmates.

"Nay," said Edwy Borup firmly. "We could—uh—parole a patient in your care only if he were rick most of the time. Those that are wrong most of the time, like poor Dr. Noggle, have to stay here."

It was all very definite. But Park had known lots of people who were just as definite until pressure was brought to bear on them from the right quarter.

The nearer the Sunday service came, the colder became Allister Park's feet. Which, for such an aggressive, self-confident man, was peculiar. But when he thought of all the little details, the kneeling and getting up again, the facing this way and that . . . He telephoned Cooley at the cathedral. He had, he said, a cold, and would Cooley handle everything but the sermon? "Surely, Hallow, surely. The Lord will see to it that you're fully restored soon, I hope. I'll say a special prayer for you . . ."

It was also time, Park thought, to take Monkey-face into his confidence. He told him all, whereat Dunedin's eyes grew very large. "Now, old boy," said Park briskly, "if you ever want to get your master back into his own body, you'll have to help me out. For instance, here's that damned sermon. I'm going to read it, and you'll correct my pronunciation and gestures."

Sunday afternoon, Park returned wearily to the bishop's house. The sermon had gone off easily enough; but then he'd had to greet hundreds of people he didn't know, as if they were old friends.

And he'd had to parry scores of questions about his absence. He had, he thought, earned a drink.

"A highball?" asked Dunedin. "What's that?"

Park explained. Dunedin looked positively shocked. "But Thane P—I mean Hallow, isn't it bad for your insides to drink such cold stuff?"

"Never mind my insides! I'll—hullo, who's that?"

Dunedin answered the doorbell, and reported that a Th. Figgis wanted to see the bishop. Park said to show him in. There was something familiar about that name. The man himself was tall, angular, and grim-looking. As soon as Dunedin had gone, he leaned forward and hissed dramatically: "I've got you now, Bishop Scoglund! What are you going to do about it?"

"What am I going to do about *what*?"

"My wife!"

"What about your wife?"

"You know well enough. You went up to my rooms last Tuesday, while I was away, and came down again Wednesday."

"Don't be an ass," said Park. "I've never been in your rooms in my life, and I've never met your wife."

"Oh, yes? Don't try to fool me, you wolf in priest's clothing! I've got witnesses. By God, I'll fix you, you seducer!"

"Oh, that!" Park grinned, and explained his ladder-and-rope procedure.

"Think I believe that?" sneered Figgis. "If you weren't a priest I'd challenge you and cut your liver out and eat it. As it is, I can make things so hot for you—"

"Now, now," interrupted Park, "Be reasonable. I'm sure we can come to an understanding—"

"Trying to bribe me, huh?"

"I wouldn't put it just that way."

"So you think you can buy my honor, do you? Well, what's your offer?"

Park sighed. "I thought so. Just another goddam blackmailer. Get out, louse!"

"But aren't you going to—"

Park jumped up, spun Figgis around, and marched him toward the door. "Out, I said! If you think you can get away with spreading your little scandal around, go to it. You'll learn that you aren't the only one who knows things about other people." Figgis tried to wriggle loose. Park kicked him into submission, and sent him staggering down the front steps with a final shove.

Dunedin looked awedly at this formidable creature into which his master had been metamorphosed. "Do you really know something to keep him quiet, Hallow?"

"Nope. But my experience is that most men of his age have something they'd rather not have known. Anyway, you've got to take a strong line with these blackmailers, or they'll raise no end of hell. Of course, my son, *we* hope the good Lord will show our erring brother the folly of his sinful ways, don't we?" Park winked.

Being a bishop entailed much more than putting on a one-hour performance at the cathedral every Sunday, as Park soon learned. But he transacted as much of his episcopal business as he could at home, and put the rest onto Cooley. He didn't yet feel that his impersonation was good enough to submit to close-range examination by his swarm of subordinates.

While he was planning his next step, an accident unexpectedly opened the way for him. He had just settled himself in the Isleif Street apartment the evening of Tuesday April 26th, when a young man rang his doorbell. It took about six seconds to diagnose the young man as a fledgling lawyer getting a start on a political career as a precinct worker.

"No," said Park, "I won't sign your petition to nominate Thane Hammar, because I don't know him. I've just moved here from Dakotia. But I'd like to come around to the clubhouse and meet the boys."

The young man glowed. "Why don't you? There's a meeting of the precinct workers tomorrow night, and voters are always welcome."

The clubhouse walls were covered with phoney Viking shields and weapons. "Who's he?" Park asked his young lawyer through the haze of smoke. "He" was a florid man to whom several were paying obsequious attention.

"That's Trigvy Darling, Brahtz's parasite." Park caught a note of dislike, and added it to the new card in his mental index file. Brahtz was a Diamond thingman from a western province, the leader of the squirearchy. In this somewhat naive culture, a gentleman had to demonstrate his financial standing by supporting a flock of idle friends, or deputy gentlemen. The name of the parasite was not merely accurate, but was accepted by these hangers-on without any feeling of derogation.

Through the haze wove an unpleasantly familiar angular figure. Park's grip on the edge of the table automatically tightened. "Haw, Morrow," said Figgis, and looked at Park. "Haven't I met you somewhere?"

"Maybe," said Park. "Ever live in Dakotia?"

Morrow, the young lawyer, introduced Park as Park. Park fervently hoped his disguise was thick enough. Figgis acknowledged the introduction, but continued to shoot uneasy little glances at Park. "I could swear—" he said. Just then the meeting was called. Although it would have driven a lot of people to suicide from boredom, Park enjoyed the interplay of personalities, the quick fencing with parliamentary rules by various factions. These rules differed from those he was used to, being derived from those of the ancient Icelandic Thing instead of the English Parliament. But the idea was the same. The local members wanted to throw a party for the voters of the hide (district). A well-knit minority led by the parasite Darling wanted to save the money for contribution to the national war chest.

Park waited until the question was just about to be put to a vote, then snapped his fingers for the chairman's attention. The chairman, an elderly dodderer, recognized him.

"My friends," said Park, lurching to his feet, "of course I don't know that I really ock to say anything, being just a new incomer from the wilds of Dakotia. But I've always voted Diamond, and so did my father and his father before him, and so on back as far as there *was* any Diamond Party. So I think I can claim as solid a party membership as some folks who live in New Belfast three months out of the year, and spend the rest of their time upholding the monetary repute of certain honorable country thanes." Park, with satisfaction, saw Darling jerk his tomato-colored face around, and heard a few snickers. "Though," he continued, "taking the healthy skin you get from country life, I don't know but what I envy such people." (More snickers.) "Now it seems to me that . . ."

Twenty minutes later the party had been voted: Park was the chairman (since he alone seemed really anxious to assume responsibility); and Trigvy Darling, at whose expense Park had acquired a frothy popularity by his jibes, had turned from vermillion to magenta.

After the meeting, Park found himself in a group of people including the chairman and Figgis. Figgis was saying something about that scoundrel Scoglund, when his eye caught Park's. He grinned his slightly sepulchral grin. "I know now why I thock I'd met you! You remind me of the bishop!"

"Know him?"

"I met him once. Say, Dutt," (this was to the aged chairman) "what date's set for your withdrawal?"

"Next meeting," quavered the ancient one. "Ah, here is our crown prince, heh, heh!" Darling, his face back to normal tomato-color, advanced. "Do you ken Thane Park?"

"I ken him well enough," growled Darling with the look of one who has found a cockroach in his ice cream. "It seems to me, Thane Dutt, that part of a chairman's duty is to stop use of personalities on the part of speakers."

"You can always plead point of personal privilege, heh, heh."

Darling did something in his throat that was not quite articulate speech. Figgis murmured: "He knows the boys would laugh him down if he tried it."

"Yeah?" said Darling. "We'll see about that when I'm chairman." He stalked off.

Park wasted no time in exploiting his new job. Knowing that Ivor MacSvensson was due back in New Belfast the next day, he went around—as Allister Park—to the law office used by the boss as a front for his activities. The boss was already in, but the outer office was jammed with favor seekers. Park, instead of preparing to spend the morning awaiting his turn, bribed the office boy to tell him when and where MacSvensson ate his lunch. Then he went to the nearby public library—movies not having been invented in this world—and took his ease until one o'clock.

Unfortunately, Ivor MacSvensson failed to show up at the restaurant indicated, though Park stretched one tuna-fish lunch out for half an hour. Park cursed the lying office boy. Plain bribery he was hardened to, but he really became indignant when the bribee failed to deliver. So he set about it the hard way. A nearby knick gave him the locations of the five highest-priced restaurants in the neighborhood, and in the third he found his man. He recognized him from the pictures he had studied before starting his search—a big, good-looking fellow with cold blue eyes and prematurely white hair.

Park marched right up. "Haw, Thane MacSvensson. Bethink you me?"

MacSvensson looked puzzled for a fraction of a second, but he said smoothly: "Sure, of course I bethink me of you. Your name is—uh—"

"Allister Park, chairman of the amusement committee of the Tenth Hide," Park rattled off. "I only met you recently, just before you left."

"Sure, of course. I'd know you anywhere—let's see, Judge Vidolf of Bridget's Beach wirecalled me this morning; wanted to know if I kenned you. Told him I'd call him back." He gripped Park's hand. "Come on, sit down. Sure, of course, any good party worker is a friend of mine. What's the Tenth Hide doing?"

Park told of the party. MacSvensson whistled. "Saturday the thirtieth? That's day after tomorrow."

"I can manage it," said Park. "Maybe you could tell me where I could pick up some sober bartenders."

"Sure, of course." Under Park's deferential prodding, the boss gave him all the information he needed. MacSvensson finished with the quick, vigorous handshake cultivated by people who have to shake thousands of hands and who don't want to develop a case of greeter's cramp. He urged Park to come around and see him again. "Especially after that fellow Darling gets the chairmanship of your committee."

Park went, grinning a little to himself. He knew just what sort of impression he had made, and could guess how the boss was reacting to it. He'd be glad to get a vigorous, aggressive worker in the organization; at the same time he'd want to keep a close watch on him to see that *his* power wasn't undermined.

Park congratulated himself on having arrived in a world where the political setup had a recognizable likeness to that of his own. In an absolute monarchy, for instance, he'd have a hell of a time learning the particular brand of intrigue necessary to become a king's favorite. As it was . . .

The Bridget's Beach knicks stood glowering at a safe distance from the throng of picnickers. Although they were anti-MacSvensson, the judges were pro, so what could they do about it if the party violated the ordinances regarding use of the beach? Since Park's fellow committeemen were by now too sodden with beer to do anything at all, Park was dashing around, clad in a pair of tennis shoes and the absurd parti-colored belt that constituted the Vinland bathing suit, running everything himself. Everybody seemed to be having a good time—party workers, the more influential of the voters and their families, everybody but a morose knot of Darling & followers at one end.

Near this knot a group of anti-Darlings was setting up a song:

> "Trig Darling, he has a foul temper;
> "Trig Darling's as red as can be;
> "Oh, nobody here loves Trig Darling,
> "Throw Trigvy out into the sea!
> "Throw—Trig,
> "Throw—Trig,
> "Throw Trigvy out into the sea!"

Park hurried up to shush them. Things were going fine, and he didn't want a fight—yet, at any rate. But his efforts were lost in the next stanza:

> "Trig Darling, he has a pot-bellee;
> "Trig Darling's as mean as can be . . ."

At that moment, apparently, a giant hit Allister Park over the head with a *Sequoia sempervirens*. He reeled a few steps, shook the tears out of his eyes,

and faced Trigvy Darling, advancing with large fists
cocked.

"Hey," said Park, "this isn't—" He brought up his
own fists. But Darling, instead of trying to hit him again,
faced him for three seconds and then spat at him.

Park glanced at the drop of saliva trickling down
his chest. So did everyone else. One of Darling's
friends asked: "Do you make that a challenge, Trig?"

"Yes!" boomed the parasite.

Park didn't really catch on to what was coming
until he was surrounded by his own party. He and
Darling were pushed together until their bare chests
were a foot apart. Somebody called the knicks over;
these stationed themselves around the couple. Somebody else produced a long leather belt, which he
fastened around the middies of both men at once,
so they could not move farther apart. Darling, his red
face expressionless, grabbed Park's right wrist with his
left hand, and held out his own right forearm, evidently expecting Park to do the same.

It was not until a big sheath-knife was pressed into
each man's right hand that Park knew he was in a
duel. Somehow he had missed this phase of Vinland
custom in his reading.

Park wondered frantically whether his mustache
would come off in the struggle. One knick stepped
up and said: "You know the rules: no kicking, biting,
butting, or scratching. Penalty for a foul is one free
stab. Ready?"

"Yes," said Darling. "Yes," said Park, with more
confidence than he felt.

"Go," said the policeman.

Park felt an instant surge of his opponent's muscles.
Darling had plenty of these under the fat. If he'd only
had longer to train the bishop's body . . . Darling
wrenched his wrist loose from Park's grip, threw a
leg around one of Park's to trip him, and brought his
fist down in a lightning overhand stab.

It was too successful. Park's leg went out from under him and he landed with a thump on his back, dragging Darling down on top of him. Darling drove his knife up to the hilt in the sand. When he jerked it up for another stab, Park miraculously caught his wrist again. A heave, and Darling toppled onto the sand beside him. For seconds they strained and panted, a tangle of limbs.

Park, his heart laboring and sand in his eyes, wrenched his own knife-arm free. But when he stabbed at Darling, the parasite parried with a curious twisting motion of his left arm, and gathered Park's arm into a bone-crushing grip. Park in agony heaved himself to his knees, pulling Darling up too. They faced each other on their knees, the belt still around them. Darling wrenched his knife-arm loose again, whipped it around as for a backhand stab, then back for an overhand. Park, trying to follow the darting blade, felt as if something had exploded in his own left arm. Darling's point was driven into it and into the bone. Before it had a chance to bleed, Darling tried to pull it out. It didn't yield on the first pull. Park leaned forward suddenly. Darling unwound his left arm from Park's right to catch himself as he swayed backwards. Park stabbed at him. Darling blocked the stab with his forearm, making Park feel as if his wrist was broken. He played his last improvised trick: tossed up the knife, caught it the other way to, and brought it around in a quick up-and-out thrust. To his surprise, Darling failed to block it at all—the blade slid up under the parasite's ribs to the hilt. Park, warm blood running over his hand, twisted and sliced his way across Darling's abdomen . . .

Trigvy Darling lay on his back, mouth open and sand in his sightless eyeballs. The spectators looked in awe at the ten-inch wound. Park, feeling a bit shaken, stood while they bandaged his arm. The knicks gravely took down the vital information about the dead man, filling the last line of the blank with: "Killed in fair fight with Allister Park, 125 Isleif St., N.B."

Then people were shaking his hand, slapping his bare back, and babbling congratulations at him. "Had it coming to him . . ." ". . . never liked him anyway, only we had to take him on account of Brahtz . . ." "You'll make a better chairman . . ."

Park stole a hand to his upper lip. His mustache was a little loose on one side, but a quick press fixed that. He gradually became aware that the duel, so far from spoiling the party, had made a howling success of it.

Leading a double life is a strenuous business at best. It is particularly difficult when both one's identities are fairly prominent people. Nevertheless, Allister Park managed it, with single-minded determination to let nothing stop his getting the person of Joseph Noggle in such a position that he could make him give his, Park's, wheel of if another half-spin. It might not be too late, even if the Antonini case was washed up, to rehabilitate himself.

His next step was to cultivate Ivor MacSvensson, burg committee chairman for the Diamond Party of the Burg of New Belfast. This was easy enough, as the chairman of the hide committee was ex-officio a member of the burg committee.

They were dining in one of the small but expensive restaurants for which MacSvensson had a weakness. The burg chairman said: "We'll have to get Anlaaf off, that's all there is to it. Those dim knicks should have known better than to pull him in it in the first place."

Park looked at the ceiling. "Even if it was Penda's daughter?"

"Even if it was Penda's daughter."

"After all, spoiling the morals of a ten-year-old—"

"I know, I know," said MacSvensson impatiently.

"I know he's a dirty bustard. But what can I do? He's got the twenty-sixth hide in his fist, so I've got to play cards with him. Especially with the thingly choosing coming up in three months. It'll be close, even with Bishop Scoglund lying low the way he has been. I had a little plan for shushing the dear bishop; it didn't work, but it seems to have scared him into keeping quiet about the ricks of the Skrellings. And the Thing meeting next month . . . If that damned equal-ricks changelet goes through, it'll split the party wide open."

"If it doesn't?" asked Park.

"That'll be all right."

"How about the Dakotians and the rest?"

MacSvensson shrugged. "No trouble for fifty years. They talk a lot, but I never saw a Skrelling that would stand up and fick yet. And what if they did try a war? New Belfast is a long way from the border; and the choosing would be called off. Maybe by the time it was over people would get some sense."

Park had his own ideas. His researches had told him something about the unprepared state of the country. New Belfast had hundreds of miles between it and the independent Skrellings; in case of a sea attack, they could count on the friendly Northumbrian fleet, one of the world's largest, to come over and help out. Hence the New Belfast machine had consistently plugged for more money for harbor improvements and merchant-marine subsidies and less for military purposes. . . . However, if the Northumbrian fleet were immobilized by the threat of the navy of the Amirate of Cordova, and the Skrellings overran the hinterland of Vinland . . .

MacSvensson was speaking: ". . . you know, that youngest daughter of mine, she wants to marry a *school teacher?* Craziest idea . . . And that boy of mine has the house full of his musical friends; at least that's what he calls 'em. They'll play their flugelhorns and yell and stamp all night."

"Why not come up to my place?" asked Park with the studied nonchalance of an experienced dry-fly fisherman making a cast.

"Sure, of course. Glad to. I've got three appointments, thinging, but hell with 'em."

There was no doubt about it; Ivor MacSvensson was good company even if he did have a deplorable scale of moral values. Park, having made the necessary soundings, finally suggested getting some company. The chairman's blue eyes lit up a bit; there was some lechery in the old war horse yet. Park telephoned his little waitress friend. Yes, she had a friend who was just *dying* to meet some big political pipes. . . .

Many residents of New Belfast were wont to say of Ivor MacSvensson: "He may be a serpent (crook), but at least he leads a spotless home life." MacSvensson was at pains to encourage this legend, however insubstantial its basis. These people would have been pained to see the boss an hour later, smeared with lipstick, bouncing Park's friend's friend on his knee. The friend's friend was undressed to a degree that would have shocked Vinlanders anywhere but on a beach.

"Stuffy, isn't it?" said Park, and got up to open a window. The unsuspecting MacSvensson was having too good a time to notice Park thrust his arm out the window and wag it briefly.

Five minutes later the doorbell rang. By the time MacSvensson had snapped out of his happy daze, Park had admitted a small, wrinkled man who pointed at the friend's friend and cried: "Fleda!"

"Oswald!" shrieked the girl.

"Sir!" shouted Dunedin at the boss, "what have you been doing with my wife? What have you been doing with my wife?"

"Oh," sobbed Fleda, "I didn't mean to be unfaithful! Truly I didn't! If I'd only thock of you before it was too late . . ."

"Huh?" mumbled MacSvensson. "Too late? Unfaithful? Your wife?"

"Yes, you snake, you scoundrel, you bustard, my wife! You'll suffer for this, Boss MacSvensson! Just wait till I—"

"Here, here, my man!" said Park, taking Dunedin by the arm and pulling him into the vestibule. For ten minutes the boss listened in sweaty apprehension to Park's and Dunedin's voices, rising and falling, the former soothing, the latter strained with rage. Finally the door slammed.

Park came back, and said: "I got him to promise not to put in any slurs or tell any newspapers for a while, until we talk things over again. I know who he is, and I *think* I can squelch him through the company he works for. I'm not sure that'll work, though. He's mad as a wet hen; won't believe that this was just an innocent get-together."

The imperturbable boss looked badly shaken. "You've got to stop him, Al! The story would raise merry hell. If you can do it, you can have just about anything I can give you."

"How about the secretaryship of the burg committee?" asked Park promptly.

"Surely, of course. I can find something else for Ethelbald to do. Only keep that man shut up!"

"All right, old boy. Right now you'd better get home as soon as you can."

When MacSvensson had been gone a few minutes, Eric Dunedin's ugly face appeared in the doorway. "All clear, Hal—I mean Thane Park?"

"Come on in, old boy. That was a neat piece of work. You did well too, Fleda. Both you girls did. And now—" Park started to drive a corkscrew into another cork, "we can have a *real* party!"

"Damn it, Dunedin," said Park, "when I say put your breakfast down on the table and eat it, I mean it!"

"But Hallow, it simply isn't done for a thane's thane to eat with his master—"

"To hell with what's done and what isn't. I've got more for you to do than stand around and treat me as if I were God Almighty. We've got work, brother. Now get busy on that mail."

Dunedin sighed and gave up. When Park chose to, he could by now put on what Dunedin admitted was a nearly perfect imitation of Bishop Scoglund. But unless there were somebody present to be impressed thereby, he chose instead to be his profane and domineering self.

Dunedin frowned over one letter, and said: "Thane Callahan wants to know why you haven't been doing anything to push the glick-ricks changelet."

Park mentally translated the last to "equal-rights amendment." "Why should I? It isn't my baby. Oh, well, tell him I've been too busy, but I'll get around to it soon. That's always the stock excuse."

Dunedin whistled suddenly. "The kin of the late Trigvy Darling have filed a wergild claim of a hundred and fifty thousand crowns against you."

"What? What? Let's see that! . . . What's that all about? Have they got the right to sue me, when I killed him in self-defense?"

"Oh, but of course, Hallow. There's nay criminal penalty for killing a man in fair fight. But his heirs can claim two years' earnings from you. Didn't you know that when you took up his challenge?"

"Good lord, no! What can I do about it?"

"Oh, deary me, glory be to Patrick. You can try to prove the claim too big, as this one may be. I don't know, though; Darling got a big stipend from Brahtz as a parasite."

"I can always withdraw Allister Park from circulation and be just the bishop. Then let 'em try to collect!"

❖   ❖   ❖

It would be wearisome to follow Allister Park's political activities in detail for the three weeks after his
use of the badger game on MacSvensson. But lest his
extraordinary rise to power seem improbable, consider
that it was not until the 1920s in Park's original world
that a certain Josef Vissarianovitch Dzugashvili, better known as Joseph Stalin, discovered what could
really be done with the executive secretaryship of a
political committee. So it is not too surprising that,
whereas Park knew what could be done with this
office, the politicians of Vinland did not. They learned.
Among other things, the secretary makes up the
agenda of meetings. He puts motions in "proper" form,
since a motion is seldom intelligible in the form in
which it is presented from the floor. He prompts the
chairman—the nominal head of the organization—on
parliamentary procedure. He is the interim executive
officer; wherefore all appointments go through his
hands, and he has custody of all records. He is
ex-officio member of all committees. Since a committee seldom has any clear idea of what it wants to do
or how it wants to do it, an aggressive secretary can
usually run as many committees as he has time for.
Whereas the chairman can't speak at meetings, the
secretary can not only speak but speak last. He gets
the gavel when an appeal is made from the chair. . . .

At least, that is how it is done in *this* world. In
Vinland the rules were not quite the same, but the
similarity was close enough for Park's purpose—
which was still to get back to good old New York
and that judgeship, if there was still any chance of
getting it.

It was after the burg committee meeting on the
first of June that Park faced Ivor MacSvensson in the
latter's office. Park intended to start needling the boss
about the body of Joseph Noggle. But MacSvensson
got there first, demanding: "What's all this about your
making up to the committeemen?"

"What's that?" asked Park blandly. "I've been seeing them on routine duties only."

"Yeah? Not according to what I've been told. And I've found out that that girl you had up for me wasn't wedded at all. Trying to put one down on the boss, eh? Well, you can go back to hide-walking. You'll call a special committee meeting for Friday night. Get those seeings out today without fail. That's all."

"Suits me," grinned Park. The chairman can demand special meetings, but the secretary's the man who sends out the notices.

When Friday evening arrived, two thirds of the seats in the committee room in Karlsefni Hall remained empty. MacSvensson, blue eyes glacial, fretted. Park, sending out thunderheads of smoke from the bishop's largest pipe, lolled in a chair, glancing surreptitiously at his watch. If MacSvensson were down at the far end of the hall when the hand touched sixty, Park would simply arise and say: "In the absence of the chairman, and of any other officers authorized to act as such, I, Allister Park, acting as chairman, hereby call this meeting to order. . . ."

But MacSvensson, looking at him, divined his intention. He snatched out his own watch, and dashed to the chair. He made it by one and a half seconds.

Park was not disturbed. He took his place, hearing the boss's growl: "Did you send out all those seeings when I told you to, Park? There's just barely a quorum here."

"Absolutely. I can't help it if they go astray in the mail." Park neglected to add that, with the proper cooperation from a postal clerk, it is sometimes possible to make sure that certain of the notices, though duly postmarked as of the time they are received, are accidentally misplaced in the post office and completely overlooked until the day after the meeting.

"The meeting will kindly come to order," snapped MacSvensson. He did not like the look of the quorum at all; not one of his tried and true friends was in sight, except Sleepy Ethelbald.

He continued: "This is a special meeting called to hold in mind the good and welfare of the committee. As such there will be no reading of the minutes. The meeting will now consider items for the agenda."

MacSvensson caught the eye of Sleepy Ethelbald, who had been primed for just this occasion. Before Ethelbald could rouse himself, another committeeman popped up with: "I move that we take up the fitness of Chairman MacSvensson to last in his present office." "Twothed." "I move the agenda be closed." "Twothed."

MacSvensson sat up for a few seconds with his mouth open. He had had revolts before—plenty of them—but never one with the devastating speed and coordination of this. He finally mumbled: "All in favor—"

"Aye!" roared most of the quorum.

MacSvensson ran fingers through his hair, then squared his shoulders. He wasn't licked yet, by any means. There were more tricks. . . . "The meeting will now consider the first item on the agenda."

"I move the impeachment of Chairman MacSvensson!" "Twothed!"

For the second time the chairman sat with his mouth open. Park said gently: "You take up the motion and give me the gavel."

"But—" wailed MacSvensson.

"No buts. A motion to impeach the chairman self-movingly shifts the gavel to the secretary. Come on, old boy."

An hour later Ivor MacSvensson stalked out, beaten. Park could have had the chairmanship himself, but he astutely preferred to keep the secretaryship and put the ancient of days, Magnus Dutt, in that exposed position.

❖   ❖   ❖

Mayor Offa Greenfield knew his own mind, such as it was. He banged his fist on his desk, making all his chins quiver. "Nay!" he shouted. "I don't know what you're up to, Allister Park, but by the right ear of Hallow Gall, it's something! The freedom of a free people—"

"Now, now, we're not talking about the freedom of a free people. I'm sure we agree on that matter. It's just a question of the person of Joseph Noggle—"

"I won't be dictated to! I won't take orders from anybody!"

"Except Ivor MacSvensson?"

"Except Iv—nay! I said anybody! Go practice your snaky trick on somebody else, Allister Park; you'll get nothing from me! I won't interfere with Borup's running of his Institute. Unless, of course," (Greenfield lowered his voice to normal) "you can get MacSvensson to back you up."

Greenfield, it seemed, had the one virtue of loyalty. He intended to stick by the fallen boss to the bitter end, even though nearly all the rest of MacSvensson's staunch supporters had deserted him when the effectiveness of Park's coup had become patent.

But Greenfield was not elected, as were the members of the burg thing. He was appointed by a committee of the Althing, the national legislative body. So Park, for all his local power, could not displace Greenfield at the coming elections by putting up a rival candidate. He could only do it by acquiring sufficient power in the Althing. He set himself to study how to do this.

New Belfast elected six members to the Althing. As the city was firmly Diamond, nomination implied election. Therefore the six thingmen, however much they bragged about their independence in public, were careful to obey the whims of the boss of New Belfast.

The repeated efforts of Yon Brahtz to impose his control on the New Belfast Diamonds, by planting

stooges like the late Trigvy Darling in their hide committees, had aroused some resentment. Park decided
that he could trust his most active supporters, and
the six thingmen, to back him in a gigantic double-
cross: to desert the Diamond Party altogether and join
the Rubies. The goats would be, not merely Brahtz
and his squirearchy, but the local Ruby politicians of
New Belfast. However, as these had never accomplished anything but draw some patronage from the
Althing in the periods when the Rubies were in power
there, Park thought he would not find much resistance to their sacrifice on the part of the Ruby leaders. And so it proved.

Twenty men, though, seldom keep a secret for long.
The morning of June 9th, Park opened his paper to
find the report of a defiant speech by Yon Brahtz,
in which he announced bluntly that "the thanes of
the Cherogian March of Vinland will defend the ricks
they inherited from their heroic forebears, by any
means needful, and moreover the means for such
defense are ready and waiting!" Park translated this
to mean that if the Scoglund amendment were passed
by a coalition of Rubies and insurgent New Belfast
Diamonds, the squirearchy would secede.

But that would mean civil war, which in turn would
mean postponement of the elections. What was even
more serious, the Diamond thingmen from the seceding provinces would automatically lose their seats,
giving the Rubies a clear majority. Since the Rubies
would no longer need the support of Park's insurgents,
they would be disinclined to make a deal with him
to appoint a mayor of his choice.

Park privately thought that, while in theory he supposed he believed in the Scoglund amendment, in
practice both his and the Ruby leaders' interests
would be better served by dropping it for the present,
despite the growls of the Dakotians and Cherogians.
However, the Ruby leaders were firm; that huge block

of Skrelling votes they would get by emancipating the aborigines was worth almost any risk.

As for such questions as the rights of the Skrellings as human beings, or the unfortunate Vinlanders who would be killed or haggled up in a civil war, they were not considered at all.

Park, holed up in the Isleif Street apartment with a couple of bodyguards, answered a call from Dunedin. "Haw, Hallow? Thane Callahan is here to see you."

"Send him over here. Warn him ahead of time who I—" Park remembered the guards, and amended: "warn him about everything. You know."

Lord, he thought, all this just to get hold of Noggle, still shut up in the Psychophysical Institute! Maybe it would have been simpler to organize a private army like Brahtz's and storm that fortresslike structure. A long-distance call for the mobilization of his Sons of the Vikings, as he called his storm troopers. Kedrick, the Bretwald of Vinland, had refused to mobilize the army because, he explained, such an action would be "provocative" . . . Maybe he secretly favored the squire-archy, whose man he was; maybe he was just a pacific civilian who found the whole subject of soldiers, guns, and such horrid things too repulsive to discuss; maybe he really believed what he said. . . .

Callahan arrived with a flourish. Since MacSvens-son was no longer boss of New Belfast, the Sachem went openly about the city without fear of arrest and beating-up by the police.

He told Park: "It would be worth my life if some of my fellow Skrellings knew I'd told you. But the Dakotians have an army secretly assembled on the bounds. If the Vinlanders start fickting among them-selves, the Dakotians'll jump in to grab the north-western provinces."

Park whistled. "How about the Cherogians?"

"They're holding back, waiting to see how things

are turning out. If the war seems to be fruitbearing, they'll try a little rickting of the bounds themselves."

"And what will your Skrellings do then?"

"That depends. If the Scoglund changelet is lost, they'll join the foe to a man. If it goes through, I think I can hold most of them in line."

"Why do you tell me this, Callahan?"

The Sachem grinned his large disarming grin. "Two reasons. First, the bishop and I have been friends for years, and I'll stick to his body no matter where his soul may be. Twoth, I'm not fooled, as some of my Skrellings are, by talk of what fine things the Dakotians'll do for us if we help them overthrow the palefaces. The Dakotian realm is even less a folkish one than the Bretwaldate's. I know a thing or two about how they treat their ain folk. So if you'll stick to me, I'll stick to you."

Park would have liked to appear at the opening of the Althing as Bishop Scoglund. But, as too many people there knew him as Allister Park, he attended in his mustache, hair dye, and spectacles.

The atmosphere was electric. Even Park, with all his acumen, had been unable to keep up with events. The risks were huge, whichever way he threw his insurgents' votes.

He kept them shut up in a committee room with him until the last possible minute. He did not yet know himself whether he would order them to vote for or against the amendment.

The clock on the wall ticked around.

A boy came in with a message for Park. It said, in effect, that the Sons of the Vikings had received a report that the amendment had already been passed; had mobilized and seized the town of Olafsburg.

Who had sent that mistaken message and why, there was no way of finding out. But it was too late for anybody to back down. Park looked up and said,

very seriously: "We're voting for the Scoglund Amendment." That was all; with his well-trained cogs no
more was necessary.

The bell rang; they filed out. Park took his seat
in the visitors' gallery. He said nothing but thought
furiously as the session of the Althing was opened with
the usual formalities. The chairman and the speaker
and the chaplain took an interminable time about
their business, as if afraid to come to grips with the
fearful reality awaiting their attention.

When the first motions came up, a dead silence fell
as Park's men got up and walked over to the Rubies'
side of the house. Then the Rubies let out a yell of
triumph. There was no more need of stalling or delicate angling for marginal votes. Motion after motion
went through with a roar. Out went the Diamond
chairman and speaker, and in went Rubies in their place.

In an hour the debate had been shut off, despite
howls from Diamonds and their sympathizers about
"gag law" and "high-handed procedure."

The amendment came up for its first vote. It fell
short of the two-thirds required by eleven votes.

Park scribbled a note and had it delivered to the
speaker. The speaker handed it to the chairman. Park
watched the little white note drift around the Ruby
side of the house. Then the Ruby leader got up and
solemnly moved the suspension of thingmen Adamson,
Arduser, Beurwulf, Dahl, Fessenden, Gilpatrick,
Holmquist . . . all the thingmen from the seceding area.

Most of those named didn't wait; they rose and
filed out, presumably to catch airwains for their home
provinces.

The amendment passed on the second vote.

Park looked up the Ruby leader after the Althing
adjourned. He said: "I hear Kedrick still won't order
mobilization. Talks about 'Letting the erring brethren
go in peace.' What's your party line on the matter?"

The Ruby leader, a thin cool man, blew smoke through his nose. "We're going to fick. If Kedrick won't go along, there are ways. The same applies to *you*, Thane Park."

Park suddenly realized that events had put him in a suspect position. If he didn't want himself and his cogs to be damned as copperheads, or the Vinland equivalent, he'd have to outshout the Rubies for unity, down with the rebels, etcetera.

Well, he might as well do a good job of it.

That afternoon the guards at the Psychophysical Institute were astonished to have their sanctuary invaded by a squad of uniformed knicks with the notorious Allister Park at their head flourishing a search warrant. The charge was violation of the fire ordinances—in a building made almost entirely of tile, glass, and reinforced concrete.

"But, but, but!" stuttered Dr. Edwy Borup. Park merely whisked out another warrant, this time for the arrest of Joseph Noggle.

"But, but, you can't stop one of my patients! It's— uh—illegal! I'll call Mayor Greenfield!"

"Go ahead," grinned Park. "But don't be surprised if you get a busy signal." He had taken the precaution of seeing that all the lines to the mayor's office would be occupied at this time.

"Hello, Noggle," said Park.

"Haw. Who are you? I think I've met you—let me see—"

Park produced an air pistol. "I'm Allister Park. You'll figure out where you met me soon enough, but you won't talk about it. I'm glad to see my figuring came out right. Can you start a man's wheel today? Now?"

"I suppose I could. Oh, *I* know who you are now—"

"Nay comments, I said. You're coming along, brother, and doing just as you're told."

The next step was when Park walked arm in arm with Noggle into the imposing executive building.

Park's standing as a powerful boss saw him through the guards and flunkeys that guarded the Bretwald's office on the top floor.

The Bretwald looked up from his desk. "Oh, haw, Thane Park. If you're going to nag me about that mobilization order, you're wasting your time. Who's— eeee! Where am I? What's happened to me? Help! Help!"

In bounded the guards, guns ready. Park faced them sadly. "Our respected Bretwald seems to have had a mental seizure," he said.

The guards covered the two visitors and asked Kedrick what was the matter. All they could get out of Kedrick was: "Help! Get away from me! Let me out! I don't know who you're talking about. My name's not Kedrick, it's O'Shaughnessy!"

They took him away. The guards kept Park and Noggle until a message from the acting Bretwald said to let them go.

"By the brazen gates of Hell!" cried Park. "Is *that* all?"

"Yep," said the new Secretary of War. "Douglas was a Brahtz man; hence he saw to it that the army was made as harmless as possible before he skipped out."

Park laughed grimly. "The Secretary of War sabotages—"

"He does what?"

"Never mind. He raises hell with, if you want a more familiar expression. Raises hell with the army for the benefit of his party, with the Dakotians about to come whooping in. I suppose it oughtn't to surprise me, though. How many can we raise?"

"About twenty thousand in the burgish area, but we can arm only half of them rickly. Most of our quick-fire pipes and warwains have been hurt so it'll take a month to fix them."

"How about a force of Skrellings?"

The Secretary shrugged. "We can raise 'em, but we can't arm them."

"Go ahead and raise 'em anyway."

"All right, if you say so. But hadn't you better have a rank? It would look better."

"All right. You make me your assistant."

"Don't you want a commission?"

"Not on your life! Your generals would go on strike, and even if they didn't I'd be subject to military law."

The army was not an impressive one, even when its various contingents had all collected at what would have been Pittsburgh if its name hadn't been the lovely one of Guggenvik. The regulars were few and unimpressive; the militia were more numerous but even less prepossessing; the Skrelling levy was the most unmilitary of all. They stood around with silly grins on their flat brown faces, and chattered and scratched. Park thought disgustedly, so these are the descendants of the noble red man and the heroic viking! Fifty years of peace had been a blessing to Vinland, but not an altogether unmitigated one.

The transport consisted of a vast fleet of private folkwains and goodwains (busses and trucks to you). It had been possible to put only six warwains in the field. These were a kind of steam-driven armored car carrying a compressor and a couple of pneumatic machine guns. There was one portable liquid-air plant for charging shells and air bombs.

The backwardness of Vinland chemistry compared to its physics caused a curious situation. The only practical military explosives were a rather low-grade black powder, and a carbon-liquid-oxygen mixture. Since the former was less satisfactory as a propellant, considering smoke, flash, and barrel-fouling, than compressed air, and was less effective as a detonant than the liquid air explosive; its military use was largely confined to land mines. Liquid oxygen, however, while as powerful as trinitrotoluol, had to be manufactured on the spot, as there was no way of preventing its evaporation. Hence it was a very awkward thing to use in mobile warfare.

Park walked into the intelligence tent, and asked the Secretary of War: "What do you think our chances are?"

The Secretary looked at him. "Against the squires, about even. Against the Dakotians, one to five. Against both, none." He held out a handful of dispatches. These told of the success of the Sons of the Vikings in extending their hold in the southwest, not surprising considering that the only division of regulars in that area were natives of the region and had gone over to the rebels. More dispatches described in brief fragments the attack of a powerful and fast-moving Dakotian army west of Lake Yanktonai (Michigan). The last of these was dated 6 P.M., June 26th, the preceding day.

"What's happened since then?" asked Park.

"Don't know," said the Secretary. Just then a message came in from the First Division. It told little, but the dateline told much. It had been sent from the city of Edgar, at the south end of Lake Yanktonai.

Park looked at his map, and whistled. "But an army *can't* retreat fifty miles in one day!"

"The staff can," said the Secretary. "They ride."

Further speculation about the fate of the First Division seemed unnecessary. The one-eyed Colonel Montrose was dictating an announcement for the press to the effect that: "Our army has driven off severe Dakotian attacks in the Edgar area, with heavy losses to the foe. Nine Dakotian warwains were destroyed and five were captured. Other military booty included twenty-six machine-pipes. Two foeish airwains were shot down. . . ."

Park thought, this Montrose has a good imagination, which quality seems sadly lacking in most of the officers. Maybe we can do something with him—if we're still here long enough. . . .

The Secretary pulled Park outside. "Looks as though they had us. We haven't anything to fickt with. Not even brains. General Higgins is just an easygoing parade-ground soldier who never expected to have to shoot at anybody in his life. For that matter neither did I. Got any ideas?"

"Still thinking, brother," said Park, studying his map. "I'm nay soldier either, you know; just a thingman. If I could give you any help it would be political."

"Well, if we can't win by fickting, politics would seem to be the only way left."

"Maybe." Park was still looking at the map. "I begin to have a thock. Let's see Higgins."

Fortunately for Park's idea, General Higgins was not merely easygoing; he was positively comatose. He sat in his tent with his blouse unbuttoned and a bottle of beer in front of him, serene in the midst of worry and confusion.

"Come in, thanes, come in," he said. "Have some beer. Piff. Got any ideas? Blessed if I know where to turn next. Nay artillery, nay airwains to speak of, nay real soldiers. Piff. Do you guess if we started fortifying New Belfast now, it'd be strong enough to hold when we were pushed back there? Nobody knows anything, piff. I'm supposed to have a staff, but half of 'em have got lost or sneaked off to join the rebels. Blessed if I know what to do next."

Park thought General Higgins would make a splendid Salvation Army general. But there was no time for personalities. He sprang his plan.

"Goodness gracious!" said Higgins. "It sounds very risky—get Colonel Callahan."

The Sachem filled the tent opening when he arrived, weaving slightly. "Somebody want me?" Belatedly he remembered to salute.

Higgins barked at him: "Colonel Callahan, do you ken you have your blouse on *backwards*?"

Callahan looked down. "So I have, ha-ha. Sir."

"That's a very weighty matter. Very weighty. No, don't change it here. You're drunk, too."

"So are—" Callahan suppressed an appalling violation of discipline just in time. "Maybe I had a little, sir."

"That's very weighty, very weighty. Just think of it. I ought to have you shot."

Callahan grinned. "What would my regiment do then?"

"I don't know. What would they do?"

"Give you three guesses, sir. *Hic.*"

"Run away, I suppose."

"Right the first time, sir. Congratulations."

"Don't congratulate me, you fool! The Secretary has a plan."

"A plan, really? Haw, Thane Park; I didn't see you. How do you like our army?"

Park said: "I think it's the goddamndest thing I ever saw in my life. It's a galloping nightmare."

"Oh, come now," said Higgins. "Some of the brave boys are a little green, but it's not as bad as all that."

A very young captain entered, gave a heel-click that would have echoed if there had been anything for it to echo against, and said: "Sir, the service company, twentieth regiment, third division, has gone on strike."

"What?" said the general. "Why?"

"No food, sir. The goodwains arrived empty."

"Have them all shot. No, shoot one out of ten. No, wait a minute. Arrived empty, you say? Somebody stole the food to sell at the local grocers. Take a platoon and clean out all the goods shops in Guggenvik. Pay them in thingly I.O.U.'s."

The Secretary interjected: "The Althing will never pay those off, you know."

"I know they won't, ha-ha. Now let's get down to that plan of yours."

❖ ❖ ❖

The names were all different; Allister Park gave
up trying to remember those of the dozens of small
towns through which they rolled. But the gently
rolling stretches of southern Indiana were much the
same, cut up into a checkerboard of fields with
woodlots here and there, and an occasional snaky line
of cottonwoods marking the course of a stream. The
Vinlanders had not discovered the beauties of bill-
board advertising, which, to Park's mind, was something. Not having a businessman's point of view, he
had no intention of introducing this charming feature
of his own civilization into Vinland. The Vinlanders
did have their diabolical habit of covering the landscape with smoke from faulty burners in their wains,
and that was bad enough.

A rising whistle and a shattering bang from the rear
made Park jump around in the seat of his wain. A
mushroom of smoke and dust was rising from a hillside. The airwain that had dropped the bomb was
banking slowly to turn away. The pneumatics clattered
all along the column, but without visible effect. A
couple of their own machines purred over and chased
the bomber off.

Those steam-turbine planes were disconcertingly
quiet things. On the other hand the weight of their
power plants precluded them from carrying either a
heavy bomb load or a lot of fuel, so they were far
from a decisive arm. They rustled across the sky with
the dignity of dowagers, seldom getting much over
150 miles an hour, and their battles had the delib-
eration of a duel between sailing ships-of-the-line.

They wound down to the sunny Ohio (they called
it the Okeeyo, both derived from the same Iroquois
word) in the region where the airwains had reported
the rebel army. A rebel airwain—a converted transport ship—came to look them over, and was shot
down. From across the river came faintly the rebel
yells and the clatter of pneumatics, firing at targets

far out of range. Park guessed that discipline in
Brahtz's outfit was little if any better than in his own.

Now, if they wanted to, the stage was set for an interminable campaign of inaction. Either side could try to
sneak its men across the river without being caught in
the act by the other. Or it could adopt a defensive program, contenting itself with guarding all the likely cross-
ings. That sort of warfare would have suited General
Higgins fine, minimizing as it did the chance that most
of his musical-comedy army would do a lightning
advance to the rear as soon as they came under fire.

It would in fact have been sound tactics, if they
could have counted on the rebels' remaining on the
south bank of the Okeeyo in that region, instead of
marching east toward Guggenvik, and if the Dakotians
were not likely to descend on their rear at any moment.

The Secretary of War had gone back to New
Belfast, leaving Park the highest-ranking civilian with
Higgins' army. He had the good sense to keep out
of sight as much as possible, taking into account the
soldier's traditional dislike of the interfering politician.

General Etheling, commanding the rebel army, got
a message asking if he would hold a parley with a
civilian envoy of General Higgins' army. General
Etheling, wearing a military blouse over a farmer's
overalls and boots, pulled his long mustache and said
no, if Higgins wants to parley with me he can come
himself. Back came the answer: This is a *very* high-
ranking civilian; in fact he outranks Higgins himself.
Would that island in the middle of the Okeeyo do?
Etheling pulled his mustache some more and decided
it would do.

So, next morning General Etheling, wearing the
purely ornamental battle-ax that formed part of the
Vinland officer's dress uniform, presented himself off
the island. As he climbed out of his rowboat, he saw
his opposite number's boat pull away from the far side

of the little island. He advanced a way among the cottonwoods and yelled, "Haw!"

"Haw." A stocky blond man appeared.

"You all alone, Thane?"

"Yes."

"Well, I'll be jiggered! You boys kin go along back; I'll holler when I need you. Now, Thane, who be you?"

"I'm Bishop Ib Scoglund, General."

"*What?* But ain't you the wick who started the whole rumpus with all that silly talk about ricks for the Skrellings?"

The bishop sighed. "I did what I believed right in the sight of the Lord. But now a greater danger threatens us. The Dakotians are sweeping across our fair land like the hosts of Midian of old! Surely it were wise to sink our little bickerings in the face of this peril?"

"You say the lousy redskins is doing an invasion? Well, now, that's the first I heered of that. What proof you got?"

Park produced an assortment of papers: dispatches, a copy of the *Edgar Daily Tidings*, et cetera.

The general was at last convinced. He said: "Well, I'll be tarnally damned. Begging your pardon, Hallow; I forgot as how you were a preacher."

"That's all rick, my son. There are times when, even in a cleric like me, the baser passions rise, and it is all I can do to refrain from saying 'damn' myself."

"Well, now, that's rick handsome of you. But what does old Cottonhead Higgins want me to do? I got my orders, you know."

"I know, my son. But don't you see the Divine Will in these events? When we His children fall out and desecrate the soil of Vinland with our brothers' blood, He chastises us with the scourge of invasion. Let us unite to hurl back the heathen before it is too late! General Higgins has a plan for joint doing all worked out. If you take it up, he will prove his good faith by letting you cross the Okeeyo unopposed."

"What kind of plan is it? I never knew Cottonhead had enough brains to plan a barn dance, not to mention a campaign."

"I couldn't give you all the details; they're in this paper. But I know they call for your army to put itself in the path of the invaders, and when you are engaged with them for our army to attack their left flank. If we lose, our brotherly quarrel will be one with Sodom and Gomorrah. If we win, it will be surely possible to settle our strife without further bloodshed. You will be a great man in the sight of the people and a good one in the sight of Heaven, General."

"Well, I guess maybe as how you're right. Give me the rest of the day to study these here plans. . . ."

They shook hands; the general made a fumbling salute, and went over to his side of the island to call his boat. Thus, he did not see the bishop hastily don his mustache and spectacles.

When General Etheling's rebels crossed the river next morning, they found no trace of Higgins' force except for the usual camp litter. Following directions, they set out for Edgar.

General Higgins, goaded to hurry by Allister Park, sent his army rolling northward. People in dust-colored work clothes came out to hang over fences and stare at them.

Park asked one of these, a strapping youth with some Skrelling blood, if he had heard of the invasion.

"Sure," said the man. "Reckon they won't git this fur, though. So we ain't worrying." The young man laughed loudly at the suggestion of volunteering. "Me go off and git shot up so some other wick can sit on his rump and get rich? Not me, Thane! If the folks in Edgar gets scalped, it serves 'em right for not paying us mair for our stuff."

As the army moved farther and farther toward Edgar, the expressions of the civilians grew more anxious. As they approached the Piankishaw (Wabash) River, they passed wains parked by the roads, piled with household goods. However, when the army had passed, many of these reversed their direction and followed the army back north toward their homes. Park was tempted to tell some of these people what idiots they were, but that would hardly have been politic. The army had little enough self-confidence as it was.

Higgins' army spread out along the south bank of the Piankishaw. All those in the front line had, by order, stained their hands and faces brown. The genuine Skrellings were kept well back.

Park took an observation post overlooking the main crossing of the river. He had just settled himself when there was a tremendous purring hum from the other side of the bridge. An enemy warwain appeared. Its ten tires screeched in unison as it stopped at the barrier on the road. Pneumatics began to pop on all sides. The forward turret swung back and forth, its gun clattering. Then a tremendous bang sent earth, bridge, and wain into the air. The wain settled into the water on its side, half out. Some men crawled out and swam for the far shore, bullets kicking up little splashes around their bobbing heads.

Up the river, Park could see a pontoon boat putting out from the north shore. It moved slowly by poling; passed out of sight. In a few minutes it reappeared, drifting downstream. It came slowly past Park and stopped against a ruined bridge abutment. Water gradually leaked through the bullet holes in the canvas, until only one corner was above water. A few arms and faces bobbed lazily just below the surface.

The firing gradually died down. Park could imagine the Dakotians scanning the position with their field glasses and planning their next move. If their reputation was not exaggerated, it would be something devastating.

He climbed down from his perch and trotted back

to headquarters, where he found Rufus Callahan, sober for once.

Ten minutes later the two, preceded by an army piper, exposed themselves at the east end of the bridge. Park carried a white flag, and the piper squealed "parley" on his instrument. Nobody shot at them, so they picked their way across the bridge, climbing along the twisted girders. Callahan got stuck.

"I'm scared of high places," he said through his teeth, clinging to the ironwork.

Park took out his air pistol. "You'll be worse scared of me," he growled. The huge man was finally gotten under way again.

At the far end, a Skrelling soldier jumped out of the bushes, rifle ready. He crackled something at them in Dakotian. Callahan answered in the same language, and the man took them in tow.

As the road curved out of sight of the river, Park began to see dozens of warwains pulled up to the side of the road. Some had their turrets open, and red men sat in them, smoking or eating sandwiches. There were other vehicles, service cars of various kinds, and horse cavalry with lances and short rifles. They stopped by one warwain. Their escort snapped to a salute that must have jarred his bones. An officer climbed out. He wore the usual mustard-colored Dakotian uniform, topped off with the feathered war bonnet of the Sioux Indian. After more chattering, Park and Callahan were motioned in.

It was crowded inside. Park burned the back of his hand against a steam pipe, and cut loose with a string of curses that brought admiring grins to the red-brown faces of the crew. Everything was covered with coal soot.

The engineer opened the throttle, and the reciprocating engine started to chug. Park could not see out. They stopped presently and got out and got into another warwain, a very large one.

Inside the big machine were a number of Dakotian officers in the red-white-and-black war bonnets. A fat one with a little silver war club hanging from his belt was introduced to Park and Callahan as General Tashunkanitko, governor of the Oglala and commander-in-chief of the present expedition.

"Well?" snapped this person in a high-pitched, metallic voice.

Callahan gave his sloppy salute—which at first glance looked alarmingly as though he were thumbing his nose—and said: "I'm representing the commander of the Skrelling Division—"

"The what?"

"The Skrelling Division. We've been ordered by the Althing to put down the uprising of the Diamonds in the southwest of Vinland. They have a big army, and are likely to win all Vinland if not stopped. We can't stop them, and on the other hand we can't let them take all the south while you take all the north of Vinland.

"My commander humbly suggests that it is hardly proper for two armies of men of the same race to fick each other while their joint foe takes over all Vinland, as Brahtz's army will do unless we join against it."

General Tashunkanitko crackled something to one of his men, who rattled back. The general said: "It *was* taled that your men looked like Skrellings, but we could not get close enough to be sure, and did not believe the tale. What do you offer?"

Callahan continued: "My commander will not try to push the Dakotians from the area west of the Piankishaw, if you will help him against the rebels."

"Does that offer bind your thing?"

"Nay. But, as our army is the only real one at present under their command, they will have nay way of enforcing their objections. To prove our good faith we will, if you agree, let you cross the Piankishaw without fickting."

The general thought for some seconds. He said: "That offer ock to be put up to my government."

"Nay time, sir. The rebels are moving north from the Okeeyo already. Anyway, if we make a truce aside from our thing, you should be willing to do the same. After we've overthrown the Brahtz army, I'm sure we can find some workable arrangement between our armies."

Tashunkanitko thought again. "I will do it. Have you a plan worked out?"

"Yes, sir. Right here . . ."

When the Dakotians crossed the Piankishaw the next day, there was no sign of the large and supposedly redskin army that had held the passage against them.

Across the rolling Indiana plain came the rattle of pneumatic rifles and the crack of air- and mortar-bombs. General Higgins told Park: "We just got a message from General Etheling; says he's hard pressed, and it's about time we did our flank attack on the Dakotians. And this General Tush—Tash— General Mad-Horse wants to know why we haven't attacked the flank of the rebels. Says he's still pushing 'em back, but they outnumber him twa to ane and he's had a lot of mechanical breakdowns. Says if we'll hit them now they'll run."

"We don't want to let either side win," said Park. "Guess it's time to start."

With considerable confusion—though perhaps less than was to be expected—the Army of the New Belfast got under way. It was strung out on a five-mile front at right angles to the line of contact of the Dakotian and rebel armies. The right wing was the stronger, since it would meet stronger resistance from Tashunkanitko's hardened professionals than from Etheling's armed hayseeds.

Park squeezed into the observation turret of the headquarters wain beside Higgins. They went slowly

so as not to outrun the infantry, lurching and cant-
ing as the huge rubber doughnut-shaped wheels pulled
them over walls and fences. They crunched through
one corner of a farmyard, and the countryside was at
once inundated by fleeing pigs and chickens. Park had
a glimpse of an overalled figure shaking a fist at the
wain. He couldn't help laughing; it was too bad about
the farmer's livestock, but there was something ultra-
rural about the man's indignation over a minor private woe when a battle was going on next door.

Men began to appear ahead; horsemen leaping
fences and ditches, scattered scouts dodging from tree
to fence, firing at unseen targets, then frantically
working the pump-levers of their rifles to compress
the air for the next shot. One of them was not a
hundred yards away when he saw the advancing
wains. He stared stupidly at them until the forward
machine-gunner in the headquarters wain fired a burst
that sent the gravel flying around the scout's feet. The
scout jumped straight up and came down running.
Others ran when they saw the wains looming out of
the dust. A few who didn't see soon enough ran
toward the advancing line with their hands up.

They met larger groups of redskins, crawling or
running from right to left with faces set. Each time
there would be one face the first to turn; then they
would all turn. The group would lose its form and
purpose, sublimating into its component human atoms.
Some stood; some ran in almost any direction.

Then they were in a half-plowed field. The plow
and the steam tractor stood deserted among the brown
furrows. On the other side of the field crouched a
hostile wain. Park felt the engine speed up as the two
machines lumbered toward each other. Bullets pattered
about his cupola. It gratified him to see the general
wince when they struck on and around the glass.

The wains came straight at each other. Park
gripped the handholds tight. The other wain stopped

suddenly, backed swiftly, and tried to run in at them from the side. Their own jumped ahead with a roar. Its ram dug into the side of the other machine with a terrible crash. They backed away; Park could see lubricating oil running out of the wound in the other machine. It still crawled slowly. His own mechanical rhinoceros charged again. This time the other machine heaved up on its far wheels and fell over. . . .

The fight went out of the Dakotians all of a sudden. They had made a terrific assault on twice their number; then had fought steadily for two days. Their wains were battered, their horses hungry, and their infantry exhausted from pumping up their rifles. And to have a horde of strangers roll up their flank, just when victory was in sight—no wonder General Tashunkanitko, and his officers, let a tear or two trickle when they were rounded up.

General Etheling's rebels fared no better; rather worse, in fact. The Skrelling regiment ran wild among the rural Vinlanders, doing what they had wanted to do for generations—scalp the palefaces. Having somewhat hazy ideas about that ancestral ritual, they usually made the mistake of trying to take off the whole top of a man's head instead of the neat little two-inch circle of scalp. When they started in on the prisoners, they had to be restrained by a few bursts of machine-gun fire from one of Higgins' wains.

The train back to New Belfast stopped at every crossroads so the people could come out and whoop. They cheered Allister Park well enough; they cheered Rufus Callahan; they yelled for Bishop Scoglund. The story had gone ahead, how Park and General Higgins had devised a scheme for the entrapment of both the rebel and Dakotian armies; how the brave bishop had talked Etheling into it; how Etheling had treacherously shot the brave bishop; how Callahan had swum the Okeeyo with Bishop Scoglund on his back. . . .

It was rumored that the city politician Allister Park had had something to do with these developments, but you never want to believe anything good of these politicians. Since he was Assistant Secretary of War, though, it was only polite to give him a cheer too . . .

Park did not think it would be prudent to show himself to the same audience both as Park and as the bishop, so they were all informed that his hallowship was recuperating.

As they rolled into New Belfast, Park experienced the let-down feeling that comes at such moments. What next? By now Noggle would have been rescued from Park's knicks and returned to Edwy Borup's hatch. That was bound to happen anyway, which was why Park hadn't tried to use that method of getting Noggle into his power before. The whirling of the wheel of if was a delicate business, not to be interrupted by people with warrants, and he would have to see to it that somebody was left behind to force Noggle to stop the wheel when the right point had been reached.

It ought not to be difficult now, though. If he couldn't use his present power and position to get hold of Noggle, he'd have enough after election—which would come off as scheduled after all. First he'd make Noggle stop poor old Kendrick's wheel. Then he'd have Callahan or somebody stand over Noggle with a gun while he spun his, Park's, wheel through another half turn. Then, maybe, Noggle would be allowed to halt his own carousel.

For the first three days after his return he was too busy to give attention to this plan. Everybody in New Belfast seemingly had written him or telephoned him or called at one of his two homes to see him. Although Monkey-face was a lousy secretary, Park didn't dare hire another so long as he had his double identity to maintain.

But the Antonini trials were due in a week, back in that other world. And the heirs and assigns of

Trigvy Darling had had a date set for a hearing on their damage claim. And, if Park knew his history, there would probably be a "reconstruction" period in the revolted territories, of which he wanted no part.

For the second time Edwy Borup had his sanctuary invaded by Allister Park and a lot of tough-looking official persons, including Rufus Callahan. Borup was getting resigned if not reconciled to this. If they didn't let his prize patient Noggle escape before, they weren't likely to this time.

"Haw, Noggle," said Park. "Feel a little more with-doing?"

"Nay," snapped Noggle. "But since you have me by the little finger I suppose I'll have to do what you say."

"All right. You're honest, anyway. First you're going to stop Bretwald Kedrick's wheel. Bring him in, boys."

"But I daren't stop a wheel without my down-writings. You bethink last time—"

"That's all right; we brought your whole damn library over."

There was nothing to it. Noggle stared at the fidgety Bretwald—the period of whose cycle was fortunately just twice his, so that both were in their own bodies at the same time. Then he said: "Whew. Had a lot of psychic momentum, that ane; I just did stop him. He'll be all rick now. What next?"

Park told everybody but Callahan to go out. Then he explained that Noggle was to give his wheel another half turn.

"But," objected Noggle, "that'll take seven days. What's going to be with your body in the mean-time?"

"It'll be kept here, and so will you. When the half-cycle's done, you'll stop my wheel, and then we'll let you stop your own whenever you like. I've made sure that you'll stay here until you do the right thing by my wheel, whether you cure your own case or not."

Noggle sighed. "And MacSvensson thock he'd get some simple-minded idealist like the bishop! How is it that your pattern of acting is otherly from his, when by the laws of luck you started out with much the same forebearish make-up?"

Park shrugged. "Probably because I've had to fick every step of the way, while he was more or less born into his job. We're not so otherly, at that; his excess energy went into social crusading, while mine's gone into politics. I *have* an ideal or two kicking around somewhere. I'd like to meet Bishop Scoglund some time; think I'd like him."

"I'm afraid that's undoable," said Noggle. "Even sending you back is risky. I don't know what would happen if your body died while his mind indwelt it. You might land in still another doable world instead of in your ain. Or you mick not land anywhere."

"I'll take a chance," said Park. "Ready?"

"Yes." Dr. Joseph Noggle stared at Park.

"Hey, Thane Park," said a voice from the doorway. "A wick named Dunedin wants to see you. Says it's weighty."

"Tell him I'm busy—no, I'll see him."

Monkey-face appeared, panting. "Have you gone yet? Have you changed? Glory to Bridget! You—I mean his hallowship—what I mean is, the Althing signed a treaty with the Dakotians and Cherogians and such, setting up an International Court for the Continent of Skrelleland, and the bishop has been chosen one of the judges! I thock you ock to know before you did anything."

"Well, well," said Park. "That's interesting, but I don't know that it changes anything."

Callahan spoke up: "I think you'd make a better judge, Allister, than *he* would. He's a fine fellow, but he will believe that everybody else is as uprick as he. They'd pull the wool over his eyes all the time."

Park pondered. After all, what had he gone to all this trouble for—why had he helped turn the affairs of half the continent upside down—except to resume a career as public prosecutor which, he hoped, would some day land him on the bench? And here was a judgeship handed him on a platter.

"I'll stay," he said.

"But," objected Noggle, "how about those thirteen other men on your wheel? Are you going to leave them out of their rick rooms?"

Park grinned. "If they're like me, they're adaptable guys who've probably got started on new careers by now. If we shift 'em all again, it'll just make more trouble for them. Come along, Rufus."

The funeral of Allister Park, assistant Secretary of War, brought out thousands of people. Some were politicians who had been associated with Park; some came for the ride. A few came because they liked the man.

In an anteroom of the cathedral, Bishop Scoglund waited for that infernal music to end, whereupon he would go out and preach the swellest damn funeral oration New Belfast had ever heard. It isn't given to every man to conduct that touching ceremony for his own corpse, and the bishop intended to give his alter-ego a good send-off.

In a way he was sorry to bid Allister Park goodbye. Allister had a good deal more in common with his natural, authentic self than did the bishop. But he couldn't keep up the two identities forever, and with the judgeship on one hand and the damage suit on the other there wasn't much question of which of the two would have to be sacrificed. The pose of piety would probably become natural in time. The judgeship would give him an excuse for resigning his bishopric. Luckily the Celtic Christian Church had a liberal attitude toward folk who wished to leave the church. Of course he'd still have to be careful—girlfriends and such. Maybe it would even be worthwhile getting married . . .

"What the devil—what do you wish, my son?" said the bishop, looking up into Figgis's unpleasant face.

"You know what I wish, you old goat! What are you going to do about my wife?"

"Why, friend, it seems that you have been subject to a monstrous fooling!"

"You bet I—"

"Please, do not shout in the house of God! What I was saying was that the guilty man was none other than the late Allister Park, may the good Lord forgive his sins. He has been impersonating me. As you know, we looked much alike. Allister Park upowned to me on his deathbed two days ago. No doubt his excesses brought him to his untimely end. Still, for all his human frailties, he was a man of many good qualities. You will forgive him, will you not?"

"But—but I—"

"Please, for my sake. You would not speak ill of the dead, would you?"

"Oh, hell. Your forgiveness, Bishop. I thock I had a good thing, that's all. G'bye. Sorry."

The music was coming to an end. The bishop stood up, straightened his vestments, and strode majestically out. If he could only count on that drunken nitwit Callahan not to forget himself and bust out laughing . . .

The coffin, smothered in flowers, was, like all coffins in Vinland, shaped like a Viking longboat. It was also filled with pine planks. Some people were weeping a bit. Even Callahan, in the front row, was appropriately solemn.

"Friends, we have gathered here to pay a last gild to one who has passed from among us. . . ."

Author's Note & Pronunciation Guide

In our world, the Inca Empire was conquered by the Spaniards in 1532. The Incas did not write. The conquerors, naturally, recorded names, places, and other things peculiar to the Incas in the orthography of Spanish. Thus they called the Empire's dominant language *Quechua*. Had English speakers first encountered the Incas, that would have been written down as something like *Kechwa*.

In the world of *The Wheels of If* and *The Pugnacious Peacemaker*, the Inca civilization survived as an independent state. When its people learned to write, they, like the other Skrelling (Indian) nations of the continent of Skrelleland (the Americas), borrowed their alphabet from the Bretwaldate of Vinland. The Bretwaldate's system of spelling, however, is not quite the same as ours. Here are some suggested pronunciations for letters and combinations that may seem unfamiliar:

VOWELS	CONSONANTS
ai = *i* of find	j = *y* of yes
au = *ow* of how	lj = *lli* of million
ej = *ay* of day	nj = *ny* of canyon
ii = *ee* of seek	s = always the *s* of self,
oo = *o* of hold	not of is
uu = *oo* of moo	sj = *sh* of should
	tj = *ch* of chip

The Pugnacious
Peacemaker

Harry Turtledove

"*Aka,*" the wire recorder said. "*Aka, aka, aka.*"

"*Aka,*" Eric Dunedin repeated. "*Aka, aka, aka.*"

Dunedin's boss, Judge Ib Scoglund, burst out laughing. The thane's pinched, rather simian face twisted into a reproachful frown. Scoglund could guess what he was thinking: *you didn't act like this back in the days when you were a bishop.*

The judge knew Dunedin was right. He *hadn't* acted this way when he was a bishop, not up until the very end. Of course, the mind of an up-and-coming New York assistant DA named Allister Park hadn't come to inhabit this body till then, either.

"I beg forgiveness, Eric," he said, more or less sincerely. "But you have to say forth that twoth wordpart down in the back of the throat, like this: *aka*. Do you hear the otherness?"

"Nay, Hallow, er, Judge," Dunedin said.

Allister Park breathed through Ib Scoglund's nose in exasperation. "Well, you're going to have to learn to hear it if you ever aim at speak Ketjwa. The way you spoke it, the way the letters look on paper to someone who's used to English, *aka* doesn't mean 'corn beer.' It means"—at the last moment, he decided to have mercy on his servant's sensibilities— " 'dung.' "

Dunedin looked ready to burst into tears. "I never wanted to learn to speak Ketjwa, or aught save English. All these Skrelling tongues tie my wits up in knots."

Privately, Scoglund, or rather Park, agreed with him. But he said, "I'm learning it, so that shows you can. And you'll have to, for no one in Kuuskoo but a few men of letters and spokesfolk to the Bretwaldate knows even one word of our speech. How will you keep us in meat and potatoes—to say naught of *aka*— if you can't talk with the folk who sell them?"

"I'll—try, Judge," Dunedin said. "*Aka.*" He pronounced it wrong again.

Park sighed. Nobody could make his thane a linguist, not in the couple of days before their steamship docked at Uuraba on the northern coast of the landstrait of Panama, not in the new sea journey down from the land-strait's southern coast to Ookonja, the port nearest Kuuskoo—and not with twenty years to work, either. A talent for languages simply wasn't in Monkey-face. The most to hope for was that he would learn more with Park bullying him than without.

"I'm going up on deck for some fresh air," Park announced. "You stay here till you've played that record two more times." Dunedin gave him a martyred look, which he ignored. The cabin was hot and

stuffy; no one in this world had thought of air
conditioning.

Park grabbed a hat and a couple of books and
climbed the narrow iron staircase to the deck. The
air there was no less humid than it had been inside,
and hardly cooler: summer on the Westmiddle Sea
(Park still thought of it as the Caribbean, no matter
what the map said) was bound to be tropical. But
here, at least, the air was moving.

The deck chairs were deck chairs, right down to
their gaudy canvas webbing. Park threw himself into
one. It complained about his weight. He sighed again.
All the alter egos on his wheel of if seemed to run
to portliness. They were all losing their hair, too; he
put on the hat in a hurry, before the sun seared his
scalp.

Soon he forgot sun, humidity, everything: when he
studied, he studied hard. And he had a lot of studying
to do. He felt like a student dropped into a class the
week before exams. Ever since his—actually, Ib
Scoglund's—appointment to the International Court
for the continent of Skrelleland the year before, he'd
done little but study this world's languages, history,
and legal systems. They were still strange to him, but
as soon as he got to Kuuskoo he would have to start
using them.

He wished he'd been assigned a case involving
the Bretwaldate of Vinland. Its customs were rec-
ognizably similar to the ones he'd grown up with.
But assigning legal actions to disinterested outsiders
made a certain amount of sense. Disinterested,
Allister Park certainly was. Nothing like either country involved in this dispute existed in the world he
knew.

Tawantiinsuuju was, he gathered from the text in
his lap, what the Inca Empire might have become
had Spaniards not strangled it in infancy. In this
world, though, Arabs and Berbers still ruled Spain.

Among other places, Park thought. That was part of the problem he'd have to deal with. . . .

A shadow fell on the book. After a moment, Park looked up. A man was standing by his chair. "You are Judge Scoglund?" he asked in Ketjwa.

"Yes, I am," Park answered slowly, using the same language. He was just glad he was talking with a man. Men and women used different words for kin and for other things in Ketjwa, and he wasn't any too familiar with the distaff side of the vocabulary. "Who are you, sir?"

"I am called Ankowaljuu," the fellow answered. He was in his late thirties, close to Park's own age, with red-brown skin, straight black hair cut a little below his ears, and a high-cheekboned face dominated by a nose of nearly Roman impressiveness. He wore sandals, a wool tunic, and a black derby hat. "I am *tukuuii riikook* to the Son of the Sun, Maita Kapak." At the mention of his ruler's name, he shaded his eyes with one hand for a moment, as if to shield them from the monarch's glory.

"*Tukuuii riikook,* eh?" Park looked at him with more interest than he'd felt before: Ankowaljuu was no ordinary passenger.

"You understand what it means, then?"

"Aye," Park said. A *tukuuii riikook* was an imperial inspector, of the secret sort outside the usual chain of command. Most empires had them under one name or another, so the rulers could make sure their regular functionaries were performing as they should. Frowning, the judge went on, "I do not understand why you tell me, though."

Ankowaljuu smiled, displaying large white teeth. "Shall I speak English, to make sure I am clear?"

"Please do," Park said with relief. "I am working to learn your tongue, but I am not yet flowing in it."

"You have the back-of-the-throat sounds, which are most often hardest for Vinlanders to gain,"

Ankowaljuu said. "But to go on: I tell you because I want you to know you may count on me—I speak for myself now, mind you, not for the Son of the Sun—for as long as you have a hand in judging this dealing between my folk and the Emirate of the Dar al-Harb."

"Oh? Why is that?" Park hoped his voice did not show his sudden hard suspicion. His years in the DA's office told him no one ever offered anything for nothing. "You must understand I cannot talk with you about this dealing—all the more so *because* you are a *tukuuii riikook*, a thane of your emperor."

"Yes, of course I understand, That you naysay shows your honesty. I must tell you, the Son of the Sun was sorry he gave our quarrel with the Emir to the International Court when he learned the judge would be from Vinland."

"Why is that?" Park asked again, this time out of genuine curiosity. "My country has little to do with either yours or the Emirate."

"Because so many Vinlanders are forejudged against Skrellings," Ankowaljuu said grimly. "But when I came up to New Belfast to find out what sort of man you are, I found his mistrusts were misplaced. No one who has swinked so hard for the ricks of the Skrellings in Vinland could be anything but fair in his judgments."

"Well, thank you very much," Park murmured, a little embarrassed at taking credit for work that had actually been Ib Scoglund's. "I won't needfully choose for you, either, just *because* you're Skrellings, you know."

Ankowaljuu made a shoving motion, as if to push that idea aside. "I would not reckon anything of the sort. But it is good to know you will not turn against us just because the folk of the Dar al-Harb are incomers to Skrelleland like you Vinlanders."

"I never thock of that." Park clapped a hand to

his forehead. "This bounds strife is quite embrangled enough without worries of that sort."

"So it is." Ankowaljuu chuckled, a bit unpleasantly. "At least I need not trouble myself about any faithly forejudgment on your part. As a one-time Christian bishop, no doubt you will have glick scorn for the Emir and his Allah on the one hand and our hallowing of the sun and Patjakamak who put it in the sky on the other."

"I think all faiths can be good," Park said.

Ankowaljuu's eloquent grunt showed just how much he believed that. The funny thing was, Park really meant it. Anyone who wanted to play politics in New York had to feel, or at least act, that way. And nothing in Park's experience with criminals had shown him that people who followed any one religion behaved conspicuously better than those who believed in another.

Trouble was, both the Tawantiinsuujans and the Emir's subjects took their religions so damned *seriously*. "Dar al-Harb" itself meant "Land of War"— war against the pagans the Moors of Cordova had found when they crossed to what Park still sometimes thought of as Brazil. Since *all* the Skrellings in the southern half of Skrelleland were pagan, the past few hundred years had seen a lot of war.

"Well, maybe this is one war we'll stop," he muttered.

He didn't know he had spoken aloud until Ankowaljuu said, "I hope we do." The *tukuuii riikook* raised a hand to the brim of his derby and walked off.

Park opened his book to the place his thumb had been keeping. Religion, politics, greed . . . *embrangled* wasn't nearly a strong enough word for this case. A word that was came to mind, but not one suited for polite company. He said it anyhow, softly, and plunged back in.

❖   ❖   ❖

Reed flutes whistled mournfully. Allister Park didn't think it was fit music for a fanfare, but nobody'd asked him. "Judge Ib Scoglund of the International Court of Skrelleland!" a flunky bawled in Ketjwa. Park bowed at the doorway to the big reception hall, slowly walked in.

Slowly was the operative word, he thought. Kuuskoo was more than two miles above sea level; the air was chilly and, above all, thin. He'd come by train from the broiling tropical port of Ookonja in less than a day. Any sudden motion made his heart pound wildly. He looked around for a chair.

He spotted one, but before he could sit down, a big, red-faced man came over to pump his hand. "Haw, good to meet you, Hallow, er, Thane, er, Judge Scoglund," he boomed. "I'm Osfric Lundqvist, the Bretwaldate's spokesman to the Son of the Sun."

"Thank you, Thane Lundqvist," Park said.

"My joyment." Lundqvist did not let go of Park's hand.

"Thank you," Park repeated, trying to find some polite way to disengage himself from the ambassador. Lundqvist was, he knew, an amiable nonentity who drank too much. Because several nations lay between Vinland and Tawantiinsuuju, this was a safe enough post for a rich squire with more influence than ability. No matter how badly he blundered, he could not start a war by himself.

As if by magic, Eric Dunedin appeared at Park's elbow. "Judge, the Son of the Sun's warden for outlandish dealings wants to meet you."

"Outlandish dealings?" Then Park made the mental leap between the English he was used to and the Bretwaldate's dialect: the foreign affairs minister, Monkey-face meant. "Oh. Of course. Thanks, Eric."

"Here, let me inlead you to him," Lundqvist said eagerly.

"That's all rick, your bestness, but I ock to go alone.

I'm here as judge for the International Court, after all, not as a burgman of Vinland." *And,* Park thought, *I'll get you out of my hair.* Lundqvist looked disappointed but managed a nod.

The warden for outlandish dealings was a middle-aged Skrelling with iron-gray hair cut in a pageboy bob like Ankowaljuu's. Unlike Ankowaljuu, though, he wore in each ear a silver plug big enough to stopper a bathtub. Only the high nobility of Tawantiinsuuju still clung to that style.

Park bowed to him, spoke in Ketjwa: "I am glad to meet you, Minister Tjiimpuu."

Tjiimpuu bowed in return, not as deeply, and set his right hand on Park's left shoulder. "And I you, Judge Scoglund. How fare you, in our mountain city? The climate is not much like that to which you had grown accustomed traveling here, is it?"

"No indeed." Park tried a Ketjwa proverb: *"Patjam kuutin*—the world changes." As soon as the words were out of his mouth, he wished he had them back; the saying's implication was, *for the worse.*

But Tjiimpuu laughed. "Lowlanders always have trouble catching their breath here. Sit down, if you need to." Park gratefully sank into a chair.

Tjiimpuu gestured to a servant, spoke rapidly. The man nodded and hurried away. He returned a moment later with a painted earthenware cup full of some gently steaming liquid. Tjiimpuu took it from him, handed it to Park. "Here. Drink this. Many lowlanders find it helps give them strength."

"Thank you, sir." Park sniffed the contents of the cup. The liquid was aromatic but unfamiliar. He tasted it. It was more bitter than he'd expected, but no worse than strong tea drunk without sugar. And by the time he'd finished the cup, he did indeed feel stronger; for the first time since he'd reached Kuuskoo, his lungs seemed to be getting enough air. "That's marvelous stuff," he exclaimed. "What is it?"

"Coca-leaf tea," Tjiimpuu said.

Park stared at him. Back in New York, he'd spent part of his time throwing cocaine peddlers and cocaine users in jail. He wondered if the foreign minister was trying to trap him in an indiscretion. Then he noticed Tjiimpuu had a cup of the stuff too. "Oh," he said weakly. "Most, uh, invigorating."

"I thought it would do you good," Tjlimpuu said. "I still should warn you not to exert yourself too strenuously for the next moon or two, or you may fall seriously ill."

"I will remember," Park said. After a moment, he added, "Could you please send some over to my servant?" Of the two of them, Dunedin would likely be doing more physical work.

A waiter soon gave Monkey-face a cup. Park caught Dunedin's eye, nodded. His man had been looking doubtfully at the stuff. Now he drank, though he made a face at the taste. Park nodded again, sternly this time, and watched him finish the tea. When Dunedin felt what it did for his insides, he grinned at his boss, which only made him look more like a monkey than ever.

"Now to business," Tjiimpuu said in a tone of voice different from the one he'd used before. "I must tell you that the Son of the Sun will not permit the boundary between ourselves and the Emirate of the Dar al-Harb to be moved from where his father, the great Waskar, fixed it twenty-eight years ago." Under Waskar, Tawantiinsuuju had won the most recent clash with its eastern neighbor.

"Setting conditions at the start of talks is no way to have them succeed," Park said.

"For the Son of the Sun to abandon land his father won would disgrace him before Patjakamak, the creator of the world, and before the holy Sun that looks down on all he does," Tjiimpuu said icily. "It cannot be, Judge Scoglund."

That was the wrong tack to take with Allister Park.
"Do not tell me what can and cannot be," he said.
"When Tawantiinsuuju agreed to let the International
Court decide your latest quarrel, you put that power
into its hands—and, through it, into mine."

"I could order you out of my land this very
instant," Tjiimpuu growled. "Perhaps I should, for
your insolence."

"Go ahead," Park said cheerfully. "I'm sure you will
make the Son of the Sun happy by disgracing Tawantiinsuuju before all Skrelleland, and for showing it
thinks itself above the International Court. You and
the Emir had me brought down here to do a job, and
by God—Patjakamak, Allah, or plain old Father, Son,
and Holy Ghost—I'm going to do it."

Someone behind Park spoke up: "Well said."

He turned. The newcomer was a tall, smiling man,
dark but not Skrelling-colored and wearing a neat
black beard no Skrelling could have raised. He had
on flowing cotton robes and a satin headscarf held
in place by an emerald-green cord. He was, in short,
a Moor.

Bowing to Park, the fellow said, "Allow me to
introduce myself, sir, I pray: I am Da'ud ibn Tariq,
ambassador from the Dar al-Harb to the pagans of
Tawantiinsuuju. I greet you in the name of Allah, the
Compassionate, the Merciful. He is himself perfect
justice, and so loves those who end disputes among
mankind." His Ketjwa was elegant and eloquent.

Park got to his feet. Even with the coca tea, it took
a distinct physical effort. Also in Ketjwa, he replied,
"I am honored to meet you, Your Excellency."

Tjiimpuu had risen too, his face like thunder. Da'ud
smiled, a smile, Park guessed, intended to get further under the skin of his rival. The ambassador
suddenly shifted to English: "He's a rick ugly misbe-
got, isn't he?"

Park glanced at Tjiimpuu. He hadn't understood,

but he didn't look happy about Da'ud's using a language he didn't know. Park decided he couldn't blame him.

He stayed in Ketjwa as he bowed to Da'ud: "If you admire justice so much, Excellency, you will see it is only just to keep to a language all of us know."

"As you say, of course," Da'ud agreed at once. "I hope, though, that you have also applied yourself to learning the tongue of the Dar al-Harb, for where is justice if the judge knows one speech and not the other?"

He was smooth where Tjiimpuu was blunt, Park thought, but he looked to be equally stubborn. Park kept a poker face as he sprang his surprise: "I am working on it, yes," he said in the Berber-flavored Arabic of the Emirate. "*Inshallah,* I shall succeed."

Tjiimpuu burst out laughing. "He has you there," he told Da'ud, also in Arabic. Park had figured he would know that language.

"So he does." Da'ud plucked at his whiskers for a moment as he studied Park. "Tell me, Judge Scoglund, did you know either of these tongues before you were assigned our dispute?"

Park shook his head. This world had no international diplomatic language. The dominance of English and French in his own world sprang from the long-lasting might and prestige of those who spoke them. Power here was more fragmented.

"How does it feel, studying two new languages at the same time?" Tjiimpuu asked.

Park thumped his temple with the heel of his hand, as if trying to knock words straight into his head. The minister and ambassador both laughed. Park was pleased with himself for defusing their hostility. Maybe that would prove a good omen.

It didn't. Tjiimpuu's frown returned as he rounded on Da'ud. "I got a report on the wirecaller this afternoon that raiders from the Emirate attacked a town called Kiiniigwa in Tawantiinsuujan territory. They burned the sun-temple, kidnapped several women from the sacred virgins there, and fled back toward the border. How say you?"

Taller than Tjiimpuu, Da'ud looked down his long nose at him. "I could answer in several ways. First, my ruler, the mighty Emir Hussein, does not recognize your seizure of Kiiniigwa. Second, surely you do not claim this was carried out by the army of the Dar al-Harb?"

"If I claimed that," the Tawantiinsuujan foreign minister growled, "my country and yours would be at war now, International Court or no International Court, and you, sir, would be on the next train out of Kuuskoo."

"Well, then, you see how it is." Da'ud spread his hands. "Even assuming the report is true, what do you expect my government to do?"

"Tracking down the raiders and striking off their heads would be a good first step," Tjiimpuu said. "Sending those heads to the Son of the Sun with a note of apology would be a good second one."

"But why, when they've broken no law?" Again Da'ud smiled that silky, irritating smile.

"Wait a bit," Allister Park broke in sharply. "Since when aren't arson and kidnapping—and probably rape and murder too—against the law?"

"Since they are worked against pagans by Muslims seeking to extend the sway of Islam," answered Da'ud ibn Tariq. "In that context, under the *shari'a*, under Islamic law, nothing is forbidden the *ghazi*, the warrior of the *jihad*."

He meant it, Park realized. He'd read about the holy war Islam espoused against what it called paganism, but what he'd read hadn't seemed quite real to him. *Jihad* smacked too much of the Crusades (which hadn't happened in this world) and of medieval times in general for him to believe the concept could be alive and well in the twentieth century. But Da'ud, a clever, intelligent man, took it seriously, and so, by his expression, did Tjiimpuu.

"Ghazi." The Tawantiinsuujan made it into a swear word. "The Emirate uses this as an excuse to send its criminals and wild men to the frontier to work their crimes on us instead of on its own good people—if such there be—and to lure more criminals and wild men to its shore from the Emirate of Cordova, from North Africa, even from Asia, so they too can kill and steal in our land to their hearts' content."

"The answer is simple," Da'ud said. Tjiimpuu looked at him in surprise. So did Allister Park. If the answer were simple, he wouldn't have been here, halfway up the Andes (Antiis, they spelled it here). Then the ambassador went on, "If your people acknowledge the truth of Islam, the frontier will no longer be held against pagans, and strife will cease of its own accord."

"I find my faith as true as you find yours or the one-time Bishop Scoglund here finds his," Tjiimpuu said. Park had the feeling this was an old argument, and sensibly kept his mouth shut about his own occasional doubts.

"But it is false, a trick of Shaitan to drag you and all your stubborn pagan people down to hell," Da'ud said.

"Aka." Tjiimpuu pronounced the word as Eric Dunedin had, but he did so deliberately. "Patjakamak is the one real god. He set the sun aflame in the sky as a token of his might, and sent the Sons of the Sun down to earth to light our way. One day the whole world will see the truth of this."

The ache that started pounding inside Park's head had nothing to do with the altitude.

"Gentlemen, please!" he said. "I've come here to try to keep the peace, not to see you fight in the hall."

"Can there be true peace with pagans?" Da'ud demanded. "They are far worse than Christians."

"Thank you so much," Park snapped. The Moor, he thought angrily, was too fanatical even to notice when he was insulting someone.

Tjiimpuu, though, was every bit as unyielding. "One day we will rid Skrelleland of you hairy, sun-denying bandits. Would that we were strong enough to do it now, instead of having to chaffer with you like potato merchants."

"Potatoes, is it? One fine day we will roast potatoes in the embers of Kuuskoo." Da'ud ibn Tariq whirled around and stormed off. His exit would have been more impressive had he not bumped into the envoy from Araukanja, the Skrelling land south of Tawantiinsuuju, and knocked a mug of corn beer (*aka* in the other sense of the word) out of said envoy's hand. Dripping and furious, Da'ud stomped out into the chilly night.

Even in summer, even within thirteen degrees of the equator, early morning in Tawantiinsuuju was cold. Allister Park pulled his llama-wool cloak tighter as he walked through the town's quiet streets.

The exercise made his heart race. He knew a cup of coca-leaf tea would be waiting for him at the foreign ministry. He looked forward to it. Here it was not only legal but, he was finding, necessary.

A goodwain chuffed by, its steam engine all but silent. Its staked bed, much like those of the pickup trucks he had known back in New York, was piled high with ears of corn. Probably taken from a *tamboo*—a storehouse—to feed some hungry village, Park supposed. A third of everything the locals produced went into *tamboos*; Tawantiinsuuju was more socialistic than the Soviet Union ever dreamed of being.

The goodwain disappeared around a corner. The

few men and women on the streets went about their business without looking at Allister Park. In New York—in New Belfast in this world—such an obvious stranger would have attracted staring crowds. Not here.

The town was as alien as the people. It had its own traditions, and cared nothing for the ones Park was used to. Many buildings looked as old as time: huge, square, made from irregular blocks of stone, some of them taller than he was. Only the fresh thatch of their roofs said they had not stood unchanged forever.

Even the newer structures, those with more than one story and tile roofs, were from a similar mold, and one that owed nothing to any architecture sprung from Europe. Vinland's close neighbors among the Skrelling nations, Dakotia especially, had borrowed heavily from the technically more sophisticated newcomers. But Tawantiinsuuju had a thriving civilization of its own by the time European ideas trickled so far south. It took what it found useful—wheels, the alphabet, iron-smelting (it had already known bronze), the horse, and later steam power—and incorporated that into its own way of life, as Japan had in Park's home world.

The foreign ministry was in the district called Kantuutpata, east of Park's lodgings. A *kantuut*, he knew, was a kind of pink flower, and, sure enough, many such grew there in gardens and window boxes. The Tawantiinsuujans were often very literal-minded.

The ministry building was of the newer sort, though its concrete walls were deeply scored to make it look as if it were built of cyclopean masonry. The guards outside, however, looked thoroughly modern: they were dressed in drab fatigues very much like the ones their Vinlandish counterparts wore, and carried pipes—compressed-air guns—at the ready. Their commander studied Park's credentials with scrupulous attention before nodding and waving him into the building.

"Thank you, sir," the judge said politely. The officer nodded again and tied a knot in the *kiipuu* whose threads helped him keep track of incoming visitors.

Inside the ministry building, Park felt on more familiar ground. Bureaucrats behaved similarly the worlds around, be they clerks in a DA's office, clerics, or Tawantiinsuujan diplomatic officials. The measured pace of their steps; their expressions, either self-centered or worried; the sheaves of paper in their hands—all were things Park knew well.

He also knew all about cooling his heels in an outer office. When some flunky of Tjiimpuu's tried to make him do it, he stepped past the fellow. "Sir, the excellent Tjiimpuu will see you when it is convenient for him," the Skrelling protested.

"He'll see me when it's convenient for me."

Tjiimpuu looked up in surprise and annoyance as the door to his sanctum came open. So did the man with him: a solidly built Skrelling of middle years, dressed in a richer version of the gray-brown uniform the ministry guards wore. The two men stood over a map table; the maps, Park saw, were of the area in dispute with the Emirate of the Dar al-Harb.

"Judge Scoglund, you have no business intruding uninvited," Tjiimpuu said coldly.

"No? By your companion, I'd say I have every business. If you are talking with a soldier at the same time you talk with me, that tells me something of how serious you are about my mission." Unlike Da'ud's, Park's nose was not really long enough to stare down, but he did his best.

The soldier said, "I will handle this." Then he surprised Park by shifting to English: "'Let him who wants peace foreready himself for war.' Some old Roman wrote that, Judge Scoglund, in a warly book. It was a rick thock then, and rick it stays in our ain time. Vinland regretted forgetting it last year, nay?"

"You have a point," Park admitted; with any sort

of decent army to overawe potential rebels, the Bretwaldate would not have gone through a spasm of civil war. "But still, ah—"

"I am Kwiismankuu, *apuu maita*—marshal, you would say in your tongue—of Tawantiinsuuju." Kwiismankuu returned to Ketjwa: "Now I will leave this matter in the hands of you two gentlemen, so learned in the arts of peace. If you fail, I will be ready to make good your mistakes." Bowing to both Tjiimpuu and Park, he tramped out of the foreign minister's office.

Park walked over to the table and examined the map Tjiimpuu and Kwiismankuu had been using. Little *kiipuu* figures, with knots drawn in different ways, were scribbled by towns. Park suspected they stood for the sizes of local garrisons, but could not be sure. To the uninitiated, *kiipuus* were worse than Roman numerals.

He noticed how far east the Tawantiinsuujan map put the border: well into what he thought of as Venezuela. Clicking tongue against teeth, he said, "Not even Tjeroogia or Northumbria recognizes your claim to so much territory, and they're the best friends Tawantiinsuuju has."

"We won the land; we will keep it," Tjiimpuu declared, as he had at the reception a few days before. If this was what he thought negotiating was all about, Park thought gloomily, the upcoming sessions would be long, boring, and fruitless.

He tried another tack. "How many folk in the land you conquered in your last war with the Emirate are still Muslims?" he asked.

"A fair number," Tjiimpuu said, adding, "though day by day we work to convert them to the true faith of Patjakamak and the sun."

Thereby endearing yourselves both to the locals and to the Emirate, Park thought. He didn't know whether the Tawantiinsuujans had borrowed the idea of one exclusive religion from Christianity and Islam or thought of it for themselves. Either way, they had their own full measure of missionary zeal.

"Dakotia is neutral in this dispute," Park said, "not least because it borders no state that has a boundary with yours. Dakotian maps"—he drew one out of his leather briefcase to show to Tjiimpuu—"show your border with the Emirate running *so*. This might be a line from which you and Da'ud could at least begin talks."

"And abandon everyone east of it to the Muslims' savagery and false faith?" The foreign minister sounded appalled.

"They feel the same way about your worship of Patjakamak," Park pointed out.

"But they are ignorant and misguided, while we possess the truth."

Park resisted a strong temptation to bend over and pound his forehead against the top of the table. That Tjiimpuu was sincere made matters no better. If anything, it made them worse. A scoundrel was much more amenable to persuasion than someone honestly convinced of the righteousness of his cause.

Sighing, Park said, "I had hoped to sound you out before we began face-to-face talks with Da'ud ibn Tariq. Maybe this will work out better, though. If he is as stubborn as you, the whole world will see neither side is serious about ending your life of war after war."

Tjiimpuu's face turned a darker shade of bronze. "I will speak with you again when these talks begin. Till then, I want nothing to do with you. You are dismissed."

Let the Moors try to claim I'm biased toward Skrellings now, Park thought as he walked out to the street. On the whole, he was more pleased than not over his confrontation with Tjiimpuu. He would have been happier yet, however, had the Tawantiinsuujan

foreign minister shown even the slightest sign of
compromise.

Kuuskoo's streets, nearly deserted an hour before,
now swarmed with life. The locals, quiet and orderly
as usual, all seemed to be going in the same direction. "What are you doing?" Park asked a man walking by.

The man turned, stared in surprise. For all Park
knew, he had never seen a pink-cheeked, sandy-haired
person before; neither travel nor communication
between distant lands was as easy here as in the
judge's native world. Still, the Kuuskan's answer was
polite enough: "We go to the festival of Raimii, of
course."

"Raimii, eh?" That was the most important religious
festival in Tawantiinsuuju, the solemn feast of the sun.
Curiosity got the better of Park, though he knew the
original inhabitant of ex-Bishop Ib Scoglund's body
would not have been caught dead attending such a
pagan rite. *Too bad for old Ib,* he thought. "Maybe
I'll come with you."

The local beamed, shifted the big cud of coca
leaves in his mouth. "I always thought foreigners were
too ignorant and depraved to understand our religion.
Perhaps I was wrong."

Park only grunted in response to that. He walked
with the crowd now, instead of trying to cut across
it. The Skrellings' low-voiced talk grew louder and
more excited as they filed into a large plaza near the
center of Kuuskoo.

The square was as big as two football fields side
by side, maybe bigger. Park tried to work out how
many people it could hold. *Let's see,* he thought,
*assuming each person needs a little more than a
square foot to stand in, if this place is, say, 400 feet
by 300—*

He gave up the arithmetic as a bad job, for he
suddenly saw that the walls of two sides of the square

had a golden chain stretched along them, a little
above man-high. Each link was thicker than his wrist.
Instead of figuring out people, he started reckoning
how many dollars, or even Vinland crowns, that chain
would be worth. A lot of them, for sure.

The Tawantiinsuujan who had told him of the
festival was still beside him. He saw Park staring at
the chain. "This is as nothing, stranger. This is but
the common people's square; we call it Kuusipata. The
Son of the Sun and his kin worship one square over,
in the plaza called Awkaipata. There you would see
gold and silver used in a truly lavish way."

"This is lavish enough for me," Park muttered.
Just one link of that chain, he thought, and he
wouldn't have to worry about money for the rest of
his life. For the first time, he understood what
Francisco Pizarro must have felt when he plundered
the wealth of the Incas back in Park's original world.
He'd always thought Pizarro the champion bandit
of all time, but the sight of so much gold lying
around loose would have made anyone start breathing hard.

Several men strode out onto a raised platform at
the front of the square. Some wore gold and silver
wreaths, and had plates of the precious metals adorn-
ing their tunics. Others used the hides of pumas and
jaguars in place of robes, with their own faces peering
out under the big cats' heads. When one man held
his arms wide, others had to step aside, for his costume included huge condor wings, feathered in black
and white.

One of the priests, for such they were, raised his
hands to the sky. All the people in the square somehow found room to squat. Park was a beat late, and
felt rather like an impostor trying to pretend he
belonged in a marching band. His knees creaked as
he held the squat. He grumpily wondered why the
Tawantiinsuujans couldn't kneel when they worshiped,

like everyone else. That would have been a lot more
comfortable.

The locals tilted their heads back so they looked
up toward the sun. They must have had a trick for
not looking right at it. Park didn't know the trick. He
kept on staring blearily upwards, dazzled and blinking, his eyes full of tears.

The Tawantiinsuujans held their hands up by their
faces and loudly kissed the air. Somehow, again a beat
slow, Park managed to do the same without toppling
over into one of the people by him.

The priests on the platform began to sing a hymn.
Still squatting, the squareful of worshipers joined in.
Everybody—everybody but Park—knew the words.
Some voices were good, others not. Taken all together,
they were impressive, almost hypnotic, the way any
massed singing becomes after a while.

The hymn was long. Park's knees hurt too much
to let him be hypnotized. Back in his New York days,
he'd never thought much of baseball players as ath-
letes, but now he started feeling no small respect for
what catchers went through.

At last the hymn ended. People stood up. Another
hymn started. When it was done, the Tawantiinsuujans
squatted again. So, stifling a groan, did Allister Park.
Yet another hymn began.

By the time the service was finally done, Park felt
as though he'd caught a double-header. He also des-
perately needed to find a public jakes.

"Is that not a magnificent festival?" asked the
Skrelling who'd inveigled him into going to the square
of Kuusipata.

Well, maybe it hadn't happened exactly like that,
but at the moment Park's memory was inclined to be
selective. "Most impressive," he said, lying through
his teeth.

"Raimii will go on for nine days in all," the local
told him, "each day's worship being different from the

last. Will you come to Kuusipata tomorrow, your foreign excellency?"

"If I can," Park said, that seeming a more politic response than *not on your life*. After nine days of squatting, he was convinced he would walk like an arthritic chimp forevermore. Then something he had noticed but not thought about during the service sank home. "Nine days!" he exclaimed. "I saw no books for prayer among you. Do you remember all your songs and such?"

"Of course we do," the Skrelling said proudly. "They are graven on our hearts. Only people whose faith is cold have to remind themselves of it. Books for prayer, indeed!" The very idea offended him.

Park was thoughtful as he filed toward the edge of the square. Reading was obviously easier and more trustworthy than memorizing, and therefore, to him anyway, obviously more desirable for keeping records straight. The Tawantiinsuujans, though, as he had already discovered in other contexts, did not think the same way he did.

Maybe that was what made him notice the goodwain parked near a wall fifty yards or so beyond the edge of the square. In New York, or even in New Belfast, he would not have given it a second glance: parking spaces were where you found them. In Kuuskoo, though, it surprised him. It impeded the flow of people coming out of Kuusipata, and that was unlike the orderly folk here.

The locals must have thought the same. A man climbed up onto the running board, reached out to unlatch the driver's-side door so he could get in and move the truck out of the way.

The door wasn't locked. Few were, in law-abiding Thwantiinsuuju. He yanked it open.

The goodwain blew up.

Park felt the blast more than he heard it. The next thing he knew, he was on the ground. The cobbles were hard and bumpy. As if from very far away, he heard people shrieking.

He shook his head, trying to clear it, and scrambled to his feet. The carnage closer to the goodwain was appalling. He shivered as he saw how lucky he was. Only the bodies of the people in front of him had shielded him from the full force of the explosion.

Half a dozen men sprang up from behind the wall, which was of ancient megalithic stonework and hence undamaged by the blast. For a moment, Park thought they'd got up there to direct help to the writhing victims near them. Then he saw they all had air rifles. They raised them to their shoulders, started shooting into the crowd.

Allister Park had seen combat as a young man in his own world, and again during his brief tenure as Vinland's assistant secretary of war. At the sound of the first sharp *pop*, he threw himself flat. He knocked over the person behind him. They fell together.

The men with guns shouted in unison as they fired. Park took a moment to notice, first that the shouts were not in Ketjwa, then that he understood them anyhow. *"Allahu akbar!"* the gunmen cried. "God is great! *Allahu akbar!"*

Someone screamed, right in Park's ear. Only then did he realize he was lying on a woman. Her fist pounded his shoulder. "Let me go!" she yelled. She tried to push him off her.

"No! Stay down!" By some miracle, he remembered to speak Ketjwa instead of English. As if to punctuate his words, a bullet felled a man standing not three paces away. The woman screamed again, and shuddered, but seemed to decide Park was protecting rather than attacking her. She quit struggling beneath him.

Around them, the noise of the crowd changed from horror to animal fury. People surged toward the men on the wall. Had the gunmen been carrying the

automatic weapons Park's world knew, they would
have massacred their assailants. With air rifles that
had to be pumped up after every shot, they slowed
but could not stop the outraged mob.

"Allahu akbar!" Park lifted his head just in time
to see the last gunman raise a defiant fist and jump
down in back of the wall. The locals scrambled over
it to give chase. One was shot, but more kept on.
Others, men and women both, began to tend the
scores of injured people near the twisted wreckage
of the goodwain.

Park cautiously got to his feet. After a few seconds,
he was convinced no more gun-toting fanatics were
going to spring from nowhere. He stooped to help
up the woman he had flattened when the shooting
started.

"Thank you," she said with some dignity, accepting his hand. "I am sorry I screamed at you. You saw
the danger from those—madmen"—she shivered—
"before almost anyone else."

"I am glad you are not hurt," Park said. For the
first time, he had the leisure to take a look at her.
She was, he guessed, only a few years younger than
he; one or two white threads ran through the midnight mane that hung almost to her waist. She was
attractive, in the long-faced, high-cheekboned local
fashion. Her mantle and brightly striped skirt were
of soft, fine wools.

The derby she'd been wearing was crushed beyond
repair. She picked it up, made a wry face, threw it
down again. Then she studied Allister Park with as
much interest, or perhaps curiosity, as he showed her.
"You are not one of us," she said. "Why were you
at the festival of Raimii?"

"To see what it was like," he answered honestly.
"I probably will never be in Kuuskoo again; while I
am here, I want to learn and see as much as I can."

She considered that, nodded. "Did the beauty of

the service incline you toward the worship of the sun and Patjakamak?"

Despite wearing an ex-bishop's body, Park wished people would stop asking him loaded religious questions. He temporized: "The services were very beautiful, ah—"

"My name is Kuurikwiljor," she said.

Park gave his own or, rather, Ib Scoglund's name, then said, "Kuurikwiljor—'golden star.' That's very pretty. So, by the way, are you." He played that game almost as automatically as he breathed; his attitude toward women was decidedly pragmatic. But just as genuine a sense of duty made him look around to make sure he was not needed here before he asked, "Where are you going now? May I walk there with you, so you will feel safe?"

Kuurikwiljor, he saw with approval, looked toward the wounded herself before she answered. With the usual Tawantiinsuujan efficiency, teams of uniformed medics were already on the scene. They slapped on bandages, set broken bones, and loaded the worst hurt onto stretchers for more extensive treatment elsewhere. They did not seem to need any unskilled help.

Park also saw Kuurikwiljor eye him appraisingly. He did not mind that; he was sensible enough to think well of good sense in others. Whatever Kuurikwiljor saw must have satisfied her, for she said, "Thank you. I am staying at my brother's house, in the district of Puumatjupan."

That district, Park knew, was in the southern part of the city. With Kuurikwiljor following, he started in that direction. "On to the house of your brother," he declared. He thought he sounded rather grand, but Kuurikwiljor giggled.

He mentally reviewed what he'd just said. "Oh, hell," he muttered in English. Then he switched back to Ketjwa, more careful Ketjwa this time: "I mean the house of your *waukej*, not your *toora*." He'd tripped himself up by echoing Kuurikwiljor; *waukej* was the word men used for *brother,* while *toora* was reserved for women.

"That's better," Kuurikwiljor said. "You don't speak badly. From what I've heard, most foreigners would never have noticed their mistake, Ib Scogljund."

In his turn, he tried to get her to say the "l" in his name without pronouncing it as if it were "ly." He had no luck; the simple "l" sound did not exist in Ketjwa. After teasing her a little, he gave up. "Never mind. It sounds charming as you say it."

"But I should be right," Kuurikwiljor said seriously. "Ib Scog—Scog—Scogljund. Oh, a pestilence!" They both laughed.

The fumbling with languages and names helped break the ice between them. They talked all the way down to Kuurikwiljor's brother's house. Park learned she was a childless widow. That sort of thing was only too common in this world, which knew less of medicine—and a lot less about immunization—than his own. Kuurikwiljor sounded suitably impressed about Park's reasons for coming to Tawantiinsuuju.

"We need to find some way to live at peace with the Emir," she said. "Either that, or wipe his country from the face of the earth. Sometimes I think Muslims are viler than the dog-eating Wankas. The way those terrible men took advantage of the accident to work even more harm on us—" She shook her head. "My mantle is all splashed with blood."

Truly, Park thought, this world was more naïve than the one from which he'd come. As gently as he could, he said, "Kuurikwiljor, I don't think that was an accident. I think they made that truck blow up. I think they were waiting for it to blow up, so they would have a confused and frightened crowd to shoot at."

She stared at him. "What a dreadful thing to say!" But after walking a few steps in silence, she went on, "That does make sense, doesn't it? They would hardly be waiting with guns just in case there was an explosion."

"Hardly," Park agreed. He let it go at that; telling her the Tawantiinsuujans were little kinder to Muslims would have accomplished nothing.

Her brother's house was a large, impressive stone building next to one of the streams that defined the boundaries of Puumatjupan. Servants came rushing out when they saw Kuurikwiljor. They exclaimed over her bedraggled state and, once they found Park had helped her come home safe, praised him to the skies and pressed llama meat, cornmeal mush, and *aka* on him.

Before long, he found himself meeting Kuurikwiljor's brother, a stocky, solemn man of about his own age named Pauljuu. "Most kind of you, foreign sir, and most generous," Pauljuu said. "I know you sought none, but let me reward you for the service you have done my family." He drew a heavy gold signet ring from his right thumb, tried to hand it to Park.

"Thank you, but I must say no," Park told him. As Pauljuu's face clouded over, Park went on quickly: "I am a judge. How will people say I judge fairly if I take presents from one side?"

"Ah." Pauljuu nodded. "I have heard it said that all foreigners will do anything for gold. I am glad to see it is not so."

"Any saying that claims all of some group will do a particular thing is not to be trusted," Park observed.

"Spoken like a judge. If not gold, then, how may I express my thanks?" Pauljuu asked. "You should know my father Ruuminjavii is *kuuraka*—governor— of the province of Sausa, to the north. I need not stint."

Park bowed. "As I say, I am a judge. I will not, I must not, take your gifts." He hesitated for a moment, then said, "Still, if you would not mind me

coming to see your sister—" he carefully used the
right word, not wanting to embarrass himself "—again,
that would be very kind."

Pauljuu glanced toward Kuurikwiljor, who had been
sitting quietly while the two men talked. (In some
ways, Park thought, Tawantiinsuuju was positively
Victorian. Too bad no one here had any idea what
Victorian meant.) Kuurikwiljor nodded. "As it pleases
her and pleases you, I have no objection," Pauljuu
said.

Park bowed again to him, then to Kuurikwiljor.
"Thank you both," he said. "Have you a wirecaller
here?" In this world, the telephone had been invented
in Northumbria; its Ketjwa name was a literal translation of what English speakers called it here.

"Of course. Ask for the house of Ruuminjavii's son.
The man who connects calls will make sure it goes
through," Pauljuu said.

"Good. I will call soon. May I also use the wirecaller now, to let my own people know I am all right?
They will be wondering after me."

"Of course," Pauljuu said again. "Come this way."

He stood up to take Park to wherever he kept the
phone. Park rose too. As he followed Pauljuu out,
Kuurikwiljor called after him, "Thank you for looking after me so." Fortunately, Pauljuu's house had high
doors and tall ceilings. Otherwise, Park thought, he
was so swelled up with pride that he might have
bumped his head on them.

He let Pauljuu place the call for him. Before long,
he heard Eric Dunedin's reedy voice on the other end
of the line. "Hallow—uh, Judge Scoglund!" Monkey-
face exclaimed. "Are you hale? Where have you been?
With the burg all bestirred by the goodwain blast, I
was afeared after you!"

"I'm fine, Eric, and among friends." Park repeated
himself in Ketjwa for Pauljuu's benefit, then returned
to English: "I'll be home soon. See you then. Take

care of yourself. 'Bye." He put the mouthpiece back into the big square box on the wall, said his goodbyes to Pauljuu, and started back to the small house he and Dunedin were sharing.

He whistled as he walked north through the streets of Kuuskoo. He hadn't met a woman like Kuurikwiljor since—since he came to this world, he thought, and that was a goodly while now. She was pretty, had some brains, and seemed to think well of him. He liked the combination, liked it a lot.

Of course, he reminded himself as he walked a little farther, one reason she interested him so much was that he hadn't had much to do with women since he'd come here. Celtic Christian bishops were depressingly celibate, and he'd stayed discreet even after he left the church. Judges didn't have to avoid women, but they did need to keep away from scandal.

Yes, Park thought, if Kuurikwiljor were just one of the girls I was seeing, I might think she was pretty ordinary. But at the moment, she was the only girl he was seeing. That automatically made her special. Park grinned a wolfly grin. He'd enjoy whatever happened, and keep his wits about him while he did so.

Keeping his wits about him meant taking a wide detour around the plaza of Kuusipata. He hadn't had a good look at the gunmen there. For all he knew, they could have been converted Skrellings. Even so, the locals, especially those near the square, were liable to be jumpy about anyone who looked foreign. Better safe, he thought.

He never found out whether his precautions were needed. He did get home safe and sound, which was the idea. Tawantijnsuujan doors had neither knockers nor bells. A polite person here clapped his hands outside a house and waited to be admitted. At the moment, Park didn't care whether he was polite by local standards. He pounded on the door.

From the speed with which Dunedin opened it, he must have been waiting just inside. His welcoming smile turned into a grimace of dismay when he saw his master. "Hallow Patrick's shinbone!" he gasped. "What befell you?"

"What are you talking about?" Park said irritably. "I'm downrightly fine—nothing wrong with me at all. I mistrust I need a bath, but that's no big dealing. Why are you looking at me as if I just grew a twoth head?"

Dunedin's smile returned, hesitantly. "You do, ah, sound like your ain self, Judge Scoglund. Maybe you ock to peer into the spickle-glass, though—"

Park let his servant lead him to the mirror. His jaw dropped as he stood in front of it. He looked as though he'd been through a war—on the losing side. He was dirty, his cloak was ripped, and there was blood both on it and on the side of his face.

He'd seen how bedraggled Kuurikwiljor was after the truck blew up, yet never thought to wonder whether he was the same. As a matter of fact, he wasn't the same. He was worse. "It's not *my* blood," he said, feeling like a fool.

"Praise God and the hallows for that," Dunedin said. "Now shall I get the bath you spoke of ready?"

"Aye, put the kettle on," Park said. Kuuskoo had cold running water, but not hot, and cold water here was *cold* water. The judge looked at himself again. He was *filthy*. "I'm near lured into not waiting for it."

"When you were bishop, you'd have been well bethock for mortifying your flesh so," Dunedin said. "Shall I draw you a cold bath, then?"

"Hell, no! I'm not bishop any more, thank God, and my flesh came too damn close to being mortified for good this afternoon, thank you very much."

Dunedin's eyes got big. Hearing such language from his boss could still shock him, though he knew someone new was living in that formerly saintly brain. "I'll get the kettle filled," he said.

Park felt a prick of guilt. Turning Monkey-face's wrinkled cheeks red was a cheap thrill. "Thanks, Eric," he said. "While you're back there, why don't you see if our hosts have given us anything stronger than *aka*? If they have, find a couple of glasses and join me."

Tawantiinsuujan whiskey tasted like raw corn liquor. Park had never gotten drunk in a bathtub before. It was fun. After a couple of protests for effect, Dunedin got drunk too. Park taught him "Ninety-Nine Bottles of Beer on the Wall." He liked it. They got louder with every bottle that fell.

After some considerable while, Monkey-face asked: "Ish—is that forty-two bottles left, or forty-one?"

"I—*hic!*—can't bethink." Park tried to find an appropriately judicial solution. "We'll jusht have to start over."

But Dunedin was sprawled against the side of the tub, snoring softly. He was almost as wet as his master; a good deal of splashing had accompanied the singing. The water, Park noticed, was cold. He wondered how long it had been that way. He started to sing solo, discovered his teeth were chattering. It had been cold for a while, then.

He pulled the pottery stopper from the drain, climbed out of the tub. "Eric?" he said. Dunedin kept on snoring. Park dragged him to his bed. Then he staggered into his own bedroom and collapsed.

The next morning, altitude turned what would have been a bad hangover into a killer. Coca tea helped a little, but not enough. Park wished for aspirins and black coffee. Wishing failed to produce them.

Eric Dunedin was still out like a light. Envying him, Park got dressed and braved the vicious sunlight outside as he walked over to the foreign ministry.

The handful of guards outside the building had been replaced by a platoon of troopers. A good many of them were standing in a tight circle around someone. They waved their arms and shouted at whoever it was.

At the moment, Park disliked shouting on general principles. "What's going on here?" he said. Then he saw for himself. The man in the midst of the angry Tawantiinsuujan soldiers was Da'ud ibn Tariq.

Heads turned his way. "Another foreigner," one of the troopers growled. He lifted his air rifle, not quite pointing it at Park.

His headache made Park even more irascible than usual. "Go ahead," he said scornfully. "Shoot me and the emirate's ambassador both, why don't you? See if Tawantiinsuuju has a friend left in the world the moment after you do."

The officer who had noted—and knotted—Park's previous arrival on the *kiipuu* recognized him now. "It is the judge of the International Court," he said. "Stand aside. Let him by."

"Let Da'ud ibn Tariq come too," Park said. "I think the minister Tjiimpuu will be interested in seeing him."

"Exactly what I've been trying to tell them," Da'ud said. "I was summoned here by the minister himself."

"Maybe we don't care about that, murderer," a soldier said. "Maybe we'd sooner cut out your guts with a *tuumii-knife*." The Tawantiinsuujans' ceremonial knife had a half-moon blade on a long handle. They did not practice human sacrifice any more (even Aztecia had given it up), not officially, anyhow. But they remembered.

"Stop that!" Park yelled, and flinched at the sound of his own voice. "You are not at war with the Emirate of the Dar al-Harb. Even if you were, your own embassy in Ramiah may answer for how you treat

Da'ud. So let him come with me, and stop acting like dog-eating Wanka fools."

Park's gibe struck home. All the other tribes in the Tawantiinsuujan empire mocked the Wankas for their addiction to cynophagy. The officer said grudgingly, "The judge may be right. Our overlords will treat the wretch as he deserves. Let him through."

Sullenly, the soldiers obeyed. One of them slammed the big trapezoidal double doors behind the two foreigners, so hard that Park thought the top of his head would come off. He rather hoped it would.

"I am in your debt, Judge Scoglund," Da'ud said in English, bowing deeply.

"It's nothing. I was just trying to get them to shut up."

The Moor glanced at him. One elegant eyebrow rose. "Perhaps I should backpay the debt by talking you into ontaking Islam. That I would seek to do anyhow, for the good of your ghost. Now, though, it strikes me your body would also be the better for having wine-bibbing forbidden it."

"It wasn't wine, and it's not your dealing," Park snapped.

"Seeking to win a good man to Islam is the dealing of any Muslim," Da'ud said. Park was about to snarl at him when he went on smoothly, "But here we are at Tjiimpuu's door, so let us backturn to Ketjwa and perhaps speak of this another time."

"You were not bidden to come here, Judge Scoglund," the foreign minister's secretary said when he saw Park.

"Yes, I know, but here I am, and what are you going to do about it?" Park followed Da'ud ibn Tariq into Tjiimpuu's private office. Having failed once already, the secretary didn't do anything about it.

To Park's surprise, Tjiimpuu didn't fuss about his walking in. In fact, a grim smile briefly lit the foreign minister's face. "Well met, Judge Scoglund," he said. "Now the world will have an impartial account of the latest outrage the Emirate of the Dar al-Harb has visited upon us."

"The Emirate has done nothing against Tawantiinsuuju," Da'ud said. "I presume you are referring to yesterday's explosion here."

"And the gunmen who set it off and took advantage of the terror it caused to kill even more," Tjiimpuu said. "Ninety-one people are dead at last count, more than three hundred wounded. Two of the murderers survived being captured. Both are Muslims; both say they and the rest wanted to strike a blow against the true holy worship of Patjakamak and the sun."

"Heaven will receive our dead, as it receives all who fall in the *jihad*," Da'ud replied, "but they did not act by the will of the Emir, Allah's peace be upon him. The Emirate is blameless."

"I do not believe you," Tjiimpuu ground out. "Nor does the Son of the Sun. This looks to be—this *is*— all of a piece with the murder and banditry your people engage in throughout the border provinces. We can tolerate it no more." The foreign minister breathed heavily. "I am sorry, Judge Scoglund, but your presence in Kuuskoo is no longer required. It will be war."

"Wait!" Allister Park said immediately, then realized he had no idea what to tell Tjiimpuu to wait for. He thought frantically. "If, ah, if the Emir—without admitting guilt—expresses his sorrow for those killed at the Raimii festival, will that not show enough, ah, good feeling from him for talks to go on?"

Tjiimpuu frowned. "The Emir Hussein has never been known for his compassion."

"That is not so," Da'ud said at once. "His Highness feels more compassion for pagans than for Muslims, in fact, as he knows that when pagans die they have only the pangs of hell to anticipate."

"Then let him say so," Park urged.

"Such a statement, were it to come; would surely be looked on with pleasure by the Son of the Sun," Tjiimpuu agreed. "If you think it might arrive, Da'ud ibn Tariq, I will urge Maita Kapak—" he shaded his eyes for a moment "—to delay the declaration."

"I do not know whether the Emir would make such a statement," Da'ud said. "In any case, I do not intend to seek it of him."

"What? Why the hell not?" Park exclaimed, startled out of both his diplomatic manners and his Ketjwa; he got no satisfaction from cursing in a tongue he had just learned.

"Because of this." Da'ud drew a rolled sheet of paper from inside his robe, handed it with a sober flourish to Tjiimpuu. When the Tawantiinsuujan undid the ribbon that held it closed, Park saw the sinuous characters of Arabic. He was learning to speak that tongue, but could read it only very slowly.

Tjiimpuu, plainly, had no problem with it. He looked up in sharp surprise at Da'ud. "This is not a forgery you made up this past evening after you knew I had summoned you?"

"By Allah I swear it is not." Da'ud turned to Allister Park, explaining, "Last night I received a courier dispatch from Ramiah. Not far outside the city, a mosque was put to the torch at the hour of evening prayer some days ago. Many are dead, how many no one knows. On a wall nearby was scrawled the name 'Patjakamak.'"

"Jesus," Park said. He supposed both Tjiimpuu and Da'ud thought he was swearing by his own god. He was swearing, all right, but not in that sense of the word.

"I will take this to the Son of the Sun," Tjiirnpuu said slowly.

"Do so," Da'ud agreed. "We have as much cause

for war as you. More, since you claim lands rightfully ours."

"They are ours," Tjiimpuu said.

"Wait!" Park said again. "This whole business of the lands has been stewing for a generation. A few days more won't matter, one way or another. What we need to do right now is to get each of you to stop trying to harm the other over what you find holy. Maybe knowing how much even a few zealots can hurt you will make both sides think twice."

"I will take your words to the Son of the Sun," Tjiimpuu said. It was as big a concession as Park had seen him make. From the way Da'ud ibn Tariq bowed, it might have been as big a concession as he'd seen, too.

He and Park left the foreign minister's office together. Tjiimpuu's secretary smiled nastily. "Is it to be war?" he asked, as if he already knew the answer.

"No," Park told him, and watched his face fall.

The judge and ambassador walked out toward the doorway. Park tried his halting Arabic: "A lesson here."

"Ah? And would you deign to enlighten this ignorant one, O sage of wisdom?" Flowery in any language, Da'ud grew downright grandiloquent when using his own.

As usual, Park spoke plainly: "Keep your holy warriors in line, and maybe the other fellow will too." Not quite the Golden Rule the real Ib Scoglund would have preached, he thought, but a step in that direction, anyhow.

"Wisdom indeed, and fit for the Emir's ear," Da'ud said, "save only this: what if those who delight in fighting the *jihad* refuse to be held in check so?"

"Who is stronger then?" Park asked in turn. "The Emir, or them?" Da'ud gave his beard a thoughtful tug and did not answer.

Under the hostile glare of the soldiers outside the foreign ministry, the two men went their separate ways. Park hurried home to take care of Eric Dunedin, who, as he'd thought, still had a case of the galloping jimjams.

"You ockn't to be tending me," Monkey-face protested feebly. "I'm your thane, not the other way round."

"Oh, keep quiet," Park said. "Here, drink some more of this."

Coca-leaf tea, soup, and, finally, a small shot of Tawantiinsuujan moonshine in tomato juice restored Dunedin to a mournful semblance of life. Park had a makeshift Bloody Mary himself; he figured he'd earned it. Thus fortified, he picked up the telephone receiver. "Whom are you wirecalling?" Dunedin asked.

"Keep quiet," Park said again. He shifted to Ketjwa as the operator came on the line: "Could you please connect me to the house of Pauljuu, son of Ruuminjavii, in the district of Puumatjupan?"

When he showed up at Pauljuu's house that evening, Park was carrying a large bouquet of pink *kantuuts*. He didn't know if flowers were customary here, but didn't think they'd hurt. From the way the maid who opened the door exclaimed over them, he'd guessed right.

Kuurikwiljor exclaimed over them too, and had a servant fill a bowl with water so they could float in it. "Very lovely," she said. "Such an unusual gift." So they weren't customary, he thought. They were a hit anyhow. In a way, that was even better. It got him points for originality.

A moment later, he had to risk them: "Where shall we go?" he asked. "What shall we do? This is your city, not mine." This world had never invented movies, eliminating one obvious way for couples to spend decorous time together.

"We could walk the walls of Saxawaman," Kuurikwiljor suggested.

"The old fortress?" Park said, surprised. She nodded. He shrugged. It wasn't what he'd had in mind, but— "Why not?"

Before they could walk Saxawaman's walls, they had to walk to Saxawaman, which lay on a hill north and west of the built-up area of Kuuskoo. Park let Kuurikwiljor take the lead; to him, one poorly lit street seemed much like another.

"You don't have many robbers here, do you?" he asked, impressed by the way she confidently strode ahead. In his New York or Vinland's New Belfast, he would have been nervous about strolling around like this after dark.

But Kuurikwiljor only answered, "No, not many," as if the idea that things could be otherwise had never entered her mind. Park suspected it hadn't. She was lucky, he thought.

A path zigzagged up the hillside to the fortress. Park puffed along after Kuurikwiljor. He'd long since put Ib Scoglund's body on a calisthenics program, but no lowland man could match someone equally fit and native to this altitude. When he finally struggled up a stone stairway to the top of a wall, he panted, "Could we—rest—on the walls of Saxawaman?"

"Of course," Kuurikwiljor said. To his relief, his admission of weakness did not make her scornful. She went on, "The view is magnificent, is it not?"

"Hmm? Why, so it is." Kuuskoo lay spread out before them. Flickering torches and the occasional brighter, steadier glow of electric light defined its irregular grid of streets. One square in the northern part of the city was especially well-lit. Park pointed to it. "What's that?"

"The royal square, the square of Awkaipata," Kuurikwiljor answered.

"I should have guessed." If anyone wanted such lavish illumination, it would be the king and his court.

Park turned. They had ascended only the lowest of Saxawaman's walls. Other curtains of unmortared stone, pale in the starlight, climbed the hill behind them. And beyond those walls were the greater stone ramparts of the Andes, black against the sky.

The sky— In the north and overhead lay the constellations with which Park was familiar, though here they looked upside down. But to the south the stars were new to him, and made strange patterns. And there were so many of them! In Kuuskoo's thin, clear air, they seemed almost close enough to reach out and touch.

Kuuskoo's air was also chilly. Park had been sweating as he went up the stone stairs, but a few minutes of quietly looking about were plenty to make him start shivering. "Now I see why you wanted to *walk* the walls," he said, matching action to word. "We'd freeze if we just stood here."

"This is a fine mild night," Kuurikwiljor protested; but she fell in step beside him. "Are all people from Vinland so sensitive to cold?"

"It's like I told your brother: I don't think all people from anywhere are any one thing. In Vinland, though, most people would not think this night is mild."

"How odd," Kuurikwiljor said. "In what other small ways are our folk different, I wonder? Color is plain at first glance, and faith soon becomes clear, but I never would have thought we might find different kinds of weather comfortable."

"Tawantiinsuuju has provinces that get much hotter than Vinland, and stay hot the whole year around," Park said. "How do people from those lands like it here?"

Kuurikwiljor laughed. "They shake all the time, and wrap themselves up in blankets even at noon. I did not think you were so delicate."

"I'm not, but it's—" Park paused, trying to work out how to say it's *a matter of degree, not kind* in

Ketjwa. He was still thinking when he heard someone kick a pebble not too far away. "What was that?"
His fists bunched. Kuuskoo had to have a few foot-
pads, and no one was close by to hear him if he
needed to shout for help.

But Kuurikwiljor laughed again. "Just someone
else—or rather, some two else—walking the walls of
Saxawaman. Did you think we were the only ones?"

"I hadn't thought about it at all." Now Park did,
hard. So she'd taken him to the local lovers' lane, had
she? In that case . . . His arm slid round her waist.
She didn't pull back. In fact, she moved closer. That
was doubly nice. Not only was she a pleasant arm-
ful of girl, she was also warm.

He kissed her. She put her arms around his neck.
When at last they separated, she stared up at him,
eyes wide and wondering. "You really do still care for
me, knowing I am a widow?"

"Yes, I care for you," Park said. "And what does
your being a widow have to do with anything? I'm
very sorry you lost your husband, but—"

Kuurikwiljor's soft, breathy laugh made him stop.
She said, "Another of those small differences between
your people and mine, I see. In Tawantiinsuuju, most
widows stay chaste, and most men want little to do
with them. Indeed, if I had children it would be
against the law for me to marry again."

"That's a foolish law," Park blurted. Then, lawyer-
like, he hedged: "At least, it would be in Vinland. As
you say, our people are not the same."

He noted that she'd told him she wasn't forbidden to remarry, which probably meant she wanted to.
He thought marriage a fine institution—for people
who liked living in institutions. That didn't mean he
had anything against some of its concomitants. He
kissed Kuurikwiljor again; she responded with an
ardor he found gratifying. But when he slid a hand
under her tunic, she twisted away.

"It's fine to feel cared for, wanted," she said, "but I do not give myself to a man I've known only a day. If that is all you want from me, better you should find a *pampairuuna*, a woman of the marketplace."

"Of course it's not all," Park protested, hoping he sounded indignant. "I like your company, and talking with you. But—forgive me, because I do not know how to say this in fancy talk—you are a widow, and you know what goes on between men and women."

"Yes, I do." Kuurikwiljor did not sound angry, but she did not sound like someone who was going to change her mind, either: "I also know that what goes on between men and women, as you say, is better when they are people to each other, not just bodies. Otherwise a *pampairuuna* would be honored, not scorned."

"Hmm," was all Park said to that. She had a point, although he was not about to admit it out loud. After a moment, he went on, "I would like to know you better. May I call on you again?"

She smiled at him. "I hope you will, for I also want to know you. Now, though, I think we should go back to my brother's house. It has grown cooler."

"All right." Feeling as if he were back in high school, Park walked her home.

Just around the corner from Pauljuu's house, where none of his people could see them, she stopped and kissed him again, as warmly as she had up on Saxawaman. Then she walked on to the door. "Do call," she said as she clapped for a servant to open it.

"I will," he said. "Thanks." Just then the door opened. Kuurikwiljor went in.

Allister Park headed back toward the house where he was staying. As he walked, he wondered (purely in a hypothetical way, he told himself) how to go about finding a *pampairuuna*.

✧   ✧   ✧

For the next several days, Kuuskoo stayed quiet.
Park met with Tjiimpuu and Da'ud ibn Tariq, both
alone and together. In diplomatic language, the joint
discussions were frank and serious: which is to say,
agreement was nowhere to be found. At least, however, the two men did seem willing to keep talking.
To Park, whose job was heading off a war, that looked
like progress.

He enjoyed his wirecaller talks with Kuurikwiljor
much more. They went out to a restaurant that she
praised for serving old-style Tawantiinsuujan food.
Park left it convinced that the old Tawantiinsuujans
had had a dull time.

"What do they call this dried meat?" he asked,
gnawing on the long, tough strip.

"*Ktjarkii,*" she answered. Her teeth, apparently, had
no trouble with it.

"Jerky!" he said. "We have the same word in
English. How strange." With a little thought, he realized it wasn't so strange. The English he'd grown up
with must have borrowed the term from his world's
Quechua. For that matter, he didn't know whether
jerky was a word in the Bretwaldate of Vinland. *Have
to ask Monkey-face,* he thought.

The dinner also featured *tjuunjuu*—powdered
potatoes preserved by exposure to frost and sun. It
was as bland as it sounded.

Afterwards, they went walking on the walls of Saxawaman. Park, whose judgment in such matters was
acute, could tell he was making progress. If he pushed
matters, he thought Kuurikwiljor would probably yield.
He decided not to push. Next time, he figured, she'd
come around of her own accord. That would keep
her happier in the long run, not leave her feeling
used.

By the time he got home that night, he'd forgotten all about asking Eric Dunedin about *ktjarkii*. He
remembered the next morning, but Dunedin was still

asleep. Park never had got fully used to the idea of having a servant. He got dressed, made his own breakfast, and left for the foreign ministry with Monkey-face still snoring.

Tjiimpuu was in a towering fury when he arrived. The Tawantiinsuujan hurled two sheets of paper onto the desk in front of him, slammed his open hand down on them with a noise like a thunderclap. "Patjakamak curse the Muslims for ever and ever!" he shouted. "As you asked, we showed restraint—and here are the thanks we got for it."

"What's gone wrong?" Park asked with a sinking feeling.

"They like their little joke, making goodwains into bombs," Tjiimpuu ground out. "Here is one report from Kiitoo in the north, another from Kahamarka closer to home. Deaths, injuries, destruction. Well, we will visit them all on the Emirate of the Dar al-Harb, I promise you that. Nor will you talk me out of war this time, either."

Park sat down to do just that. After a couple of hours, he even began to think he was getting somewhere. Then a real thunderclap smote Kuuskoo. Tjiimpuu's windows rattled. Faintly, far in the distance, Park heard screams begin.

Tjiimpuu's face might have been carved from stone. "You may leave now," he said. "Your mission here is ended. When I have time, I will arrange for your transportation back to Vinland. Now, though, I must help the Son of the Sun prepare us to fight."

Seeing he had no chance of changing the foreign minister's mind, Park perforce went home. He was not in the best of moods as he walked along. Here he'd been called in to stop a war from breaking out, and it had blown up in his face. What with the Muslim zealots using trucks as terror devices, that was almost literally true. Even so, he'd failed his first major test. The other, more senior, judges on the

International Court might well hesitate to give him another.

Dunedin gaped at him when he slammed the front door to announce his arrival. "Judge Scoglund! Why are you here so soon?" His servant's wrinkled cheeks turned red. "And why did you not rouse me when you got up this morn? It's my job to help you, after all."

"Sorry," Park said. He grinned at Monkey-face: "But you looked like such a little angel, sleeping there with your thumb in your mouth, I didn't have the heart to wake you."

"I do not sleep with my thumb in my mouth!" Park had never heard Eric Dunedin yell so loud.

"I know, I know, I know." When he had Dunedin partway placated, Park went on, "If you feel you have to make like a thane, why don't you run back into the kitchen and fetch me a jug of *aka*? I'm home early because it looks like Tawantiinsuuju and the Emirate are damned well going to fick a war regardless of what I think about it. Fick 'em all, I say."

Monkey-face brought back two jugs of *aka*. Park gave him a quizzical look. "You're learning, old boy, you're learning." Each man unstoppered a jug. Park sat down, half-emptied his with one long pull.

For the first time since he'd been named judge of the International Court, he gave some thought to visiting Joseph Noggle once he got back to Vinland. Maybe whoever was currently inhabiting his body hadn't made too bad a botch of things while he'd been gone. . . .

He put that aside for further consideration: nothing he could do about it now anyhow. He finished the *aka*, got up and walked over to the wirecaller. "Get me the house of Pauljuu, son of Ruuminjavii, please." If Tjiimpuu was going to kick him out at any moment, he might as well have a pleasant memory to take home. A servant answered the phone. "May I please speak to the widow Kuurikwiljor? This is Judge Scoglund."

"Tonight?" Kuurikwiljor exclaimed when Park asked her out. "This is so sudden." She paused. Park crossed his fingers. Then she said, "But I'd be delighted. When will you come? Around sunset? Fine, I'll see you then. Goodbye."

Park was whistling as he hung up. *Aka* made the present look rosier, and Kuurikwiljor gave him something to look forward to.

He was going through his wardrobe late that afternoon, deciding what to wear, when someone clapped outside the front door. "Answer it, will you?" he called to Dunedin. Before Monkey-face got to the door, though, whoever was out there started pounding on it.

That didn't sound good, Park thought. Maybe Pauljuu was worried about his sister's virtue. Even as the idea crossed his mind, Dunedin stuck his head into the bedroom and said, "There's a big Skrelling outside who wants to see you."

"I don't much want to see him," Park said. He went out anyhow, looking for something that would make a good blunt instrument as he did so. But it was not Pauljuu standing there. "Ankowaljuu!"

"Whom were you outlooking?" The *tukuuii riikook* fixed Park with the knowing, cynical gaze he remembered from the ship.

"Never mind. Come in. I'm glad to see you." Aware that he was babbling, Park took a deep breath and made himself slow down. He waved Ankowaljuu to a chair. "Here, sit down and tell me what I can do for you."

"You came here to stop a war, not so?" the Skrelling demanded.

"Aye, I did, and a fat lot of good it's done me— or anybody else," Park said bitterly. "Tjiimpuu just gave me my walking papers." Seeing Ankowaljuu frown, he explained: "He told me my sending here was done, and that I would have to backgo to Vinland: the Son of the Sun would order war outspoken against the Emirate of the Dar al-Harb."

"That's sooth," Ankowaljuu said. "He's done it. But then, you never got a chance to set the whole dealing before Maita Kapak himself." He made the ritual eye-shielding gesture.

"Before Maita Kapak?" Park was too upset to bother with Tawantiinsuujan niceties—if Ankowaljuu didn't like it, too bad. "How could I go before Maita Kapak? The way the Son of the Sun is hedged round with mummery, it's a wonder any of his wives get to see him." He realized he might have gone too far. "Forgive me, I pray. I am not trying to wound you."

"It's all rick, Judge Scoglund. There are those among us who say the like—I not least. But as for getting the let to see him—remember, I am *tukuuii riikook*. I have the rick of a seeing at any time I think needful. I think this is such a time. A wain is waiting outside for us."

Park hadn't heard it come up, but that meant nothing, not with the silent steam engines this world used. He started for the door. "Let's go!"

"Nay so quick." Ankowaljuu sprang up, made as if to head him off. "You needs must pack first."

"Pack?" Park gaped as if he'd never heard the word before. "What the hell for? Are you shifting me into the kingly palace? Otherwise, what's the point?"

"The palace has naught to do with it. Maita Kapak"—again the eye-shielding, which had to be as automatic as breathing for Tawantiinsuujans—"left by airwain this morning, to lead our warriors to winning against the heathen who deny Patjakamak and slay his worshipers. I have another airwain waiting on my ordering at the airfield. I want us on it, as fast as doable."

Park wasted a moment regretting that Kurrikwiljor's

bronze body would not be his tonight. Then he dashed for the bedroom, shouting to Monkey-face, "Come on, Eric, goddammit, give me a hand here."

Dunedin was right behind him. They flung clothes into a trunk. "Hey, wait a minute." Park pointed to a shirt. "That's yours. We won't need it. Take it out."

His thane shook his head. "Don't need it indeed. What do you reckon me to wear on this trip?"

"I didn't reckon you to wear anything—and I don't mean I thock you'd come along naked, either. I reckoned you'd let Tjiimpuu ship you home; that'd be easiest and safest both."

"So it would, if I meant to leave. But I don't. My job is to caretake you, and that's what I aim to do." He gave Allister Park a defiant stare.

Park slapped him on the back, staggering him slightly. "You're a good egg, Eric. All rick, you can come, but don't say I didn't warn you." He thought of something: this world's steam-powered planes were anything but powerful performers. "Will the airwain bear his heft, Ankowaljuu?"

"Reckon so," the Skrelling said. "I'm more afeared for all the books you're heaving into that case, Judge Scoglund."

"I need these," Park yelped, stung. "What's a judge without his books?"

"A lickter lawyer," Ankowaljuu retorted. "Well, as may be. I reckon we'll fly. Be you ready?"

"I guess we are." Park looked around the room at everything he and Dunedin were leaving behind. "What'll happen to all this stuff, though?"

"It'll be kept for you. We're an orderly folk, we Tawantiinsuujans; we don't wantonly throw things away." Having seen how smoothly Kuuskoo ran, Park suspected Ankowaljuu was right. The Skrelling watched Monkey-face wrestle the trunk closed, then said, "Come on. Let's be off."

Ankowaljuu not only had a wain outside, but also

a driver. The fellow's face was a perfect blank mask, part Skrelling impassivity, part the boredom of flunkies everywhere waiting for their bosses to finish business that doesn't involve them. He stayed behind the wheel and let Park and Dunedin heave the trunk in by themselves.

"Go," Ankowaljuu told him.

The wain sprang ahead, shoving Park back in his seat. He was no milquetoast driver himself, but Ankowaljuu's man did not seem to care whether he lived or died. Eric Dunedin's face was white as they shot through Kuuskoo like a dodge-'em car, evading trucks by the thickness of a coat of paint and making pedestrians scatter for their lives. Park sympathized with his thane. Though he wasn't really Bishop Ib Scoglund, he'd never felt more like praying.

Ankowaljuu turned to grin at his passengers. "When Ljiikljiik here isn't swinking for me, he's a champion wain-racer."

"I believe it," Park said. "Who would dare stay on the same track with him?"

Ankowaljuu laughed out loud. He translated the remark into Ketjwa for Ljiikljiik's benefit. The driver's face twitched. Park supposed that was a smile.

Soon they were out of town. That meant less traffic, but Ljiikljiik sped up even more, rocketing south down the valley at whose northern end Kuuskoo sat.

The airfield was just that: a grassy field. Ljiikljilk drove off the road. As far as Park could tell, he didn't slow down a bit, though everyone in the car rattled around like dried peas in a gourd. When Ljiikljiik slammed on the brakes, Park almost went over the front seat and through the windshield. The driver spoke his only words of the journey: "We're here."

"Praise to Hallow Ailbe for that!" Dunedin gasped. He jumped out of the wain before Ljiikljiik could even think about changing his mind. Park followed with equal alacrity. Still grinning, Ankowaljuu tipped

the trunk out after them, then got out himself.
Ljiikljiik sped away.

Only one airwain, presumably the one at Ankowaljuu's beck and call, sat waiting on the field. Next to
a DC-3 from Park's world, even next to a Ford Trimotor, the machine would have been unimpressive. With
its square-sectioned body hung from a flat slab of a
wing, it rather reminded him of a scaled-down version of a Trimotor. It had no nose prop, though, and
the steam engines on either side of the wing were
far bigger and bulkier than the power plants a plane
of his world would have used.

The pilot opened a cockpit window, stuck out his
head, and spat a wad of coca leaves onto the grass.
That did nothing to increase Park's confidence in him,
but Ankowaljuu seemed unperturbed. "Hail, Waipaljkoon," he called to the man. "Can we still fly with
another man"—he pointed at Dunedin—"and this big
cursed box?"

Waipaljkoon paused to stick another wad in his
cheek. "Is the box much heavier than a man?" he
asked when he was done.

"Not much, no," Ankowaljuu said with a sidelong
look at Park, who resolutely ignored him.

"We'll manage, then," Waipaljkoon said. "One of
my boilers has been giving me a little trouble, but
we'll manage."

Hearing that, Park thought hard about mutiny, but
found himself helping his thane manhandle the trunk
into the airwain. Monkey-face was chattering excit-
edly; Park decided he hadn't picked up enough
Ketjwa to understand what the pilot had said. He did
not enlighten him.

Takeoff procedures were of the simplest sort. The
airfield did not boast a control tower. When everyone was aboard and seated, Waipaljkoon started
building steam pressure in his engines. The props
began to spin, faster and faster. After a while,

Waipaljkoon released the brake. The airwain bumped over the *itjuu*-grass. Just when Park wondered if it really could get off the ground, it gave an ungainly leap and lumbered into the air.

Used to the roar of his world's planes, Park found the quiet inside the cramped cabin eerie, almost as if he weren't flying at all. That was Kuuskoo flowing by beneath him, though. He wished he had a camera.

"Best you and your thane don your sourstuff masks now, Judge Scoglund," Ankowaljuu said, returning to English so Park and Dunedin could not misunderstand him. "You're lowlanders, and the air will only get thinner as we climb over the Antiis." He showed the two men from Vinland how to fit the rubber masks over their noses. "Bethink you to outbreathe through your mouths, and you'll be fine."

The enriched air felt almost thick in Park's lungs, which had grown used to a rarer mix. Before long, at Waipaljkoon's signal, the Tawantiinsuujans also started using the masks. Not even their barrel chests could draw enough oxygen from the air as the 'wain climbed higher and higher.

Tiny as toys, llamas wandered the high plateaus over which the airwain flew. Its almost silent passage overhead did nothing to disturb them. Then the altitude grew too great for even llamas to endure. The backbone of the continent was tumbled rock and ice and snow, dead-seeming as the mountains of the moon.

The cabin was not heated. Waipaljkoon pointed to a cabinet. Eric Dunedin, who sat closest to it, reached in and pulled out thick blankets of llama wool. Even under three of them, Park felt his teeth chatter like castanets.

He wanted to cheer when greenery appeared on the mountainsides below. The airwain descended as the land grew lower. The Tawantiinsuujans took off their oxygen masks. A couple of minutes later, Waipaljkoon said, "We're down to the height of Kuuskoo. Even you lowland folk ought to be all right now."

Park shed his mask, and immediately began feeling short of air. The pilot chuckled at his distress. "How well do you do in hot, sticky weather down by the sea, smart boy?" Park growled.

"That smelly soup? I hate it," Waipaljkoon said. Park laughed in turn. The pilot glared, then said grudgingly, "All right, you made your point."

They landed at a town called Viiljkabamba for the night. Park tried to phone Kuurikwiljor to tell her where he was. After assorted clicks and pops, the call went through. When someone answered it, though, the connection was so faint that he could not make himself understood at all. Finally, swearing, he hung up.

They flew on the next morning. Below them, foliage grew ever more exuberant; jungle stretched ahead as far as the eye could see. To Allister Park, viewing it from above, it might have been a great green ocean. Only an occasional cleared patch or the glint of sunlight off a pond or river spoiled the illusion.

"How do you find your way when everything looks alike?" Park asked Waipaljkoon. For all he could tell, they might have been flying in circles.

"By the blessed sun, of course, and the lodestone." The pilot tapped a compass on the instrument panel. In the profusion of other dials, Park had not noticed it. He felt foolish until Waipaljkoon went on, "And by keeping track of my air speed and guessing whether the wind is with or against me, and by a good deal of luck."

"He hasn't crashed yet," Ankowaljuu said jovially, slapping the pilot on the back.

Eric Dunedin intoned, *"Patjam kuutiin*—the world changes," in a voice so sepulchral that everyone stared at him, the two Tawantiinsuujans in surprise, Park in admiration. Monkey-face grinned. He sometimes showed unsuspected depths, Park thought.

He'd drunk *aka* with breakfast at Viiljkabamba. Now it began to have its revenge. He fidgeted in his chair. Soon fidgeting did not help. "How do I make water here?" he asked.

Waipaljkoon handed him a stoppered jug. "Make sure you put the plug back in tightly," the pilot warned, "in case we hit choppy air." Though relieved when he gave back the jug, Park reflected that Tawantiinsuuju still had a lot to learn about proper airline service.

The *aka* also left Park sleepy. He was wondering if he could doze in his uncomfortable seat when the airwain lurched in the air. "What the—" he began, while Ankowaljuu and Dunedin made similar dismayed noises.

Waipaljkoon, red-brown face grim, pointed wordlessly to the starboard engine. The steam plants' exhaust usually scrawled a big vapor trail across the sky. Now, though, vapor was spurting from several places in the engine housing where it did not belong. Park watched the spin of the three-bladed wooden propellor slow, stop.

"Boiler tubes must have failed," the pilot said.

The jungle, all of a sudden, seemed terribly far below and much too close, both at the same time. No, it *was* closer—the airwain was losing altitude. Park was glad he'd used the jug not long before. "Are we going to hit the ground hard?" he asked, not knowing how to say "crash" in Ketjwa.

Waipaljkoon understood him. "Unless we find a town or a clearing soon," he said. "We can't fly long with just one motor, that's certain."

The next few minutes were among the worst of Allister Park's life. The slow descent of the airwain only gave him more time to think about what would happen at its end. The lower they got, the hotter it grew. Park would have been sweating just as hard, though, had the engine quit during their frigid passage over the Antiis.

Just as he was wondering when some high treetop would snag their landing gear and flip them into the forest, Eric Dunedin pointed off to the left. "Isn't that a break in the trees?"

It was. Waipaljkoon fiddled with the controls. To Park's amazement, the airwain climbed a little. "Now that I have somewhere definite to go, I can give my one engine full power," the pilot explained. "Before, I had to save some to make sure it didn't fail too, before we had a place to land."

All four men cheered when the clearing proved to hold not only cultivated fields but also, snug against the riverbank, a small town. Farmers in the fields gaped up at the airwain. Park wondered if they'd ever seen one up close before.

"I'm going to set it down," Waipaljkoon said. "Hang on tight, and pray Patjakamak is watching us."

Cornstalks swished and rattled against the wings as the airwain bumped to a stop. Park's teeth clicked together several times, but he'd been braced for worse. "Thank you, Waipaljkoon," Dunedin said. That, Park thought, about summed it up.

People came rushing toward the airwain from the fields and from the town. "Probably the most exciting thing that's happened in years," Ankowaljuu said drily. "I wonder how many people here speak Ketjwa."

The locals were Skrellings, of course, but with rounder faces and flatter features than the men from the mountains. Men and women alike wore only loincloths. In the moist heat of the jungle, Park could hardly blame them. "Rude to stare, Eric," he murmured, "though I own she's worth staring at." He wondered if Kuurikwiljor would forgive him for not showing up.

Ankowaljuu was sitting closest to the door. He opened it, climbed out onto the wing. "What's the name of this town?" he called.

Someone understood him, for an answer came back: "Iipiisjuuna."

"Well, good people of Iipiisjuuna, I am *tukuuii riikook* to Maita Kapak" (they all shaded their eyes; back of beyond or no, this was still Tawantiinsuuju) "the Son of the Sun. I need your help in furthering the travels of this man here, Judge Ib Scoglund of the International Court." He beckoned to Park.

From the way the locals gabbled when he came out, Park was sure sandy-haired white men did not come to Iipiisjuuna every day. "Hello," he said in Ketjwa, and waved, as if he were making a speech on a stump.

A fat man with a large scar on his belly and streaks of gray in his hair (which looked, Park thought irreverently, as if it had been cut under a bowl and then soaked in Vaseline) pushed through to the front of the crowd. "What sort of help do you need?" he demanded in a deep, important-sounding voice. "*Tukuuii riikook* or no, sir, I, Mankoo, am chief at Iipiisjuuna."

"Of course," Ankowaljuu agreed—wisely, Park thought, for Mankoo reminded him of a red-skinned, half-naked version of Ivor MacSvensson. The way people moved aside for the chief, the way they watched him when he spoke, said that Iipiisjuuna was as much his town as New Belfast had been Mac-Svensson's. And here Park had no leverage to break his hold on it.

Ankowaljuu went on: "If you have a mechanic who can fix our airwain engine, we will be on our way very quickly."

"We have no steam engines here, save on a couple of riverboats," Mankoo said. Park's heart sank. Of all the places he did not care to be stranded, Iipiisjuuna ranked high on the list. Mankoo was saying, "—roads hereabouts aren't good enough for them. But I will have our blacksmith look at it, if you like."

"You are very kind," Ankowaljuu said, wincing almost imperceptibly. "If, Patjakamak prevent it, your smith is unable to make the repairs, how would you suggest that we go on our way northwards? We must, to stop the war that has broken out between the Son of the Sun and the Sun-deniers of the Dar al-Harb."

The crowd muttered to itself. Suddenly suspicious no longer, Mankoo said, "Word of this war has not reached us. The wirecaller lines are down again, somewhere in the jungle."

Hell, Park thought. There went another chance for calling Kuurikwiljor—and it was getting late for excuses. After this, it would be awfully late.

Mankoo went on, "I fought the Sun-deniers a generation ago. I know what war is like. Anything to stop it is worth doing." He rubbed his scar, then turned and shouted at the fellow next to him in the local tongue. The man dashed away. Mankoo returned to Ketjwa: "He will fetch the smith."

"What if he can't fix it?" Park spoke up. "You didn't answer that."

Mankoo's massive head swung his way. He boldly looked back: let the chief get the idea that he was somebody in his own right, not just tagging along with the bigshot *tukuuii riikook*. After a moment, Mankoo nodded. "If that happens, I will give you a boat and supplies. Our river, the Muura, flows into the Huurwa, and the Huurwa into the Great River. On the towns of the Great River, you may be able to command another airwain. Is it well?" Now he looked a challenge at Park.

The thought of sailing down the Amazon did not fill Park with delight. The thought of all the time he would lose left him even less happy. Unfortunately, though, he recognized that Mankoo really was doing his best to help. "It is well," he said, answering before Ankowaljuu could.

It was afternoon by the time the smith got there. He and Waipaljkoon wrestled off the engine housing. When the smith looked inside, he whistled. "That engine dead," he said in halting Ketjwa. "Melted—twisted . . . Maybe Patjakamak bring back to life, but not me." The glum look on Waipaljkoon's face said he agreed with the verdict.

"A boat, then." Ankowaljuu sighed. He turned to Allister Park. "I am sorry, Judge Scoglund—this did not turn out as I planned."

Park shrugged. "I'm just glad to be in one piece."

"And well you might be," Mankoo said. "I saw airwains fall from the sky when I fought in the war—no, it is the last war now, you tell me. Seldom did I see any flying man walk away from them afterwards. Were I you, I would offer prayers of thanks to Patjakamak for your survival."

"Tomorrow at sunrise we will be in the temple here, doing just that," Ankowaljuu said. Then he caught himself: "Or Waipaljkoon and I will, at any rate. Judge Scoglund here is a Christian. I do not know if he will join us."

All eyes turned to Park. He'd hoped to sleep late, but that didn't look politic. "I'll come," he said, and everyone beamed. He didn't much mind praying to Patjakamak; as far as he was concerned, God was God, no matter what people went around calling Him. The real Ib Scoglund wouldn't have approved, but the real Ib Scoglund wasn't around to argue, either.

"Perhaps we will win you to the truth," Mankoo said. Park shrugged his politest shrug. The chief smiled, recognizing it for what it was. He said, "And now a feast, to make you glad you came to Iipiisjuuna, even if unexpectedly."

"Nothing could make me glad I came to Iipiisjuuna," Park said, but in English. Eric Dunedin and

Ankowaljuu, the only two people who understood him, both nodded.

The food these jungle Skrellings ate was different from what Park had grown used to in Kuuskoo. He hadn't tasted tomato sauce in this world till now. The sauce in question was heated with chilies; it smothered several roundish lumps nearly the size of Park's fist.

"What are these?" he asked, poking one with his knife. "Stuffed peppers?"

"Stewed monkey heads," Mankoo told him. "The brains are a rare delicacy."

"Oh." Park wished the rare delicacy were extinct. But with the chief expectantly watching him, he had to eat. The monkey tasted like flesh; the clinging spicy sauce kept him from knowing much more than that. Just as well, he thought.

He spent the night in a hammock. The Iipii-sjuunans seemed ignorant of any other way to sleep. From the size of the cockroaches he'd seen before he blew out his lamp, he suspected he knew why. He wouldn't have wanted anything that big crawling into bed with him without an invitation.

Reliable as an alarm clock, Dunedin woke him while it was still dark. "If you're bound for this heathen church, you'd best be on time," he said primly.

"Mrff." Park, always grumpy in the morning, wondered how Monkey-face would look slathered in tomato sauce.

The service to Patjakamak and the sun went on and on and on. As at the festival of Raimii, everyone but Park (and now Dunedin) had all the prayers and responses memorized. After things finally ended—it was nearly noon—Park asked Ankowaljuu, "How do you folk heartlearn all those words, all those songs?"

The *tukuuii riikook* also used English: "By beginning with them as soon as we begin to speak, of course. How else would one do such a thing? We have a saying: 'Everyone is a faithly *kiipuukamajoo*'—a knowledge-keeper, you might say."

"I've seen that you speak sooth," Park agreed, admiring such diligence without sharing it. He continued, "Now we have one mair thing to do." His stomach rumbled, interrupting him. "No, two mair—first lunch, then on to the steamboat."

"You'd never make a worshiper of Patjakamak," Ankowaljuu chuckled, glancing at Ib Scoglund's incipient bay window (all along the wheel of if, Park's analogs ran to plumpness). "For some of our festivals, we fast three days straickt."

That idea did not appeal to Park at all. Eric Dunedin came to his defense: "Aye, Judge Scoglund's not thin—" ("Thank you too much, Eric," Park said, but Monkey-face was going on) "—but he's wild for bodily fitness: he drills himself most mornings, with sitting-ups and I don't ken what all else."

"Is that so?" Ankowaljuu stood face-to-face with Park, set his right foot next to the judge's, and seized his right hand. "Let's see what his swink has got him, then." He locked eyes with Park. "First man to pull the other off kilter wins."

"All rick, by God!" Park said, going into a half-crouch. "Eric, count three, to give us a mark to begin at."

He almost lost the match in the first instant, when the absurdity of Indian-wrestling a veritable Indian hit him. But the painful jerk Ankowaljuu gave his arm made him stop laughing in a hurry; He and the *tukuuii riikook* swayed back and forth, tugging, yanking, grunting. Finally Park, with a mighty heave, forced Ankowaljuu to take a couple of staggering steps to keep from falling. "Ha!"

Ankowaljuu opened and closed his hand several times to work out the numbness. "You cauckt me by surprise there, Judge Scoglund," he said reproachfully.

"I didn't know that wasn't in the rules." Park grinned.

Ankowaijuu raised an eyebrow. "You should be a *tukuuii riikook* yourself. You look to getting around rules that make trouble, not just blindly carrying them out."

"Not so much to getting around them. That would be bad in a judge. But in reckoning the rick onputting of them—"

"Aye, there's the rub," Ankowaljuu said. Park blinked; Ankowaljuu, most certainly, had never heard of Shakespeare. The Skrelling went on, "I will own, this not being any hick holy day, my belly could do with filling too. Shall we see what good food Mankoo has in store?"

"Not mair monkey heads, I hope," Park and Dunedin said in the same breath.

Ankowaljuu laughed. "Sooth to tell, so do I."

Had anyone told rising young prosecutor Allister Park that within three years he would be sailing down tributaries of the Amazon, he would have called the teller crazy. Had the fellow gone on to say he would be bored doing it, he would have laughed in his face.

But bored he was, in short order. Neither the Muura nor the Huurwa was a big enough river to be impressive in its own right, and one stretch of jungle looked much like another. Of the riverboat's crew of three, only Iispaka the pilot spoke Ketjwa, and he was so taciturn he might as well have known no language at all.

Thrown back thus on his own resources, Park plunged into his books. By both inclination and training he was a creature of the printed page; he was convinced the answer to the endless strife between Tawantiinsuuju and the Emirate of the Dar al-Harb was set forth there, could he but find it.

Monkey-face had learned to leave him severely

alone when such fits came upon him. In them, he
often bit his thane's head off. Other times, as when
he was learning Ketjwa, he insisted that Dunedin
share his zeal. To his servant, that was worse.

Even the air of good cheer Ankowaljuu cultivated
wore thin as Park kept his nose in his books and
spoke almost as little as Iispaka. Only the swarms of
mosquitoes that buzzed endlessly round the steamboat made him sit up and take notice—their bites
roused him to brief spasms of insecticidal frenzy.

Then one day, about a week after they had left
Iipiisjuuna, Park slammed shut the volume in which
he'd been lost. "Tell me," he asked Ankowaljuu, his
voice suddenly so mild that the *tukuuii riikook* gave
him a suspicious glance, "does your faith out-and-out
forbid you from writing down what you believe in?"

"No one ever does," Ankowaljuu said after a
moment of frowning thought. "As you've seen, we of
Tawantiinsuuju pride ourselves in heartlearning everything we need to know."

"Aye, aye," Park said impatiently, "but that's not what
I asked. I want to know if you *may*, not if you *do*."

"But why would we want to?" Ankowaljuu persisted.

Park rubbed his chin. "Hmm. Reckon you had an
upgrown man like, like me, say, who wanted to become
a changer to the faith of Patjakamak. Upgrowns aren't
as good at heartlearning as children. Would you be
allowed to put things in writing to help him grasp your
faith?"

"Like you?" Ankowaljuu said. "Is that why you've
been toiling so hard: because you're thinking on
joining the brotherhood of the sun and the All-
Maker?" His English failed him; with shining eyes,
he switched to Ketjwa: "We would welcome you, my
friend."

"I thank you." Park felt like a heel—he had no
intention of converting—but plunged ahead: "Could
you make such a writing for me?"

"Aye, and I will," Ankowaljuu promised. After that first moment of emotion, he had his English back. "You are rick: the writing in itself is naught shameful nor sinful, and so you will have it as quick as is doable."

That did not prove so quick as either Ankowaljuu or Park, for rather different reasons, hoped. A search of the ship revealed only three or four sheets of paper. "Why more?" Iispaka demanded when the two eager men upbraided him for the lack. "I don't write."

"Where's the nearest storehouse?" Ankowaljuu asked. Public storehouses in the towns and along the highways of Tawantiinsuuju kept vast quantities of all sorts of supplies against time of need.

"Next town is Tejfej," Iispaka said. "Maybe two days away."

Ankowaljuu fumed at the delay. He spent as much of the intervening time as he could preaching at Park, perhaps expecting oral argument to work as well as written. To the *tukuuii riikook*'s disappointment, Park responded by diving back into his books. While he was studying, he could ignore distractions.

He could not so escape Eric Dunedin. When they were bedding down on deck under mosquito netting, his servant whispered, "Do you really have truck with that heathen foolishness? I ken you're truly no hallow, and even if you were, you left the church to take up your judgeship. But I thock you still a Christian wick."

"I am," Park said after some moments' thought. "All the same, though, I need to learn as much as I can about faithly dealings here, for the strife between Tawantiinsuuju and the Emirate is ungetawayably tied up in 'em." He paused again. "D'you believe me?"

The answer mattered to him. Dunedin was friend as well as thane. Relief flowed through him as the small, wrinkled man said, "Reckon I do. If I can't trust you, I can't trust anyone."

"Thanks, Eric," Park said softly. He got no reply and repeated himself, a little louder. Still no answer, only soft, regular breathing. Monkey-face was asleep. Park let out a snort of laughter and joined him.

That night, they passed from the Huurwa to what Park persisted in thinking of as the Amazon. It was as if a giant hand had pushed the jungle back from either side of the steamboat: the Great River was a couple of miles wide. Its own mighty current added to the speed the steamboat's engine could produce.

As Iispaka had predicted, they reached Tejfej toward evening of the second day after Ankowaljuu had asked for paper. The little town lay on the south bank of the Amazon, just past a tributary smaller than the Huurwa. A few Kuuskoo-style public buildings of massive stonework contrasted oddly with the huts of leaves and branches all around them.

One of the massive buildings was the storehouse. Using his authority as *tukuuii riikook*, Ankowaljuu requisitioned a ream of paper. He would sooner have commandeered an airwain, but Tejfej had none.

"Maybe this is for the better," Ankowaljuu said as they steamed away the next morning. "Now I will in sooth have the time to write out what you need to know."

And write he did, with a furious intensity that reminded Park of his own obsessive leaps into projects. Each evening he delivered to Park the pile of papers he had filled that day. Then Park had to wrestle with written Ketjwa, for Ankowaljuu expected him to read every word and absorb it with proper convert's zeal.

"How can you keep track of so much?" Eric Dunedin asked one night, seeing his boss studying by lamplight and occasionally batting away the big bugs the lamp attracted.

Park looked up, grinned wryly. "It is rather like

baptism by thorough indunking, isn't it?" He wondered for a moment what the real Bishop Ib Scoglund would have thought of that comparison, then went back to his labors.

Even in the first couple of days, he saw how much constant exposure to Tawantiinsuuju's written language improved his command of it. He also learned enough about the local religion to develop a considerable respect for it.

Patjakamak, Ankowaljuu wrote, was the creator and sustainer of the earth and heavens. He had placed the sun above all the stars and made them the sun's handmaidens. The moon was the sun's sister and wife, a pattern echoing that of the ruling house of Tawantiinsuuju, which sprang from the sun.

The sun's warmth and light was the medium Patjakamak used to shape the world and everything in it. The sun deserved worship for its light, heat, and beauty, and also for its legendary descent to earth to give rise to the empire's royal family.

Patjakamak, by contrast, did not allow himself to be seen. Nevertheless, he was the supreme god and lord, worshiped inwardly by every Tawantiinsuujan. That appealed to Park: the sun's cult had more show, but the invisible god behind it was the more powerful.

Patjakamak judged the souls of the dead. Those of the good went up to a heaven—literally, an *anan patja,* an upper house—of rest and pleasure, while those of the bad went to hell—*uuka patja,* the lower house—where they had toil and pain and sickness forevermore.

It was, in short, a faith about as sophisticated as Christianity or Islam, though growing from different roots. It had its own pride; Ankowaljuu wrote tartly, "Christians say God's Son died; we know Patjakamak's Sun lives." A man who followed its tenets would live a good life by any reasonable standard.

None of that was enough to convince Allister Park

that he needed to switch religions, but he didn't see that the Tawantiinsuujans needed to have their beliefs changed, either. He carefully stowed away every sheet that Ankowaljuu gave him.

A little more than a week after they left Tejfej, they came to Manaus, at the junction of the Great River and the almost equally impressive Black River. Iispaka moored the steamboat at one of the floating docks that let the town cope with the river's ever-shifting level. "You find airwain here," he said.

Park felt sure he was right. Manaus was a real city, nearly as big as Kuuskoo. Bigger ships lay to either side of Iispaka's vessel; though Manaus was a thousand miles from the Atlantic, ocean-going craft could sail up the Amazon to it.

None would, though, not any time soon, not if the war went on: the mouth of the Great River lay inside the Emirate of the Dar al-Harb.

As soon as Ankowaljuu was off the docks and on ground that stayed at the same level, he stepped in front of a wain. The driver slammed on the brakes, though the *tukuuii riikook* was not that close. He stuck his head out the window and loudly wished Ankowaljuu down to *uuka patja;* the orderly Tawantiinsuujans did not take kindly to having order flouted.

Then Ankowaljuu announced his rank and demanded to be driven to the residence of the local *kuuraka.* The Skrelling in the wain sang a different tune. He jumped out, helped Park and Dunedin load their trunk inside, and whizzed off to the governor's palace.

Impressed at such complete and instant obedience, Park asked, "How often does someone get into hot water for feigning that he's a *tukuuii riikook*? He could have a rare old time till he was cauckt."

"Only seldom," Ankowaijuu said. "Most folk here would never think of it."

"It's not like that in New Belfast," Park said.

"So I ken, but our way suits us."

The *kuuraka* of Manaus was a thin, aging man named Anta-Aklja. He hustled the *tukuuii riikook* and his companions out to the airfield with breathtaking celerity. Park again spoke in English to Ankowaljuu: "Is he falling all over himself to be helpful, or does he have something going on here that he doesn't want a *tukuuii riikook* to see?"

"You have a mistrustful turn of thock, Judge Scoglund," Ankowaljuu said in the same language. "Were my sending with you less weighty, I might want to infollow that more closely. As is—" one eyelid fell, rose "—well, I am not the only *tukuuii riikook* in Tawantiinsuuju."

The airwain to which Anta-Aklja's minions hurried the newcomers was of the same model as the plane that had crash-landed at Iipiisjuuna. Eric Dunedin crinkled up his face at it. "I'd not like to have this twoth one fail," he said, also in English.

"What's that?" Waipaljkoon asked in Ketjwa. Monkey-face made the mistake of translating. The pilot burst out; "You keep quiet! It was just after you came out with your cursed *patjam kuutiin* that the other airwain had trouble. Are you some *jatiirii*, some coca-leaf reader, trying to illwish everything we do?"

He took several minutes to calm down. So, Park thought: under the fine cult of Patjakamak and the sun, superstition lives. He was unsurprised, as anyone who has ever decorated a Christmas tree would be.

Manaus' airfield was smoother than Kuuskoo's. Park's teeth rattled only a couple of times before the airwain climbed off the ground. Below, he could see the Black River's clear dark water flowing side by side with the red-brown stream of the Great River; only after some miles would they fully mix together.

"Where now?" Waipaljkoon asked as he swung the airwain northward.

"The Son of the Sun flew to Mavaka, near the head-waters of the Ooriinookoo," Ankowaljuu said. To Park, that meant they were heading for southern Venezuela. Here, though, it was a town in the province Tawantiinsuuju had wrested from the Emirate after their last clash.

Waipaljkoon gradually shifted course to the northwest. "This would be a faster, easier flight if we hadn't had to sail halfway down the Great River to find another airwain," he grumbled.

"When next you tell Patjakamak how to order the universe, I suggest you take that up with him," Ankowaljuu said. Waipaljkoon grunted and shut up.

The flight was as boring as the earlier one had been—until that plane's engine went out, Park reminded himself. He too hoped this leg of the trip would not be so strenuously interrupted. He sat back and watched jungle go by below, now dark green, now yellow-green. Again it reminded him of the sea with its unending not-quite-sameness.

Then, suddenly, not long before Waipaljkoon expected them to reach Mavaka, they saw a great cloud of smoke rising high into the air from below. The pilot scowled, pursed his lips. "I've seen big fires before, aye, but seldom one that size," he said.

"That's no fire!" Ankowaljuu said as they got closer. "That's a cursed battle, is what that is!" He got the words out only an instant before they burst from Allister Park. He too had seen the flashes from exploding shells down there. Men were too small to spot from several thousand feet, but goodwains and machine-gun-carrying warwains were visible in clearings carved from the jungle.

Waipaljkoon needed no urging to steer wide of the battlefield. As the airwain was approaching from the southeast, he chose to fly more nearly due north, saying, "We'll cross the line in a quieter place, then swing west to Mavaka." That sounded good to Park, who had no desire to catch antiaircraft fire from either side in a war not his own.

Unfortunately, though, airwains rushing up to the front to add their pinpricks to the fighting spotted the intruder. Two peeled off to give the strange aircraft a once-over. In a quavering voice, Eric Dunedin said, "They have the star and sickle moon on their tails."

Waipaljkoon turned west with everything his airwain had. That was not nearly enough. The Emirate's fighters would have been sitting ducks for a Messerschmitt or Spitfire, but they were like sharks against a fat ocean sunfish compared to the slow, lumbering transport the Tawantiinsuujan was flying.

One zipped past the airwain, so close that Park could see the pilot's grinning, bearded face in the cockpit. The other came alongside, fired a burst from its air-powered machine gun. That fighter's pilot made a come-with-me gesture, then fired his gun again. What he meant was depressingly obvious.

"Slavery," Waipaljkoon groaned as he followed the fighter eastward. The other one stayed on his tail, to make sure he didn't try anything tricky. "They'll sell us into slavery if they don't kill us on the spot for following Patjakamak. That's all we are to the stinking Muslims, fair game."

"They won't kill us, and they won't sell us either," Park said confidently. "Remember, you're with Judge Ib Scoglund of the International Court of the Continent of Skrelleland. If they harm me, they have an international incident on their hands."

"Let's hope they bother to find that out," Ankowaljuu said. "Or that they care."

"They'll find out," Park promised. He left the other half of Ankowaljuu's worry alone; he didn't much want to think about that himself.

The fighter in front of them landed on a strip hacked out of the jungle. Waipaljkoon followed it down. Moors who had been standing around or working on other airwains came trotting over at the sight of the unfamiliar craft bouncing to a stop.

"Some of them have pipes, Judge Scoglund," Dunedin said. He didn't mean the kind from which tobacco was smoked.

"Of course they have pipes, Eric. They're warriors, for God's sake." Hoping he sounded braver than he felt, Park unbuckled his safety harness. "I have to get out first," he said. Shrugging, Waipaljkoon opened the door. Park ducked through it and scrambled onto the wing.

The bearded fighter pilot was already out of his airwain and running toward the craft he had forced down. "These are my captives!" he yelled, brandishing a large knife. "They're mine to keep and sell as the pagan dogs they are!"

Park did not follow all of that, but he caught enough. He hoped the Moors would be able to understand his self-taught Arabic—Ketjwa, at least, he'd been able to practice over the past weeks. "Not captives!" he shouted at the top of his lungs. "Not pagans either!"

The pilot understood, all right. "What do you mean, you're not a captive? You're here, lying fool, at our base, the Emirate's base, at Siimaranja. And that's a Tawantiinsuujan airwain, so you're a filthy Patjakamak-worshiping pagan!"

"I'm no Tawantiinsuujan," Park said. His fair skin, sandy hair, and light eyes told the truth of that better than any words.

"Well, who in Shaitan's name are you, then?" someone called from the ground.

Park sternly suppressed a sigh of relief. If nobody asked that question, he would have had to plunge in cold. As it was, he had the perfect chance to give them his name and impressive title. Then, into abrupt silence, he went on, "I am a citizen of the Bretwaldate

of Vinland, and a Christian by religion. You will treat
me as Muslim law requires you to treat a Person of
the Book."

The Moors started arguing among themselves.
That was as much as Park had expected. The pilot's
voice rose above the babble, loud with outrage:
"Well, what if he does belong to the *Ahl al-Kitab*,
the People of the Book? Those other three I see in
there don't. They're pagan Skrellings, and they're
mine!" When no one argued with him, he started
toward the downed airwain again, still clutching that
knife.

"One is my servant from Vinland, and a Christian
like me," Park said. The pilot shook a fist at him. He
continued, "The other two men are of Tawantiinsuuju,
yes. But they fly me—I ask them to fly me—to help
make peace between the Son of the Sun and your
Emir. You should let us go on our way, free from
harm."

He didn't expect that to happen. He figured,
though, that if he only asked for what he wanted, he'd
end up with less. One thing he'd never been short
on was gall. He stood on the wing, trying to look as
impressive as possible, while the Moors kept on
arguing. Finally, when they seemed about to come
to blows, one of them said, "Let's take it to the *qadi*."

"Yes," Park said at once. "Take us to the *qadi*. He
will judge the truth."

"They're mine, curse it!" the frustrated fighter pilot
said again, but most of the Moors on the airstrip
shouted him down.

"Come down," one of them said to Park. "By Allah,
the Compassionate, the Merciful, you will all stay free
and unhurt till the *qadi* lays down his judgment."

"Agreed." Park stuck his head back into the airwain.
"Come on out. One of their judges is going to figure out what to do with us."

Despite the Moor's promise, men crowded close

to Park and his companions to make sure they did
not break and run. He wondered where they could
run to, but on second thought was just as glad to have
a lot of bodies around—the pilot never had put away
that knife.

The *qadi*'s tent was at the edge of the jungle, close
by several dozen man-sized rugs spread on the
ground: the airfield crew's worship area, Park realized. "Excellency!" a Moor said.

Everyone bowed when the *qadi* came out. Park was
slower than the Muslims, but quicker than Dunedin,
Ankowaljuu, or Waipaljkoon. When he straightened,
he got his first good look at the Muslim judge; all
he'd noticed before was the Arab-style robes the man
wore.

The *qadi* was no Arab, though. With his round,
copper-skinned face, he was plainly of jungle Skrelling
stock. Park knew he shouldn't have been surprised.
Just as Vinland's Skrellings were Christian, so naturally those of the Emirate would follow Islam. He
needed a moment to adjust all the same.

The *qadi* said, "Who are these strangers? Why do
you bring them before me?"

Park spoke up before anyone else had a chance:
"Excellency, I am *qadi* myself—a judge of the International Court of the Continent of Skrelleland. Your
pilot made my airwain land by mistake."

"They are my prisoners, my battlefield booty!" the
fighter pilot cried. "Even this Christian who calls
himself a *qadi* admits that these"—he pointed at the
two Tawantlinsuujans—"are but pagans, deserving only
death or slavery."

The *qadi* frowned. "This is too complicated to
decide at once. Come into my tent, Muawiyah" (that
was evidently the pilot) "and you foreign folk as well.
And, to keep anyone from getting ideas perhaps he
should not have, you come too, Harun, and you,
Walid, with your weapons."

The tent was crowded with so many people inside, but it held them. The Muslims with pipes sat behind Park and his companions. The *qadi* also found a place on the rug. He picked up a book—a *Qu'ran,* Park guessed.

"Now we may begin," he said, then added, "I suppose I should tell you and yours, O *qadi* of the Christians, that I am called Muhammad ibn Nizam. Do you all speak Arabic?"

"I do, *qadi* Muhammad," Ankowaljuu said at once. Waipaljkoon and Dunedin did not understand the question, which was answer in itself.

"Translate as you need," Muhammad ibn Nizam told Park and the *tukuuii riikook.* "We shall allow the time. 'Allah's judgment surely will come to pass: do not try to hurry it along,' as Allah says in the chapter called The Bee. Now, unfold me your tale."

Park again spoke first, describing how he had been chosen to arbitrate the dispute between Tawantiinsuuju and the Emirate of the Dar al-Harb, and how, in spite of his efforts, war had broken out between them. He told how Ankowaljuu still had hopes for peace, and had arranged to have him fly to meet the Son of the Sun—and all the trouble he'd had since. "I also hope for peace now," he finished, "but not for the same reasons."

"I had heard of your mission," Muhammad said. "Beyond your Frankish look, can you prove who and what you are?"

"Yes, Excellency. My papers are in the trunk inside our airwain. Other important papers, too."

Muhammad nodded to the Moors behind Park. "Have this trunk fetched here." One of the men hurried away. The *qadi* went on, "While we wait, I will hear what Muawiyah has to say."

Park half-listened as the pilot told how he had intercepted the Tawantiinsuujan airwain and forced it to land. "The pagans, at least, are mine," he insisted, "and their airwain, as booty won in our righteous *jihad*."

Just then, two men lugged the trunk into the tent. Park opened it and extracted his credentials. He had three sets: English, Ketjwa, and Arabic, all gaudily scaled and beribboned. Muhammad ibn Nizam carefully read the Arabic version. He kept his face still until he was through. Then he nodded.

"It is as the Christian *qadi* says," he declared. "Both the Emir, Allah grant him long years and prosperity, and the pagan king have agreed to harken to his judgment. May it be wise." He bowed to Park.

"Then we *are* free?" Park asked, bowing back in delight. That was better than he'd dared imagine.

"You and your servant, yes. Not only are you an honored judge, but, as you said, a Person of the Book, even if your Christian Gospel has only in corrupted form the truth of the glorious *Qu'ran*. Still, by Allah's holy law, you may not be wantonly enslaved. That is not the case, however, for the Tawantiinsuujans with you."

"What? Why not?" Park said. "They are with me, they fly me to try to make peace—"

"There can be no peace between Islam and paganism," the *qadi* said. "In the words of the *Qu'ran,* 'Kill those who give God partners wherever you find them; seize them, encompass them, and ambush them.' " He turned to Ankowaljuu. "You, pagan who knows the Arab speech, will you and your comrade yield yourselves to the truth of Islam?"

The *tukuuii riikook* spoke briefly with Waipaljkoon, then shook his head. "No, *qadi*, we will not. We have our faith, just as you have yours."

"Then you know what must become of you. You are the pilot Muawiyah's to slay or to sell into slavery, as he alone shall decide. You men"—he nodded to the armed Moors in back of Park and his party—"help the good pilot take them away."

"No! Wait!" Park said.

Muhammad ibn Nizam shook his head. "I understand your concern, *qadi* of the Christians. I even have some sympathy for it. But under the *shari'a*, the law of Islam, this thing must be. I am sorry."

"Wait," Park said again. He was not about to let his friends go to a fate he thought worse than death, certainly not over a dispute where, as far as he was concerned, no sure right answer existed. And so he trotted out for a *qadi* of no particular importance the argument he'd intended to use on the Emir or his envoy to Tawantiinsuuju: "These men are not pagans. They too are People of the Book, for they have the truths of their religion set down in writing."

"Do you see what a liar this Christian is, *qadi*?" Muawiyah the pilot said. "We have been fighting these pagans since our ancestors crossed the sea to bring Islam to this newer land, and never yet have we seen one sign of a scripture among them. Now he invents it out of his own head. Let him show it to us, if it is there."

"With pleasure." Park dug into the trunk. He pulled out the sheets Ankowaljuu had written as they'd traveled down the Amazon, presented them with a flourish to Muhammad ibn Nizam. "I'll read this if you like, and translate into Arabic."

"No," Muawiyah burst out. "I've already said the man is a liar, ready for anything. Who knows what these papers say, and whether he translates them truly?"

"Yes, that is so," the *qadi* said thoughtfully, "the more so as lying would be to his advantage. Have we any other man here who knows the pagans' tongue as well as our own?"

One of the armed guards, a thin, grizzled man somewhere in his fifties, spoke up: "I do, excellent *qadi*. I was raised not too far from here, before

Tawantiinsuuju stole this province from us, and
learned to read and write the language so I could
better deal with the folk who knew it but no
Arabic."

"Good," Muhammad said. "Read, then, Walid, and
translate for us. By Allah, I charge you to translate
the words here as they are written."

"By Allah, I will, Excellency." Walid took the papers
from the *qadi*, studied them. "They do speak of
Patjakamak, the Tawantiinsuujans' false god," he said
grudgingly. "I begin: 'How Patjakamak made the sun
and the world and the stars . . .' "

"Enough," Muhammad said, some time later.

"More than enough," Muawiyah said loudly. "I will
take these two now, as the excellent *qadi* has justly
agreed is my right. They are not Muslims; what we
just heard proves that. Therefore their religion must
be false."

"In essence, the pilot is right," Muhammad said.
"The *Qu'ran* recognizes but three faiths as failing
under the status of Peoples of the Book: those of the
Christians, Jews, and Sabians. All others are pagans.
Truly, I admit there is more that approaches truth in
the religion of Tawantiinsuuju than I had thought, but
under the *shari'a* that has no bearing."

"What of those who follow Zoroaster?" Park said.
Not for nothing had he spent his time on the steamboat immersed in books. On this point of Islamic law,
if on no other, he was ready to do battle with the
subtlest of sages.

The *qadi* frowned. "They are not specifically mentioned in the *Qu'ran* either. What of them indeed?"

"No, not in the *Qu'ran*," Park agreed. "But when
Arabs conquer Persia, Zoroastrians write down their
holy book, their *Avesta*. Till then it had only been
recited"—he used the word on purpose, for the literal Arabic meaning of *Qu'ran* was *recitation*—"just
like faith of Patjakamak now. And Arabs recognize

Zoroastrians as People of the Book. Do you see, excellent *qadi*? Precedent for what I say." *Precedent* was one Arabic legal term he'd made sure he knew.

Of course, all his research would go down the drain if Muhammad ibn Nizam was the kind of judge who used the law only to justify what he had already decided. Park had known enough judges like that, in New York and New Belfast both. Not all of them were, though. He waited for the *qadi* to reply.

What the Muslim judge said was: "Are you sure you are a Christian? You should be made to convert to Islam, for you argue like one of us."

"*La ikraha fi'l-din,*" Park answered: " 'There is no compulsion in religion.' "

"You even quote the holy *Qu'ran* at me." Muhammad shook his head. "I find that your precedent has some validity." Muawiyah let out a howl of outrage; Ankowaljuu, and a moment later Waipaljkoon, cheered. "Be still, all of you," the *qadi* said sternly. "More learned men than I must make the final decision in this case. Until they do, I declare these two Tawantiinsuujans People of the Book, under the protection of the Christian *qadi* here. If I am overruled, however, they shall become the property of the airwain pilot Muawiyah. I have spoken."

"Now what?" Park asked him.

"Now I send you on to my more learned colleagues, which means, in the end, on toward the court of the Emir, Allah's blessings upon him." The *qadi*'s eyes were shrewd. "Which, no doubt, is what you had in mind."

"Who, me?" Park grinned at Muhammad ibn Nizam. It was always easier to do business with someone who understood him.

"You did that aforethockly," Ankowaljuu said the next day as they jounced along in one of the Emirate's military goodwains toward its ruler's headquarters.

"Did what aforethockly?" Park asked. They used English for privacy's sake; had Park been in Muhammad ibn Nizam's shoes, he knew he would have salted away a Ketjwa-speaker or two among the guards who made sure nobody tried diving out over the rear gate. Park had no intention of escaping but, since he'd fallen into the Emirate's hands in the company of two enemy citizens, was certain the Moors would not believe that.

"Had me make that faithly writing," Ankowaljuu said. "You never planned to change to Patjakamak—you wanted the writing to show the Muslims we Tawantiinsuujans are People of the Book."

"Who, me?" Park said, just as he had to the *qadi*.

"Aye, you, and don't naysay it, either. You made me so hopeful of the ghostly good coming to you that I forgot to think straight through, as a *tukuuii riikook* ock. But tell me this, Thane Ready-for-Aught: how were you thinking of getting the writing to the Muslims had we gone on to the Son of the Sun as we reckoned we would?"

"I'd have had you take me over the lines," Park answered calmly.

"I'd nay do that!"

"Oh yes, you would, if you're as hot for peace as you say you are. The best chance to get it is to show the Muslims you're no heathen country, but earnful of being treated like other folk with a godshown faith. I'd have talked you into getting me over there, all right, never fear."

"You just might have," Ankowaljuu said after a pause in which he seemed to be examining his own feelings. "I thock I was good at fingertwisting men into doing what I want, Judge Scoglund, but I own I've met my thane in you."

"That's sooth," Eric Dunedin put in. "He even got me to learn Ketjwa. He's the slyest man I ken for—"

Park never did find out why Monkey-face thought he was so sly. Just then, a beetle almost the size of a kitten flew into the goodwain's passenger compartment. Christians, Patjakamak-worshipers, and Muslims spent a couple of frantic minutes knocking it down and squashing it. By the time the remains were finally scraped off the floor and tossed out, the conversational thread was broken.

When they arrived at the base from which the Emir was directing his war, Park did not find the Arabian Nights-style encampment he had half expected. Instead, the neat rows of mass-produced shelter tents reminded him only of the Vinlandish camps he'd seen the year before. The Industrial Revolution, even this world's less complete one, inevitably brought industrialized warfare with it.

He had hoped he and his companions would be whisked straight to the Emir, but that did not happen. Muhammad ibn Nizam led them to a *qadi* he knew, one of hardly higher reputation than himself. That judge listened with the same skepticism Muhammad had shown, and only slowly came round to reluctant acceptance of the possibility that the Tawantiinsuujans might have had some long-ago share of divine revelation, however much their current doctrine distorted it. Ankowaljuu bristled at that; Park could not even kick him under the table, as they were sitting on rugs again instead.

The *qadi* said, "How ancient are these beliefs of yours?"

Park knew the cult of Patjakamak had sprung up in the fourteenth century. Before he could answer, though, Ankowaljuu said proudly, "They date from the time of the creation of the world, thousands upon thousands of years ago."

"Hmp." The *qadi* gave an audible sniff. "There were many prophets before Muhammad. Maybe one did indeed visit your folk, unlikely as I would have

thought it. Had you told me your religion grew up
after the Prophet's time, I would know it for a sure
falsehood, as he was the seal of prophecy. . . . You said
something, Judge Scoglund?"

"Nothing, Excellency." Park swallowed a gulp. He
had forgotten about that detail. A good thing Ankowaljuu had been irritated enough to interrupt with
that bragging, he thought, or all his plans would have
gone down the drain.

"Please let us deliberate by ourselves for a time
now, Judge Scoglund," Muhammad ibn Nizam said.

"Why? I am judge, too." Park was anything but
happy at having the two *qadis* decide things without
his being there to see to it they decided his way.

But the other religious judge said pointedly, "You
may be a *qadi* of *qadis* among Christians, Judge
Scoglund, but you are not a Muslim." Park knew a
warning to back off when he heard one. He got out,
taking Ankowaljuu with him.

"Even if they do ontake us as Folk of the Book,
they'll still be as faithproud as ever," the *tukuuii
riikook* said while they waited and worried. "You *are*
a Wick of the Book, and look how the *qadi* brushed
you aside. We and they will still find grounds for
ficking each other."

"I don't doubt it," Park said.

"What then?"

"If you're Folk of the Book, that makes you a
civilized country—"

"What kind of country?" Ankowaljuu asked. "I don't
know that word."

"Huh? Civi— Oh." It was a wonder, Park thought,
that he didn't absent-mindedly use his native brand
of English by mistake more often. "A burgish country, I mean, in Muslim eyes, not a bunch of savages
to be fickt whenever the mood takes the Emir, and
surely not a fit dumping ground for *ghazis* who'd
likely be in jail if they weren't out hunting heathens."

"I hope you're rick," Ankowaljuu sald, "because if you're not—"

Muhammad and the other *qadi* came out of the tent. The more senior judge looked as sour as if he'd been sucking on a lemon, but he said, "Come with us. We'll lay your case before the Emir's *qadi*, to let him make the final decision."

Getting in to see the Emir's *qadi* took most of the afternoon, though he did not seem that busy. He was one of those important people who show how important they are by making everyone else wait. His name, Muhammad ibn Nizam told Park, was Uthman ibn Umar.

Park's heart sank when he was finally led into Uthman's presence. The chief *qadi* was an ancient man whose hair and beard were white but whose bushy eyebrows somehow remained defiantly dark. The deep-set eyes that glittered beneath those brows were also dark, and as unyielding as any Park had ever seen. Convincing him of anything new was not going to be easy.

"Well, what is it?" Uthman asked peevishly.

By way of answer, Muhammad ibn Nizam handed him the sheets Ankowaljuu had composed. He put on spectacles and began to read. "You know Ketjwa?" Park said in surprise.

Those eyes, like an old hawk's, lifted from the paper. "Why should I not?" Uthman said. "Even pagans may produce worthy thoughts. Surely the Greeks did. For all their wisdom, though, they burn in hell." He read on, dismissing Park from consideration. Park glared at his turban, but did not interrupt again.

Finally Uthman set down the sheets. "So," he said, "you claim the Tawantiinsuujans are People of the Book and not pagans?"

"Yes, excellent *qadi*," everyone said together.

"From this, I might even believe it, but for one thing," Uthman said.

"What?" Park asked, wondering how he would have to finagle with the *shari'a* next.

"This book is no Book." Uthman tapped the pages with a skinny finger. "It is but one man's belief written out, not a true holy text like the Torah or the Gospels or the perfect book, the *Qu'ran*. Let the Tawantilnsuujan priests accept it and I could do the same." His laugh told how likely he thought that was.

Park winced. The *qadi* had a point, one that could be stressed if the Emirate wanted to go on reckoning the Tawantiinsuujans pagans, wanted an excuse to fight their neighbors whenever they got the whim. "How fares the war, excellent *qadi*?" he asked tensely. If the Muslims were winning—

But Uthman did not start to gloat. "Many souls have mounted to paradise, martyrs in the *jihad*," he said. "On this earthly plane—" which he obviously thought of smaller importance "—gains are small on either side."

"Then urge the Emir to call a truce," Ankowaljuu said. "He loses little, and may gain much. Consider— perhaps we will be less harsh to the Muslims in our land if you stop tormenting those who follow Patjakamak in yours.

"If they *are* People of the Book, you may *honorably* stop tormenting them," Park added.

Uthman ibn Umar plucked at his beard. "Let it be so," he said at last. "I think you will fail in your effort, thus showing that Tawantiinsuuju's faith truly is pagan. But if I am in error, if revelation did reach you in the ancient days, I would be sinning if I denied you the chance to prove it. Wait here. I shall speak to the Emir." He rose, tottered out of the tent.

A squad of soldiers soon appeared to take charge of Park and his companions. They led them to a bigger, fancier tent. One of the soldiers frisked them, quickly and efficiently, before they were allowed inside. A servant shouted, "Bend yourselves before the mighty Emir Hussein, beloved of Allah!"

Ankowaljuu and Waipaljkoon prostrated themselves as they might have before the Son of the Sun. Park and, following his lead, Eric Dunedin bowed from the waist. "Rise," Hussein said. "Uthman tells me you have a curious tale for me. I would hear it."

Hussein was not what Park had imagined an emir would be. He was short and thin and wore glasses. In the dark green uniform of the Dar al-Harb, he looked more like a corporal from the typing pool than a ruler.

He thought like a ruler, though. He proved that at once, asking, "Judge Scoglund, if I agree to seek a truce so you can try to show that the Tawantiinsuujans are in fact People of the Book, what is the advantage for me?"

Park carefully did not smile, but he felt like it. He approved of people who got down to brass tacks. He said, "If the followers of Patjakamak are People of the Book, you do not need to persecute the ones in your land any more. Make them pay *jizya* instead."

"The tax for the privilege of keeping their religion in peace, eh?" Behind the lenses of his spectacles, Hussein's eyes grew calculating. He was figuring out how much the tax would bring, Park thought— probably down to the last copper. He must have liked the sum, for he said, "Aye, that is interesting. What else?"

"If you stop persecuting those who worship Patjakamak, the Tawantiinsuujans likely will go easy on their Muslims. That gives you both one less thing to fight about."

"This could be so." Hussein was a cool one, all right. He steepled his fingers—a hell of a thing, Park thought, for a Muslim to do. "What else?"

"Damn," Park muttered. If all that wasn't good

enough— He racked his brains. At last, carefully, he
said, "Lord Emir, how do you feel about your *ghazi*
raiders?"

"Why?" Hussein was cautious too, revealing nothing.

"If you want to be without them, hope the Tawantiinsuujans do show they are People of the Book.
Then *ghazis* will have less excuse to come to your
country from overseas, and you will not need to worry
so much about what so many ruffians running around
loose in your land may do."

He wondered if he'd gone too far. But hell, if he
were running a country, the last thing he'd want in
it was a bunch of gangsters and terrorists, no matter how holy their motives were. He just hoped
Hussein thought the same way.

The Emir said, "They are men given over to Allah,"
and Park was sure he'd stuck his foot in it. Then
Hussein went on, "But it is true, they are sometimes
difficult to control." Park breathed again. Hussein
finished, "I will try to arrange a truce, then, of ten
days' time. If you fail, we fight again."

"What if I don't?" Park said. "What if I do what
I say?"

Hussein stared at him. "Do you challenge me?"

"Only this far—if I succeed, do as you agreed to
do before this stupid war started: accept my settlement of your dispute with Tawantiinsuuju. Do it on
the spot, right here, right now—or then, I mean."

"You do not lack courage," the Emir said slowly.

"Or gall," Uthman added.

Park only waited. Now he grinned. Finally Hussein said, "We have a bargain." After that, Park did
prostrate himself. Hussein, he figured, had earned
it.

Neither the Moorish officers who escorted Park
and his companions across the line of battle nor the
Tawantiinsuujans who received them seemed to have

much faith in the green-and-white-striped flags of truce both sides bore. The two parties hastily separated from each other; members of both kept looking back over their shoulders to make sure no foe was going for a weapon.

"Is the truce holding?" Park asked the Skrelling soldier next to him.

"So far," the Tawantiinsuujan replied. "Who knows how far we can trust the cursed Sun-deniers, though?" Park knew the men of the Dar al-Harb were saying the same thing about Tawantiinsuuju. He also knew that telling the soldier so would do no good.

A very young Tawantiinsuujan officer tried to take charge of the newcomers as soon as they were out of air-rifle range of the front line. "Come with me," he said. "I want to get a complete written record of everything you saw and did while under the control of the forces of the Emirate."

"No," Ankowaljuu said.

"Hell, no," Park agreed.

"But you must," the lieutenant said. "Proper procedure requires—"

Ankowaljuu said, "*Aka* to your proper procedure, boy. I am *tukuuii riikook* to the Son of the Sun. Proper procedure is what I say it is." He produced the documents that proved he was what he claimed. The young officer's eyes got big as he read them. He put a hand over his eyes, as if Ankowaljuu were the Son of the Sun himself. "Better," the *tukuuii riikook* nodded. "Now get us moving toward Maita Kapak, so I can carry out my duties."

Within ten minutes, Park found himself bucking along in a goodwain different from one of the Emirate's only in the color of its canvas top and that of the accompanying soldiers' uniforms. "I admire the efficiency," he said to Ankowaljuu, "but I wish the ride were smoother."

"You mean you want peace and kidneys both?"

Ankowaljuu exclaimed, as if he was asking much too much.

Maita Kapak's encampment proved far more impos-ing than Hussein's. The Emir was not even caliph, commander of the faithful, merely a secular prince. The Son of the Sun, though, claimed divine descent, and lived in pomp that did its best to make the claim seem real.

Prominent as his office made him, Park might have waited weeks before gaining an audience with the ruler of Tawantiinsuuju. The words *tukuuii riikook,* however, melted obstacles as if by magic. The sun was not yet down when Ankowaljuu and Park were ushered into a tent just outside the Son of the Sun's pavilion.

"His Radiance will see you shortly," a majordomo said. "Just don one of these packs——" He handed out a pair of what looked like hikers' backpacks. Anko-waljuu, who knew the routine, strapped on his without comment.

Park balked. "Why do I have to wear this silly thing?"

The majordomo sucked in a shocked breath. "It is a symbol that you would bear any burden for the Son of the Sun."

"In the old days, Judge Scoglund," Ankowaljuu said, grinning slyly, "it would have been no symbol, but a fully laden pack. Be thankful you get off so easy." Park sighed and put on the pack. If the locals didn't think it looked stupid, he supposed he could stand it.

A servant stuck his head in and said, "The Son of the Sun will see his *tukuuii riikook.*"

Maita Kapak had been conferring with his aides. As Park came in with Ankowaljuu, he nodded to Tjiimpuu and Kwiismankuu, the only two he knew. Kwiismankuu nodded back; Tjiimpuu kept his face still. Park had no chance to speak to either of them.

The servant was taking him straight to the Son of the Sun.

He followed Ankowaljuu to his knees and then to his belly as they offered the Son of the Sun their symbolic burdens. "Rise," Maita Kapak said.

As Park gained his feet, he got his first good look at Tawantiinsuuju's master. Maita Kapak was older than he, younger than Tjiimpuu. He bore something of a family resemblance to Tjiimpuu, in fact; considering the inbreeding of Tawantiinsuuju's royal family and high nobility, that was not surprising. Like the foreign minister, he wore plugs in his ears. His were of gold, and almost the size of saucers. The vestigial muscles in Park's own ears quivered at the thought of supporting so much weight.

The Son of the Sun said, "So, Ankowaljuu, why have you chosen to exercise the *tukuuii riikook*'s privilege?" As he spoke, he tossed his head. Park was sure the gesture was unconscious: instead of a crown, Maita Kapak wore a tassel of scarlet wool that descended from a cord round his head to cover most of his forehead. With that fly whisk so close to his face, Park would have done some head-tossing, too.

"Radiance, I present to you Judge Ib Scoglund of the International Court of Skrelleland," Ankowaljuu said. "He has, I believe, a plan to bring us peace now, and perhaps even an enduring peace, with the Emirate of the Dar al-Harb."

Before Park could speak, Tjiimpuu said, "Such a plan would have been easier to bring off before the fighting started. Now passions are aroused on both sides."

"Nobody listened to me before the fighting started," Park said. "You people and the Emir got me down here and then ignored me. I think the whole appeal to the International Court was just so you could feel righteous about the war you felt like fighting anyway. But this one's not as much fun as Waskar's, is it, now that you're in? No big breakthroughs here, just a bloody fight no one is winning."

"We may yet force the Muslims back," Tjiimpuu said.

"Or we may not," Kwilsmankuu said. Ignoring Tjiimpuu's glare, the marshal went on, "If you have peace terms you think fair, Judge Scoglund, I will listen to them."

"And I," Maita Kapak said. "The prospect of enduring peace especially intrigues me. The only reason we and the Emirate did not go to war years ago was that we thought ourselves too evenly matched. So it has proved on the field. I will listen."

"You may not like what you hear," Park warned him.

"If not, I will send you back to the Emir and go on fighting," the Son of the Sun said. He sounded perfectly calm and self-assured. All the Tawantiinsuujans in earshot nodded, even Ankowaljuu. If Maita Kapak said it, they would do it. *So*, Park thought, *this is what being an absolute monarch is all about*.

He began, "First, Radiance, you will have to write down and publish the tenets of the faith of Patjakamak."

"Never! 'Everyone is a religious *kiipuukamajoo*'!" Tjiimpuu and Kwiismankuu said together. They stared at each other, as if unused to agreeing.

"Your faith does not forbid it." Park looked first to Maita Kapak, then to Ankowaljuu. "So I have been told." Reluctantly—in this company he was of lowest rank—Ankowaijuu nodded.

"It may not forbid, but it certainly does not ordain," Maita Kapak said. He asked the same question Hussein had: "What is the advantage of breaking a centuries-long tradition?"

"If you put your beliefs down in writing, the Muslims will recognize you as People of the Book,"

Park said. "That means those who worship Patja-kamak in the Emirate will be able to keep their religion if they pay a yearly tax, and it means you won't be pagans to the Muslims any more. It will gain you status. Not only that, but you could put a similar tax on the Muslims of Tawantiinsuuju. It would"—he glanced at Kwiismankuu—"be only fair."

"Let me think," Maita Kapak said. He did not ask for advice, and no one presumed to offer it. One of the few advantages of absolutist states, Park thought, was that decisions got made quickly. The Son of the Sun did not have to convince or browbeat stubborn, recalcitrant thingmen into going along with him. All he had to do was speak.

He spoke: "It shall be done." Park expected some kind of protest, but none came. Having heard their ruler state his will, Tjiimpuu and Kwiismankuu would carry it out. That was a big disadvantage of absolutist states: if Maita Kapak made a mistake, nobody warned him about it. This time, Park didn't think he was making a mistake.

"Thank you, Radiance," he said, bowing. "I might add that the Emir Hussein did not think you would do this. In fact, we had a sort of—" he had to ask Ankowaljuu how to say "wager" in Ketjwa "—on it."

"Trust a Muslim to guess wrong about what we will do." Tjiimpuu's chuckle had a bitter edge. "They've been doing it since their state first touched ours, almost three hundred years ago."

Maita Kapak picked up something that went by his foreign minister. That made sense, Park thought: since no one spoke straight out to the Son of the Sun, for his own sake he'd better be alert to tone. Now he asked: "Why do you mention this wager, Judge Scoglund? What were its terms?"

"To let me settle the dispute between the Emirate of the Dar al-Harb and Tawantiinsuuju, and to accept the settlement I set down. Will you also agree to that, Radiance, or will this useless war go on?"

"Anyone would know you are not one of my subjects, Judge Scoglund," Maita Kapak said. Fortunately, he sounded more amused than angry. Park wondered just how close he'd come to lèse majesté—pretty close, by the expressions on the Tawantiinsuujans' faces. The Son of the Sun said, "Let me think"; then, after a pause, "First tell me the terms you propose."

"No," Park said. Boldness had got him this far, and suited him in any case. He went on, "You and Hussein agreed to put yourselves under the authority of the International Court when you summoned me. If you didn't mean it, keep fighting and send me home."

"I tried that," Tjiimpuu said. "It didn't seem to work."

Park grinned at him. "No, it didn't, did it?" He worried a little when he saw the look the foreign minister was giving Ankowaljuu. If Maita Kapak went along, though, the *tukuuii riikook* couldn't be in too much hot water. If . . .

The Son of the Sun had screened out the byplay. He was like Allister Park in that: when he was thinking, he let nothing interfere. Finally he said, "Very well, Judge Scoglund. If the Emir thinks you have terms that will satisfy both him and me, I too will put myself in your hands. How shall we become friends?"

"I doubt you will," Park said. "Being able to live next to each other is something else again. Your becoming People of the Book will go a long way toward solving that, as the Muslims will lose their ritual need to persecute you out of existence."

"What about our need to show them the truth of our religion?" Kwiismankuu said.

Park scowled; he'd forgotten that Patjakamak had his holy terrorists too. After some thought, he said, "I do not know, sir, if you have heard that, before I became a judge, I was a Christian bishop, a senior priest. I am not trying to change your religion—you and the Muslims have both had enough of that, I think. But I will tell you one of the things we Christians try to live by. We call it the Rule of Gold: do to others what you want them to do to you." For once, he thought, the real Ib Scoglund would have been proud of him.

"There are worse ways to live than that, perhaps," Maita Kapak said. "So. Have we heard all your terms of peace? If we have, I tell you I am well pleased."

"Not quite all," Park said. "I was summoned to give my judgment on where the border should lie between Tawantiinsuuju and the Dar al-Harb, especially in this disputed sector. My judgment is that the best line between you is the Ooriinookoo River." He walked over to a map, ran his finger along the river, and waited for hell to break loose.

The Tawantiinsuujans did not keep him waiting long. "You thief!" Tjiimpuu cried. "Did you bother to notice that we are east of the Ooriinookoo now, and in territory that has been ours for a generation?"

"Yes, I noticed that," Park said. "I—"

"It cannot be, Judge Scoglund," Maita Kapak interrupted. "Were this land I myself had won in war, I might think of yielding it. But I would be forfeiting my inheritance from my father Waskar if I gave it up. That Patjakamak would never suffer me to do."

When the Son of the Sun said *it cannot be,* his subjects heard and obeyed. He turned back in astonishment when Allister Park kept arguing: "Radiance, I have good reasons for proposing the Ooriinookoo as a border."

"What possible reasons can there be for giving up a third of what Waskar won?" Maita Kapak said in a voice like ice.

"I'm glad you asked," Park said, pretending not to notice the Son of the Sun's tone. "For one thing, the

Ooriinookoo is a wide, powerful river. That makes it a good border between countries that do not get along well—it keeps them apart. I think Kwiismankuu would agree."

The Tawantiinsuujan marshal jerked as if poked by a pin, then nodded as both Park and Maita Kapak looked his way.

"Not only that," Park went on, "but having such a border would make it harder for Muslim zealots to get into Tawantiinsuuju to work harm on your people."

Kwiismanknu nodded again, this time without prompting. Tjiimpuu, however, said, "I thought you told us we would be free of Muslim zealots if we became a People of the Book."

Damn the man for listening, Park thought. Aloud, he said, "Your problem with them will certainly be smaller. No one can promise to make all fanatics happy, though: if they could be made happy, they wouldn't be fanatics. Having the Ooriinookoo as a border will help keep them out of Tawantiinsuuju, though, because they won't be able to sneak into your land so easily as they can now."

Maita Kapak started to say something, stopped, looked annoyed at himself. Park doubted the Son of the Sun often found himself of two minds. When he did speak, it was to ask his aides, "What do you think of acting as the judge suggests?"

"Militarily, it makes good sense, Radiance," Kwiismankuu said.

"Even from the religious point of view, it could be worse; so many of the people on this side of the Ooriinookoo are still Muslims, despite our best efforts to bring them to truth." Tjiimpuu did not sound happy about what he was saying, but said it anyway. Park admired him for that. The foreign minister went on: "If Your Radiance is able to reconcile a withdrawal with your principles—"

"No!" said a man who had been quiet till then. His tunic bore a large sun image, picked out in gold thread. From the size of that sun, and from the way he had dared interrupt Tjiimpuu, Park figured him for a high-ranking priest.

"Tell me why you say no when these others agree, Viiljak Uumuu," Maita Kapak said.

"Because, Radiance, you were right when you first rejected this mad scheme," Viiljak Uumuu said. "Patjakamak would turn away from you, reject you, cast you from his grace, should you decrease his realm by so much as a clod of river mud." The priest burned with outrage at the idea.

Well, there goes the ball game, Park thought. Religious fanaticism had started this idiot war, and religious fanaticism would keep it going. Just when he was beginning to think he'd talked Maita Kapak around, too. But fire and brimstone—or whatever their Tawantiinsuujan equivalents were—could drive out logic every time.

Then Maita Kapak said, "Viiljak Uumuu, do you presume to expound the will of Patjakamak to *me*?" If his voice had been icy to Park, now it was somewhere around the temperature of liquid air.

The priest turned as pale as a Skrelling could. "N-no, Radiance, of course not. I—I only thought to remind, uh, to remind you of what you yourself always, uh, sometimes said."

"Enough," Maita Kapak said. "*I* am the Son of the Sun, and I am the instrument through which Patjakamak expresses his will. Do you doubt it?"

Viiljak Uumuu went down on his belly. "No, Radiance, never!" He sounded horrified. Arguing with the Son of the Sun wasn't merely lèse majesté, Allister Park saw—it was a lot more like blasphemy.

"What *is* your will, Radiance?" Park asked into the ringing silence that followed Maita Kapak's outburst.

"Let me think," the Son of the Sun said, and

silence stretched again. At last the Tawantiinsuujan ruler gave his decision: "The benefits that will come to us as a result of improving our standing with the Muslims outweigh, I think, the loss we suffer from restoring to the Emirate this land east of the Oorii-nookoo. Therefore Patjakamak must be seeking our acceptance of the terms Judge Scoglund has presented. Should the Emir keep the promise he made the judge to honor those terms, Tawantiinsuuju will also cleave to them. Let there be peace."

"Let there be peace," his aides echoed, Viiljak Uumuu loudest among them. Park wanted to go over and shake the big-mouthed priest's hand. If he hadn't got Maita Kapak angry, the Son of the Sun might have come down the other way. *On some different turn of the wheel of if* Park thought, blinking, *maybe he did.* He deliberately turned his back on that thought. He liked the way things had turned out here just fine.

"No one will be waiting for us, Judge Scoglund," Eric Dunedin said, a little wistfully, as the train pulled into Kuuskoo.

Park shrugged. "I didn't want a brass band." He wouldn't have got a brass band anyhow; the Tawantiin-suujans greeted their returning heroes with reed pipes, flutes, and drums made from gourds. It wasn't what Park liked in the way of music, but then it wasn't for him, either.

"Well, you *ock* to have a brass band," Dunedin said. "If not for you, all these warriors would still be out in the jungle, ficking and dying."

"The International Court will know that," Park said, "which is what counts to me. To these folk, I'm just some funny-looking outlander. That's all rick. I did what I did, whether they care or not."

Someone here would care, though, Park thought as the train, brakes chuffing, glided to a halt. He looked forward to explaining to Kuurikwiljor just exactly how exciting his adventures had been, and how important his role in making the peace. He wouldn't really have to exaggerate, he told himself, only emphasize what needed emphasizing. Of course she would be fascinated.

And then, Park thought, and then . . . He'd been imagining "and then" in odd moments ever since Ankowaljuu started banging on his door. Soon, with a little luck—and he'd only need a little—he wouldn't have to imagine any more.

The train stopped. Park leaped to his feet. "Come on, Eric," he said when his thane was slower to rise. "Let's head for our house. I want to use the wirecaller."

"What of seeing to our trunk?" Dunedin said.

"Hell with it. The Tawantiinsuujans will make sure it catches up with us sooner or later. They're good at that sort of thing: hardly a thiefly wick among 'em. We didn't pack everything, you know—there's still enough stuff to wear back at the place."

Monkey-face looked dubious, but followed Park to the front of the car. As they went down the steps, the thane's wrinkled face split in a big, delighted smile. He pointed. "Look, Judge Scoglund! Someone came to meet us after all. There's the Vinlandish spokesman to Tawantiinsuuju."

Osfric Lundqvist spotted Park and Dunedin at about the same time Dunedin saw him. He waved and used his beefy frame to push his way through the crowd toward his two countrymen.

"Haw, Judge Scoglund!" The ambassador pumped Park's hand as if he were jacking up a wain. "Well done! I say again, well done! Without your tireless swinking on behalf of peace, the Son of the Sun and the Emir would still be bemixed in uproarious war."

"The very thing I told him," Eric Dunedin chirped. "The very thing."

"You're most kind, bestness," Park murmured. He sent Monkey-face a glance that meant *shut up*. He had no interest whatever in standing in the railway station chattering with this political hack. What he wanted was to get to a wirecaller.

Dunedin, unfortunately, didn't catch the glance. He said, "Singlehanded, the judge talked Maita Kapak and Hussein into ontaking peace."

"Wonderful!" Lundqvist boomed. "Though as you said, Judge Scoglund, you came here as a forstander of the International Court and not of Vinland, still what you did here brings pride to all Vinlandish hearts."

"It wasn't as big a dealing as all that," Park said. Where he'd intended to magnify his accomplishments for Kuurikwiljor, now he downplayed them in an effort to make Lundqvist give up and go away.

That, however, the ambassador refused to do. Park had picked off Amazon leeches with less cling than he displayed. Finally he said, "Isn't that Tjiimpuu waving for you, Thane Lundqvist?"

Lundqvist looked around. "Where?"

"He's behind those two tall wicks now."

"Reckon I ock to learn what he wants of me. I'll see you later, Judge Scoglund; I have much mair to talk about with you." Lundqvist plunged back into the crowd, moving quickly in the direction Park had given him.

"I didn't see the warden for outlandish dealings back there," Eric Dunedin said.

"Neither did I," Park told him. "Let's get out of here before Lundqvist finds out and comes back."

He and his thane hurried off, going the opposite way from Lundqvist. Soon they were standing outside the station. Park had hoped to flag a cab, but saw none. For one thing, they weren't as common here as in Vinland. For another, as he realized after a moment, cabbies didn't come swarming to meet a troop train, not in Tawantiinsuuju, where anything pertaining to military transportation was a state monopoly. As he watched, soldiers started filing onto government folkwains—by now, Park seldom thought of them as buses.

The station was a couple of miles from the house he'd been assigned. He was about to give up and start walking—though his lungs, newly returned to two miles above sea level, dreaded the prospect—when a familiar-looking wain pulled up nearby. Ankowaljuu stuck his head out. "Need a ride, Judge Scoglund?"

"Yes, and thank you very much." Park and Dunedin climbed into the wain. Park shifted to Ketjwa. "Hello, Ljiikljiik," he told the *tukuuii riikook*'s driver.

Ljiikljiik nodded, then set off at the same break-neck pace he'd used before. Ankowaljuu said, "You have a fine recall, to bethink yourself of the name of a man you met just for a brief while."

"Thanks." Park didn't point out that any aspiring politician learned to remember people's names. He also didn't say that he wouldn't forget Ljiikljiik's driving if he lived to be ninety.

It had its uses, though. Faster than Park would have thought possible, the wain pulled up in front of his house. "I hope everything is still in there," he said.

"It will be," Ankowaljuu said confidently. "In the olden days, a Tawantiinsuujan who was going out put a stick across his door to show he was not home, and no one ever bothered his goods. We're not so lawful now, worse luck, but I was sad when I got to New Belfast and saw lodging-room doors with three locks."

"You'd have been sadder yet if you hadn't used them," Park said. Still, despite the years he'd spent in the DA's office battling crime, he found slightly inhuman the idea of letting the world know a house was standing empty. If anywhere, though, it might have worked in Tawantiinsuuju.

As Ankowaljuu had predicted, the inside of the house was untouched. The *tukuuii riikook* clasped his hand. "I wish I could stay, Judge Scoglund, but I have dealings elsewhere that will not wait."

"It's all rick," Park said. "But I thank you again—for everything. Without you, no one would have had the chance to listen to me up there in the jungle."

"You were the needful one. No one would have listened to me." The *tukuuii riikook* nodded one last time, hurried out the door and back into his wain. Ljiikljiik zoomed off.

"At last!" Park said. He fairly ran to the telephone. "Get me the house of Pauljuu, Ruuminjavii's son, in the district of Puumatjupan."

The phone rang and rang. Just as Park began to lose patience, a servant answered: "Yes? Who is it?"

"This is Judge Ib Scoglund," Park said grandly. "I'd like to speak to Kuurikwiljor, please."

"Oh! Judge Scoglund!" the woman exclaimed. "Just one moment, please." She set down the receiver. Faintly, Park heard her calling someone. He preened while he waited; just hearing his name, he thought, had been enough to impress the servant.

A voice he knew came on the line: "Judge Scoglund! How are you today, excellency?"

"Fine, thanks, Pauljuu," Park answered, frowning a little. "But I asked to speak with your sister, not with you.

"Kuurikwiljor—is not here."

"When should I call back, then?"

"Judge Scoglund—" Pauljuu hesitated, as if unsure how to go on. "Judge Scoglund, the last time you called here, some weeks ago, you made arrangements to see my sister that evening—and then never came."

"I couldn't help it," Park said. "I was called away—I was almost dragged away—on the mission to make peace with the Dar al-Harb. The mission that succeeded, I might add."

"I know that now. So does Kuurikwiljor, and we honor you for it. But we only learned the truth in the past few days. At the time—at the time, Judge Scoglund, all we knew was that you had not come. My sister was not pleased."

"I see. I was afraid of that. I'm sorry. I did try to get in touch after I left, but I had no luck. But if she isn't angry any more, Pauljuu, perhaps—"

"I am sorry too, Judge Scoglund, but I fear you do not see yet. A few days after you—well, after you disappeared, as we thought then—a noble named Kajoo Toopa made an offer of marriage for Kuuri-kwiljor. The rank of our family, which is higher than his own, made him willing to overlook her being a widow. After some thought, she accepted. The ceremony was performed eight days ago. *Patjam kuutiin*, Judge Scoglund."

" 'The world changes,' " Park echoed dully. "Uh-huh." After a moment, he remembered enough manners to add, "I hope they will be happy together. Thank you for letting me know, Pauljuu." He hung up.

Dunedin came in, saw his face. "Bad news, Judge Scoglund? The lady is ill?"

"Worse than that, Eric. The lady is wed." He had the somber satisfaction of watching Monkey-face's jaw drop.

"What now?" his thane said.

"That's a good asking." Park slowly walked into the kitchen, Dunedin tagging along behind. When he opened the pantry, his eye lit on a jug whose shape he knew. He undid the stopper, sniffed, nodded. This was the stuff, all right—one whiff was enough to make his eyes cross. "Here's what now, by God."

Thane's thane that he was, Monkey-face had already found two mugs. Park poured. Both men drank. Both men coughed. After the coughing was done, though, the pleasant glow remained in Park's middle and rose rapidly to his head. He poured again.

After three or four shots, Dunedin said, "Judge

Scoglund, do I rickly recall you teaching me some song—?"

"Hmm?" Then Park remembered too. "So you do, old boy, so you do." He took a deep breath, turned his baritone loose: "Ninety-nine bottles of beer on the wall, ninety-nine bottles of beer! If one of those bottles should happen to fall—"

Monkey-face chimed right in: "Ninety-eight bottles of beer!"